DEVILISH

DEVILISH

LUCIA ST. CLAIR ROBSON

Copyright © 2014 by Lucia St. Clair Robson

ISBN 10: 0990640027
ISBN 13: 9780990640028

*This preposterous tale is dedicated
to my friends and neighbors
in that magical place, Cliffs of the Severn,*

…and to my beloved ghost writer, Brian Charles Daley.

ACKNOWLEDGEMENTS

When I said I was writing a contemporary novel, a frequent response was, "So, you don't have to do any research for this one." If only that were true.

Thanks to Carl Harbaugh, Kimberly Morgan, Bill Lane, Steve Mohrbacher, Russell Smith, and Cindy Kondo for their insights on police work. Vivian Waters knows hospital protocol and all things medical. Howard Ernst filled me in on motion-activated night-vision cameras. Patti Fagnano supplied detailed information on auras and instructions on how to see them.

When I asked for recommendations of makes and models of automobiles, friends replied with their favorites. Ann McCord observed that a Southerner would only drive an American car. Gayle Pruitt said the Ford Flex can handle big guys and a policeman could afford it. Theresa Hulongbayan prefers the Honda Element for camping because it has a wipe-down interior and no carpet. Rob Scott's 1983 Mercedes sedan is on its third engine. Russell Smith likes the 1968 Pontiac Bonneville handed down to him when he got his first shield. Ed Elkins suggested a used Crown Victoria Police Interceptor bought surplus from the local police department. I went with Bill Lane's choice of the 1975 Buick Electra 225.

Special thanks to Bill Hoagland-Fuchs who is a repository of information on a variety of subjects. Debby Roberts came to my rescue with answers to formatting dilemmas. Carol Siegel sent me a link to the Catonsville campus of the Community College of Baltimore County where they include a course in Mortuary Science.

I'm especially grateful to Elaine Nash for her proof-reading skills and sage suggestions. Her insights were invaluable.

CONTENTS

Preview of Coming Distractions

She mustered will power from some secret reserve and managed to shout silently. "No! No, no, no, no!"

The demon must have sensed her lack of enthusiasm. The glowing cheroot ends softened into the big dark eyes of a Labrador puppy. Now it looked like the offspring of a Lab and a wildebeest, and when it said, *Here's looking at you, kid*, Bogart sounded more like Columbo with the hiccups.

Whatever this was, it had committed the worst sort of home invasion. It had broken into her head. And it could speak.

There was no explaining why the old advice-to-new-brides joke occurred to her. The device was too improbable to use in any plot she might have written, but there it was. "When ironing, think about sex. When having sex, think about ironing." She was out-gunned by supernatural forces, and the only weapon she had was scorn.

She avoided looking into those puppy eyes and concentrated on sending a thought. *I don't do doggy style, asshole."*

With a roar, the monster disintegrated and scattered like an explosion of dandruff in a duffel bag. In its place Hollywood heart-throbs appeared like a grainy, flickering old film montage. Hell must be experiencing transmission difficulties.

CHAPTER ONE

"DANCING IN THE DMZ"

*Bureaucracy is the epoxy that
greases the wheels of progress*
Dr. James Boren (1925-2010)

Do seahorses sing when they make love? Alice thought about that as she drove Charlie's cardinal-red Stingray through Friday morning traffic. She had left the Vette's t-tops in place to shade her from the August sun.

Seahorses were of the genus Syngnathidae. Even their name had syng in it. Alice pictured male Syngnathidae harmonizing on "Drowning in the Sea of Love."

Dunes in the desert, they sing too, she thought. Loose grains vibrate when the wind caresses them. They make a booming noise, like approaching cavalry or thunder. Or a Corvette engine in idle.

But dunes don't mate. Or maybe dunes do, their forms pale, soft, shaped like breasts. Maybe they flow together, their grains commingling.

She pulled into the lot and parked. People called the Department of Motor Vehicles the DMZ, the De-Militarized Zone. They had their reasons. She opened the car door and unfolded her long legs into the summer heat.

Alice stood five-feet-ten in her sandals. She had delicate bones, small breasts, and an assertive nose. Her eyes were the color of pool cue chalk. She wore faded denim cut-offs and an old white cotton dress shirt of Charlie's that was too big for her. She had pulled her brown hair back in a ponytail.

The big glass doors swung outward and a gust of chilled air blew out like a djinn released from his lamp. She shivered. The DMV was cold enough to crisp lettuce, and the gray walls had all the charm of a highway tunnel. The floors exuded the aroma of disinfectant. The large information desk floated like an island fortress in the center of the room. She took her place at the end of the line.

Alice expected the wait to be long one. Everyone came here expecting to wait. She intended to use the time to think about the current work-in-progress. She had a contract for a novel and it came with the usual deadline. But when Charlie died a year ago so did the ability of deadlines to compel her. Deadlines, she thought. Dead. Lines.

Don't go there, Alice.

Whales. Whales sing. Long, mournful, complicated descants that ancient mariners heard through the oaken hulls of their ships.

Alice had a recording of whale-songs. They must have scared the bejeezus out of those sailors in their hammocks below decks.

The line inched forward until the man in front of her reached the counter. He loomed as large as a walk-in freezer. Six-foot-six and two-fifty at least.

"A snake got into the glove compartment and shredded my driver's registration to make a nest," he told the clerk. "I need a new one."

"Mice tear up paper for nests, not snakes." The woman was remarkably patient, but then she probably heard more stories in a month than Alice would in a lifetime. "That'll be twenty-five dollars for a replacement. You'll need your driver's license for identification. Take a number."

"My driver's license is in the glove compartment and I can't get to it."

The clerk gave him a bored stare.

"The snake must have been pregnant," he said. "Babies by the dozens started dropping out of the dashboard and into my lap. I almost wrapped the car around a telephone pole. The glove box is full of them."

He pulled a small black, wriggling reptile from the deep pocket on the side of his cargo pants and held it up. Alice wasn't afraid of snakes, but the woman standing behind her screamed loudly enough for both of them. People had no idea what the screaming was about, but they started diving under the flimsy folding chairs and rushing for doorways.

He thrust the snake at the clerk and she retreated to the far side of her bastion. When Alice saw her pull a can of pepper spray from under the counter she stepped out of the line of fire. Two security guards hustled out from a far door, styrofoam coffee cups still in hand, but someone else arrived before they did.

"The fun's over, sir." The owner of the voice stopped where Alice had been standing. He topped out at a few inches shorter than the trouble-maker, six-foot, three-inches maybe, and in a lower weight class. Even with his back to her, she could see from the fit of his faded Levis and black t-shirt that he either had excellent genes or spent time in a gym. Or both. And he carried a motorcycle helmet.

The snake handler turned to face him. His cheeks and nose were red and he smelled like a citrus grove three days after a hard freeze. Alice assumed the source was orange-flavored vodka. She and everyone else moved back to make room for the ruckus, but the newcomer kept his voice low and steady.

"Take it outside."

"Just havin' a little fun, occifer."

"Set the snake loose in the woods beyond the parking lot."

The man swayed as he studied his opponent's chest. He saluted, put the snake back in his pocket and headed for the door. The second man turned to follow him and Alice saw why the first one had left without a fight. Printed in bold white letters across the black t-shirt were the words, "UNDERCOVER COP."

Why would an undercover cop announce it on a t-shirt? Or why would someone not on the force wear one? The questions puzzled her.

She caught a glimpse of his face as he passed and noticed it was a handsome one. She swiveled slightly to admire the rear view of his jeans and t-shirt. He walked through the glass doors and into the glare of sunshine just as the clerk called to her.

Alice explained her mission, took the next plastic number tag from the hook and joined the others sitting in rows of chairs not designed for comfort. She tried to finish her *New York Times* crossword puzzle, but her mind kept wandering. The two-second look she'd had of the Undercover Cop's face, was enough to make her want to follow him outside and try to strike up a conversation.

Don't be stupid. She stared at the LED screens displaying the numbers and available windows instead. *A man that good looking isn't walking around unattached.*

Her number finally appeared, along with words. They flashed by quickly, but she could have sworn they said, "Life a funny thing." It was one of Charlie's favorite Sonny Liston quotes.

"Charlie?" She said it out loud, but no one looked up. She was just one more person talking to herself here.

At the high counter that ran the length of the back wall, DMV personnel stood behind partitioned-off spaces. Alice's brown envelope contained every official piece of paper she could imagine needing — Charlie's will, his driver's license with the photo that made him look like a thug, the Vette's registration and title, probate papers, and the death certificate. The various documents marked the end of Charlie's life, of his hopes and humor, dreams and talents. But not the end of love. Never the end of that.

"I want to transfer the title of Charles O'Brien's Corvette to my name."

The clerk glanced at the documents. "And who are you?"

Alice paused. She never knew how to answer that. "I was his mate."

"His mate?"

"We weren't officially married."

She wanted to add, "We exchanged rings. We lived together fifteen years. We loved each other as much as two people can, and then some."

"Where's the inspection certificate?"

"Inspection?"

"Because you weren't legally married you'll have to get it inspected, the same as if the car were being sold." He gave the impression he thought she was trying to pull a fast one.

"What about common-law marriage?"

"No such thing in this state."

Alice sat down at the end of the back row. Tears blurred her view of the papers as she stuffed them back into the envelope. She looked up when an old man stopped in front of her. She guessed he was at least eighty-five.

"You promised me, Lilly."

"I beg your pardon?"

"You promised me this dance." He held out his hand.

She stood up. He put his hand on her waist and steered her into a waltz. After a stumble or two she got into the rhythm. As they waltzed around the chairs, Alice laid her head back and laughed.

A woman hurried after them and caught his arm as he went by.

"Can't leave you for a minute, Dad." She tapped the side of her head and gave Alice a sad and beleaguered look. "I apologize for my father."

"That's okay. It was fun." How long since she had said that?

The automatic doors soughed open and she walked outside. The snake man was gone, and so was the Undercover Cop. In spite of the heat radiating from the Vette, she ran a hand over the long curve of its front fender. The lush red paint job made her smile. Charlie had said he would buy it only if she painted her toenails to match.

The black leather seat felt hot on the backs of her knees. All his things remained where he had left them– maps, drink holders, pens, the clipboard and yellow legal pad. Behind the seat, he stored the tool box, umbrella, and the jumper cables in their vinyl case with the Corvette logo.

She touched the heavy silver ring hanging on a chain around her neck. It was in the form of a winged dragon and so big she could put two of her fingers through it. Only yesterday she had transferred the smaller version of it to her right hand. Her friend Esme had said it was time to do that, and Esme always gave good advice.

The rings were replicas of the ancient symbol called Ouroboros, a dragon eating its own tail. Charlie said Ouroboros came from the Greek. He said it meant something constantly re-creating itself. He said it symbolized eternity.

Alice draped both arms over the steering wheel. She leaned her forehead against its hot arc and sobbed. Charlie's ring swung forward to dangle on its chain. Alice did not see the lids blink over the dragon's ruby eyes. She did not feel the slight flutter of the silver wings folded along its back.

CHAPTER TWO

"SPIT OR MISS"

Life is a god-damned, stinking, treacherous game,
and nine hundred and ninety-nine men out of
a thousand are bastards.
Theodore Dreiser

Homicide detective Nick Shea was not in a good mood. He had investigated all varieties of criminal activity, but he never had had to scrape spit off the sun-softened surface of a parking lot. And this lot was outside a fast food restaurant in a busy shopping district. What if that tall brunette he'd noticed at the DMV yesterday happened to be behind the wheel of one of the cars stopped at the nearby traffic light?

He already felt like a fool that she had seen his Undercover Cop t-shirt. What if she saw him now, a forty-seven-year-old man hunkered next to a Crispy Chikin franchise, scooping a loogie onto a sterile cotton swab? What if she happened to pull into the lot and notice that his sweat-drenched shirt was sticking to his back and that he smelled like dirty gym socks?

Then again, the idea of her being that close was the nicest thought he'd had all day. He was not paid to think about her though. He was paid to find evil-doers, and the two-legged source of this slimy glob was definitely evil.

Everyone involved with the case considered him guilty. Nick was sure the guy's own lawyer knew he had carved up a young woman with a butcher knife, starting, according to Will the coroner, with her face.

The smug s.o.b. had almost taunted them when they questioned him a month ago, as if murder were some video game and he had won. As if the life he had destroyed had no value. As if virtual had replaced virtue.

The only evidence was circumstantial, and the suspect had exercised his right to refuse to give a saliva sample. Without it to compare to the DNA of the hair and skin found under the victim's fingernails, there was no hard evidence against him. Nick had trailed this loogie's launcher for two weeks. Now he had DNA to check out.

He had pulled the four to midnight shift. The late afternoon sun was still bouncing heat up from the asphalt, but he squatted there a few heartbeats longer. With his forearms resting on his thighs, he dangled the zippered sandwich bag from his fingers. He stared at the wad of mucous sticking to the transparent plastic.

To hell with innocent until proven guilty. He felt the rush of endorphins that made this the only work he could imagine doing. He would never say his job description was Avenging Angel, but he thought it from time to time.

One more killer would be taken off the streets. Whether he stayed locked up was another matter. A lot of criminals walked free on technicalities, but that was beyond his control.

Ten years ago, in an outbreak of a new chief's fervor, everyone on the force had been ordered to attend sensitivity training that included sessions with a zen master. Nick didn't know if the New Age touchy-feely hooey had changed the divorce rate among his comrades. He couldn't say whether it had lessened the incidents of violence in their domestic relationships. He himself, however, had gained something valuable from his brush with Buddhism: Do not beat yourself up over what you cannot control.

He took the bag-o-spit to the station and was filling out the paperwork when a call came to report that a floater had washed ashore. He went out to his car, set the cherry on top, and drove off with it flashing. The light wasn't necessary, but seeing cars pull over to let him pass almost made him feel better about shoveling sputum.

He turned it off when he reached the neighborhood. No sense luring the locals away from their evening of sit-coms and cop shows. He would be talking to them later tonight anyway, when he and his notebook went house to house.

The setting sun was staging a splendid show when he pulled into the small parking area at the community's river beach. The waterfront was hardly distinguishable from the scores of small beaches scattered along the Chesapeake Bay. He exchanged amenities with the pair of patrolmen who were keeping a few curious neighbors at bay, then he slogged through the sand. A security lamp mounted on a tall pole cast light on the scene.

He had collaborated on cases with one of the two uniformed Natural Resources police waiting for him at the water line. Cindy's long dark hair was pulled back into a no-fuss-no-bother pony tail. She looked about twenty and the top of her head barely reached his shoulder. He knew she was closing in on forty, time enough to serve with the Army's Military Police in Afghanistan. She had a third-degree black belt in aikido, and on the firing range she could bull's-eye whatever she aimed at.

She shined her military-grade spotlight in his direction. He shaded his eyes.

"Good evening, Nick."

"Hello, Cindy."

"Are you all the county's got?" Cindy's partner muttered.

"You know what Texans say, 'One severed limb. One Ranger.' " Nick waved the high beam away. "It's a weekend. My partner's out on a call. He'll be here soon."

Cindy swiveled her *uber* light to illuminate the human leg lying half in the water and half ashore. Her partner picked up a stick and poked at the blue crab cozying up to it. The crab scuttled away, but if crustaceans could feel resentment, Nick was pretty sure this one did.

"What do you think, Cindy?"

"Recent." Cindy had seen enough drowning victims to be able to say at least that much. "In summertime a leg should come to the surface in about two weeks to a month."

She didn't waste his time telling him what he already knew. Water temperatures played a part in delaying decomposition. With floaters, currents altered the advance of rigor mortis. Crabs and other marine life fed on flesh, leaving circular patterns that mimicked foul play.

Nick hunkered down to study the leg. Shaved. No tattoos or scars. No signs of trauma. The toenails painted fire engine red. Its previous owner had been a woman. Or not.

He knew he was in for a long evening. He went to a picnic bench and sat down to admire the full moon and wait for Nathan, Homicide's new guy.

Maybe the moon got him to thinking about the tall brunette again. He had been tempted yesterday to go back inside the DMZ and talk to her, or at least wait for her in the parking lot. But he was wearing that ridiculous t-shirt, and the delay would have made him late for work.

Then there was the real reason he had left without seeing her. It wasn't because he was shy, although he was. He didn't want to start a relationship that would end like all the others. Women quickly tired of his crazy hours and his preoccupation with his work. His last girlfriend called his job "That bitch."

The department's brief fling with a Zen master had been interesting, but someone else had had more of an influence on Nick's thinking. As a teenager he had read the first three Han Solo books. One of his guilty pleasures was re-reading them every five or six years. Han had a one-liner for every occasion and a come-back for every contingency.

The one that came to mind now was, "Regrets are a waste of time."

Chapter Three

"Greasing the Kids"

No, you never get any fun
Out of the things you've never done.
Ogden Nash
Portrait of the Artist as a Prematurely Old Man

Syl finished the Bloody Mary in her paper cup and launched into another joke. "Two old ladies are in a nursing home. First old lady asks the second one, 'What do you do when you get horny?' Second old lady says, 'I suck on a life saver.' The first one thinks about that then asks, 'Who do you get to drive you to the beach?'"

Esme chuckled in that soft, throaty way she had. Faye threw her head back and guffawed. Alice smiled.

Alice didn't know Syl well, but she had heard the gossip. When Syl brought a gallon thermos of Bloody Marys to the crab bash at the community's river beach, she wasn't surprised.

Until recently Syl had lived at the other end of Cliffs of the Severn, near the highway. The houses were newer and larger there. They lined up in rows, unlike the helter-skelter arrangement in this old part of the community. After her divorce she had moved into one of the old summer cottages near the water where Alice and her friends, Faye and Esme, lived. The stormy fall-out from Syl's divorce fueled much of the gossip about her.

Alice could believe the gossip. Syl's bounteous body and wild auburn curls were perfect packaging for a brassy attitude. She struck Alice as someone a man scorned at his peril. Women had better watch out too.

Alice's next-door neighbor, Faye, liked her, though, and that was enough of a recommendation. Faye had invited Syl to join them at the crab feast. Now Alice understood why she had chosen a folding table at the far end of a long row of them. Discretion and volume control were alien concepts for Syl.

Her burly blue thermos rose like a centerpiece from the crab shells and corn cobs on the long sheet of brown paper. Wooden mallets pounding on the crab carapaces provided an unruly percussion line to Jimmy Buffet's serenade from a pair of loudspeakers on tall poles. A full moon, a star-spangled sky, and strings of small, colored bulbs shed a festive light.

Syl primed the button on top of the thermos and pumped out another drink. Her fingers left a red-orange smear of Old Bay spice on the lid. She topped off Alice's and Faye's paper cups, then reached for Esme's.

Esme put a slender brown hand over it. "I'm driving."

Syl nodded toward the house perched on the nearby tree-covered ridge. "Es, I could fling Spook by her skinny ankles and hit your place from here."

"Spook?" asked Alice.

"Syl thinks I have psychic powers," said Faye.

"Hell, everyone thinks that, Spook."

"Esme has a kid, Syl." Faye ignored the jibe. "She can't be chugging your high-octane concoctions, especially not here in the nabe."

"Right. I forgot."

They turned their folding chairs around to watch the teenagers playing volleyball in the glow of a light atop a tall pole. They were fit and agile and had summer tans almost as brown as Esme's daughter, Kenya.

The music, the conversation, and the din of wooden crab mallets blended into a pleasant hum for Alice. With her elbows on the table top she looked at Syl over the ear of sweet corn she was about to eat.

"Is it true you put a dead possum in an air-con duct at your ex's house?"

"It's my house too, and no, that is not true. I stuffed two dead possums into the ductwork. That was a bad day for possums trying to cross the road."

Syl looked as if she expected Alice to take notes on the information she was about to share. "Always put at least two dead critters in the air ducts. When the furnace guy found one corpse, collected an exorbitant fee, and left, my sumbitch husband figured the problem was solved." She threw her head back and laughed. "Imagine his disappointment."

Esme poked at the crab parts lying in heaps on the brown paper covering the table. "When I was a kid, I thought crab balls were their...well, you know."

"Testicles." Syl finished the sentence.

"Speaking of testicles," Faye said, "Where's your mother tonight, Syl?"

"You know how Doc is. She thinks crab feasts should be a felony."

Alice assumed, from the name Doc, that Syl's mother was a physician. She wanted to ask what connection she had to testicles, but she didn't speak up quickly enough. The two loudspeakers commenced with "Under the Boardwalk." Syl, Faye, and Esme took up the refrain, and Alice joined in.

Almost at the top of its trajectory, the moon looked down on its reflection in the black water of the cove. Parents had gathered their younger children for the walk home. A crew of neighbors began rolling the litter up in the brown paper and stuffing it into a platoon of trash cans. Others folded chairs and tables and stacked them against the tree trunks at the edge of the beach.

Syl held the thermos to her ear and sloshed it. "I'll get more ice." She marched barefoot toward the beached dinghy full of beer, soft drinks, and ice. She returned with the thermos dangling from one hand and a watermelon cradled under the other arm. She dropped it with a thud in the middle of the table.

"It's covered with lard." Alice moved aside in case it decided to roll.

"Must be left over from the kids' races this afternoon," Esme said.

Syl climbed onto the bench, then up on the table. "We're having a greased watermelon contest," she shouted. "Last one in is a rotten egg."

The members of the clean-up crew had been marinating all evening in crab juice, Old Bay spice, melted butter, and beer. They cheered.

Syl headed for the water, but Faye, ten years younger, lithe and athletic, sprinted past her. Fully clothed, she cannon-balled off the diving board. She surfaced laughing, her reddish-purple spiked hair in disarray. She gave the one-finger salute when Syl heaved the melon at her.

Syl pulled the shift over her head and shrugged out of her bra. She slid her silk bikini briefs down around her ankles and stepped away from them. In the moon's light her body gleamed pale and curvaceous as a painting by Reubens. She gave a sweeping, one arm wave to the neighbors standing at the water line. When she bounced on the board her bow and stern were a study in Newton's Third Law of Motion: for every action an equal and opposite reaction.

She soared into a graceful arc and the water closed over her. Several others leaped in after her. Their laughter and splashing echoed across the cove.

Few meals were messier than blue crabs steamed in the shell, and Alice and Esme headed for the pump by the beach house. They took turns pumping while the other washed her hands and stuck her head under the gush of water. When Esme shook her head, beads of water flew from her elegantly short afro.

They sat on the bulkhead with their legs dangling and their toes in the water. Behind them bats chased the insects attracted to the lights of the roulette wheel in the beach pavilion. A few people were still trying their luck there.

"How are you doing, Alice?" Esme asked.

"I'm okay."

Esme turned to look at her. In daylight she had the loveliest, calmest smile of anyone Alice knew. Now, the water drops in her hair glittered like diamonds in the moon's glow. The red lights on the spinning roulette wheel reflected in her wide, dark eyes like a miniature carnival under the canopy of her long lashes. Her face, the color of coffee with just a little cream, blended with the night, leaving the lights in her eyes to shine almost disembodied.

"You always say you're okay."

"It takes more time than most people assume it will. But who knows that better than you, Es?"

Three years ago Alice had gone with Esme and her daughter to Dover Air Force Base to meet the C-17 bringing its cargo of loss and tragedy home from Afghanistan. Just the memory of that solemn ceremony for Esme's husband, with the drums, bugle, and color guard, brought tears to Alice's eyes.

"How did things go at the DMV yesterday?" Esme asked.

"I tried to change the Vette's title. I thought I had every official piece of paper they could possibly require, but since we weren't married I'll have to get it inspected as if he were selling it to me."

Still holding hands, they sat without speaking. Esme didn't feel the need to fill gaps in conversation with words. She called speech the small change of silence. That was one of the many reasons Alice liked her.

Chapter Four

"Undercover Cop"

Think twice before you speak to a friend in need.
Ambrose Bierce

Nick's shift was almost over when the last call came. Someone had complained about noise, nudity, and hooliganism at a neighborhood beach. Something about a crab feast that had gotten out of hand.

"What about the regular patrol?"

"They're checking out a bar fight. Just swing by on your way home."

With a sigh, he headed for Cliffs of the Severn. He rarely went there, which was a good sign. It meant murder and mayhem didn't happen often in that neighborhood.

He had been going off-shift the last time he got a call for the Cliffs a year ago. Some poor guy had died at home. The dispatcher mentioned the deceased was forty-five.

Nick had arrived to find the house full of police and emergency medical technicians. From a back room came the sound of a woman sobbing. He had seen people in distress many times, but that night he felt as though he had walked into a dense fog of grief. When one of the EMT's told him the death had resulted from natural causes, he was grateful for the excuse to leave.

The traffic light turned green and Nick turned onto the only road leading down into Cliffs of the Severn.

Syl and Faye waded out of the water. Faye's shorts and t-shirt clung to her thin frame. Syl nodded in her direction as she reached for her clothes.

"Look at Spook. Forty years old and no hips, no thighs. I hate her."

Syl pulled on her underwear as if the community beach were a department store dressing room. She bent over to shake her breasts into her bra before she fastened it.

"I grew up in this neighborhood, you know. Jerry and I went skinny-dipping here, back when we were first dating." Syl shrugged into her peach-colored shift and settled it over her hips. "Now I've aged out, and he's traded me in for a newer model."

"Why did you stay here?" Alice ventured with caution into Syl's personal life.

"It's more convenient for making his life a hell. Less of a commute." Syl waved a hand at the cove sparkling in the moonlight. A faint breeze had set the halyards on the sailboats to chiming softly. "Besides, this is my home. That sumbitch is not going to drive me out of it."

"He's a lawyer," Faye added, as though that explained everything.

"Every lawyer I know is a nice guy." Alice paused to remember the lawyers she knew. "Except one. She's a nice woman."

"Oh yeah. They're charming as hell at parties." Syl slid Alice an analytical look as she stepped into her flip-flops. "My guess is you've never been in a courtroom in your life."

"My guess is you have."

"Touché." Syl laughed. "But only for drunk and disorderly."

Arm in arm the four women climbed the concrete stairs to the road and started up its slope. Syl stopped to catch her breath halfway to the top.

"A guy and his alligator walk into a bar," said Faye while they waited for her to start again. "The guy asks the bartender, 'Do you serve lawyers in here?' Bartender says, 'Sure do.' Guy says, 'Good. Give me a beer and I'll have a lawyer for my 'gator.'"

They had almost reached the crest of the hill when a county police car approached. Alice and her friends moved aside and watched it pass.

"Someone must've complained," said Esme.

Alice stared at the cruiser as it passed slowly under the street light.

"I think that's him."

"Who?" Esme turned to look after it.

"The undercover cop."

"What undercover cop?"

"I saw him at the DMV yesterday. He was wearing a t-shirt that said 'Undercover Cop.'"

"That makes no sense," said Faye.

"No kidding."

"Was he do-able?" asked Syl.

"I suppose so."

"You suppose so?" Syl gripped Alice by the back of her shoulders, turned her around, and gave her a push downhill. "Go. Make his acquaintance."

"No." Alice did an about-face.

"This is what they call convenient for the author, Alice. What are the odds of a hermit like you seeing a good-looking stranger twice in two days? He is good looking, right?"

"He's probably married, Syl."

"You'll never know if you don't chat him up." Syl started down the hill. "I'm going to ask him."

"Get your lard bucket ass back here," Alice shouted. "Now."

Syl turned like a sailboat tacking into a stiff headwind and huffed up the street again. She and Alice glared at each other.

After too long a pause, Alice said. "I was speaking metaphorically about the lard bucket ass."

Another pause. Then Syl laughed so hard she grabbed a street sign's post to keep from falling over. Still chortling, she grabbed Alice's arm and started up the hill again.

"You're all right, Al."

Alice pretended not to hear when Syl leaned over and asked Faye, "What does metaphorically mean?"

They came to Esme's cottage perched on a bluff above the water. A light shone through the window curtains of Esme's daughter's room. An arched arbor gate draped with rambling roses gave entrance to the small yard. A lantern illuminated a large plaque in the center of the arch.

The plaque was a plaster cast of the Green Man, the Druids' ancient god of the woods. His bee-stung lips, broad nose, and cheeks like twin tennis balls peered from the middle of a leafy wreath.

When Alice glanced up at him he winked at her. She blinked and stared at him again, but this time he gave no sign of recognition. She decided she was drunker than she thought.

Esme kissed Alice on the cheek. "About the undercover cop," she whispered, "Coincidences are God's way of staying anonymous."

She walked under the unblinking stare of the Green Man and closed the front door quietly behind her so as not to wake her daughter, Kenya.

Syl turned off at the next corner. With arms outstretched and her damp dress clinging to her, she twirled down a narrow side street. Her voice floated back from the darkness.

"This was the best crab feast ever."

Faye put her arm around Alice's waist and Alice draped hers across her friend's thin shoulders. They walked together, matching strides.

"Syl meant well," Faye said.

"I wish people wouldn't try to fix me."

"Consider this, Al. Syl would take a cab to her garage if she could, but she was willing to climb this hill twice to help a new friend."

"I suppose you're right."

Alice remembered what Esme had said about coincidences. She was about to ask Faye to go back to the beach with her to check out the Undercover Cop when the cruiser headed up the hill. The flash of brake lights as it rounded the curve at the crest gave Alice a brief hope that he would back up, roll down his window, and say "good evening." Instead, the sound of the engine grew fainter.

Alice didn't ask Faye if she had seen the Green Man wink. She didn't want to encourage her friend's kooky notions by giving the impression she shared them.

Faye believed in seers and psychics, alien abductions, and etheric forces. She channeled a third century sage named Gundenis. She conversed with angels, saw auras, practiced acupuncture, decorated using *feng shui*, and read tarot cards. She swore by pyramids, creative visualization, and the curative powers of prayer, crystals, prisms, and aromas. Syl was right about one thing. Spook was a good name for her.

Alice and Faye paused to look down into the ravine where thousands of fireflies were putting on a spectacular show in the dense tangle of foliage. More of them flashed in unison in the canopy of oaks, elms, and walnuts high overhead. The moon shining through the branches seemed to be shepherding them.

Ducks floating on the still waters of the cove chuckled as if one of them had told a funny story. A screech owl's eerie call descended into soft purrs and trills that made the hair stir on the back of Alice's neck.

"This place is magical," said Faye softly.

"Yes, it is."

CHAPTER FIVE

"CHUM"

To like and dislike the same things,
that is indeed true friendship.
Gaius Sallustius Crispus (86 – 35BC)

Nick knew only one person who enjoyed discussing cadavers, especially over breakfast at two in the morning. He was relieved that Will had chosen a booth away from the truckers, late-shift hospital workers, carousers, party-departers, and other night owls in Chuck's Wagon, the only all-night diner on Main Street. In the past they had received horrified looks from those close enough to overhear them.

As he slid onto the bench across the table from Will, Nick saw that his friend's hair was damp, but he gave a cautious sniff anyway. It confirmed that Will had showered before he left the morgue. Talk of dead bodies at breakfast was one thing. Their lingering bouquet was another.

Nick and Will had known each too long and under circumstances too strange to bother with amenities. Will had an isosceles triangle of a face and a nose arched like the beak of an ibis. A pair of granny glasses magnified his brown eyes and enhanced the wading bird effect. His pale blond hair was short on the sides and long on top.

He glanced up from his ham slab, runny eggs, and stack of flapjacks a-drift in mock-maple syrup.

"The tox reports finally came in for your freezer geezer."

"The one the caretakers stored with Ben and Jerry and Mrs. Paul while they collected her Social Security checks?"

"Yep. Looks like they kept granny on cold for six weeks."

"If a relative hadn't come for a visit, Mrs. Jane Doe might still be chilling." Nick sighed. The longer he lived the less he understood his species. "Have you got a C.O.D.?"

"With an eighty-nine-year-old, cause of death is a crowded field, but congestive heart failure took the gold."

"Not a homicide?"

"I'd call it criminal negligence, but that's for you fellows to figure out."

"Don't have to. Unless there's evidence of foul play, storing a stiff in the family freezer is not illegal."

"Why am I not surprised?" Will mopped up egg yolk with a piece of toast. "But if I know you, and I do, you'll bull-dog it 'til not a shred of doubt remains."

The waitress brought a plate with two eggs over easy, home fries, and dry whole wheat toast. It was the breakfast she knew Nick would have ordered if she had asked him. He smiled his thanks when she set down the bottle of chipotle sauce.

As he shook the *Cholula* onto the eggs and potatoes he didn't notice her hovering a few moments before she headed back to the counter.

Will did notice. "You should get her number."

"Whose?"

"Angie's." He nodded at the waitress's back.

"Why? So another woman can inform me at full volume that I'm married to my job? Leila left in such a fury I had to screw the door hinges back on the wall."

"I warned you about dating body-builders."

"Yes, you did."

"If I had your looks my locker would be papered with phone numbers."

The subject of women and dating and the women Nick dated made him uncomfortable, so he changed it.

"The tee you gave me came in handy when I was off-duty a couple days ago."

" 'Undercover Cop?' "

"Yeah."

Nick didn't add that he'd only put it on because the day promised to be a scorcher and it was the last clean t-shirt in his drawer.

"A drunk was waving a snake around at the DMV. The shirt confused him enough to escort him outside without a fight."

"What were you doing in the Demilitarized Zone."

"Renewing my motorcycle license."

"Don't they give you boys special dispensation?"

Nick chuckled without much humor. "One of our guys gets calls from his friends and family, asking him to fix traffic tickets. So he does. You know how?"

"How?"

"He goes downtown and pays the fines for them." Nick's smile turned a little melancholy. "Only reason I know this is his wife told me."

"You know how Mafia guys claim sulfuric acid will liquefy a human body in fifteen or twenty minutes?" Will made his usual sharp conversational turn without signaling.

"I've heard that." Nick paid attention. In the past, Will's stories had helped him solve cases.

"They found tanks of acid in a Mafia hideout in Palermo, so some Italian scientists ran a study."

"Did they use a Giovanni Doe from the morgue as a test case?"

"John Doe. Cute. No. Pig carcasses. Adding water speeded up the process, but it still took twelve hours to dissolve muscle and cartilage. Two days to reduce the bones to powder." Will snorted. "I could've told them that and saved them a bundle."

"It wasn't a total waste of money. Now we know that even with five thousand dollar wrist watches, mafia *gavones* can't tell time."

"Tomorrow's the second Sunday of the month. You gonna swim with the sharks?"

"Sure."

Will shook his head in mock sorrow. "I'm going to start calling you chum, chum."

"I've told you they're small sharks. And very well fed."

"I do not want to come to work some Monday morning and find you on a slab, along with plastic baggies of whatever undigested parts of you they could recover."

"Why, Will, that's the nicest thing anyone's said to me today." Nick glanced at his watch. "But then, the day's young."

When Nick grinned, his teeth flashed beguilingly white in contrast with his tanned face and dark hair and eyebrows. The three a.m. shadow made him look dangerous and irresistible. The fact that he was unaware of it parlayed the appeal.

He wrapped the remaining piece of toast in a paper napkin and slid it into the pocket of his jacket.

"For the ladies?" Will asked.

"Yeah."

"You guys are the only cops I know of with a flock of feral hens roaming at large outside your barracks."

"They have a calming effect."

"On you boys or the perps?"

"Both."

Nick added an extra two dollars to the tip in lieu of asking Angie out, and headed for the door.

"'Night, Nick," called Angie.

"Goodnight." He waved without turning around.

Chapter Six

"Hot and Bothered"

Here's to the bull who roams the wood.
He does the cows and heifers good.
Were it not for his long, long rod,
What would we do for beef, by God?
Mark Twain

Alice had never gotten around to buying an air-conditioner. A wet t-shirt was cheaper and quieter. On days as hot as this one she supplemented the damp shirt with a small window fan. Her office occupied a long narrow room that had been the house's screen porch. Windows along two sides and a screen door on the third gave cross-lighting. The room's location high above the street made it feel like an osprey's aerie.

She leaned back in her desk chair and opened the day's newspaper. She was avoiding work by reading her favorite section, the Police Beat. Today the anonymous reporter had written, "The alleged bank robber left a to-do list in her apartment. After 'clean closet' and 'bleach teapot' she had noted, 'Buy ski mask, and police scanner, borrow gun, check MapQuest for escape route.'" He had added, "Here's to the housewife that's thrifty.'" Alice laughed out loud. She knew the line came from a poem by Richard Sheridan, but she doubted many others did.

> Here's to the maiden of bashful fifteen;
> Here's to the widow of fifty.
> Here's to the flaunting, extravagant quean
> Here's to the housewife that's thrifty.

Alice was often tempted to call the newspaper and ask who was responsible, but she never did. Maybe a woman wrote the reports. Or if a guy wrote them he was probably some pot-bellied misfit.

She put the newspaper in the recycling bin, opened a window screen and refilled the bird feeder hanging outside the window. She finally sat down and wrote a sentence. It was a lousy sentence, but it was a start and she could fix it.

She leaned back and pondered a chaser for it. After ten chaser-less minutes she wandered into the kitchen to refresh her shirt with the sink's sprayer. She got back to her office just as the screen door slammed behind Syl.

"Hi." Syl took in Alice's wet t-shirt, but made no comment.

The words, "flaunting, extravagant quean" flashed through Alice's mind. Then she reminded herself that she herself was, after all, a "widow of fifty."

Syl nodded at the glow of the computer screen. "I wanted to see where the magic happens."

"No magic happening here."

"You got what they call writer's block?"

"Big time."

Syl produced a bouquet of black-eyed Susans and a bottle of chardonnay from behind her back. "By way of apology for trying to herd you into hustling that cop last night. I was a little lit."

"I apologize too. You actually have a very nice ass."

Syl accepted the apology with an airy wave of lacquered finger-nails. "People give us drunks and grieving widows a lot of slack."

Alice grinned, relieved that she would not get the usual well-intended condolences from Syl. She took the wine and flowers into the kitchen and returned with a glass of iced tea. Syl was facing the window fan, arms outstretched.

"Is your A/C broken, Al?"

"Don't have one." Alice handed her the tea.

Syl raised an eyebrow at Alice's lapse in sanity. She took a sip and raised the glass. "Do you have something to put in it?"

"Lemon? Sugar?" Alice knew Syl had something stronger in mind, but she didn't feel like acting as enabler so early in the day.

"Never mind."

Syl sipped her tea and stared at the garland of gold finches clinging to the mesh bag of thistle seed hanging outside the window. From there she circumnavigated the room. She studied the maps, notes, and clippings pinned to a large bulletin board on the only windowless wall. She paused in front of a framed photo of Charlie and Alice barefoot and arm-in-arm at the river beach.

"He looked so damned good in that Vette with the t-tops off. We all envied you, you know." She stared out the window. "What's up with Spook? She's wandering around her yard like she's lost the way to her own front door."

Alice's house stood on one of several bluffs running through the neighborhood. She and Syl went out onto the small deck built thirty feet above the street. They set their glasses on the railing, leaned on their elbows, and looked next door.

Barefoot and wearing a faded blue cotton shirt and jeans cut-offs, Faye stood still as a statue amidst the low-growing wild flowers and rampant ground cover she called a lawn. She stared fixedly at the turquoise pendulum she dangled from a black nylon cord. After a minute or two she retrieved a piece of cardboard from the ivy. She moved a few paces to the left, laid it out again, and repeated the process.

"What the hell is she doing?"

"She's dowsing for a new septic tank. The pendulum swings left or right above a numbered chart and tells her if the site's suitable."

"You're kidding."

"Faye says Albert Einstein used a dowsing rod. He believed its powers had to do with electromagnetism. She says migrating birds follow the earth's magnetic field, so why can't we use it too?"

"But hocus-pocusing a septic tank?"

"Welcome to the old section of the Cliffs. Every yard has abandoned sumps, grease pits, cess pools, septic tanks, waste pipes, dry wells. Faye's way of avoiding them is as good as any."

"Doc says she has to replace her septic tank."

A red hybrid cruised slowly past, heading downhill toward the water. Its bumpers were plastered with "Save the Bay" stickers.

"Speak of the devil," muttered Syl. "There goes Doc now, off on some anti-perc test crusade.

"Doc is Logan?" Alice recognized the car. She often saw it in pursuit of some septic company's truck. "Logan is your mother?"

"Hard to believe, huh."

Alice did find it hard to believe. "Logan's a hero in this part of the neighborhood. She's a regular at building permit hearings."

"Doc lives to obstruct."

Alice didn't bother explaining that if someone could obtain a positive percolation test for a septic tank, they could finagle a permit to build on the smallest, most perpendicular lot. This close to the water, land was expensive. Wealthy newcomers wanted to build big and they didn't care whose view they blocked or where their effluvium ended up.

Alice remembered the remarks about crab balls and testicles at the crab feast. She was about to ask what Syl's mom had to do with them when a telephone truck pulled over and parked across the street. The driver, a lineman wearing sunglasses and earbuds, got out.

Syl gave a low whistle to get Faye's attention. By the time Faye put her elbows next to theirs on the railing, the lineman had buckled his tool belt low on his hips and strapped on his climbing harness. The tools clanked as he started up the pole in his cleated boots. They shaded their eyes and stared up at him. With his boots braced on the pole and his legs holding him out from it, he looked as relaxed in the harness as if it were a porch swing.

Several women appeared from houses up and down the street. A couple of them pretended to sweep their porches and walkways. In spite of the ninety-degree heat, some seemed struck by a sudden urge to garden. Others decided to check their mailboxes even though this was Sunday.

"Most of these old cottages down here are occupied by women," said Alice. "They appeal to us nesters."

"They're small and quirky," added Faye.

Syl wasn't amused. "By quirky you mean they have no closet space, you can't run a hair dryer and a vibrator at the same time, and only a mountain goat can navigate the stairs to the front door."

"You use a vibrator while you're drying your hair?" Faye laughed. "Why am I even asking?"

"Hey," said Syl, "Sometimes a girl's late for work."

Chapter Seven

"Indian Summer"

Be happy while y'er leevin,
For y'er a long time deid.
Anonymous (Scottish)

Taking the Indian out on the highway always cheered Nick up, but heading north on I-97 toward Baltimore was the best. He rode a 1939 Indian four-cylinder motorbike rather than the more popular 1947 Chief twin-cylinder for two reasons. He was a southpaw and he liked the Four's left-hand tank shift. The second reason was subtler. He thought of himself as an Indian, not a chief.

The crimson Chief was flashier, but Nick had refinished the Four in the original cream and white colors. The company's logo on the gas tank was the head of a warrior in a wind-swept war bonnet. Nick had re-painted the curved black pinstripes around it.

He didn't mind throttling back when he left the highway. He didn't even mind the snarl of traffic around the Inner Harbor. He had grown up in Baltimore and he remembered when the waterfront was crowded with abandoned warehouses. In those days, sensible people did not go there after dark.

As a rookie twenty-five years ago he had walked a beat in less charming areas of Charm City. Baltimore had taught him more in his first week on the job than the entire course at the police academy. Riding past Camden Yards he thought he caught a phantom whiff of the spice factory the Orioles' stadium had replaced. He knew it was an olfactory mirage, but he was already smiling when he saw the National Aquarium's huge glass tetrahedrons soaring above the water.

He parked the bike to one side of the Aquarium's entrance. The security guard standing inside gave him a high sign. He would keep watch on the Indian.

Nick slipped his scanner inside the small duffle bag with his wetsuit and flippers. He clipped the chin strap of his helmet into a stainless steel clasp on the outside of the bag. With the duffle slung over one shoulder he pushed through the doors and into the rush of cool air. The crowded lobby was lofty and flooded with light from the glass ceiling twenty-five feet overhead.

Nick and the other three members of his team spent half the morning preparing food for the 16,500 inhabitants of the sprawling, underwater fairyland. When he finished, he picked up the yellow and white plastic boxes he had packed with shrimp, smelt, squid, and mackerel. Wearing a SCUBA tank and his black wet suit and carrying his face mask and swim fins, he walked with the other three to the public area.

The dive platform cantilevered out over the concrete pool called the Ray Tray. The volunteers and staff had named it for the skates, stingrays, and manta rays living in it.

When he stepped up onto the platform he was aware of hundreds of pairs of eyes watching him. He had gotten over being embarrassed by the attention, but he still didn't know how to deal with women who seemed to consider a lanky guy in goggles, a squeaky wetsuit, and flapping fins sexy. Some tried to hit on him before he went into the water. Some were waiting when he came out. Some did both. Once, one slipped him a house key with an address written in indelible ink on the plastic tag attached to it. On the back of the tag she had thoughtfully added a schedule of her husband's work hours.

As Nick eased into their world, the rays, triggerfish, nurse sharks, and one very large three-legged sea turtle swarmed around him. The triggerfish, resplendent in iridescent stripes and polka dots, were crowd favorites, but Nick liked the mantas. They were also called Devilfish, but even in the wild, giant mantas sought out contact with human divers. Nick especially liked the charmer named Ray.

Ray measured five feet from the tip of one wing-like fin to the other. His twelve foot length included his barbed tail. For reasons no one could explain, he always ignored the other three divers stationed around the tank and came to Nick. He took the shrimp from Nick's fingers with the delicacy of a diner at the Four Seasons. After Ray had eaten he continued to circle while Nick stroked his back at each pass.

The next assignment was the man-made, glass-enclosed coral reef five stories high. When Nick had emptied his yellow box of chum, he scooped white gravel from the bottom of the tank and let it drift out from between his fingers. The smaller fish swam under the gentle fall of it so it could clean their scales. Nick thought of one of the clown fish as female. She hovered almost vertically to let the gravel fall past her face and down the length of her body. Nick would have sworn the look on her face was blissful.

What made Nick's heart as buoyant as the rest of him was the acceptance of these creatures as one of them. Almost as good as that, whatever issues they might have with each other were not his problem.

If anyone had asked him right then if he were happy, he could have said, "Yes."

Nick started the Indian and headed for home. The warm glow of endorphins lasted until he saw the ranks of red brake lights on the highway ahead and heard chatter on the scanner. A pair of helicopters circled.

He turned onto the median and bucketed over rough ground toward the flashing lights of police cars, fire engines, ambulances, and tow trucks. Most were clustered around two wrecked cars and the tractor trailer truck lying on its side across the oncoming lanes. A med-evac chopper lifted off as Nick reached the scene.

Traffic was backed up to the horizon and beyond. State troopers, police, and firemen were walking in a circle expanding out from the two cars. Nick put a pair of latex gloves into his pocket, and approached the state trooper directing traffic. No cars were moving in either direction so he had time to talk.

Nick nodded at the searchers. "What are they looking for?"

"Driver of the Lexus is missing his head." As the trooper talked he watched the cars inching past. "The piece of the hood that came through the windshield must've sheared it off. The force of the crash must've sent it ballistic."

Nick made the same visual sweep of the traffic. No telling who might boil out of his car with a glove-box Glock in hand.

"What caused the pile-up?"

"Truck driver says the Lexus drove across the median and headed straight up the lane at him going at least a hundred miles an hour. The trucker swerved to avoid him, crossed the median, and rolled. The Lexus smashed into the Ford traveling behind him. We found a note in the grass. Looks like the Lexus was a suicide."

Nick surveyed the two twisted, crumpled heaps of metal. "I assume no one walked away from this one."

"Just the semi driver. A man and a woman were in the front seat of the Ford."

A shout came from the searchers. They had found the head. Paramedics unloaded a stretcher and went running across the field with it.

The trooper eye-balled the distance. "If the guy's noggin had been a football he would've made a record goal."

Night had landed with a sullen thud when Nick reached home. He lived in a community of people who did work the average citizen could not. They built Bungalows and skyscrapers. They repaired cars, replaced roofs and plumbing. They installed locks, re-wired houses, kept furnaces running, and cleared snow in the depths of winter. They knew the difference between a widget and a thingamajig.

Nick didn't feel qualified to live among them, but at least he could try to protect them if they needed it. Not that many of them needed protecting. Most of them owned guns. Anyone who tried to burglarize a house here was as suicidal as the guy in the Lexus.

He drove past the small houses, old cars, pickups, and panel vans. He hit the garage door opener and rode the Indian inside. Feeling every one of his forty-seven years, he stood on his porch in the dark and took ten slow, deep, calming breaths before he unlocked the door.

He lit the lamp on an end table next to the threadbare couch. He kicked off his boots and threw his leather jacket across an easy chair near the fireplace. The boots and jacket instantly became the only items out of place in a room lined with bookcases.

The computer on the desk near a corner window gave asylum to the novel he had been working on for several years. He kept a bottle of Maker's Mark in the cupboard for Will's infrequent visits to play poker or watch a Ravens' game. He dropped a few ice cubes into a tumbler and splashed some of the whiskey over them.

He took his grandfather's copy of *Bartlett's Quotations*, the 1938 edition, from the shelf above the desk. He laid his six-foot-three-inch frame out on the sofa with his head resting on one of the armrests and his feet propped up on the other. He put on his glasses and opened the Bartlett's. The index listed over four hundred entries under Death.

Nick began with "Death, thou'rt a cordial old and rare," by Sidney Lanier. Then he read them all. In alphabetical order.

When he finished he looked up Love. He counted five hundred and seventeen entries. The fact that there were more of them than for death gave him comfort. He refilled his glass and started reading at random through the book.

Chapter Eight

"Plight of the Iguana"

Twinkle, twinkle, little bat!
How I wonder what you're at.
Lewis Carroll
Alice's Adventures in Wonderland.

Alice knew bats in flight did not entangle their tiny claws in people's hair. She had read that they didn't, but she only believed it because Faye had told her so. She had believed Faye, that is, until this particular bat started executing Immelmanns and reverse half-Cuban eights in her living room. His aerobatics brought him so close she could feel the sough of wind when he zipped by. She pulled down the upper halves of all the sash windows and waved a throw pillow around, trying to shoo him out into the night. He wasn't buying it.

When Esme opened the front door, the bat's trajectory brought him within an inch of her face. She screamed and crouched with her arms over her head. She scuttled into the living room and huddled next to Alice on the sofa. Alice pulled a comforter over both their heads. They peered out from under it.

"Have you called Faye?" asked Esme.

"She's in the shower. She said she'll be over as soon as she dries off."

"What's the problem, Al?" The voice belonged to Faye.

Alice and Esme peered over the back of the couch. They were both curious to see if Faye would duck or flinch when the bat came careening toward her. She didn't.

She unfolded a large white cambric handkerchief and tossed it upward. As it floated down, the bat must have thought it was the biggest moth he ever had seen. Faye said bats consumed 600 to 1000 insects an hour. Maybe this bat figured if he ate this moth, he could chill for twenty minutes or so. He flew into it, became entangled, and fell to the floor. Faye wrapped him gently in the handkerchief.

"Shouldn't you wear gloves?" Esme asked. "What if it's rabid?"

"I'll be alright. Turn off the outside light please, Al."

Faye went out onto the porch with Alice and Esme behind her. She stood at the railing and held up the cambric bundle. She slowly opened it, letting the ends drape over her cupped hands. A street lamp illuminated the bat as a dark angular object on the white cloth. After half a dozen heartbeats he flitted away so fast Faye seemed to have hocused him into vanishing.

The three friends went into the kitchen to mix margaritas. It was a two-butt kitchen, but they were used to operating above maximum capacity.

"Alice, would you take care of 'Zilla for a few days?" Esme emptied ice trays into the blender. "Faye works afternoons and nights, and…"

Alice finished the sentence for her. "…and I'm always home."

She knew about Esme's daughter's Rhinoceros iguana, Godzilla. He was almost four feet long and mostly teeth and tail. He was a familiar figure at the beach and playground, waddling along in his harness and leash.

"Are you going away?"

"No." Esme blushed. "About this time of year 'Zilla goes into season."

Alice enjoyed Esme's blushes. The color against her brown skin reminded her of something Monet would paint.

"What does that mean?"

"When I'm menstruating he gets aroused. I can handle him, but Kenya's cycle follows mine and he freaks her out."

"Lizard love?" Alice glanced at Faye, the expert on critters.

"I've heard it happens when no adult human male lives in the house."

"The last time I had my period Zilla grabbed my wrist in his mouth," Esme said. "He mounted my arm and, um, you know."

"He jacked off?" asked Faye.

"He gave it the old college try. If I stick a pacifier in his mouth he calms down. I'm afraid he'll get kennel cough if I board him."

"I'll keep him, Ez, but have you thought about trading him in for a female?"

"He's not a library book or a used car, Al. By the time we discovered his gender, Kenya had already bonded with him."

"You can bond with a lizard?"

"Sure. He's house-trained too. On my way to work tomorrow I'll drop off his box, some kitty litter, and lizard chow. Kenya will walk him over before the school bus comes."

"Bring the pacifier."

"You probably won't need it."

"Bring it anyway."

They took the pitcher of frozen margaritas out onto the porch. They faced three canvas sling chairs into the light breeze whiffling off the water, and sank into them. They sat in silence looking up at the spangle of stars and listening to the chorus of crickets. Now and then a duck chuckled on the creek below.

The clinking of ice in their glasses must have alerted Syl as she was walking home from her mother's house. She climbed the stairs, opened out another chair, and propped her heels next to theirs on the railing. Esme handed over her glass. Syl raised it in thanks.

"I'm worried about Doc." She didn't waste time with amenities.

"Why?" asked Alice.

"Her *jihad* against developers is kicking into high gear."

Faye laughed. "Doc's motto is 'anything worth doing is worth overdoing.'"

Syl didn't find that funny. "Now she's going gangbusters against that proposed shopping center and apartment complex."

"Lots of people are angry about that monstrosity," said Esme.

That didn't reassure Syl. "I heard about a woman who had a stroke and lost her ability to experience fear."

"Well, maybe the hapkido lessons make her feel invincible," said Faye.

"Hapkido?" Alice tried to imagine diminutive Logan throwing people around.

"She's been doing it for years. She's barely five feet tall and weighs ninety pounds with rocks in her pockets. No way that chop-socky mumbo-jumbo will save her skinny ass." Syl started to say something else, stopped, then started again. "Doc found a note under her windshield wiper today when she came out of the grocery store."

"What did it say?"

"'Back off.'"

"That's it?" asked Faye.

"Yeah. Doc laughed it off, but I'm worried."

Alice agreed with Syl. Those two words delivered a threat more effectively than a manifesto.

Esme had her own way of diverting a conversation. She started to sing in a resonant, sweet soprano. " 'Oh, give me land, lots of land under starry skies above. Don't fence me in…' "

It was their anthem of sorts. Alice and Faye sang alto softly so as not to disturb the neighbors or the crickets. " 'Let me ride through the wide open country that I love. Don't fence me in.' "

Syl was new to the group and whistled the tune. Her whistling was so melodic, so evocative of a lone rider silhouetted against a sunset sky, it gave Alice goose bumps.

When they finished, Esme stood up. "Early shift tomorrow."

"I envy you, Es," said Syl. "The airport is a great place for meeting men."

Esme smiled. "And how did your date with that handsome pilot go?"

"Touché."

"You can't say I didn't warn you."

"Yes, you did."

"Married?"

"Probably." Syl's sigh was audible.

"Sweet dreams." Esme turned and walked down the stairs.

"Speaking of men," said Syl. "I have a guy for you, Alice. His name's Russell. He's successful and good-looking. And he has a body as hard as advanced calculus."

"Then why aren't you going after him?"

"He's a client and there's that bothersome ethics thing. Besides, he asked about you. Says he sees you at the gym."

"You mean the guy who struts around in spandex shorts and mesh tank tops."

"I see he caught your attention."

"For all the wrong reasons."

"What have you got to lose?" Syl was unfazed.

"Thanks, but no thanks." Alice made a mental note to go to the gym at a different time of day.

"What about you, Faye?" Syl asked. "You must see a hundred guys at the bar every night."

"Don't get me started."

Faye hesitated, and Alice expected her to launch into one of her outrageous bar stories.

Instead, she said, "An incubus visited me last night."

"What's that?" asked Syl.

"A male sexual demon."

"Really?"

"They can be anything or anyone you want them to be." Faye probably didn't expect to be taken seriously. "I've named him Harry."

"Why Harry?"

Faye shrugged. "Why not?"

"Better than your ex, right, Spook?" Syl gave Faye a fist-bump to the shoulder, and turned to Alice. "Did she tell you her hubby turned out to be a cross-dresser?"

"Yes, she did."

"At least he's easy to shop for at Christmas and birthdays," said Faye. "And he's a kind, considerate guy."

"So how was Harry, this incubus guy?" asked Syl. "Did you get his card? Does he have a friend or a toll-free number?"

"Sorry I brought it up. Must've been the margaritas talking."

Faye and Syl stood up. As they handed over their empty glasses Faye gave a flicker of a smile, reassuring Alice that she would keep her secret.

Not long before Charlie died he gave Alice a vibrator. She had confided in Faye that for the past year it had been haunted.

CHAPTER NINE

"CANE AND ABLE"

Don't hesitate trying to protect your arse.
As soon as an opportunity appears, take it.
Yamaoka Tesshu 1836-1888
(Advice on wrestling river demons who try to
pull their victims' livers out through their anuses)

The radio crackled into static-packed action as Nick upended his thermos and tapped the bottom to flush out the trickle of coffee black as midnight in a subterranean cave. Someone had called in a report of a disturbance outside the nearby bingo parlor.

Nick wasn't surprised. The place catered to senior citizens. Its parking lot was prime turf for muggers and carjackers. That was one reason he chose to drink his morning coffee in this small industrial park.

He rarely arrived in time to see the crime occurring, so this was a stroke of luck. At the far end of the lot an elderly woman and a young man were engaged in a grim tug-of-war with a shoulder bag. What followed was so bizarre he assumed the guys at the station were playing an elaborate joke on him.

With her free hand the woman whacked the boy on the head and face a few times with her cane. These weren't the usual desperate, flailing sort of blows. She delivered them with whip-like wrist action at short range.

He recognized the technique. It was called the three-inch punch. He had seen his sensei use *chi* force to send an opponent across the room with a jab that didn't look powerful enough to rattle a housefly.

He stepped out of the car and started to shout "Police," but stopped, fascinated. The "victim" entwined the cane with the boy's hand grasping the purse strap and the extended arm attached to it. She braced the end of it in her dazed assailant's armpit. Using the cane as a lever on the fulcrum of his wrist and forearm, she twisted it in a way never intended for the human anatomy. He fell on his knees and she gave the cane a slight jerk, pinioning his elbow behind his back.

The snatcher looked about eighteen years old. He howled in pain and sprawled on his stomach with his cheek pressed against the hot asphalt. The cane held his arm behind him and bent it at the elbow like a third of a pretzel. The woman shifted her weight onto the knee pressed into the small of his back. When he tried to free it she gave the cane enough of a twist to make him yelp again.

She let go of the cane with one hand and rapped her knuckles on the crown of his head to get his attention. She interrupted his steady freshet of cursing in which the F and B words predominated.

"Listen to me." She enunciated slowly, as if speaking to a troublesome child. "If you move I will break your arm. If that doesn't stop you I will crack your skull and thread your eye onto the end of this cane like a shish kabob." She paused for effect. "And I will leave you singing soprano."

"Police, ma'am." Nick knew it was past time to start doing his job. "I can take it from here."

"Good morning, officer." She smiled up at him. "Do you suppose this child even knows what a shish kabob is?"

He helped her to her feet. With one cheek pressed against the pavement the boy looked up with a flounder eye, but he didn't move.

"What happened?"

"I caught him keying my car." She nodded toward the long gash on the door on the driver's side. "And then he tried to steal my purse. Martha must've called 9-1-1." She waved at a middle-aged woman who waved back.

"That old bitch attacked me." The mugger seemed sincerely aggrieved that his victim had turned on him so viciously.

Nick didn't feel like chasing someone less than half his age. He fastened ankle restraints before he helped him up. The boy's mouth was already starting to puff up like a toadstool, and blood trickled from a small cut over his eye. Nick handed him a tissue.

As the boy wiped away the blood, he whined, "The bitch broke my wrist, man.".

"The bitch broke my wrist, man."

"Watch your mouth."

"I could have broken it, son," said the woman. "but I didn't."

Nick felt the wrist. It was only sprained, but the boy screamed as if he were being eviscerated.

"Empty your pockets onto the hood of my car."

After the would-be felon had used his good hand to fish a few items from the depths of his sagging camo pants, Nick cuffed his wrists. He patted him down, then frog-marched him to the cruiser.

He ignored the hail of claims of police brutality coming from the back seat and took his latex gloves and plastic bags out of the glove box. The boy's keys were clean, but a box cutter had flakes of high-gloss red paint on it. He found a driver's license in the wallet. It was obviously stolen, but he called in for an ID check anyway. Only then did he notice that the rear end of Dr. Brant's car was rapidly sinking. The kid had punctured both back tires.

The bingo parlor was just outside city limits, so three more county cars came wailing into the parking lot. No one, however, left the bingo hall to see what the ruckus was about.

Nick gave his colleagues a quick summary and they got busy surveying the rest of the lot, interviewing Martha, the witness, and checking out the stolen driver's license. Nick recorded the name and age of the woman who was technically the victim, although this was a case of "You shoulda seen the other guy," if ever he had witnessed one.

Dr. Logan Brant wore crisply-creased jeans, running shoes, and a faded blue Aloha shirt with palm trees, parrots, and orchids on it.

Her wavy gray hair was ear-lobe length and combed back from her chiseled chin and high cheekbones. Her eyes were the same pale blue as the shirt. She looked about sixty, but Nick wasn't surprised to learn she was sixteen years older.

"Finally got to use a couple hapkido cane moves," she said. "I've been taking lessons since the Gipper left office." She beamed up at him. She could've sheltered under his chin with inches to spare. "The Gipper is Ronnie Reagan."

"I know, ma'am. We'll call an ambulance for you."

"Not necessary."

"Then I'll have to ask you to go to the station so we can fill out a report. You can ride with one of the other officers."

"Will I be back in time for the afternoon bingo session?"

He stifled a smile. Apparently she didn't consider vandalism, mugging, a possible hijacking, a knock-down fight, and vilification from a punk kid cause enough to miss bingo.

"Probably."

"I'll drive her to the station." Corporal Len Smoot held his car door open.

"Thank you, officer, but I can drive myself."

"Your back tires are flat, Dr. Brant," said Nick. "In any case forensics will want to check your car for fingerprints, and match the paint flakes on the box cutter. When they finish we can notify you to arrange to have the tires fixed."

"Then I prefer to ride with you…," She came close and peered at Nick's nametag. "…Detective Shea."

"Yes, ma'am. Officer Smoot, would you transfer the boy to your car?"

"Why can't he ride with us?" asked Logan.

"He's agitated, ma'am. No telling what he'll say."

"Please, Detective Shea. I don't mind."

The glass isolating the rear of the cruiser was shatter-proof and bullet-proof but not sound-proof. The kid raged that the old hag was a menace and he would press charges.

"I think souls are developing glitches." The sadness in Dr. Logan Brant's voice surprised Nick.

"I beg your pardon, ma'am?"

"The conservation of energy is an empirical law of physics. In a closed system, energy can neither be created nor destroyed. It can only be changed from one state to another, like ice to water to steam."

This wasn't the conversation he expected.

"Souls are recycled, but our species has reproduced so successfully that maybe souls are getting worn out, the way a template loses its crisp edges. Maybe some children are being born with defective souls."

"It's about brain wiring, ma'am. Criminals have made up a large part of our species since they first started burglarizing caves and stealing mastadon steaks."

"That's true, but I like my theory."

In spite of the distractions from the back seat and the front, Nick took a tour of the lot. He knew the city police were on the job, but he surveyed all the parked cars. The only vehicle damaged was Dr. Logan Brant's.

A couple questions nagged at him. Why would a two-bit petty thief bother to key his victim's car before he tried to steal her purse? And if he intended to hijack the car, why would he want to damage it and flatten the tires?

"I don't know who might have paid that boy to vandalize my car, Detective Shea."

Dr. Brant had the angelic look of Nick's own diminutive grandmother. Despite that, he was sure she was lying. But why?

She rested her elbows on his desk. "What's going to happen to him?"

"They'll book him and put him up in a holding cell until his initial appearance in the magistrate court, then a preliminary hearing, a bail bond hearing, and arraignment."

"Have you learned his name?"

The booking officer had told him that the wanna-be mugger had given up that much information. It was enough to find out he had priors. He was eighteen so his name would probably appear in the newspaper's Police Beat anyway.

"He calls himself Hot Dog," said Nick, "but his name is Emanuel Boyd."

"God Is With Us."

"I beg your pardon?"

"Emanuel means 'God Is With Us.'"

"If you think of anything that might be of help, or if anyone threatens you, give me a call." He handed Dr. Brant his card. "Someone will notify you when they finish with your car." Nick saw a hint of consternation in her eyes. "Don't worry about it. I know a good mechanic who'll tow it, and fix the tires."

He beckoned to Len Smoot. Smoot was twenty-three and fresh from the academy. New recruits bore the generic nickname "Boot," which made Len's surname unfortunate. Losing the moniker Smoot the Boot might take a couple years.

"I have to fill out paperwork, Dr. Brant, but Officer Smoot will take you wherever you want to go."

"The bingo hall is not far. I can walk."

"I'd rather you ride with an officer."

If she went on foot in this part of town, some other lowlife might think she'd be easy pickings. The emergency room had enough patients without the good doctor and her cane sending them more. As they left, Nick wondered if she would enlighten Len on the recycling of souls.

He got a copy of the booker's form and went to his desk to work on his report. Maybe he could shave a few minutes off the hours of station time the average arrest consumed. He snatched half a dozen forms from the racks on the wall and opened his laptop.

He hadn't set out to amuse readers and inspire reporters for the Police Beat. Bored one day, he had indulged in a bit of philosophizing in his after-action report. He hadn't intended to become a repeat offender, but like potato chips and tattoos, it was hard to stop with one ad-lib in a scripted exercise.

Today he began with, "On Saturday, rough justice stood five feet tall, wielded a cane, and wore high tops and an aloha shirt."

He expected to see few changes in his prose when it appeared in the *Chronicle*. Maybe the Police Beat reporter Joe Stone would add something original this time, but he doubted it.

Chapter Ten

"Bingo!"

You can take it as understood
that your luck changes only if it's good.
Ogden Nash
Roulette Us Be Gay

Alice rocked back in her squeaky desk chair and thought about thought. Did a thought become tangible when it was written down? And did writing a thought capture it or set it free? Did sharing it with others alter it like the colors of a mood ring on different fingers? If unwritten, did it exist in some sort of half-life, wandering in the brain's maze? She pictured the unwritten thought as a helmeted space traveler, umbilical cord cut from his ship, adrift in the vastness of the universe.

She stopped thinking about thought and went back to staring into the poker face of her monitor's blank screen. Esme's daughter's iguana, Godzilla, slept under her bare feet like a scaly ottoman with a pulse. His rough skin felt good on her soles, like a mini-reflexology session. The soft tweets and whiffles of his snores lent a subtle sort of domestic bliss to her usual solitude.

The phone rang. Syl was on the other end. Alice had noticed that Syl didn't drop in unannounced now that 'Zilla was cohabiting.

"Come with me to pick up Doc."

"Is her car in the shop?" If Alice had been making any progress on the novel she would have been annoyed at the interruption.

"She was mugged this morning outside that damned bingo den."

"Is she alright?"

"She says she is. But did she call her only daughter?" Syl's question was rhetorical. "No. She did not. The only reason I know about it is because a reporter showed up at my office with some story about her beating the crap out of an 'alleged' attacker. He said he had heard the report of Doc and her cane o' death on his scanner." Syl snorted. "I told him where he could put his scanner."

"Is Logan at the police station?"

"I called there and they said she's back at the bingo hall. They're keeping her car for evidence or something." Syl paused, "I'm worried about Doc, Alice."

"That's understandable. Someone attacked your mother in a parking lot."

"Besides that. Her eyesight is going and she's starting to forget things. Could she be coming down with Alzheimer's?"

"Get her to make an appointment with a neurologist."

"She says doctors don't know squat."

"And yet…"

"I know. Ironic, isn't it, her being an MD and all."

"Is she a urologist?"

"How'd you guess?"

"The testicles remark at the crab feast."

"Don't mention her work, Al. She'll start talking shop, and oh man, does she have stories."

"I'll meet you out front in five." Alice rubbed 'Zilla's head with her toes before she slid her feet into her sandals.

But Syl wasn't finished. "By the way, this morning Doc phoned to ask me to invite you to dinner tonight."

"Why me?"

"She likes you."

"She hardly knows me."

"Maybe she wants to get to know you better."

When Alice closed the front door behind her, she saw Syl's Mercedes out front with the motor purring. Elvis was crooning "Are You Lonesome Tonight?" on the stereo and the air-conditioner was going full blast.

On the way out of the neighborhood Syl slowed in front of the house her ex occupied. She rolled down her window, letting in a gust of toasty air. She stuck out her arm and gave a vigorous middle finger salute as she passed.

"I still miss the son of a bitch, but my aim is improving."

Alice was disappointed when Syl rolled her window up, cutting off the warm breeze. "Why did you marry him?"

Syl lowered her sunglasses and glanced over the rims at her. Under purple-shadowed lids, like shades half drawn, her green eyes looked as though she'd just waked from a sexy dream. Add a tousle of dark chestnut curls and a pair of thirty-six double D's and it was not surprising Syl attracted the salivating sort.

"Jerry was handsome. He was sweet, and funny. He really was. And a very shrewd lawyer."

"What happened?"

"Time happened. First the fortieth birthday and the Lamborghini. Then the forty-fifth and hair plugs. Finally the fiftieth and he started screwing his friends' daughters."

They rode for half a mile before Syl broke the silence. "I woke up the other day sober enough to realize I'd put out for a guy with a play-off bracket on the back of his closet door."

"What's that?"

"A flow chart of winners and losers for sports teams in tournaments."

"So he likes sports?"

"He likes sporting. This bracket had photos of naked chicklets, all ID'd and ranked."

"Don't tell me…"

"Oh yeah. He'd already printed out my picture and posted it. And the bastard had tacked it up in the middle of the pack." Being ranked as mediocre obviously rankled her.

"Didn't you know what he was up to?"

"I might've passed out."

This time Alice's look had a hint of reproof.

"I know. I have to cut back on the sauce."

"What did you do?"

"While he was in the shower I tore up the picture and emptied my bottle of Shalimar onto his mattress."

"Shalimar? Do they still make that?"

"Focus, Al."

"Right."

"He'd left his smart-ass phone on the nightstand with the whole lot of us stored in it. I dropped it in the toilet while he was still showering and flushed. He screamed like a girl when the hot water hit him."

They rode in silence for a minute, then Syl asked, "What do you make of Faye's nocturnal admission, Al?"

"You mean the visit from the incubus? The sex demon?"

"Yeah."

"She doesn't lie," said Alice. "But she does occupy an enhanced reality."

Syl pulled into the parking lot at the Bingo Palace. "Some advice before we go in. Don't talk to anyone. Don't sit down. If someone finds you in her regular seat things will turn ugly. And for Pete's sake, don't yell 'Bingo!' as a joke."

A mirrored ball hung in the middle of the big room as a relic of the hall's former disco hip-ness. Some of the fluorescent lights in the ceiling had burned out, their rectangular translucent covers dark as fallow fields among the acoustic tiles. Smoke from scores of candles and incense formed a haze over the long tables.

The players, most of them women, sipped tepid coffee from Styrofoam cups. The hollow popping of numbered balls dancing inside a glass globe was punctuated by the whiskey-and-cigarettes voice of the caller, a lank-haired land mass in a muumuu.

Besides the candles and incense, each player had set out other objects in precise arrangements. Alice saw photos, statuettes of saints, religious medals, stuffed animals, dolls, and bronzed baby shoes. Angels were popular. Stuffed, molded, glazed, carved, and crocheted angels. Angels made of metal, glass, bread dough, pipe cleaners, handkerchiefs, and yarn.

The place reminded Alice of the post-World War II cargo cults on the island of New Guinea. The candles resembled the rows of fires the natives set out to imitate landing lights and lure the big cargo planes back.

Someone yelled "Bingo," and Syl threaded her way among the tables with Alice behind her. Over the low hum of conversation, a cricket-like clicking rose as players swept magnetic wands across their cards to collect the metal markers.

"Oh shit," muttered Syl. "She's wearing that gawd-awful shirt. She thinks it's lucky. It looks like someone threw up on her after too many mai-tais."

Syl gestured for her mother to come, but Logan ignored her.

"It's late, Doc, and Alice has to get back to work."

"Hi, Alice."

"Hi, Logan."

Logan collected her marking pens, a small statue of Buddha, and a popsicle stick frame holding a photo of a small girl with pigtails and a cherubic smile. Alice guessed this particular little angel was Syl.

Are you a vegetarian, Alice?" Logan asked.

"Yes."

"I thought so."

"May I bring anything to dinner tomorrow night?"

"A copy of your latest book." Logan's eyes widened, as if a thought had just occurred to her. "I met the nicest police officer today. A detective."

"So, how much did you win, Doc?" Syl diverted the subject.

"It's not about winning and losing, Sylvana."

"Yes it is, Doc, and you know it."

CHAPTER ELEVEN

"LOVE IS JUST AROUND THE CORONER"

I Smell a Rat.
Ben Jonson (1573? – 1637)
Tale of a Tub

A hundred or more pleasure craft twitched and tugged on their tethers at the piers fingering out into the bay. The crowd was typical for a mid-week summer night at the Red Eye Dock Bar and Marina. Nick walked out onto the rambling expanse of wooden decks cantilevered over the water on pilings. He gave a slight salute to the two beefy bouncers. They nodded back.

The Red Eye's security personnel wore chinos and headsets, running shoes and red tee-shirts with a large, bloodshot eye stretched across their bulging pectorals. They stood one each next to the big wooden planters located at thirty-foot intervals around the edge of the deck. The throb of top-forty covers blared from speakers mounted on poles above them.

A body of legend had grown up around the bouncers. The belief was that they had the perceptive ability of a C.A.T. scan, the strength of a bulldozer, and the martial arts abilities of Bruce Lee. That was one reason why Nick came here. Whatever disturbance might erupt, they could take care of it. Also, Nick felt the need now and then to mingle with fellow bipeds who were not engaged in criminal activity. At least he was pretty sure most of them weren't.

He scanned across the three thatched bars, the outdoor stage, and dance floor. Will was at his usual place at the bar in the smallest and most distant of the tiki huts. Conversation was possible there without shouting.

Will sat on the barstool he referred to as the Tippler's Antipode. Nick guessed he called it that because no one else in that happy hour horde knew what either tippler or antipode meant. Will preferred to put mental, emotional, and physical distance between himself and the up-and-comers trolling for love around the bandstand.

Nick settled on a stool to the leeward of Will's as Faye, the bartender, slid the usual double Jack on the rocks down the polished teak that once had graced some sea-going yacht. Will and Nick glanced at the hopefuls doing their best to put the happy in happy hour. Nick raised the sparkling ice and dark amber.

"'The wombat lives across the seas,'" he recited. "'Among the far Antipodes. He may exist on nuts and berries, or then again on missionaries.'"

Will clinked his glass against Nick's. "Here's to being poles apart."

Will wore ripped jeans, sockless docksiders, and his favorite shirt. The black tee featured a bold white graphic of a grinning skull in a cowboy hat. Circling it like a lasso were the words, "Death. It's a Living." A Goth crowd would have appreciated it, but not this bunch.

"Did you know," Will said, "That forty percent of women have hurled footwear at a man?"

"Poor bastard." Nick stared into the glass, more fascinated by the irridescent play of jewel-toned light than by its promise of oblivion. "But in my experience they fling china and stemware."

Will already had moved on. "The shop hired a new rat wrangler."

"Tell me again what a rat wrangler does."

"Interns are given the shit jobs. Our rat wranglers are assigned forensics for crime scenes smaller than a breadbox."

"You mean dead rodents found in cereal boxes or loaves of pumpernickel?"

"Doesn't have to be the whole cadaver. Parts will do. The question is, did the deceased get into the not-so-happy meal by accident, or did it have help?"

"And the answer is…?"

"… for the rat-wrangler to find out. First he looks for tooth marks on the container. Dead rats don't gnaw. Next comes neck-cropsy. Ligature abrasions on the neck mean the critter perished in a mouse trap. You don't find many of those in boxes of Chocolate Frosted Honey Nut Frute-O's. Green dye in the stomach indicates rat poison. When only bones or tufts of fur remain, the case becomes more interesting. The newbies hate it, but it's good training."

"At least your customers are silent."

Will chuckled. "Speaking of which, your Antique Avenger is all the chatter among your scanner fans."

"I assume you mean the set-to in the bingo hall's parking lot this morning."

Nick knew that a large portion of civilian scanner owners were marijuana growers hoping police would let slip their next bust plan. But he also was vaguely aware he had a following among police groupies. He didn't mean to put wit into his calls, but sometimes a sardonic remark slipped out. He didn't remember using the term Antique Avenger, but he might have.

"She has a rap sheet." Nick didn't usually run a check on victims, but this was not the average mugging.

"No shit? The old lady and her cane o' chaos?"

"She's been written up for rowdiness at demonstrations. Blocking traffic, disturbing the peace, assault with a protest sign. One law suit called her a menace."

Nick realized that was the second time today he had heard Dr. Brant called a menace.

Will stepped in front of his train of thought. "What did the sign say?"

"'There is no planet B.'"

"So, she likes to go out and wave a sign around now and then. Big deal."

"I found out her neighbor has filed a lot of complaints. He claims she nailed his cats with a paint gun. Says they're now purple and green. She also shot out his bug zapper and his motion-triggered flood light. He wanted her arrested."

"She shot out the bug zapper with a paint gun from across the street?"

"He claimed she used a semi-automatic assault rifle for that. I talked to the investigating officer. He said he only found bb's on the scene. When he knocked on her door she invited him in for tea. He didn't have a search warrant and he didn't see a gun. But at the station they're talking about recruiting her for the S.W.A.T. team."

"Do you suppose the neighbor hired some street punk to etch a racing stripe on her car and take her purse as pay back?"

"I'll be talking to the neighbor."

Faye the bartender returned to top off their glasses. "We're featuring a new drink tonight. Fallen Angel."

"What's in it?" asked Will.

"Three quarters sambuca. Wild Turkey floating on top. No blending so the amber band of whiskey rests on the liqueur."

"I'll try one," said Will.

Faye performed her sleight-of-hand with the two bottles and set the Fallen Angel in front of Will.

While she waited to see how he liked it she said, "Nick, I know you don't like set-ups, but I have a friend…"

"Thanks, Faye, but I'm not interested."

"Yeah, yeah. You've told me. Married to your job. Yadda, yadda. But you would like her."

"Maybe some other time."

Nick watched her and her magenta mohawk move to the other end of the bar to confront a drunk who was pounding on the teak with his beer mug. Nick couldn't see auras often, but he'd caught a glimpse of Faye's once. It was the same color as her hair. He liked Faye, but if her friends were as outlandish as she was he could not imagine falling in love with one of them.

"I met someone interesting," Will said. "An ER nurse."

"A nurse." Nick nodded. "That makes sense."

"Vivian says if she had it to do over she'd become a coroner. She says the colors inside the human body are extraordinary. She says she wishes she had a cocktail dress the color of aortal blood."

The E.R. nurse has a name, thought Nick. Will didn't usually divulge such intimate information this early in the mating ritual.

"So, are you two dating?"

"We start swing-dance lessons next Saturday."

Nick tried to imagine Will doing the jitterbug and failed.

He had never seen such an expression of cautious euphoria, mixed with chagrin, hope, and terror on his friend's face before. Maybe this was the real thing. Nick hoped so. Whenever Will came down he made a hard landing.

Cops usually only hung out with other cops, but it was no surprise Nick liked Will. Cops and coroners. Both had difficulty making small talk at parties.

Nick remembered the rest of Will's favorite poem about wombats.

> His distant habitat precludes
> Conclusive knowledge of his moods,
> But I would not engage the wombat
> In any form of mortal combat.

CHAPTER TWELVE

PRIVATE DICK STORIES

*The ghost that got into our house raised such a
hullabaloo of misunderstandings that I am sorry
I didn't just let it keep walking, and go to bed.*
James Thurber
My Life and Hard Times

Alice closed the gate behind Esme and herself, but the act was a formality. The fence's unpainted pickets leaned helter-skelter like drunks in a conga line. A large mound of dirt rose beside a deep hole in the rear of the side yard, a septic pit in progress. The rest of Logan's over-grown garden pulsed with light and shadow, insect calls and birdsong. The anarchy there gave Alice a sense of serenity.

Not everyone shared her attitude.

Across the street her neighbor finished manicuring his putting green of a lawn. He shut off his mower with a twenty-four horse-power engine and tight turn capability. He dismounted into a rever-berating silence as though climbing off a rodeo bull. He replaced the family of yard gnomes and their little plaster cart full of plastic flowers.

The silence was short lived. He revved up his leaf blower and began redistributing the debris into the street and adjoining yards. In the middle of the swirling storm of leaves and grass clippings, the gnome family with their cart looked like bewildered refugees from a hurricane. The sudden din also startled the family cat. Alice paused on Logan's front porch to watch the big gray tom with chartreuse ears and a purple caboose dodge through the gnome obstacle course and disappear under the porch. Then she opened the screen door.

Inside, tendrils of wisteria undulated through holes in the screens. Swags of philodendron lolled like emerald pythons along curtain rods made of bamboo. Virtual tropical fish swam across a monitor screen while its computer hummed like a monk under a cowl of loose papers. A baby grand piano filled one corner of the living room. Books rose in angular stalagmites from the heart-pine floor. Posters, paintings, and family photos left little of the wood paneled walls visible.

An aroma of sautéed mushrooms and onions followed Logan out of the kitchen. "Alice, I met the nicest policeman today."

"You mentioned that at the bowling alley."

"A very handsome young man. And tall too. He's a police detective."

Alice was saved from having to respond when Syl arrived waving a can of wasp spray.

"Doc, what's this I hear about a rat in your mailbox?"

"It's probably just a prank."

"Like hell. It's the Grim Mower." If looks could kill, the across-the-street neighbor would already be a goner. "This is war."

Logan focused on the can in Syl's hand. "Sylvana, you know I don't condone insect spray."

"This is for two-legged pests, not six-legged ones, Doc. It's better than mace or pepper spray. It's more accurate and comes out in a harder stream." Syl set it on the kitchen counter by the stove.

That confirmed what Alice had suspected. For all Syl's complaints about her mother she was worried about Doc's safety.

After dinner, Logan said thanks, but no thanks to offers of help with the dishes. Alice and Esme stood at the rail of the rear deck outside the French doors. The far side of the deck was cantilevered out over the deep ravine with its dense growth of trees, vines, and tall bushes. A doe and a fawn ghosted along the bottom of it. As dusk turned to darkness a raccoon and her two little ones trundled up the steps. They sat in an expectant row and stared fixedly at Alice and Esme.

"Syl," Esme called softly. "Your friends are here."

Syl arrived with a dog dish of kibbles. "They're no friends of mine, the mangy little moochers." Grumbling about rabies, she stood back while they gathered around it.

"Syl feeds them when Logan's away." Esme smiled at Alice. "I even caught her in the grocery store buying them cat treats."

Logan's voice came from the kitchen. "Cut it out, Nelly."

"Who's Nelly?" asked Alice.

Syl rolled her eyes. "Ignore her."

"Nelly's the resident ghost," said Esme. "She came with the house."

They clustered in the kitchen doorway and watched Logan fuss at the toaster. She flipped the handle up and the red glow in the element faded.

"I wish Faye weren't working tonight. She usually can quiet her down."

"I'm telling you, Doc, it's that old wiring. It has more shorts than Wimbledon."

A scratching of nails on glass came from the French doors, and the raccoons stared in at them, their eyes glittering red in the dark. Syl returned to the deck and handed out cat treats like candy at Halloween.

Esme returned to the subject of the haunted toaster. "Faye says Nelly's a discarnate. A ghost."

"Doesn't that frighten you, Logan?" asked Alice.

"She made me uneasy at first, but I've gotten used to her."

The small washing machine in the alcove rumbled into action. Logan banged on it with the flat of her hand.

"Faye says spirits come back for a reason, usually to deliver a message to a loved one. But ghosts hang around because they want someone to help them complete unfinished business. Even Faye's had no luck getting this one to leave."

The kettle started whistling on the stove and Alice put a tea bag into each of the four cups on a tray. Esme carried the plate of lemon cake slices to the living room, leaving the kitchen to Annie.

Esme and Logan shared the small couch. Syl and Alice settled into the two overstuffed chairs that took up most of the rest of the small room.

"I've invited Freddy to dinner next week, Sylvana."

"Bad idea, Doc."

"Who's Freddy?" asked Alice.

"He's in cahoots with the skeevy developer of that mall project," said Syl.

"Destroying a wetland is bad enough," added Logan. "He's also let slip that they have plans to build condos and a marina at the mouth of our creek."

"Doc's been busting Freddy's chops for months now."

"What makes you think he'll come to dinner here, Logan?"

"He's my nephew."

"Cousin Freddy is the poster child for birth control," added Syl. "And to make it even more incestuous, my ex, Jerry, is his mouthpiece."

"Freddy's not that bright. His business associate, Sam Hare, is the real culprit. He's using Freddy's very generous inheritance as seed money."

"Why don't you go after him instead of Freddy?"

"I've tried, but he hides behind a wall of administrative assistants and lawyers. Maybe over dinner I can persuade Freddy to pull out of the project."

"Don't tell me you're going to lecture him again about saving the horned pad weed and the widgeon grass."

"If reason doesn't work, I'll blackmail him."

"Not the vacuum cleaner story, Doc. It's not the sort of letter-to-the editor the newspaper will print."

"I know folks at Freddy's yacht club. At his country club. His favorite bar. His gym. And then there's the internet. I do love the internet. Its anonymity circumvents patient confidentiality. Although, technically, Freddy isn't one of my patients."

"How could you, Logan?" Esme came as close to scolding as Alice had ever witnessed.

"Gloves are off with someone as ethically-challenged as Freddy, my dear."

"What about the vacuum cleaner?" Alice asked.

"Just before I retired, Freddy came into my office with his willy in a sling. I referred him to my partner in the practice, but not before he told me he'd gotten high on weed and stuck his penis into the sucking end of the vacuum cleaner."

"Is that even possible?"

"You'd be amazed at what's possible, Alice. Next thing he knew, blood was spurting all over his new carpet."

"The vacuum cleaner cut off his penis?"

"Mangled it pretty badly. Freddy didn't realize there's a fan inside to blow the dust into the collection bag. He got caught by the blades. It happens more often than you'd think."

Alice and Esme said "Ouch" in unison.

"Men also have a tendency to slam them in toilet seats. Don't ask me how."

"I told you not to get Doc started on dick stories," said Syl.

"Faye tells me you had her over to dowse for a septic tank site," said Esme.

"I did. They started digging the hole today."

The dryer rumbled in the kitchen alcove, then shut off with a loud click.

Logan called out, "I'll read to you later."

"Reading to a major appliance is stupid, Doc. Ghosts don't exist."

"Tell that to your father, Sylvana." Logan nodded at the recliner with a crocheted afghan draped across it. "I saw him in his chair yesterday."

"You had one too many vodka tonics, Ma." Syl rattled her car keys. "I'm going to the Red Eye for a nightcap. Al, Esme, want to come with me?"

"I have to work early tomorrow," said Esme. "Give my love to Faye."

"And I'm going to try to start a new chapter before bedtime."

At the door, Logan put a hand on Alice's. "You're a spirit now too, my dear, and so am I. They're part of us – your Charlie, Esme's Aaron, my Mitch."

As Alice and Esme started up the street toward home, Alice said, "Logan's right."

"About what?"

"I use Charlie's favorite expressions. I've adopted some of his habits. I ask him for advice."

"Does he answer?"

"No, but I imagine what he would say. Have you seen Aaron?"

"I thought I caught a glimpse of him once. And he visits in dreams."

"Charlie's never come back."

"Why do you think he hasn't?"

"I guess he knows I'd freak out."

"Is there another reason?"

Alice stopped. "Yes." The second reason had not occurred to her before.

"What is it?"

Alice had a feeling her friend already knew. That was why Esme was the best customer relations person at the airport.

"Because he knows if I see him, I'll want to join him."

Chapter Thirteen

"Home Is Where the Heart Is"

Something will come of this.
I hope it mayn't be human gore.
Charles Dickens
Barnaby Rudge

Nick wasn't surprised to see Joe Stone's old Buick Skylark among the police vehicles at the scene. Stone yelled to him, but he pretended not to hear. So far, the reporter had been content to use Nick's reports practically verbatim and not bother him when he was working. This time he tried to make his way through the crowd of police and firemen to reach Nick. To Nick's relief the cop on duty in front of Logan's house made him go across the street.

Nick introduced himself to the burly foreman of the septic company's excavation crew. He and his men were standing outside the yellow crime-scene tape.

"We found them down there when we came to work this morning," the foreman said. "Them and the other thing."

Nick locked looks with him. "We request that you and your men tell no one about the other thing. If anyone asks, you found a pig's heart."

"Understood." The foreman nodded, then added, "Someone from Natural Resources is on the way."

"Thanks."

But the "other thing" was why Nick had been called.

The foreman checked his watch and looked at the sun climbing higher in the morning sky. Maybe he was fretting about time lost, or maybe not. He put his hands in the pockets of his khaki pants and rocked from the heels to the toes of his work boots while he watched Megan, the police photographer, taking pictures from every angle.

The forensics team had designated a narrow path to the crime scene. Nick ducked under the yellow tape and walked to the pit in Dr. Logan Brant's side yard. The freshly-turned soil was a mosaic of the vibrum-soled prints of work boots. Making casts and matching all of them to the shoes of the septic company crew to rule them out would keep forensics busy. Even then, the possibility existed that one or more of those workmen were the perpetrators. They all would have to be checked out.

Nick stood under the toothy jaws at the end of the excavator's long neck. With the toes of his perfectly-polished shoes at the edge of the hole he studied the two corpses lying on the bottom of it. Their magnificent wingspreads were six feet at least. He gave his head a slight shake to clear out the haunting image of dead angels.

The two eagles would require a necropsy to determine time and cause of death. He wondered if the morgue's new rat-wrangler would get the job. Already he was assessing implications in the murder of two members of an endangered species in the front yard of an environmental activist. An activist who had been mugged two days before.

This was what police called a "one-off." Not the casual, garden variety felony. Nor was it a "gimme." No smoking gun here. But given what everyone knew about the hostility between the developers and the environmentalists, the list of possible perpetrators was already assembling in Nick's head.

He sensed someone standing next to him and turned to find Cindy, the Natural Resources officer, staring at the eagles too.

"So this is where they ended up." Maybe the slant of the morning sun made her eyes sparkle with what looked like tears.

"You know where they came from?"

"Not that many nesting pairs of bald eagles around here." She pretended to have something in her eyes and wiped them with her sleeve. "A couple days ago we checked out a report of a dead dog, road kill, on the beach at that island in Herald Bay."

"The one where the developer, Hare, built his mansion with a kiss-my-ass instead of permits?"

"He's the one who reported the dog's body. Since there aren't any dogs on the island he wanted someone to investigate for trespassing. The dog was laced with strychnine, though, and the eagles haven't been seen since."

So the prime suspect phoned in the report of the poisoning he himself might have done. Misdirection or innocence? Maybe this wouldn't be the slam-dunk Nick was hoping for.

As he looked into the excavation he felt a pang of envy for the foreman's muddy work boots. The dispatcher who sent him here had codes for everything else about a crime scene. Why not a dress code to warn him that he would be tobogganing down the side of a mud hole and slogging around in the bog of wet clay at its bottom?

The foreman called from the street. "It's under the wing of the biggest bird. When our guy saw it he put everything back the way he found it and we called you all."

"Thanks." Nick hoped the workman had left his gloves on when he did it. But then, styrofoam and meat were hard to lift prints off of anyway.

"I'll wait 'til you're through," said Cindy.

He accepted the certainty that he could not do this with dignity nor without a dry-cleaning bill, and went over the edge of the hole. He slid most of the way to the bottom on the seat of his pants. He put on his latex gloves and gently raised the eagle's wing.

He found the heart where the men said it would be. It was neatly packed in a styrofoam take-out container, like a leftover from some macabre all-you-can-eat buffet. The septic company's employees opined it must be a pig's heart planted by some prankster, but he knew better. Maybe a homicide and maybe not.

The police must have been distracted, because Dr. Logan Brant's face appeared at the hole's rim. The business end of the shaft of morning sunlight formed a penumbra, like a halo around her head. She was clearly and understandably distraught and angry.

"Who would commit such a despicable act, Detective Shea?"

Len Smoot ushered her off before Nick could say he did not know. He sniffed the heart before he left the container in place for the deputy coroner and the forensics team. Not much odor of decay. It was either fresh or, as they advertised in fish markets, pre-frozen. He saw a search for a heartless body in his near future.

Careful not to step on any footprints, he made a reconnaissance loop outside the perimeter of the tape. When he reached the rear of the house he stood for several minutes staring down into the deep, green ravine. Nothing caught his eye, and if anything important was down there the investigating team would find it.

He went to his patrol car to call in and saw that the dead-end street was filling with curious neighbors. He didn't notice the man making his way through the crowd and confusion until the guy started yelling.

"God dammit!" He kept shouting as he strode across the street and up to Nick. "That god-damned bitch!"

"Sir, this is a crime scene. Please move back."

"Crime scene? I'll show you a crime scene." He pointed to his immaculately manicured lawn across the street. "That's a goddamn crime scene."

"Has anyone been murdered or injured there?" Nick saw what was troubling him and he tried to keep the sarcasm out his voice. He really did.

"No. But that old biddy is a menace."

Nick added a third checkmark in Dr. Brant's menace column. "When we're through here we'll send an officer to talk to you about your complaint."

He added this guy to the list of suspects, although frankly, he seemed too goofy to pull off something this complicated.

Only two dead eagles could have distracted everyone from the tableau in the yard across the street. He walked over for a closer look at the neighbor's gnomes.

Mama Gnome wielded a whip of black leather strips. She wore a studded dog collar, an outsized push-up bra, and a satin garter belt over a clump of wiry hair glued on at crotch level. The hair looked like a poodle's or the sweepings from under a beauty salon chair. Nick put some of the hair into a bag for a DNA sample.

Dad sported a black lace string bikini, a feather boa, and a woman's cloche hat. He tottered on red spike heels that had been glued to his feet. The vandal, or vandals, had added imps' horns and strap-on dildos to the gnomes' three offspring. The scene had bored, but creative, teenagers written on it as clearly as the beards and pendulous breasts drawn in magic markers.

Nick sat back on his heels to inspect the items in the gnomes' cart. It contained a vibrator, penis rings, nipple clips, dildos, chains, and gadgets that even he didn't recognize. And he had worked Vice along Charm City's East Baltimore Street red light district back when strip clubs, peep shows, and sex shops flourished there.

The cart's cargo changed his assessment of the situation. Teenagers relied on youthful stamina and illicit substances for their kicks. These weren't the sorts of sex toys most of them had access to, unless they had some kinky parents.

Were the front-to-front crime scenes a coincidence, or was some psycho prankster on the loose in the neighborhood? And if so, had he or she been responsible for the trouble in both yards? Did Dr. Brant think the neighbor had put the kid up to defacing her car and trying to rob her? Was this her pay-back?

The underside of the street's tree canopy lit up with the flashing lights on the police cruisers, the Natural Resources big green Ford four-by-four, and the volunteer fire department's truck and ambulance. A crowd of first-responders stood in clumps inside the festoons of yellow tape. Dr. Brant was handing out homemade cookies and glasses of iced tea to all of them.

The fellow with the kinky gnomes was patrolling the street side of his property line to make sure no one tried to park on his grass. The workmen and the gawkers milled around in the road and neighboring yards. Most of them held their cell phones over their heads so they could photograph and film the scene.

Nick had seen his share of bizarre situations, but this one made the short list. Cliffs of the Severn had always seemed quiet and innocuous, but now it took on a sinister vibe. He felt as though he had fallen down a rabbit hole and landed in an alternate universe.

Chapter Fourteen

"A Trolling Stone"

...in this world nothing can be said to be certain
except death and taxes.
Benjamin Franklin (1706-1790)

On Friday afternoon Alice decided to visit Faye at the Red Eye. Like a race horse, the Vette needed exercise. She hadn't driven it much in the week since that strange encounter with the drunk and his snake at the Department of Motor Vehicles.

While she changed into new-ish jeans and a clean shirt she hoped the snake was adjusting to life outside the confines of an automobile glove compartment. She also wondered who the Undercover Cop was. Whenever she went to the grocery store or the library or post office now, she couldn't help looking for that black t-shirt.

She put on her best sandals and combed her hair. She folded the letter that had come in the mail that morning and stuck it into her jeans' back pocket. The letter was the real reason she felt the need to talk to her friend Faye. She took the back route out of the neighborhood and didn't see the remaining police and fire vehicles still parked at Logan's house.

On Friday afternoons Faye's elbow benders were a docile bunch. Unlike the crowd that would swarm in later, they were more in search of an eighty-proof placebo for loneliness than scoring a one-night affair.

The Red Eye had no door, but it did have a door-man, a formidable individual named Ralph. Faye must have spotted her friend bantering with him. She had a margarita on the rocks, no salt, waiting on the bar when Alice sat down.

"So you've left your cave and ventured out into the wide world." Faye put her forearms on the polished teak and leaned forward. She knew better than to ask how the writing was going. "What's new?"

Alice took the envelope from her back pocket and handed it to her. Faye read the return address.

"The IRS sent Charlie a letter?"

"I replied to an earlier notice and told them he was deceased."

Faye opened the letter and scanned it. "That would explain why the heading reads, 'Charles Deceased O'Brien.'" Her laugh was as dry as one of her martinis. "So, they want to know if he's changed his address."

"Yeah. Should I tell them what's left of him resides in a quart-sized beer stein at 619 Avon Road? That would be easier than trying to list where we've scattered the rest of his ashes."

"Ignore them." Faye folded the letter and handed it back to her. "You and Charlie weren't legally married. They don't have a choke hold on you."

Alice stood up to return it to her back pocket while Faye went to take care of the other five customers at the bar. When she returned Alice detected worry in her eyes.

"What's wrong?"

"I haven't heard from Kelly in a few weeks."

"Maybe he's taken the boat on a trip somewhere."

"I went by the marina. It's still at the dock."

Alice understood why Faye was worried about her ex-husband. For the first five years of their marriage she had thought him wonderfully romantic, buying her beautiful lingerie and expensive spike-heeled shoes. Then she came home early from work one night and found him wearing her black silk high-cuts and matching push-up bra.

At the time she told Alice that at least she realized then why she kept running out of lipstick and eye shadow. As she put it, "When he came out of the closet he had on everything in it."

Alice put a hand lightly on Faye's wrist. "I'm sure he's okay. Being out, as it were, in public is new for him."

"That's what I'm afraid of. He's a sweet, considerate, affectionate guy, but he says the danger of discovery is an aphrodisiac for him."

"File a missing person report."

"I'll give him a few more days." Faye glanced over Alice's shoulder. "By the way, the pudgy little guy in the safari jacket is staring at you."

"Do you know him?"

"His name's Joe Stone. He shows up now and then. Always alone. He says he's a reporter for the *Chronicle*. Wears those ridiculous hiking boots. Dresses like John Wayne in *Hatari*." Faye gave a slight eye-roll. "And he's heading your way."

Faye went off to see to the others at the bar, although Alice suspected she wanted to avoid conversation with the reporter. Stone hitched up onto the bar stool next to her. The tuft of thin, pale hair sticking up from his cowlick reached to about the height of her earlobe.

"What're you drinking, gorgeous?"

She glanced over at him. "I've had my limit, thanks."

"The name's Stone. Joe Stone." He extended a hand that felt like soft putty in an old sock. "And you are...?"

"Alice."

"What do you do for a living, Alice?"

She was tempted to say chicken-sexer or rodeo clown or alligator wrestler, but those might encourage further conversation.

"I'm in used golf ball sales."

"Well, that's fascinating. I'm a journalist. You might have read my stuff in the Police Beat section of the *Chronicle*."

Could this be the guy who described Logan in yesterday's paper as "rough justice in high tops and an aloha shirt?" Her romantic notions about that anonymous wit did a belly flop.

"I'm working on a really big story that just broke this morning." He handed her a business card, then pulled a pen and notebook from one of the many pockets of his khaki jacket.

"What's your address and phone number? I'll sign a copy of the story and send it to you when it breaks."

Alice started to say she didn't give out personal information to strangers when Faye beckoned from the far end of the bar.

"Excuse me." As she hurried away she called over her shoulder. "Good luck with the story."

Faye held up her cell phone. "Syl sent a text a couple hours ago. Something's wrong at Logan's house."

Alice leaned close, trying to decypher the message. " '2 egles n dox setpic hole.' What the hell is a setpic? And what are egles n dox? Does she mean bagles and lox?"

"I'd think it means two eagles in Doc's septic hole."

"How in the world do you know that?"

"I've heard that texting is re-wiring the human brain. After a while you start to see the *gestalt*. Besides, I've been getting texts from Syl for a few years now. This one is crystal clear compared to some."

"Why would eagles be in a septic pit? Did you call her and ask what's going on?"

"No one answers. And I have to stay here until eleven tonight."

Syl's failure to answer her phone seemed to alarm Faye more than the message itself. Syl never turned her phone off or left it anywhere. It was rarely out of her hand. Faye said she carried a lipstick-sized charger in her purse.

"I'll go find out."

Alice left in such a rush she didn't notice that the I.R.S. envelope dropped out of her back pocket. Faye was so distracted texting Syl she didn't see Joe Stone pick it up.

Chapter Fifteen

"Mocking Bach"

The act of dying is not of importance,
it lasts so short a time.
Samuel Johnson

The yard gnomes looked respectable again, as though they were trooping home at twilight from whatever work gnomes did. Nick imagined them singing, "Hi, ho, hi, ho" in the lengthening shadows. But something was amiss with the lawn. He walked closer.

The grass was impeccably mowed, natty as a crew cut, but several varieties of weeds were beginning to sprout among the blades of grass. Weeds were not a felony, however, so it was none of his concern. In Dr. Brant's yard the lei of yellow crime scene tape was still around the excavation and the company's workmen had covered the pit with plywood.

Nick was relieved to see a patrol car parked in the cul-de-sac at the end of the street. The boys on the beat were honoring his request to check up on Dr. Brant. The patrolman must have noticed his arrival because the headlights came on. The car drove slowly past, turned the corner, and headed out of the neighborhood.

He climbed the three wooden steps to the small porch and brushed past the wisteria and honeysuckle vines shinnying up the roof's support posts. His knuckles were poised for a third business-like rap on the door when it flew open and his reflexes kicked in. He pulled his forty-five, stepped to one side, and stood with his back pressed against the cedar shake siding.

Dr. Brant peered out into the gathering shadows. "Go bother someone else," she snapped. "I told you I have nothing to say."

Then she spotted him. He noticed she carried a baseball bat.

"Detective Shea. Forgive me. My eyesight is going bad. I thought you were that reporter who's been skulking around." She led him into the small living room and leaned the bat against the wall by the door.

"Don't you have somewhere else to stay tonight, Dr. Brant?"

"Why?"

Why do you think? sounded rude, so Nick just looked at her.

"Oh that." She glanced toward the window with the view of the Big Dig. "It's deeply distressing that two eagles were murdered because of me. But this is my home, and one's home is one's castle, is it not?"

"It is until someone starts leaving body parts in the moat."

"I'm having a gin and tonic, Detective Shea. May I fix you one?"

"No, thank you, Dr. Brant."

"Please call me Logan." Wearing a faded green chenille robe and a pair of fake-suede scuffs, she padded into the galley kitchen. "Limeade then?"

"Yes, thank you." Nick sat on the edge of the couch to make it clear he was here on business.

Logan set the tall glass and a plate of peanut butter cookies on the battered army trunk that served as a coffee table. When she took the afghan off the nearby easy chair and sat down, it seemed about to swallow her.

"I suppose the to-do here yesterday added to your list of questions, Detective."

"It did. Who do you think put the eagles and the heart in your yard?"

She leveled a look at him over the top of her glasses. "I would be disappointed in you if you hadn't checked me out already."

Nick nodded.

"So you know who dislikes me. Who do you think might have done it?"

"Do you expect your patients to tell you how to do your job?"

"Touché." Logan smiled. "But I can tell you the culprit isn't my neighbor Bernie, although I suspect he put the rat in my mailbox the other day."

"What rat? When?"

She shrugged. "A few days ago. I figured he was angry with me for paint-gunning his cats."

"What did you do with the rat?"

"I threw it into the ravine for the foxes."

"Was there a note with it?"

"No. Just a rat. Not long dead."

"Why do you say he wouldn't have put the eagles and heart in your septic pit?"

"I've known him since he was a kid. He's all bluster. And where would he get a human heart?"

"I'll be talking to him tomorrow."

"He's away tomorrow. Some rider-mower rally in Pennsylvania, but he'll be back by seven a.m. Sunday, in time to make the usual morning racket with his mower and blower."

"Do you know who…" Nick paused. Vandalized was too dignified a word. "…tampered with his property?"

"No." Logan chuckled. "But I can guess."

He raised a dark eyebrow.

"My daughter Sylvana calls him Grasstapo. They've disliked each other since kindergarten. And Sylvana is a prankster. She must have gotten that from her father."

Nick had checked up on Sylvana Gant, nee Brant, and mischief fit her profile. Her ex-husband, Jerome Gant, had filed the latest complaint. He claimed she had put two dead opossums in his ductwork, but he couldn't prove it. Even if the police had wanted to investigate, lifting prints off a rotting 'possum wasn't possible. The cops and Animal Control folks still chuckled about it though.

"I'll stop by and talk to her after work tomorrow."

"I'll give you her phone number, but I haven't been able to reach her at home."

"She hasn't come by to see if you're okay?"

"She called from work yesterday." If Dr. Brant was disappointed in her daughter's lack of concern she didn't show it.

"What about your nephew, Fredrick Brant? You've been giving him flak lately."

"You've done your homework." Logan sighed. "Freddy is too milquetoast for a stunt like that. In fact, if he had grown the *cajones* to do it, I'd be impressed. He's coming here for dinner Friday night and I plan to reason with him."

"Anyone else on a suspect list?"

"Freddy has a partner."

Nick took a small notebook from his shirt pocket. "His name?"

"Sam Hare."

"Samuel Hare of Longview Development?"

"The one and only, and thank goodness for that."

"Do you think he's capable of this sort of thing?"

"Sam? Oh, no, not personally. He pays people to do his dirty work. He hides behind a phalanx of toadies, publicity flacks, legal hacks, purchased politicians, and, I suspect, seriously bad-ass goons."

Phalanx. Nick pictured solid ranks of heavily armed Greek soldiers, all wearing Armani suits, their shiny brief cases held up side by side to form a wall around Mr. Hare.

He asked a few more questions, then Logan had some of her own.

"Do you know whose heart that was?"

"We're waiting for lab tests —DNA and all that." No sense telling her "all that" could take weeks.

"And do you know what killed the eagles?"

"The Natural Resources people say it looks like strychnine, but we're waiting for test results on that too. They weren't wearing tags, but their legs were rubbed where they used to be."

"I can't begin to express how much I regret being responsible, in a way, for their deaths."

"The one who killed them probably considered that an added reason for doing it."

Dr. Brant perked up, as though a thought had just occurred to her. "Detective Shea, did I mention that I know someone I think you would like?"

"Yes, you did, Logan, and I said 'Maybe some other time.'"

"I take it this isn't the time."

"No, ma'am."

He assumed she was trying to set him up with her daughter. Now that he had the scoop on her daughter, his answer would always be "Some other time." He didn't mention the drunk and disorderly charge that had earned Sylvana a night in the county jail a few years ago.

The ceiling light flickered in the kitchen. Logan gave it an annoyed glance over her shoulder.

"A short in the wiring?"

"No, not short. Nelly stood about five foot eight. Tall for her time."

Nick wondered where he'd lost track of the conversation. "Tall for what time?"

"Her husband beat her to death in this house in 1939, twenty-five years before I moved in. Until recently a few neighbors were alive who knew her. They told me about her."

The light flickered again, then went out. Nick felt the hair stir on his arms. What was it about this neighborhood?

Logan got up and opened the window nearest the piano. She set her drink on a coaster on top of the polished lacquer.

"Music seems to quiet her down. Do you mind if I play a short piece, or do you have to go?"

"I'm technically off duty."

He didn't mention how many late night calls he and his colleagues went out on, only to be met by some lonely citizen craving nothing more than human interaction.

"We can provide a safe house for you, Dr. Brant... Logan."

"This house is safe."

"I could open your front door lock with a credit card."

"Death is not important. Living is."

"But death does interfere with living, doesn't it."

She laughed as her fingers rippled across the keyboard. She sang along with their sprightly beat.

Oh Death, where is thy sting-a-ling-a-ling,
O Grave, thy victoree?
The bells of Hell go ting-a-ling-a-ling
For you but not for me.

"British soldiers sang that in World War One." She finished with a flourish. "Ten million young men died in that useless slaughter. A generation gone. So what does a single random human death matter? We are not an endangered species."

Nick had no answer, nor did he think Logan wanted one.

She smiled brightly, as if at a recital. "This next piece will be a duet."

"You must mean Nelly, because I don't play the piano or sing."

"Of course you sing, Detective. Everyone sings. You sing in the shower, don't you?"

He shrugged an answer.

"I thought so." She nodded toward the open window. "This vocalist lives in the dogwood tree outside."

She started to play Bach's "Jesu, Joy of Men's Desiring." Nick sat back on the sofa and leaned his head against the cushion. He folded his arms across his chest, extended his long legs with the ankles crossed, and closed his eyes. He sank into that rarest of states. Tranquility. He remembered Pascal's quote from his father's old Bartlett. *All human evil comes from a single cause, man's inability to sit still in a room.*

To his disappointment, Logan stopped twelve bars in. He opened his eyes and saw her put her fingers to her lips. Outside, a mockingbird repeated the tune, singing as if he were on stage at the Met. When he finished he started over.

"We do this most nights," Logan said. "I think he waits out there for me. He knows a little Beethoven and a Boccherini guitar quintet that I transcribed."

"Good god." He didn't realize he had said it aloud.

"Good God indeed."

When the mocking bird finished, Logan started the Boccherini. Nick closed his eyes again and let the music soak into his tired bones. The sound of the piano was lovely, but the mockingbird's rendition was magical.

Chapter Sixteen

"Raising Hell"

If men knew how women pass the time
when they are alone, they'd never marry.
O. Henry
Memoirs of a Yellow Dog

On the way home from the Red Eye Alice saw yellow crime scene tape glimmering in the street lamp's light, but only one vehicle sat outside, an old Ford Bronco. She parked the Vette and walked back to Logan's house. She was debating a knock on the door when she heard "Jesu, Joy of Men's Desiring" float out through the open window.

If Logan was playing the piano she must be alright. Rather than disturb her, Alice started for home. Bach and this summer's crop of lightning bugs turned the tree-lined street into a landscape of fugue and fire.

She lay on the couch and worked on a crossword puzzle while she watched *Casablanca*. She had lost count of how many times she'd seen the movie, but it was on and she couldn't pass up the chance to watch it again. She had just murmured "Louie, I think this is the beginning of a beautiful friendship" along with Bogart when the phone rang. She had never heard panic in Faye's voice before.

"Al, we've got to go to Syl's house. Now."

Alice glanced at the mantle clock. Eleven-forty-five. "Isn't she with Logan?"

"If only. I just got home and found a phone message she left an hour ago. She wanted me to come over and help her summon an incubus. She said she'd found the instructions on the internet. She said she figured I'd know if they were legit or not. I'm pretty sure she was drunk."

"So she's up to one of her antics. She'll sleep it off."

"This is serious, Al. It's not safe to mess around with the Devil or his minions."

"Minions? Haven't you dated a minion?"

"I know I told you an incubus visited me, but I didn't summon him. No time for chit-chat. Meet me out front."

Clouds scudded across the full moon overhead and thunder rumbled in the distance. Faye's inseam measured four inches shorter than Alice's, but she had to hustle to keep up with her.

"I know an incubus is a male sexual demon and a succubus is female. But how do you summon them and what do they do?"

"No time for details, Al. Look it up in *Wikipedia*."

"Your incubus hasn't caused you problems, has he?"

"No, but I'm… I don't know… maybe he came to me as sort of an introductory offer."

"You're saying other worlds exist?"

Alice couldn't tell if Faye's snort was anxiety or exasperation.

"Some locations have a thinner wall between this world and the others. This old section of the neighborhood is a portal. I never mentioned it because I figured no one would believe me."

Alice remembered the Green Man winking at her from Esme's garden arch.

"I believe you."

Faye's sidelong glance said, *It's about damned time somebody did.*

The air conditioning unit in the window of Syl's bungalow rumbled like the turbines on an aircraft carrier. The front door was unlocked and when Alice and Faye went inside the temperature there would have chilled a mint julep. Alice took a quick look around the living room as she followed Faye to the back hallway and the stairs to the basement.

The walls were covered with photos of the King. Elvis statues, plates, shot glasses, mugs, dolls, and lunch boxes populated all the horizontal surfaces. His face adorned the wall clock, throw pillows, and afghan. A life-sized painting of him on velvet covered much of the wall behind the sofa.

Syl's voice drifted up the stairwell leading to the basement. Faye and Alice went to the open door and peered down. Dozens of candles brightened the usual gloom.

"Now we know where old exercise equipment goes to die," muttered Alice.

A treadmill, stationary bike, rowing machine, cross-trainer, and a home tanning bed were ranged like hulking spectators along the walls. Syl sat naked and cross-legged in the middle of a circle drawn in black chalk on the concrete floor. The circle was inside a pentagram also in chalk. Syl clutched a rosary in one hand and other objects surrounded her. A sheet of paper, probably a computer print-out, lay in front of her. With eyes closed she intoned something in a language Alice had never heard.

"*Aglon, tetragram, vacheo stimulatum ezphares retragrammaton.* Amen."

Faye shouted, "No!" just as Syl said "Amen." A flash of lightning must have hit the wiring. It sent sparks from the naked bulb hanging over the washing machine. The crash of thunder that followed sent a bolt of fear through Alice.

"What do you think you're doing?" shouted Faye.

"It's okay." Syl held up the book. "It says here the cross and these other things will protect me."

The three of them held their breaths. A distant moaning riffled the hair at the nape of Alice's neck, but she tried to convince herself it was the wind in the trees outside. They all stayed motionless and silent. Alice could hear her heart thumping out the seconds in the longest two minutes she had ever experienced. When nothing happened, Syl looked disappointed but not surprised.

"Looks like it's booga-booga bullshit after all."

Alice wanted to run out of the house and not stop until she'd closed her own door behind her and locked it. She sat at the top of the basement stairs instead. Below her the flickering candles threw grotesque shadows on the walls. The exercise machines looked like torture devices.

Faye walked downstairs. "Why'd you do this, Syl?"

"I read up on incubi. That's the plural of incubus, by the way."

"I know."

"They're not dangerous. They can't make you pregnant. Most people can't even see them. They give you blissful ecstasy unlike anything a mortal can provide."

That sounded like hype from an infernal infomercial to Alice. But wait, there was more.

"You don't have to cook meals for them or wash their dirty underwear or pamper their egos. And they're easily sent packing if you tire of them."

"Where did you read that?" Faye asked.

"Some website."

"Do you remember the name of it?"

"Something called CMHS. They seemed very knowledgeable."

"That's the Church of the Most Holy Satan. You can't believe anything they post. They claim incubi and succubi are the perfect sexual companions for prison inmates, for cryin' out loud." Faye took the plush robe off the newel post and handed it across the chalk line to Syl.

"I was bored. I figured it was worth a shot. It doesn't matter anyway, because nothing happened." Syl stood up and high-stepped out of the ring as though it were a low wall. "I also asked the boogey man to give me a promotion to partner at the firm. And while I was at it, I ordered a case of genital warts for Jerry."

Syl shrugged into the robe and tied the sash. She pulled a dozen or more small plastic bags from the pockets.

"I forgot these were in here. I bought them on-line."

"I wouldn't have pegged you for a gardener, Syl," Alice called down from her perch at the top of the stairs.

"These aren't just any seeds." Syl read the labels. "Dandelions. Crab grass. Crown Vetch. Devil's Shoestring. That last one is my favorite."

"Again... you don't strike me as the gardening type."

"They aren't for me. I added them to Grasstapo's lawn one night about a week ago. The little buggers are already beginning to sprout. I must've left the packages in my pocket when I took a shower afterward." She stuffed them back into her pockets. "You two want to join me for a nightcap?"

Faye said "No." Alice said "Hell no."

Alice was relieved to flee Syl's house and walk up the middle of the deserted street with Faye. Thunder still grumbled occasionally in the distance. As Alice started up the stairs to her front door Faye called softly after her.

"Be very careful who you let into the house, Al. And check their reflections in your mirror by your front door."

"You said your... your visitor... showed up without an invitation."

"All the more reason to be as careful as possible."

"Looks like it was bogus anyway. No harm, no foul."

"Maybe. But if anything strange happens at your place call me right away, even if I'm at work."

Alice turned to look at her friend. Lamplight illuminated half of Faye's elfin face. The other half disappeared into shadow. With her magenta Mohawk, Faye looked like a sprite herself.

A thought hit Alice like the first glimpse of a bus advancing fast from the blind side of her car. "We didn't make the request, but we were present when Syl made it, and we were outside the circle. We had no protection against forces of evil."

"Correct."

"How big an area does a spell encompass? Are Syl's next door neighbors involved or someone walking a dog in the street outside?"

"I don't know, but look on the bright side. Black magic is not one of Syl's specialties. Maybe she bungled the incantation."

That was small consolation. As Alice walked up the stairs to her door she heard Humphrey Bogart's edgy voice in her head. "You'll regret it," he said. "Maybe not today. Maybe not tomorrow, but soon, and for the rest of your life."

Chapter Seventeen

"Russell the Love Muscle"

*His mother should have thrown him away
and kept the stork.*
Mae West (1893 – 1980)

Alice was taking clothes from the dryer in the basement when she saw the small black snake disappear behind the utility shelving. She was glad that he, or she, had returned. The crickets had started reproducing like… well… locusts. Their aptitude for multiplication probably had brought the snake inside.

"Welcome back, Slim," she murmured. "*Bon appetit.*"

She carried the warm clothes upstairs, inhaling their fresh-from-the-dryer aroma as she went. She dumped them on the couch and was in the process of folding them when a knock rattled the screen door. The man standing in the gathering dusk outside looked familiar.

"Who is it?"

"Syl's friend."

"You'll have to be more specific."

"Russell Wright. Russ. I've seen you at the gym, Alice. I had a client in this area and thought I'd drop by for a visit to get better acquainted."

"I'm busy, Russell. Some other…"

Before she could finish he barged in. She could tell he had been drinking, and she wondered if he had been this deep in the bag when he saw his client. If there was a client. She remembered Faye's warning about strangers and glanced at the hall mirror by the door.

The belief that supernatural beings didn't have reflections was silly, but she was relieved to see his image there.

"I brought you a present." Russell waved a bottle of tequila, the cheapest brand.

The fact that he thought she could be had at clearance bin prices annoyed her almost as much as his intrusion.

"I have work to do." She could tell diplomacy would be wasted on him so she didn't bother with it. "Go away."

"Do you believe in the hereafter, Alice?" He advanced into the room, unbuttoning his shirt as he came.

Alice backed up. *Oh shit. He's one of those drunks who gets deaf and horny.*

She spoke loudly, enunciating clearly. "Get out of my house."

He whipped off his belt and tossed it aside. "'Cause if you believe in the hereafter, then you know what I'm here after."

"You've been warned, Russell."

Alice wished she were as confident as she hoped she sounded. She'd taken a self-defense course after Charlie died. She knew how vulnerable certain parts of the human body were, but she had never applied the techniques to a real adversary.

As he stepped out of his docksiders and peeled off his $125 dirty-wash skinny jeans she took a mental inventory of the options covered in the self-defense class. A broken nose. A knee to the groin. A heel stomp and grind on his instep. A blow with the sole of her foot on his patella, bending it in a direction not recommended. Three rigid fingers to the trachea. A thumb against the bundle of nerves under his jawbone, just below the ear.

As Russell wriggled out of his tight jeans she saw the words emblazoned on the front of his red bikini briefs, "The Love Muscle." Under them an arrow pointed down to his lad and his 'nads, as Syl called them. Alice laughed.

He must have taken her laughter as an invitation. He grabbed her with arms that had morphed into tentacles. Pressed against his bare chest, she brought her left elbow in and her forearm vertical, palm out, against her own chest. She pistoned the heel of her hand upward, smashing the base of his nose into an accordion configuration. He let go of her as though she had caught fire, but the pain wasn't all that caused the bulge in his briefs to deflate.

Godzilla had sunk his teeth into Russell's ankle. Like a football player with an opposing lineman clinging to his calves, Russell whirled with his leg outstretched. The centrifugal force caused the iguana to fly across the room, but he didn't stay there. He launched at Russell and chomped down on the now much smaller bulge in the briefs.

Russell screamed, backed up, and fell over a side table. Godzilla landed on top of him, his tail lashing. His claws gouged deep crimson pinstripes down Russell's bare thighs as Alice pulled him off. She held the hissing iguana in her arms like a shield with attitude and a twitching tail while Russell hauled himself to his feet.

He grabbed his clothes and bolted for the door. On the porch he struggled to pull on his jeans and put an arm through a shirt sleeve. He held only one shoe as he thundered down the wooden stairs. Alice heaved its mate at him, glancing it off the side of his head.

He retrieved it from a thicket of overgrown hostas and ivy and shook it at her. "You'll be hearing from my lawyer."

"Will he bring me a bottle of cheap-ass tequila too?" Alice went back into the house and latched the screen door. "*Putz!*" she muttered.

She sat on the living room floor with her legs crossed. Godzilla insinuated his front half onto her lap. She kissed the top of his head on one side of his spiked crest, then stopped her hands from shaking by scratching him under his chin.

When she had calmed down some and her heart wasn't pounding loud enough to drown out a conversation, she dialed Esme.

"Es, can you take 'Zilla back?"

"Sure. Kenya's period is almost over and she's at her grandmother's tonight. Is he causing trouble?"

"He chased away an intruder."

"Are you alright?"

"Yes. It was Russell. That jerk Syl knows. He was drunk and got grabby. 'Zilla chewed him up and might need a perp protection program."

"I'm heading out for work soon, but bring him over."

With hands still shaking, Alice put Zilla's leash and harness on him. Then in case Russell was lurking outside somewhere, she pocketed her cell phone and locked the door behind her.

Esme greeted her with a long hug. "Are you alright?"

"Yes. I guess I'll have to lock my door during the day too."

Esme cocked one eyebrow.

"I know. I know. You've told me to keep the door locked, but I hate being locked in."

"The next intruder could be a thief, or worse, Al."

Alice sat on the edge of the bathtub while Esme put on her makeup. Her navy blue uniform was perfectly pressed and fitted. Each glossy curl of her short afro was in place. Alice had always envied her friend's image of having the details of life under effortless control.

Esme finished applying her lipstick then asked. "Are you going to file a complaint? I'll go with you, if you want."

"No. It'd be my word against his. Charlie would have kicked his sorry ass down the stairs, although he might have killed him first."

Her voice faltered and the tears started. Esme sat next to Alice on the rim of the tub, put her arms around her, and held her as she sobbed.

Esme pulled a couple feet of tissue off the roll and passed them to Alice who wiped her eyes and blew her nose.

"Guess what was printed on Russell's briefs."

"I'm afraid to guess."

"'The Love Muscle.'"

"You're kidding."

"I'm not. 'Zilla sank his teeth into Russell's bundle like it was a cabbage. A very small cabbage. More like a brussel sprout."

Esme laughed. The two of them joked about Russell and talked about life as Esme ate a plate of leftover macaroni and cheese and cold asparagus with hollandaise. She had to work the late shift, so at ten o'clock they walked outside.

"I'll miss that green Galahad," Alice said.

"Kenya can bring him by for visits."

Singing "He's a Love Muscle" with an R and B vibe, Esme slid behind the wheel of Aaron's old Corvair. Alice laughed as she waved goodbye. Then she headed home and opened her front door.

She tried to scream, but no sound came out. Afraid to turn her back on the house, she stumbled down the stairs in reverse and fled into the deserted street. She didn't like to call Faye at work, especially not on a Saturday, but this was an emergency. With shaking fingers she dialed by the light of the street lamp.

Chapter Eighteen

"Spare Parts"

A little necrophilia never killed anyone.
Unknown

N ick sat on the tall stool, his long legs wound around the rungs. With his forearms framing his glass he stared over it as if admiring the scantily clad young women dancing in front of the Red Eye's bandstand. His real aim was to scan the exuberant Saturday night crowd for signs of the Spitter. This was where hook-ups happened and that made it a perfect place for the killer to acquire another victim.

The Spitter probably thought he had beaten the rap, and he might get careless. In a way he had, temporarily anyway. Nick never got over resenting the time required for DNA lab results. He wondered if more young women would be sliced into pieces before he and his new partner could make an arrest. As he watched the dancers he felt like a father with way too many daughters he had to worry about.

Will had seen him in this state before. "Nick." He raised his voice to get his attention. "I heard you talked to our Rat Wrangler today. What'd you find out?"

"He was snorkling in Belize that week." Nick sat up straight, but his eyes kept scanning. "He showed me his phone log and the dated photos on his computer."

"He could be one of those snotty young cyberspooks who can dick around with data."

"He's still on my list."

"It's not like rodents are in short supply. Is this particular rat in custody?"

"No. Dr. Brant threw it into the ravine behind her house. She said it was a treat for the foxes."

"Any prints on the mailbox?"

"Just the mailman's and hers."

"How's the hunt for the heartless cadaver going?"

"It didn't come from a fresh kill."

"How do you know?"

"I smelled formaldehyde."

"So you gave it the sniff test." Did a flash of satisfaction cross Will's face, as if Grasshopper had learned well?

"Today we started on the list of hospitals, funeral homes, clinics, labs, med schools, morgues. I didn't know so many places have body components lying around and how casually they're disposed of."

"Yes, you did. I told you. You can cop a spare heart or brain as easily as a fan belt or a muffler from a junk yard. It's illegal to steal dead guy's pinky ring, but okay to take the pinky."

"Did you know that six hundred thousand to a million tons of medical waste are produced every year in this country? A million tons."

"We at the county morgue try our best to contribute our share to the national effort."

"What do you do with it all?"

"What isn't claimed or shipped off for scientific study, a company collects and incinerates. Blood and other bodily fluids we hose into the sewer system."

"Do you keep an inventory?"

"Do you inventory your toenail clippings or the whiskers left in the sink when you shave?"

A deep voice with a velvety nap of Georgia Sea Isles Gullah dialect said, "I have it on good authority that Detective Shea does, in fact, inventory his nail parings and whiskers."

A well-tailored suit sat down on the other side of Nick. The suit's occupant was the approximate size and density of a refrigerator and the color of Kahlua. The bar stool creaked, but held steady.

Nick called to the barkeep. "Faye, a Bud straight up for my new partner."

When Faye set the bottle on the bar icy drops of condensation glittered in the glow from the rope lights overhead. "How are you tonight, Nathan?"

"Fine as frog hair, Miss Faye."

Will leaned across Nick and held out a hand and arm. "Will Mabry, county coroner."

The newcomer's hand engulfed it. "Nathan Hale."

"No shit?"

"No shit."

"What do they call you for short?"

"Nathan." He took a swig, tilted his head back, and savored the beer.

"So, you two are at bat for the Spitter?" Will knew better than to discuss the details of open cases in public.

"And the birds and the carry-out carton." One of William Blake's lines ran through Nick's head. *Does the eagle know what is in the pit, or wilt thou go ask the mole?*

"Since Shea's had me nosing around gross anatomy labs all day," said Nathan, "...and you're a coroner, Will, I assume you two were talking about deceased folks."

Will jerked a thumb in Nathan's direction. "He's good, Nick."

"Is it true you all take out the brains and stuff the skulls with tissue paper?"

"That's why Will's handle is Scoop," put in Nick.

"We take out all the soft organs," said Will. "What you see in a casket is a meat taco shell, without the lettuce, tomatoes, guacamole, jalapenos or shredded jack."

"I took three showers tonight and I can still smell the nasty." Nathan looked at the beer as though he wished he could pour it over his head, or better yet swim in it. "When they say gross anatomy they aren't kidding. At one point I was standing in a puddle of brain slushy. Smell wouldn't come off my shoes. I tossed them into a dumpster."

Will brightened. He liked to talk about this subject and so rarely had the opportunity.

"We've improved in the disposal of the dead. In Scotland in the 1700's medical school tuition could be paid in corpses."

"Where'd they get them?"

"Enterprising men dug them up."

"They were called Resurrectionists." Nick had heard this lecture before.

"Did you know your skin occupies enough space to cover the top of a twin bed?" asked Will.

"In Nathan's case make it a double."

"Here's an anatomy factoid. If you took all the veins in your body and laid them end-to-end…" Nathan paused. "You'd die." He lowered his voice. "Is it true that having sex with a corpse is not against the law in this state?"

Nick and Will answered together. "Yes and no."

"Yes and no?"

"Before 1965 there were no laws against necrophilia any-where in the country. About nine states still don't prosecute those who do it." Nick shrugged. "Here it's dealt with on a case by case basis. Sometimes it's considered desecration of mortal remains. Sometimes they book a perv for disturbing the peace or lewd and lascivious behavior if they're caught at it."

"It's illegal in Georgia." Nathan stopped short of sounding smug about it.

"As what?" Nick already knew the answer. It was pretty much the same for all the states that had necrophilia laws on their books.

Sheepish looked odd on a face as rugged as Nathan's, but there it was. "A misdemeanor at most."

"Legislators can't figure out how to classify it," said Nick. "And who wants to introduce the subject in the legislature's hallowed halls, much less debate it?"

"After death the genitals become enlarged." Will went into his professorial mode and then out again. "Rigor mortis puts the stiff in stiffies."

"A mortuary worker was arrested while driving a hearse home with a good-looking twenty-five-year-old corpse in the back," said Nick.

"The incident happened in another county." Will wanted to make that clear.

"Arrested? You said it wasn't illegal."

"She was pulled over for speeding, but when the trooper came up to ask for her license, she floored it and tried to escape. Almost ran over the Smokey. Led him on a helluva chase before colliding with a tree."

"I guess she didn't want the trooper to find the defunct hunk with the junk in her trunk," added Will.

As Nick headed for the door labeled "Buoys," he called back to Nathan, "Will's been saving that up for some poor sucker who hasn't heard it yet."

At the end of the bar Faye was bent over. With her head down she was talking in a low voice on her cell phone. Nick could tell something was wrong. He slowed reflexively as he passed and heard her end of the conversation.

"Oh, shit, Al. I was afraid of this." Silence. Then, "They prefer enclosed places. Stay out on the porch. I'll come over as soon as I get off work in an hour and a half."

A short silence. "Okay, then. Go to Esme's mom's place. She'll be awake."

When Nick returned Faye was staring out across the water. He stopped to pay for the last round of drinks.

"Everything alright, Faye?"

She gave her head barely enough of a shake to ripple her Mohawk. "I'm fine, Nick." Her smile was a little too perky. Faye was not the perky sort.

He looked at her a couple extra seconds, long enough to let her know she wasn't fooling him. Then he rejoined Will and Nathan. He pretended to listen to their banter, but he was replaying Faye's end of the phone conversation.

Al must be her boyfriend, but who preferred enclosed places and why should Al take refuge from them?

CHAPTER NINETEEN

"MISS MARJORIE"

What happens if you get scared half to death twice?
Unknown

A wind sent clouds scudding across the moon. Alice stood in front of the garage door and debated opening it. What if the garage were infested also? She looked longingly up the street toward Logan's house, but she didn't have her phone number and she didn't want to bother her at this late hour. Knowing Logan and what she'd been through these past few days, she might shoot first with her air rifle and apologize later.

Alice looked down the hill toward Syl's. No way was she going there. Syl was responsible for whatever was lurking in the house now. Alice didn't know Esme's mother, Mrs. Mayhew, very well, but Faye must have had good reasons for suggesting her house as a refuge.

Besides, Alice knew she would have to go into the garage sometime. She had locked the front door of the house when she left for Esme's earlier, so she had her keys with her. She could thank Russell the Love Muscle's intrusion for that.

Alice was backing the car out when a battered old rattletrap with a bungee cord holding up the front bumper cruised slowly down the street and stopped, blocking her. Alice put the stick in park and set the hand brake. She grabbed the small mirror in the glove compartment. She walked outside and stood with her back to the garage wall.

The car door opened and Joe Stone got out. He hastily unbuttoned his blue denim shirt enough to expose a deep vee of hairless pink skin. He was wearing the same beige safari jacket, cargo pants, and felt slouch hat he had had on at the Red Eye the afternoon before. Tonight he had added a "press" badge pinned to the hat band. The long zoom lens of the camera hanging around his neck looked more than a little phallic.

Alice aimed the mirror at him. The street lamp and the garage light illuminated his image in the glass. He was a pain in the ass, but not a demon. She surveyed him from the crown of his hat to his high-tech hiking boots. The shoes almost certainly had lifts inside them.

"Good evening, Miss Lewis. We meet again. What luck."

Luck, my ass.

She wondered how he had found out her last name. Faye wouldn't have given it to him.

"I'm in a hurry, Mr. Stone."

"This'll just take a minute. I'm writing an in-depth article on the use of alligators as guard animals. The police scanner reported one in this neighborhood today."

"What kind of reporter skulks around at this hour?"

Stone didn't seem to notice the irritation in her voice. "I just heard the report and thought I'd check it out. You happened to be here, so I'd like to get your take on it."

"There are no alligators in this neighborhood." She glanced up at the house, expecting to see grotesque faces peering out of the windows. The fact that it seemed normal and innocent wasn't much comfort.

"Then why would someone claim an alligator attacked him here?"

"You're the investigative reporter. You tell me. Now move your car."

As Alice backed out of the garage, thunder prowled in the restless canopy of the trees. A sudden rain hit the roof of the car like buck shot.

⚜ ⚜ ⚜

Esme's mother, Marjorie Mayhew, lived in an old riverfront community upstream from the Cliffs. A wooded lot next to her house shaded a small cemetery that post-dated the Civil War by a few months. Miss Marjorie said of the graveyard's earliest inhabitants that President Lincoln freed them just before God called them.

The wood-frame cottages were owned by families whose ancestors had lived there when white folks' polite word for them was "darkies." The houses were small, solidly built, and neatly kept. They were what realtors and developers referred to as "tear-downs." Given their proximity to riverfront views and deep water anchorage, plenty of realtors and developers were in a froth to tear them down. Miss Marjorie had joined forces with Logan to throw a spanner into their wrecking balls, but their obstructionism had had only limited success.

Alice ran through the rain to the covered porch, and knocked. Miss Marjorie held the door open for her as though people often appeared on her doorstep in the rain at eleven at night.

"Faye called to say you'd be coming, Alice."

With the light behind her she cast a formidable shadow. She was close to six feet tall and probably weighed one-eighty, none of it excess. Alice wanted to throw her arms around her and hold on.

Miss Marjorie nodded toward the McMansion-in-progress across the street. "Another TGN going up."

Alice guessed that TGN meant There Goes the Neighborhood. In this neighborhood, the phrase was literally true. Alice turned to look. The labyrinth of unfinished walls sent a shiver through her. Given the way tonight had been going, she would not have been surprised if a Minotaur, the half man, half bull of Greek myth, came charging out in search of seven maidens for a late-night snack.

The walls of the building were raw and angular in the glare of arc lights mounted on tall poles. Maybe the contractor also put lights up elsewhere to discourage construction site pilferage, but they seemed an affront here. They implied that folks in this community could not be trusted.

"I would've called you, Miss Marjorie, but I didn't have your number."

"You're always welcome, darlin.' The bathroom's down the hall. I'll put the kettle on while you dry off. Kenya's in her bedroom if you want to say 'Hi.' "

The tea was ready when Alice returned to the living room. The over-sized chenille cushions of the big easy chair embraced her as she sank into them with a grateful sigh. Family portraits covered the walls. Hanging among them, as though they too were members of the family, were Jesus and the twelve Apostles breaking bread in DaVinci's vision of the Last Supper. Another portrait of a gentle-eyed Jesus hung next to a large crucifix over the fireplace.

The dignified presence of the people in the pictures, like a host of friendly partisans, calmed Alice a little. Still, the china teacup jittered as she put it back on the saucer. That did not escape Miss Marjorie's attention. She was a teacher. Very little escaped her attention. Faye called her Miss Polly, short for polygraph.

Alice knew Miss Marjorie was curious about what had brought her to the door this late on a rainy Saturday night. She also knew she couldn't lie. She could tell part of the truth, but she doubted Miss Marjorie would buy it.

"I thought I heard critters in my house and Faye said she would help me with them when she got off work."

"What sort of critters?"

"I'm not sure."

Miss Marjorie gave her the Look. It worked on her ninth grade English students and it worked on Alice.

Alice got as far as, "It's Syl." Then she lost her resolve. Miss Marjorie went to church every Sunday. What would she think of Syl handing out her calling card to the Devil's disciples?

"Oh good Lord. What has that child gone and done now? Esme called from work and told me Syl sicced some low-life hustler on you. Did he show up again? Or was it some other devil?"

"I think it's another one." *Or more likely several.*

"Then call the police, honey."

"Maybe it's a raccoon."

"What's a raccoon got to do with Syl?" Then Miss Marjorie held up a finger next to her jaw, a teacher's gesture, and shook it to show she had the answer. "She put those 'possums into her ex's house, didn't she. She's a prankster, Syl is."

"Yes, she is."

Alice sucked in a breath of relief. Maybe she could get past Miss Marjorie's exquisitely-tuned instincts without telling the entire preposterous, appalling story. She wasn't surprised that the relief only lasted until she exhaled.

Miss Marjorie held up the finger again, this time just behind her ear and motionless, as though she were receiving a message from the part of her brain in charge of bullshit detection.

"A dead 'possum can be picked up with a shovel. But I don't see Miss Sylvana Brant getting herself involved with live creatures."

"She gets involved with two-legged rats and skunks on a regular basis."

Miss Marjorie threw her head back and laughed. "You're right about that."

Alice knew that didn't dispel Miss Marjorie's curiosity, but she was too tired to think of anything better. She yawned. "May I wait here until Faye calls?"

"Of course. Make yourself comfortable on the couch."

"This chair is fine, thanks." She closed her eyes and surrendered to exhaustion.

As the late August nighttime coolness set in, she didn't feel Miss Marjorie drape a hand-knitted afghan over her or hear the brief prayer she murmured before she turned out the lights and went to bed.

Alice drifted into a dreamless sleep, the calm before her personal storm.

CHAPTER TWENTY

"ELEMENTAL, MY DEAR WATSON"

"The Universe is full of magical things,
patiently waiting for our wits to grow sharper."
Eden Phillpotts (1862-1962)

Alice was shaking so badly that Faye put her arms around her as the two of them sat on the couch with their legs drawn up. Alice wanted to turn on every lamp in her house, but Faye insisted on darkness.

Except the house wasn't dark.

The ceiling fan had a diaphanous blue glow around it like a tattered, backlit chiffon prom dress. Small points of red-gold light twinkled among the undisciplined ranks of potted ferns, peace lilies, and philodendrons on the sun porch. Alice heard a faint rustling coming from the plants.

"You're awfully calm, Faye."

"I'm relieved. The way you were babbling on the phone I thought you had a serious demon infestation, but these are only elementals."

"What are elementals? Why are they here? Did Syl call them up?"

"I have them in my house too. Everyone does. There are trillions of them, but they vibrate at a higher wave frequency than most people can detect. They're the visual equivalent of dog whistles."

"Have you always been able to see them?"

"I'd catch glimpses now and then, out of the corner of my eye. The hocus-pocus in Syl's basement must have made us more sensitive to them. I expect I'll see them plainly when I go home. I don't know why you haven't caught sight of elementals before."

"What do you mean?"

"You're intuitive, open-minded, unpredictable, Al. A natural."

"Faye, no one is more predictable than I am."

"In real life, maybe, but you're a writer. Your mind can go anywhere. You can make anything happen."

"I wish I could make something happen in my real life. Something other than this, I mean." Alice waved at the vapor-draped fan and the twinkling lights in the ferns. "Should I hire an exorcist?"

"They're benign, and besides, they'd only come back. There are four types – earth, air, fire, and water. The earth sprites in the plants are called gnomes."

"You're kidding."

"No, I'm not. Sir Arthur Conan Doyle believed in them. Nicola Tesla and Thomas Edison tried to invent a device to photograph them. Not surprising, I suppose. Tesla and Edison were both experimenting with electricity and photography."

"How do you know all this?"

Faye did an eye roll. "I've been talking about this stuff for years and none of you took me seriously."

"You're right. I apologize."

Faye nodded toward Alice's barely domesticated jungle from which emanated a low-pitched hum. "See how those little red lights are more concentrated among the Boston ferns?"

"Yes." Alice felt as if she had discovered an alternate universe in her living room. Which was exactly what she had done.

"Ferns have the oldest lineage of all the plants on earth. They go back four hundred million years. My guess is the gnomes are more comfortable with them."

Alice wanted to ask if these particular elementals had been around that long. And if not, what was their life span and how did they reproduce? Were they pure energy or did they have material-istic needs? She settled on two questions that were more pertinent.

"Who created them? Why are they here?"

"Who knows." Faye shrugged. "Maybe God created them. Their job is to clean up the negativity humans generate, so it would make sense that God is involved."

"This is a lot to believe." *And yet there they are, plainly audible. And visible.*

"The fire elementals are called salamanders." Faye said it as though she were introducing a parks-and-recreation softball team at a sports bar. "The domestic variety gather around the pilot lights in ovens and furnaces. The crew in the water are called undines. The airborne ones are sylphs. They're my favorites."

Faye stepped onto the old trunk that served as a coffee table. She reached a hand toward the fan whose blades were turning at the lowest setting and beckoned with the other one.

"Check this out, Al."

Alice brought the step stool from the kitchen and set it next to the trunk. She held her hand up into the translucent rags of pale blue light. She felt the rhythmic stir of air from the fan's blades, but something else too. Subtler than the movement of moths' wings, she saw vague shapes fluttering. She sensed feather-frail kisses on the tips of her fingers. They sent shivers down her arm and stirred the hair at the nape of her neck. A feeling of love washed over her.

"They look like fairies," she murmured.

"In a way, they are. Young kids who haven't lost their inner vision believe in fairies and pixies and gnomes because they've seen them." Faye smiled at her. "You're taking all this very well, Al."

"If these creatures are harmless, I'm relieved. But what should we do about Syl?"

Faye chuckled. "If the Devil is taking on Syl, he'd better bring his A-game."

"The Devil? She only called up an incubus."

"I have a feeling Old Scratch is a micro-manager. He and his flunkies are a package deal."

"The Devil? Shit." Faye was right. Alice was starting to believe in all of it. "We should check up on her."

"You're right." Faye stood up. "Let's go."

"Now? It's after midnight. What if she's asleep?"

"I don't give a damn."

As she and Faye walked up Syl's driveway, Alice noticed a curtain stir in the window across the lane. Had the neighbors noticed Syl's flirtation with demons? Or had her personal life been providing entertainment, titillation, and gossip before she started dabbling in the supernatural? Alice hoped for the latter.

Faye rang the doorbell while Alice waited in the shadows just beyond the porch's pool of light. Syl opened the door a crack and peered into the night. She swayed and blinked in the half-hearted glow of the porch light. Mascara ringed her eyes. Her hair radiated outward in coils. She looked like a Medusa who'd just gotten her snake 'do fluffed and blow-dried. Her pink robe hid very little. It hung open and off one shoulder halfway to the elbow.

The voice of The King singing "Love Me Tender" flowed out around her like audible honey. Alice didn't mention that the lyrics should be "Love Me Tenderly." This was not the time to correct grammar, but Mark Twain's dictum came to mind. "The road to hell is paved with adverbs." It had never seemed more appropriate.

When Syl saw Alice in the shadows she pulled the robe closed and moved a pace or two out onto the porch. Alice got the impression she assumed Faye had come to scold her. Maybe she figured Alice would serve as a mediator and take the edge off Faye's ire.

Syl always had a ready-to-romp air about her, but her demeanor tonight was far sexier. She seemed more ready-to-rumble than romp. If sex were a drug, Syl looked on the verge of an O.D.

"Wassup?"

Faye got right to the point. "Have you gone to see Logan today, or yesterday for that matter?"

Syl hesitated. That obviously wasn't the question she'd expected from Faye.

"I've been busy. I talked to her on the phone."

"Do you even know what's been going on at her house?"

"Something about a couple dead eagles. I'll check on her tomorrow. You wanna come in for a nightcap?"

Faye and Alice snapped in unison. "Hell, no."

Was Syl drunk, high, possessed or all three? And was that a whiff of sulphur?

"You're right." Faye glowered at her. "Tomorrow would be better."

She turned abruptly and Alice followed her down the steps. When Alice looked back over her shoulder, the door had already closed, muffling the sound of Elvis asking them to love him tender.

The porch light clicked off.

CHAPTER TWENTY-ONE

"HARE-BRAINED SCHEME"

The Antiseptic Baby and the Prophylactic Pup
were playing in the garden when the bunny gamboled up;
They looked upon the creature with a loathing undisguised—
It wasn't Disinfected and it wasn't Sterilized.
Arthur Guiterman (1871-1943)
Strictly Germ Proof, Stanza I

Monday had been uneventful so far. Nick hoped it stayed that way at least until he finished breakfast and yesterday's newspaper. He turned to the "Police Beat" and wasn't surprised to find almost verbatim excerpts from his own reports. If imitation was the sincerest form of flattery, then the reporter the other cops called "Nick's Knock-off" was one sincere guy.

> Workmen found two endangered representatives of
> the nation's proud symbol dead in an open pit being
> dug for a septic tank in a suburban neighborhood.
> Keeping the bald eagles company was a cardboard
> carton containing what might be a pig's heart, giving
> a grisly twist to the term "take-out."

What might be a pig's heart? Nick usually shrugged off Stone's plagiarism, but this time he wanted to pull the guy's safari hat down over his semaphore ears. In his report he had written pig's heart with no qualifiers. To carry on the investigation he needed to discourage speculation that it had belonged to a human being. He added to his day's agenda a visit to newspaper's editor.

With that out of the way he started on his eggs and home fries and the Sunday crossword puzzle.

The eight booths in Chuck's Wagon restaurant jutted out at right angles to the wall across from the long counter. The Governor's mansion and the State Legislature building stood a couple blocks away so each of the dozens of sandwiches on the menu was named for a local politician. A favorite pastime of Chuck's patrons was speculating on why the ham-on-rye was named after one legislator and baloney-on-white bread after another.

With his shoulders wedged into the corner of the rear wall Nick could see everything, including the tables on the second level, six steps up at the back of the room. Starched white shirts preferred the booths. Blue collars occupied the four-tops above them. The blue collars referred to the recreational boaters below them as the "yellow people" for the color of their weekend foul weather gear.

This was the usual breakfast crowd. The lyrics of the conversational hum consisted mostly of politics and boats. Political preferences were too mixed to call, but when it came to boats, the booths discussed rigging, regattas, and escalating flush-out fees. The four-top talk covered diesel engines, fishing limits, and the crab-pot thievery of the yellow people.

Nick was halfway through the destruction of his eggs and home fries and stumped by a five-letter word for a logarithmic unit when the rabbit arrived. Not including his ears, the bunny stood about five-foot-six in a costume intended for someone several inches taller. He appeared to be in a hurry. "I'm late, I'm late for a very important date" floated up from his subconscious.

The rabbit slid to a halt in front of the 1950's-era brass rococo cash register as though, on the spur of the moment, he had decided to pick up a pack of gum while checking out at the grocery line. He waved a flare gun at the wide-eyed young woman behind the counter. In a voice muffled by the silvery-gray plush mask with its black rubber nose, plastic bucked teeth, and bristling whiskers, he demanded she hand over the contents.

Many of the diners recorded the drama with their phone-cams. They had just finished the morning tradition of standing up, facing the American flag, and reciting the Pledge of Allegiance. Maybe they assumed Chuck had staged this as a surprise.

While the cashier opened the drawer and collected the bills, the rabbit danced from one polyester velveteen foot to the other. His pink-lined ears swayed as his attention swiveled from the cashier to the front door. Nick slid from the back corner of the booth to the outside edge of the bench seat.

He moved slowly. Crime-fighting, like comedy, was about timing.

The rabbit snatched the cash as two city policemen threw their shadows across the front threshold. He sprinted down the narrow aisle toward the back exit, unzipping the front of the costume and stuffing bills inside while glancing back over his shoulder. When he was almost abreast of the booth, Nick stretched one lanky leg into the flight path. The ankle supported a size 14-C foot in a perfectly-polished Finley loafer.

Bugs's left rear paw slid neatly under the ankle. He performed a devil-may-care forward dive, followed by a flailing tuck-and-roll. His back hit the floor with a thud, his arms and legs forming an X the width of the aisle.

The flare gun flew upward. Nick already had his handkerchief out and draped over his palm. He made a one-handed catch as the gun came down. When the two city cops arrived, he moved back to the bench to get out of their way. He was well enough acquainted with them to know they weren't in the habit of sprinting. They both were panting.

"Thanks, Shea."

"Glad to help, Carter."

They ordered the rabbit to roll onto his stomach so they could cuff him.

"He picked the lock on the rear door of the pharmacy up the street about an hour ago." Carter helped his partner haul Bugs to his feet and took the gun from Nick. "When the alarm went off he must've run down the alley and dodged in through the kitchen of the Ark and Dove Hotel. He hid in a coat closet near the front desk."

"We looked all over this end of town," added his partner. "If he'd stayed put we might have given up."

"But he found the rabbit costume hanging in the closet and tried to sneak out the front door in it."

"A criminal genius he ain't."

"The concierge saw him, realized Easter is seven months away, and called 911."

Carter pulled off the rabbit headpiece and mask and Nick let out a gust of exasperation.

"Emanuel, why are you out of jail?"

Emanuel, aka Hot Dog, glanced up at him with the look of a high school quarterback who had just missed a winning pass in the finals.

"The old lady dropped charges and paid my bail."

Nick was used to coincidences like the Chuck's Wagon rabbit and the name of the developer, Sam Hare, but they made him uneasy anyway. Coincidences encouraged his suspicion that life was a joke the cosmos played on humanity.

The old poem, "The antiseptic baby and the prophylactic pup," came to mind. Nick liked the idea of being the prophylactic pup. He was the bloodhound who would thwart whatever further foul play someone had in mind for Dr. Brant.

His job would be easier though if Logan would take up bridge or yoga or better yet, go on a 'round-the-world cruise. But no. Here she was marching back and forth in front of Longview Development's office building waving a "Shame on You" sign.

The dozen or so protesters with her wielded signs with messages more specific than that, but Nick had to smile at hers. Logan could be depended on to get to the crux of the matter. Before she noticed him he went to a side entrance. He would drop by her house later this evening, and tell her how her boy Emanuel had spent his first day of freedom. He would request that she leave justice to the justice system, imperfect as it might be.

Longview Development's top floor reception area was faux-'50's with minimalist chairs and boomerang-shaped end tables. The receptionist's desk was constructed of melamine-coated particle board. The pastel walls looked like an explosion in a sherbet shop. It must have cost Hare's company the equivalent of a year of Nick's salary to create décor this cheap-looking and uncomfortable.

He wasn't surprised when the receptionist ushered him into her boss's office after the metal sunburst clock on the wall had ticked away only four and a half minutes. He could imagine the conflict in Hare's head. Should he establish superiority by keeping the cop cooling his heels in a room chilled to appletini temperature, or should he be smart and not vex the constabulary? A four and a half minute delay was long enough to give the impression of a busy titan of progress, but not enough to arouse antipathy.

The '50's decade ended at the heavy oak door of Hare's inner sanctum. Teddy Roosevelt would have felt at home on the other side of it. Portly Moroccan-leather easy chairs hunkered in clusters around the room. On the wood-paneled walls above them the stuffed heads of elk, moose, grizzly, and bison stared with melancholy in their glass eyes. On the wall behind Hare's desk hung an ornate frame with a quote from Nietzsche's *Faust* written in calligraphy on parchment. *Mit den Fursten der Finsternis habe ich Wurfel gespielt.*

Hare stood up. He was almost as tall as Nick and easily as slender. He had ice-blue eyes, whip-thin lips, and a perfect nose that Nick suspected wasn't God-given. His black hair was sleeked back and gelled in place. It conspired with his receding chin to giving him the profile of a seal. Slick was the best way to describe him, but slick on the cusp of slimy.

He gestured to a upholstered chair on the passenger side of a desk shaped like an aircraft carrier's landing deck. Nick could see his reflection in the polished mahogany. He had come prepared to be patronized. He didn't have to wait long.

Hare slid back two wall panels to expose an alcove with a hutch and wet bar on one side. Next to it was an antique shaving stand, basin, and all the accessories. The shaving brush looked to be made of black silver-tipped badger hair in an ivory handle. If Hare thought Detective Shea would notice details like that and intended to impress him, he was half right. Nick noticed details.

Hare took a bottle of Johnny Walker Scotch Gold from the hutch. He poured himself a shot glass, then held up the bottle. Nick shook his head. He knew the bottle probably cost under six hundred dollars and Hare offered it to not-so-important visitors. The really good stuff was behind the closed cupboard doors on the top shelf. With wildly expensive limited releases, high-end liquor companies were peddling the image of prestige and exclusivity these days. His friend Will called the phenomenon the Lush Life.

"Glad the department sent someone over so quickly, Detective Shea." Hare sat down on the other side of the desk. "I only called this morning. Thievery on our construction sites is costing us hundreds of thousands."

He opened a tooled leather humidor with Cohiba cigars and held it out so Nick could reach it.

"No thanks."

"Coffee then, Detective?"

"No thank you. I'm not here because of thefts on your construction sites."

He had heard Hare's secretary tell her boss that Detective Shea from the Homicide Division was there to see him. Only a numbskull would think Homicide would be sent to investigate theft, and Hare was not a numbskull.

"Then what can I do for you, Detective?"

"Interesting quote on the wall."

Hare swiveled in his chair to look at it. "Ah yes." He laughed. "Someone gave it to me as a joke. Do you know what it means?"

" 'With the Prince of Darkness I have gambled at dice.' "

"Right."

Nick made a mental note to confer with the division that investigated reports of Satanism and voodoo. If Hare had had any connections with that sort of activity it would explain the eagles and the heart in the septic pit and the dead rat in Logan's mailbox. There was also the fact that a strychnine-laced dog carcass had been found on Hare's property about the time the pair of eagles disappeared from their nesting site.

He had no proof, yet, of wrong-doing on Hare's part. He knew this interview would be a fishing expedition, and so did Hare. If the man didn't own the distinction of beating the Devil at dice, he possessed something almost as good, that phalanx of lawyers. But even the slickest operators slipped up occasionally.

"How well do you know Dr. Logan Brant?" Nick asked.

Chapter Twenty-Two

"A Bump in the Night"

There is no fate that cannot be surmounted by scorn.
Albert Camus (1913-1960)

Alice and Faye walked in silence up the street from Syl's house. Finally Alice asked, "Do you think Syl has hooked up with an incubus?" She thought she knew the answer though.

"You saw her. What do you think?"

"I don't know what to think. Maybe the tabloids are right. Maybe Elvis really isn't dead." The thought that the tabloids might have been right all these years after all surprised Alice into grinning. "Or maybe his ghost has chosen to have a fling with our friend."

When they reached the foot of the stairs to Alice's front deck they both looked up. The house never had looked ominous before.

"Do you want to stay at my place, Al?"

"No thanks. I'm okay. I didn't call up an incubus. And those creatures, those elementals, have been here all along, right?"

"Right." Faye refrained from pointing out that incubi didn't have to be summoned. Longing and loneliness were enough to attract one. "But in case anything sinister is on the loose beyond Syl's house..." Faye held out a crucifix. "...take this to bed with you."

"Faye, you know I'm agnostic at best."

"Before we straighten this out, Al, I'll bet my house and retirement fund that you'll believe in God, the Devil, angels, demons, the hereafter, where-after, forever-after. All of it." Faye kissed her on the cheek and waved good night.

Alice climbed the stairs and opened her front door slowly. When nothing came boiling out at her, she took a few cautious steps inside. She left the solid front door open and stood with her back against the screen door and her hand on the handle, in case she had to bolt. Aside from the pale-blue glow around the ceiling fan and the twinkle of tiny red lights in the house plants, everything seemed to be what she already was beginning to think of as the new normal.

She knew that worrying about disturbing her recently discovered roommates was silly, but she tiptoed upstairs and set the crucifix on the nightstand. She threw her clothes onto a chair and didn't bother putting on her old cotton nightshirt. Nighttime hadn't cooled the air much so she lay on top of the sheets.

She missed Charlie the most each morning when she woke up and realized his death was not a terrible dream. Nighttime was difficult too, without his strong arms around her and his warm breath stirring her hair.

When the beast loomed in the doorway she didn't know if she was awake or asleep. She hoped she was asleep, but real or a nightmare, it paralyzed her with terror. The creature lurched toward her on hind legs whose knee joints bent in the wrong direction. It had a wildebeest's broad, flat snout and curved horns. Its super-sized rat tail switched from side to side. Its eyes glowed like the business ends of twin cheroots.

She knew she was awake and naked when she felt its sharp talons sink into her breasts. She moaned more in pleasure than pain as a tidal wave of sensuality swept over her. The alligator teeth jutting from its raw, red wound of a mouth seemed to grow larger as it bent down and snuffled in her ear.

Shudders of ecstasy radiated from her groin out to the ends of her fingers and toes, but she sensed that climaxing would surrender her to forces darker than she could imagine. She mustered will power from some secret reserve and managed to shout, "No! No, no, no, no!"

The demon must have sensed her lack of enthusiasm. The glowing cheroot ends softened into the big dark eyes of a Labrador puppy. It looked like the offspring of a Lab and a wildebeest, and when it said, *"Here's looking at you, kid,"* Bogart sounded more like Colombo with the hiccups.

Whatever this was, it had committed the worst sort of home invasion. It had broken into her head. And it could speak.

There was no explaining why the old advice-to-new-brides joke occurred to her. The device was too improbable to use in any plot she might have written, but there it was. "When ironing, think about sex. When having sex, think about ironing." She was out-gunned by supernatural forces, and the only weapon she had was scorn.

She avoided looking into those puppy eyes and concentrated on sending a thought. *I don't do doggy style, asshole."*

With a roar, the monster disintegrated and scattered like an explosion of dandruff in a duffel bag. In its place Hollywood heart-throbs appeared like a grainy, flickering old film montage. Hell must be experiencing transmission difficulties.

Agent 007 cocked a bushy eyebrow. Johnny Castle held out a hand in an invitation for dirty dancing. Lieutenant "Maverick" Mitchell gave her a come-hither look over the rims of his Top Gun shades. She finally fell asleep, but her own voice woke her.

"Charlie." She called his name aloud and her eyes flew open.

She was not alone in the dark room. Hell's IT department must have gotten back on-line. Standing at the foot of the bed was a man so handsome he would have stopped traffic on the New Jersey Turnpike. But he didn't look like Charlie. In the midst of all this, she realized that none of them had looked like Charlie, and she thought she knew why.

She held the cross aloft with one hand, and with the other, took Charlie's silver dragon ring and chain from the nightstand's top drawer. For good measure she also retrieved the vibrator with two large knobs from the bottom drawer. Its official purpose was massaging aching shoulders, but Charlie had dubbed it the "two-humped camel of love." Neither of them had spoken of its foreshadowing of loss, grief, and loneliness.

During the year since Charlie's death the camel had taken on a life and a purpose of its own. It did more than provide multiple happy endings with every use. Each one finished with such an intense, universal feeling of love, it left Alice shaking and sobbing. She held the cross in one hand and the ring in the other and cradled the vibrator with both arms. The incubus vanished. Alice stared at the ceiling for an hour or more before sleep finally came. It was blessedly dreamless.

CHAPTER TWENTY-THREE

"UP TO HER ASS IN ALLIGATORS"

A truth that's told with bad intent
Beats all the lies you can invent."
William Blake

Night faded into a pale promise of dawn. Alice lay curled like a caterpillar in the 600-thread-count cocoon suspended between sleep and consciousness. What helped her fight back panic were the bats coming home to roost in the attic.

These night-roving intruders were real. They were natural. Nothing figmentish about them. Their muffled rustling sounded like a congregation settling into the pews. For weeks, evicting them had been on Alice's to-do list, but now they seemed the least of her troubles.

After the bats stopped squeaking, the earliest bird tuned up. A second cardinal responded, melodically re-establishing his territory. A wren chimed in with counterpoint. By the time the sun made an appearance, a chorus of birds sounded among the tree tops outside Alice's window.

She sat up in bed and leaned over to check the floor for scattered demon debris. The area rug was so clean that Faye would have nodded sagely and said, "So, you're blocked again." Faye was wise to the fact that when her friend Alice couldn't get her fictional house in order, she vacuumed her physical one.

Remembering Syl's satisfied-customer look of the night before, Alice wanted to call Faye. She was sure than whatever was servicing

Syl did not look like what had visited her a few hours ago. She wanted to ask Faye why that was the case, but being awakened earlier than noon made her cranky.

Alice wandered, naked and shaken, into the bathroom. The clean rug and the birds' familiar morning rave almost had her believing that last night's hell-bent attempt at seduction had been a horrific nightmare. A glance at the mirror dispelled that notion. Like the neon border of a bar's beer sign, a lavender glow outlined her head and shoulders. The vivid color shimmered against the white wall behind her.

She stared at it, tallying the good news and bad news of opening a door to the Other Side.

The good news: auras existed and she had one. That was like discovering her IQ was thirty points higher than the number recorded in her high school records. The bad news: the nightmare she'd had a few hours ago wasn't her imagination.

She knew with a gut-wrenching certainty that her life had taken a turn for the worse and she had no clue as to how to put it back the way it was. She couldn't fix it by installing an alarm system and putting double locks on the doors. She couldn't call the police and complain about a home invasion. She didn't know how to reverse whatever spell had spilled over from Syl's recklessness.

As she retrieved the cotton drawstring pants and rumpled t-shirt from the chair where she'd thrown them the night before, she took stock of what assets she had. Faye was a brave and resourceful friend and together they should be able to figure a way out of this. Ironically, last night's proof of hell's existence meant heaven was real too and wherever it was, she knew she had a protector there.

She fastened the chain around her neck and covered Charlie's ring with her palm, pressing it against her sternum. She would not take it off again. She turned back to the mirror and stared at her third ally. Herself. As bad as last night's apparitions had been, they also had demonstrated weakness. With her hand still on the dragon ring, she resolved to deal with whatever happened with as much calm, courage, and common sense as she could muster. The decision wasn't a difficult one. It wasn't as though she had a choice.

She padded barefoot downstairs. Low-slanting rays of morning sunshine streamed through the floor-to-ceiling windows of the sun porch and into the living room. In their light, the ethereal glow from the furniture and artwork was visible. Alice stood at arm's length from the softly luminous sofa and touched the back of it with the tips of her fingers.

No electricity caused her hair to stand on end. No imps or demons popped out from behind the cushions. The sofa didn't rear up on its stubby hind legs and snarl at her. She exhaled the breath she had been holding. The party in the house plants was so subdued Alice had to walk close to hear it.

Alice had lots of questions about the natural history of unnatural beings and not even *Wikipedia* could give her reliable answers. Foremost, was it possible to communicate with the elementals? And if so, did she want to?

She approached the kitchen as if it were a dark alley in a bad neighborhood. Brandishing the small iron skillet in one hand, she turned on the gas burner, and put on her glasses. With fry pan at the ready, she bent down for a closer look.

Two vaguely humanoid creatures the size of carpenter ants danced in the gas jets, their hair in flames. Alice's first impulse was to throw water on them, even though she knew they weren't on fire. They were fire. These were the elementals Faye called salamanders.

How should she prepare breakfast now that she knew her stove was a habitat for non-humanity? She put a piece of bread in the toaster and pushed down the lever. She stared into the slot but saw no revelry among the glowing coils. Actual flames must be necessary.

She hesitated at setting the heavy skillet on top of the burner until reason prevailed in what was a completely unreasonable situation. After all, they must have been there all along, dancing in the fire that cooked her fake bacon, grits, and fried egg, over easy. She put the iron skillet gently on the burner and made a conscious decision to calm down.

Faye said the elementals were allied with angels, and so far they had presented no threat. She already shared her house with bats, mice, spiders, ants, stink bugs, crickets, lizards, the small black snake in the basement, and the occasional squirrel trying to move into the bats' neighborhood above the ceiling. And those were just the roommates she knew about.

Alice flipped the egg. She softly sang the first four lines of "Don't Fence Me In," and turned off the burner. She shoveled the bogus bacon and the over-easy onto a plate and carried it to the table. In the brightening sunlight, the sylphs around the fan looked like a pale blue haze. The glow from the furniture and artworks was barely discernible.

Okay. So I have unusual pets and mood lighting with a continuous power supply... and very, very, very bad dreams.

When she finished washing the dishes she sat warily in her desk chair. She put her left hand on the mouse and stared into the slumbering computer's rectangular eye. What if it was infected? She doubted the silicon valley whiz-kids had programmed the anti-virus software to handle demonic possession.

She pushed her chair back a couple feet as the monitor's inner light came on and the computer hummed to life. When nothing leaped out at her she opened the file containing the not-much-work-in-progress. She stared at the screen a long minute or so, then she went outside and threw peanuts to the squirrels.

While she was up she walked down to the street to fetch the morning newspaper and read it at her desk. After more communion with a page that had only a chapter title she took the plunge and went on-line.

Alice was tempted to look for sites selling exorcism software or offering advice on demonic cyber-possession, but she decided to leave that Pandora's box unopened. The Devil's minions must include damned hackers collecting the cookies of candidates for eternal perdition. And by the way, when did "minion" become part of her working vocabulary?

While on her EVA through cyberspace Alice found the perfect screen saver. The video loop of a pair of courting seahorses had no audio, but for ten minutes she watched their silent, sensual ballet in a garden of undulating kelp. They would have kept her entranced longer, but the jangle of the doorbell broke the spell.

Two policemen were waiting outside. One looked like a lanky kid hardly old enough to be a policeman. The other resembled one of Santa's elves who'd come out of retirement and donned a police uniform. He wore granny glasses and an artful arrangement of the wisps of hair left on the perimeter of his skull.

Alice joined them on the porch and tried to look casual. Had neighbors complained about suspicious activity in the Lower Cliffs? Had someone complained about strange noises coming from her house last night? Had something terrible happened to Logan? Was Syl's affair with a horny demon named Harry a felony?

The elf spoke. "I'm Sergeant Staub, ma'am, and this is Corporal Smoot. Yesterday we received a complaint about a vicious alligator at this address."

"An alligator?"

"Yes, ma'am. An anonymous caller claimed a six-foot alligator attacked him."

She wanted to point out that alligators only had four feet, but she figured Sergeant Staub wouldn't appreciate it.

"I don't have an alligator." She was grateful that Russell had given her the chance to lie by telling the truth.

"He was insistent about checking it out, ma'am. Menace to society and all that."

Alice smiled. The sergeant harbored a fugitive sense of humor after all. She opened the door, stood aside, and gestured them in, then paced the front deck like a lion in a cage several sizes too small.

What if. What if they heard the gnomes whooping it up in the houseplants or noticed the sofa had a glow on? Worse, what if that monster from last night appeared? And oh yes, she hadn't made the bed this morning.

She grasped the irony. Come hell or high water, bad housekeeping was a no-no.

She gave Staub and the earnest-looking Smoot enough time to search from the second floor to the basement. When they didn't reappear she pushed off from the porch railing, as if she needed to propel herself inside. She found them standing in her office. They were staring, transfixed, at the seahorses making languid love on her monitor screen.

Alice's presence startled them. They mumbled their apologies for disturbing her, and she was amused to see Smoot blushing. She watched them walk down the steps to the street and get into their patrol car.

She carried a sense of relief back inside. The translucent blue sylphs were still riding the ceiling fan's carousel, and the gnome hum radiated from the plants. Now Alice had the comforting assurance that other people were as oblivious to all of that as she once had been.

She decided to get out her grandmother's recipe and bake some chocolate chip cookies. Her personal music delivery system was her old stereo. She put on her favorite Tom Waits album.

When she turned on the oven, she leaned down to look inside. The salamander elementals slithered up from the pilot light hole. They danced in the flames like children in a gush of water from a fire hydrant on a hot summer's day.

She measured and stirred and spooned the batter onto a pair of cookie sheets. With a "Heads up, girls and boys," she slid the pans onto the oven racks.

As the aroma filled the house, Alice wondered if it was her imagination or did the hum from the house plants sound more excited. She cut open a brown paper bag and spread it out on the kitchen counter. When the cookies finished baking she used a spatula to shovel them onto the paper in neat rows.

After they cooled she broke two of them into pieces and distributed them among the plants. Alice was surprised when silence ensued the way it did around a Thanksgiving table when the turkey and dressing were divvied out.

Chapter Twenty-Four

"Match. Set. Game."

*Every normal man must be tempted at times
to spit on his hands, hoist the black flag,
and begin slitting throats.*
H. L. Mencken

Nick rocked back in his swivel chair and propped his feet, ankles crossed, on the desk. He opened Tuesday's newspaper, a day old now, and held it up in front of him. The killer his colleagues called the Spitter was still at large and probably cruising the clubs. Nick was not in the mood for bullpen banter. The newspaper was the flimsiest of screens, but better than none.

A piece on the first page of the second section caught his attention. Joe Stone had finally gotten a byline over an article about the hostilities between the Defenders of the Chesapeake and Longview Development Corporation. It occupied sixteen column inches above the fold. It wasn't a front page spread, but it was the first time Nick had seen an attribution to Stone.

This article named Dr. Logan Brant as the head of the environmentalist group. Stone also detailed the charges against her for assault and vandalism, and mentioned her arrest for disturbing the peace. He ended by quoting talking points from Hare's usual media puff-pieces. "Millions in tax revenues." "Thousands of jobs." "Partnership with the community." "Preservation of the Chesapeake's natural beauty." "Conservation of wildlife."

In the past thirty years Nick had heard all that horse hockey more times than he could count. He wondered how Logan Brant was reacting to it. Knowing her she was probably taking it better than he was. Then Sheila arrived and his day got better, although he didn't know it yet.

Most of Nick's colleagues recognized the sanctity of his newsprint rampart, but not Sheila from Records. As a rule Sheila hardly slowed down when she made deliveries, shying folders onto desks like drink coasters as she passed by. Today she came to a full stop and dropped three manila folders onto the neatest desk in the room. Nick folded the newspaper into a precise rectangle with the crossword puzzle showing and slid it into his bottom desk drawer. He reached for the folders and looked up, surprised to see her still there.

"Good afternoon, Sheila."

"This is your lucky day, Shea." Sheila was not one for amenities. "The lab set a speed record for DNA results on your spitter." Her mouth twitched in a phantom smile although her lager-amber eyes hadn't gotten the memo. "Maybe your girlfriend, the coroner, put in a good word for you at the lab."

Nick had wanted to tell her many times before that she didn't have to try so hard to be one of the boys, and he resisted the impulse now too. He opened the top folder and scanned the report on the condition of the heart in the cardboard container in Dr. Brant's septic pit. He was relieved to see that it had been frozen for weeks. If the Spitter had killed its owner he had done it before Nick found the telltale mucous in the Crispy Chikin parking lot. There was no identification of a body to go with it.

He picked up the second file with information about the severed leg that had washed ashore. Anyone watching Sheila would not have noticed her lean half an inch closer, but Nick did without even looking up. While he read the results and studied the photos of the leg he could feel the slight shove of air as she intruded a little farther into his personal space. The ability to sense the *chi* force of others had saved his life on occasion, but only his friend Will knew about it. Will occasionally referred to him as Obi-wan.

The leg had been floating for a couple weeks, so it hadn't shared an address with the previously-deceased heart either. Nick indulged in a moment of what-if anyway. If he had collected the spittle three weeks earlier, the leg and its owner might be attached and alive. If, in fact, the Spitter was the murderer. He didn't want to think about the possibility of two serial killers with butcher-knives on the loose.

He leaned back in his chair, more to increase that psychic elbow room than to ease the ache in his lower spine. "So, the pedicure belonged to a guy."

He could tell that Sheila was disappointed by his lack of surprise. It was a shapely leg, except for the turtle bites, and well cared for. He knew everyone had been anticipating an ID and photos of the woman once attached to it. He himself would have been surprised by this turn of events if anything could surprise him anymore.

"No DNA matches in the data banks." Sheila shifted from one foot to the other. She gave the impression of a kid waiting impatiently for someone to open a present. "And no one-legged bodies have turned up."

Can't get dental records from a pedicure, Nick thought.

He opened the third folder with the DNA results. It contained a name, Russell Wright, a home and a business address, plus a photo taken from an article in the local paper's business section a year earlier. As he stared at the good-looking, self-satisfied face of the man he'd been shadowing, he replayed the scene that had haunted him. Once again he was standing in the blood spattered apartment, looking down at the young woman raped and bludgeoned until her face was unrecognizable. Plus the DNA linked Wright to three cold cases from a couple years earlier.

He took his shoulder holster from the back of the chair and put his jacket on over it. He positioned the two-way radio over his left lapel, clipped the helical receiver cord to the back of his collar, and put in the ear bud. He took the handcuffs out of his desk drawer and attached them to the clip on his belt.

"You going after the son of a bitch?"

"Yes."

That was what Sheila had been waiting for. She hiked off with a satisfied smile.

Nick's former partner in this case had died of a heart attack while bowling three months ago. Because until recently it had been a cold case and the department was short-handed, he had been working it alone.

Nathan was in Baltimore checking out voodoo shops as part of Dr. Brant's case. After years on the Miami police force, he knew more about obeah, voodoo, and santoría than everyone else here put together. Nick called him on his private line. Nathan wasn't officially assigned to the Spitter's case, but he'd be irritated if he were left out of the collar.

When he hung up he glanced at his watch. Three o'clock on a midweek afternoon. He talked strategy with the platoon commander on deck, then notified Kimberly in Dispatch. Time to call in the cavalry. He gave Kim a rendezvous location out of sight of Wright's building. She would put out the call to all available units.

She called back to tell him a patrolman had reported Wright's car in the garage. That meant they wouldn't have to wait for him to come home. Nick went looking for the rookie, Len Smoot, and found him in the kitchen. What Smoot the Boot lacked in longevity on the force he made up for in enthusiasm.

"We have a match on the one-eighty-seven."

"You got the Spitter?"

"Yeah. Meet me at the car."

Len's eyes lit up. He abandoned his pizza and soda and triple-timed to his locker. Nick maintained a stoic expression when Len exited the station wearing his Kevlar, radio, Glock, and duty belt studded with at least ten pounds of spare magazines, tools, and gadgets. Smoot glanced at the car's empty back seat, then at Nick's jacket, radio, and handcuffs.

"Where's your gear, Shea?"

"You're wearing enough for both of us."

As the elevator door opened, Nick turned on his radio and adjusted the ear piece. He could hear the subdued footsteps of men taking up positions in the hallways and stairwells leading off this one.

"Should I break leather?" Len spoke from way too close behind his right shoulder.

He'd have to talk to Len about that. It could get him seriously hurt some day, if not dead.

"No."

Break leather? Was slang a course in Cop School 101? Or had Smoot been watching too much television? No matter. He'd make an outstanding cop one day.

Russell Wright's over-priced unit was on the top floor of a condo the management claimed had a water view. The sales brochures didn't mention that the wet stuff was a shopping mall's holding pond only visible from the roof.

Len left his Glock in the holster, but the unspoken question, Are you sure? hovered in the air behind Nick as he walked down the hall. The weight of his own Sig Sauer under his jacket felt good though.

The police outside had stayed hidden on side streets and in the garage, but maybe the doorman had tipped off the Spitter that a pair of strangers had hit the elevator button for his floor. As Nick and Len approached the apartment, the door slammed open. Wright charged out with a half empty bottle of vodka dangling from his left hand. In his right he brandished a meat cleaver almost as big as a briefcase. Nick couldn't detect a gun's bulge, but that didn't mean Wright wasn't carrying.

"Stop! Drop your weapons and put your hands on top of your head."

Wright kept coming. With his Sig still holstered Nick strode inside the Spitter's reach. In a motion too swift to track, he held up his right hand and forearm as a guard. He planted his left palm on the man's chest and gave a quick shove. It was the flat-hand equivalent of the three-inch punch.

Russell Wright flew backward with both feet off the ground. His head hit the vinyl parquet floor with a thwack. The bottle shattered.

The cleaver soared upward in a steep trajectory. Len stepped forward and caught the short handle, his arm following its downward path to ease the weight of the blade attached to it. Nick rolled the stunned killer onto his stomach and cuffed him.

His radio had broadcast the showdown to the waiting units. In less than half a minute the hallway swarmed with uniforms, all with weapons aimed at the Spitter.

"Awesome!" Len probably didn't mean to blurt it.

"Awesome yourself. Where did you learn to catch like that, Smoot?"

Len's pale round face turned pink. "In college I juggled knives at Ren fairs."

"Looks more like a cleaver."

"It's old." Len fished a handkerchief out of his pocket and used it between to minimize his prints. The blade was almost a foot square, gracefully curved along its top and leading edges. "Chinese. Carbon steel with the tang inserted into the plum wood handle."

From the rapt expression on Len's face, Nick figured if the knife ever disappeared from the evidence room he'd know where to look for it.

Nathan arrived in time to help four patrolmen wrestle Russell into a squad car. As the car drove away Nick felt a flutter in the air. Maybe it was an errant draft from the building's air conditioning unit, but he thought of it as a disturbance in the Force.

His preoccupation with the killer was decamping. His brain was cleaning house. It was making room for the heart in the septic tank hole, Samuel Hare, and the search for the leg's owner. He'd also have another talk with Emanuel Hot Dog Boyd. No matter how much Boyd swore he had mugged Dr. Brant for drug money, he was positive someone had put him up to it.

Nathan joined him on the sidewalk and the two of them headed back inside behind the forensics squad. They had planned to canvas farther a-field in Dr. Brant's neighborhood this evening, knocking on doors as people came home from work. No time now for a leisurely sunset stroll through the quiet, shaded streets overlooking the Cliffs' watery vistas.

"When we're done here I'll write up the report," Nick said. "You can do the house-to-house in the Cliffs."

"So I finally get to meet the Antique Avenger?"

"Sure. Give her my regards."

Antique Avenger might be how people referred to Doctor Brant around the station house, but Nick had his own nickname for her, inspired by a childhood hero. In the privacy of his thoughts he called her Doc Savage.

Chapter Twenty-Five

"Hump Day"

The camel's hump is an ugly lump
Which well you may see at the Zoo;
But uglier yet is the hump we get
From having too little to do.
Rudyard Kipling
("How the Camel Got His Hump"
from *The Just So Stories*)

Alice and Faye carried the cooler between them down to the river. It knocked against their legs, but Faye was too angry at her ex-husband to notice.

"He said he'd return my cashmere sweater weeks ago."

"A sweater? It's August, Faye. What's really bothering you?"

"He's my friend, Al. I'm worried."

"Did you turn in a missing person report?"

"You know I'm allergic to filling out official documents."

Alice was nursing her own preoccupations. "I had a bad night."

"What happened?"

"Harry happened. And in a seriously hideous form."

They set the cooler on the bench attached to a picnic table in a scruffy patch of grass near the beach's perimeter. Alice shrugged out of her back pack with more picnic supplies.

"What did he do?"

"He appeared in my bedroom as one horny freak after another. He tried impersonating movie stars, but he couldn't hold the poses for long. Apparently he can't duplicate Charlie at all."

"Charlie was one of a kind alright. So, how did you get rid of Harry?"

"I told him to go piss up a rope. Then I waved the crucifix and the vibrator at him. He exited like an explosion in a talcum powder factory."

"Is Charlie's two-humped camel of love still haunted?"

"Not so much now." Alice couldn't keep the wistful out of her voice. "What about you and Harry?"

"He still visits now and then, but it's more of a sex dream than reality."

"He was way too real at my house. I have to get rid of him."

"We both do." Faye sighed. "Harry went after the furnace guy this morning. I heard rattling and banging and moaning in the basement and found him draped across the dryer with his ass in the air and his pants around his ankles."

"What did you say to him?"

"Nothing. He obviously didn't have chit-chat on his mind. He cleared out through the basement door without leaving a bill. But he did clean the cum off the top of the dryer."

"Maybe there's a do-it-yourself exorcism site on-line."

"And I'll ask around."

With a plan in hand, even if it was a half-assed one, Faye spread a tablecloth on the table and set her wireless speaker on it. She selected steel drum calypso on her phone and the two of them danced while they unpacked the plates and utensils. They set out baked camembert and crackers, raw vegetables, onion dip, and Alice's cookies. Faye had brought four stemmed glasses and a lidded pitcher full of her Hump Day specialty, tequila sunsets. Syl and Esme would be working late, so they sat across from each other and started on the sunsets.

"I don't like keeping secrets from Es," said Alice. "But how do we tell her?"

"Saying 'Syl screwed up' always works for me."

As if on cue, Syl arrived in her Mercedes with the top down and Elvis blasting from the speakers. With a level of energy unusual for her she trotted down the cement steps from the small parking area. She sat next to Faye and pulled a frosty bottle and four slender champagne flutes from her insulated shoulder bag.

"Impressive." Faye held up the bottle. "Cattier Brut Blanc de Noirs."

"You're looking at the new partner in Swivens, Alcott, Jenkins, and Brant. It comes with a raise, a corner office, and my own parking space."

"Brant?"

"When I stopped at the liquor store for the champagne I ran into Jerry's secretary. She told me the paperwork had finally come through to get my maiden name back. No more Mrs. Brant Gant. What was I thinking?"

"Congratulations." In the slanting rays of the setting sun Alice noticed that the purplish pouches under Syl's eyes were gone. So were the faint wrinkles and the broken capillaries.

"What can I say?" Syl shrugged. "I'm on a roll."

"You know why this is happening." Faye glared at her.

"When you're dealing with Evil there's no free lunch," Alice added.

"Elvis had lunch on me last night. It was so good the neighbors wanted a cigarette afterward." As Syl poured the champagne she caught Alice's eye. "Sorry about Russell, Al. I had no idea he was such a jerk."

"To hell with Russell. A monster from hell tried to rape me last night and it's your fault."

"No it's not. You crashed the party in my basement. I didn't invite you."

Alice stood up. She looked about to reach across the table to deliver a left hook. Faye put a hand out, like a crossing guard at a dangerous intersection.

"I don't get it." Alice leaned forward with her knuckles on the table. "Why is Syl dating Elvis and I get scared shitless by the Thing?"

"Maybe they don't know what to do with you, Al," said Faye. "You've experienced true love. Maybe love does conquer all. Even Hell."

"But what if Harry keeps trying?"

"He can't impersonate Charlie," said Faye. "He can try to hijack a soul, but he can't fake a soul mate. What is it you say about sex with other guys?"

"It feels good, but it doesn't feel right."

"Feeling good feels pretty damned good." Syl held her champagne flute up in a salute to feeling good.

"You're right about the 'damned' part," muttered Alice. "If a blind date feels like an eternity, what do you think eternity feels like?"

Before Syl could think of a come-back, Esme arrived. She wore a pair of denim cut-offs, sandals, and a tank top. She looked good in them. But then, she looked good in everything.

"Happy Hump Day." She sat down hard across from Alice, as if her ankles had given out on her. "Give me a sunset. Immediately. And keep 'em coming."

"Bad day?" asked Alice.

"Is it my imagination, or are more people becoming insufferable?"

"What happened, Es?" Faye handed her the glass.

"Another Dykwim. Five minutes before quitting time."

"What's that?" asked Syl.

Alice knew the answer. "It's short for 'Do you know who I am.'"

Faye elaborated. "A Dykwim is a guy who tries to bull his way to the head of the line. If people object, he demands to know if they know who he is."

"Esme's job is to keep a fight from breaking out."

"Did you give him the usual response?" asked Faye.

Esme nodded.

"What'd you say, Es?"

Alice answered for her. "She takes the microphone and announces loudly, 'There's a gentleman here who doesn't know who he is. Would anyone who can identify him please come to gate six'… or whatever."

Syl guffawed. "My god, don't they try to get you fired?"

"Almost every time." Now that her bad day at BWI was off her mind Esme sensed tension at the table. "Is everything all right? Is Logan okay?"

"She's fine, all things considered," said Syl. "She's invited cousin Freddy to dinner Friday night, and she plans to try to talk sense into him."

"Will you go too, Syl?"

"Hell no. I'd rather be poked in the eye with a sharp stick than spend an evening with cousin Freddy."

They talked until the sun had ducked behind the tops of the trees. When Alice finally worked up the nerve to tell Esme about Harry, she realized she'd be talking to herself. The other three had focused like lasers on the man walking through the sand in the glow from the beach's light pole.

"Oh, brother," Esme murmured.

He stood six-foot-two or three. His trousers had knife-blade creases in the legs. The navy-blue jacket hung on his athlete's frame with casual elegance. Under it was a starched white shirt and paisley tie. His shoes were polished to the sheen of obsidian.

Syl raised her glass in invitation. "Howdy, stranger."

"Good evening." He spoke with a southern drawl.

"Care to join us for a sundowner?" asked Syl.

"Maybe another time." He showed them his badge. My name is Detective Hale. I'm with the County Police department."

As they all introduced themselves Alice noticed that Hale stared at Esme a couple beats longer. She noticed that Esme noticed it too.

"We're gathering information about the deceased eagles found in your neighbor's yard last Friday.

"You mean my mother's yard," said Syl.

"Then you're Sylvana Gant?"

"Brant. I just got my old name back."

Detective Hale pulled a notebook and pen from his jacket's inside pocket, and made note of the names. Pen and paper. How retro. Alice was charmed.

"We heard they found a heart in the hole," she said.

"A pig's heart, ma'am."

Faye held up a hand to get his attention. "And don't forget the rat in Dr. Brant's mailbox and her vandalized car and the attempted mugging,"

"Have you seen anyone unfamiliar in the neighborhood, or heard anything that might identify who's behind the harassment?"

"I imagine you know about Dr. Brant's objections to some local development projects, Detective Hale." Esme's voice was silkier than usual.

By now Faye and Syl had picked up on the electricity arcing between her and Hale. When he finished with his questions Syl said, "Don't rush off. Who else do you have to talk to tonight?"

"You all are the last ones." He handed each of them a card. "If you think of anything else that might be helpful, no matter how inconsequential it seems, please call me or Detective Shea at this number."

"So you're off duty, right?" Syl didn't wait for an answer before pouring him a sunset.

Alice stood up. "I'd like to stay, but I have to get back to work." She extended a hand and Hale's engulfed it. "Why don't you sit here, Detective?"

The seat across from Esme creaked when he sat down, but it held.

"I have to go too," said Faye. But curiosity made her and Alice linger.

"You don't sound like you're from around here," said Faye.

"I'm from Georgia."

"Esme went to college in Georgia," said Alice.

"Spelman," added Esme.

"I graduated from Morehouse."

Alice threw Syl a go-thither look. Syl caught it and stood up.

"Esme lives in that white house overlooking the water." Syl pointed to the tree-covered ridge above them. "Why don't you help her carry home the leftovers?"

Faye started to go, then turned around. "Detective Hale, how does someone file a missing person report?"

"Call me tomorrow at the number on the card. I'll tell you what you need to bring to the station – photos, list of medications, physical description, that sort of thing."

"Thanks."

Faye and Alice followed the tail lights of Syl's Mercedes. The acoustics of the green slopes surrounding the cove amplified the laughter floating up from the beach. As Alice and Faye reached the crest of the hill they heard Esme and Detective Hale reciting Stephen Vincent Benet in unison. The detective was drumming a complex cadence on the wooden table. They both knew all the verses.

> Oh, Georgia booze is mighty fine booze,
>> The best yuh ever poured yuh,
> But it eats the soles right offen your shoes,
>> For Hell's broke loose in Georgia.

Chapter Twenty-Six

"A Life of Grime"

Life is just one damned thing after another
Frank Ward O'Malley

The sun was about to throw some light on Thursday morning by the time Russell Wright had been booked and Nick had taken care of the paperwork and gone home. He slept until almost nine o'clock. He was looking forward to a couple hours at the computer with his novel-in-progress. He showered, shaved, and dressed, then fired up the frying pan for bacon and a couple eggs over easy. His phone went off as the toast popped up.

"Detective Shea?"

"Yes, Kimberly."

"We have a 10-54. I'm texting the address. Two units are on scene."

"Cause of death?"

"Looks like natural causes, but they want to be sure. It's a decomp. It smelled so bad the neighbors complained." The dispatcher lowered her voice, as if that would make the news easier to take. "The uniform in charge on scene says it's a hummer."

"Damn." He knew she didn't use the word hummer in a fun, fellatio way. Hummer meant flies, lots of them. It meant maggots, stench, and probably a hoarder. Cops called hoarders dirt bags.

Patrol cars, an assortment of fire department vehicles, and a fleet of the county's Public Works dump trucks narrowed the tree-shaded street to one lane. A policeman directed the sporadic civilian traffic to an alternate route. Nick pulled in behind the last cruiser in line and walked toward the dilapidated house that was attracting so much attention. It filled the role of eyesore in the cast of fresh new faux-colonial facades on the block.

The fire department had smashed in the front door with axes. Public Works personnel were trying to clear an entrance through the solid wall of debris behind it. The county workers wore white Level-A hazmat suits made of tyvek. Cops, firemen, and Public Works folks called them bunny suits. The police had parked the plastic bags with their bunny suits in a pile or they held them dangling at their sides. Thermometers must be hovering at ninety. No one wanted to climb into an impermeable union suit until he or she had to.

The operation had attracted so much attention that no one took notice of the body sprawled on its back beside a "No Trespassing" sign next door. Not even the homeowner watching the neighboring hullabaloo from his front porch seemed concerned about the two-legged litter on his own lawn. Nick figured the human clutter was sleeping off a bender, but he couldn't pass up a possible corpse. He detoured to take a look at it.

"Filthy," "disheveled," and "smelly" over qualified as understatements. The empty 1.75-liter Smirnoff bottle cradled like a vitreous teddy bear in his arms indicated a code-390, a drunk. His age could be anywhere from thirty to fifty, adjusting for the effects of too much alcohol for too many years.

Nick crouched and pressed two fingers to the left side of the man's neck. The steady surge of arterial blood beat like tropical surf against Nick's fingers. He counted silently.

"One hippopotamus. Two hippopotamus."

The math was simple and awesome in its ontological implications. In spite of the abuse and neglect it must have suffered, the 390's heart was beating once a second. Faithful as the family dog, it measured out the minutes of one sorry-ass existence.

"Good afternoon, Shea."

The Zen sessions must have had an effect. Nick didn't jump when Len Smoot spoke too close behind him.

Len kept his voice low so the guy on the porch wouldn't hear him. "I got the call to bring in Rip van Wrinkled here."

Nick chuckled *sotto voce*. So Smoot the Boot had a sense of humor.

The stench emanating from the gaping front entry of the house next door explained why Len looked pleased at having drawn the short straw for pickled-trespasser transport. He shrugged toward the unhappy homeowner, leaning with his hip against the railing on the poop deck of his porch.

"Joe Somebody over there called in the complaint and ID'ed our friend here. He said before the guy passed out he was raving about his grandmother being dead." Len glanced toward the problem lying at their feet. "At least we can haul him away without a shovel and trash bags."

Len pulled on his latex gloves. No telling how many varieties of cooties the 390 was incubating. Nick took a pair of gloves from his back pocket and posted a mental memo to requisition more. A lack of latex signaled a busier-than-usual week, and this was only Thursday. Few civilians realized cops pulled out the latex gloves far more often than they drew their side-arms.

Len grabbed the wrists, Nick took his ankles, and they carried him to the curb. Len unlatched the rear door of his squad car with his elbow and bumped it open with his hip. Nick helped him slide the unconscious man, limp as a two-hundred-pound sack of Play-Doh, across the back seat. Nick didn't often entertain the second deadly sin of envy, but he had a flash of it as Len drove away.

One dump truck had reached capacity and left as Nick headed for the inevitable. In their hooded one-piece suits, boots, gloves, and bug-eyed respirators, Public Works looked like creatures from the Bleak Lagoon. He walked through the obstacle course of the thirty-nine-gallon, black plastic bags of garbage they were hauling outside. On the way, he noticed a torn "Condemned" sign on the shattered wood of the former door.

The precinct's captain, his *café au lait* skin shiny with perspiration, handed him a large baggie with his disposable hazmat *ensemble* and the items to accessorize it – booties, gloves, and a mask. Nick didn't mention that no one had told him this would be a white tyvek affair. He didn't need cop-clairvoyance to know the captain wouldn't appreciate it.

The good news was that instead of a heavy respirator he had a simple mask with a charcoal filter. The bad news was the filter didn't keep out the rich bouquet of rotting food, rat, mouse, raccoon, cat, and human excretions, all of which had been festering for months in the summer heat. This wasn't the first hoarder lair he had seen, but he needed fewer than five seconds to realize it was the worst.

Public Works made slow progress, their miner's lamps creating a Halloween horror-house light show in the maze of tunnels. They proceeded slowly, with a dog sniffing for explosives. They knew the place was booby trapped. Their advance man had found trip wires. The police followed with their body-dog.

Broken furniture, bales of newspapers, unidentifiable debris, and old take-out cartons green with rotten Big Burgers made progress even slower. Nick didn't indulge the thought that he didn't get paid enough for this. The public works people didn't get paid enough either.

After almost an hour they reached what the Level-A hazmat suits called a "nest," a room with maybe sixty square feet of wadeable space. They stood aside to let him and the other police go in. A window on the far wall provided a faint light at the end of this particular tunnel. The buzz of flies signaled the end of the search.

Flies were entropy's agents, turning solid into liquid and liquid into gas. Whatever too, too solid flesh they were recycling now through their tiny digestive tracks wasn't going anywhere on its own. Nick had to wait for the deputy coroner anyway, so he kicked aside rubbish in the path to the window. A ladder leaned against the side of the house. It solved the question of how the grandson entered and left.

He stared out at the oak's leafy canopy, then turned and surveyed the room. An avalanche of furniture, crates, and assorted rubbish covered most of a torn, filthy mattress. Sticking out from under the pile was a pair of feet, toes pointing up and splayed outward.

The left foot was bare, the yellowed nails so long they curved over the tops of the toes. The right foot wore a new red satin scuff that glittered in the miner's lamp light. Images of the wicked witch from the Wizard of Oz flashed through Nick's mind.

He stood aside as the county's crew uncovered the body. He wasn't surprised that it seethed with fly larvae. The only good news: this probably did not qualify as a homicide. He stared down at the putrifying heap that once had been a child, a young woman, a mother. He hoped she had died in her sleep.

By the time the assistant medical examiner arrived and he could leave, night had arrived. He went outside, shed the suit, and sucked in a lungful of fresh air. Now if only he could walk directly into a shower stall and lather up.

A truck with a wrecking ball was parked out front, waiting for sun-up. The police captain was conversing with the driver. He was no doubt telling him that demolition would have to wait until forensics finished.

On the way to his car he over-handed the suit and booties into one of the dump trucks. When he walked past the house next door the porch light was still on and Joe Somebody sat with his feet propped up on the railing. Joe raised a glass of champagne in salute as Nick passed. He didn't blame him for the satisfied grin.

The "No Trespassing" sign no longer graced the yard's elegant landscaping.

Chapter Twenty-Seven

"Scat!"

1: Interjection used to drive away a cat
2: an animal's fecal dropping
Merriam Webster's Collegiate Dictionary

At first Alice thought the music was coming from her computer. She leaned almost close enough to put an ear to the monitor. The computer was mute, but the melody lingered in the sound box of her skull. There was no mistaking Tom Waits' six-miles-of-gravel-road voice, but was "Heart Attack and Vine" real or infrasonic?

Now that Alice could see auras and elementals and had had an offer of supernatural sex, could she also hear sound waves at a frequency below 20 hertz? She felt like James Thurber's mother who lived "with the horrible suspicion that electricity dripped invisibly all over the house."

She stood in her office doorway and surveyed the living room. It shimmered with afternoon sunlight. Multi-colored auras wrapped like neon ribbons around the furniture, artifacts, artwork, and photographs. It also pulsed with Waits' lyrics.

I'm living in Las Vegas, she thought. *…and I hate Las Vegas.*

Alice walked to the bookcase where the early '90's-era stereo components occupied two shelves. She leaned down to listen. The stereo was silent, but the song still played in her head.

How did Harry know she had a particular fondness for Waits? And why did he choose this song from her collection of oh-so-obsolete compact disks? Then she heard, "Don't you know there ain't a Devil, there's just God when he's drunk."

She almost laughed. Did Harry have a sense of humor? Or had he and his boss rifled through her mental file cabinet and learned she wasn't on the best of terms with the Almighty?

"Get lost, Harry."

As soon as the words came out she feared she had made a mistake. She had addressed the creature, even though it wasn't his official name, if he had one. She didn't know what the rules were in alternate planes of existence, but getting on a first name basis with one of Old Scratch's flunkies couldn't be wise.

As if to affirm her fears, Harry shimmered into view in the sun porch at the far side of the living room. He lounged, barefoot, in the big easy chair with a muscular arm thrown across the back of it. His legs sprawled, one outstretched and one bent at the knee. The trouser tent rising from his crotch signaled that his personal circus was a bonanza. The chiseled features of his face were too perfect and his unbuttoned shirt exposed a matched set of sculpted pectorals. If he was aiming for the cover-boy look, he'd succeeded. If he thought Alice would fall for the buff and baby-oiled cliché, he'd failed.

Good afternoon, Alice.

His smooth baritone sounded inside her, not as words, but as if her flesh and bones had become permeable to cognizance. Her ears weren't immune either. His voice vibrated the 31,000 tiny hair cells in each ear. The sensation extended to the humble nub some ex-boyfriend once had called the "love-button." He'd only referred to it that way once because she didn't answer his phone calls after that.

"I said get lost."

As long as I'm here, why don't we finish what we started?

An intense physical desire engulfed her main-frame and networked out to her fingers and toes. Okay, maybe Harry's efforts at seduction hadn't totally failed.

She backed up against the wall by the entryway to the kitchen. At the far end of the kitchen was an outside door, but she didn't intend to flee. She would not surrender her home to the Devil himself, and certainly not to Harry.

She stamped her foot, waved her hands, and shouted "Scat!"

Like any horny drunk in a bar, unequivocal rejection didn't faze him. He stood up and shed his shirt. He unzipped his tight jeans and wriggled out of them, revealing a lack of underwear. He turkey-winged his elbows out to each side and pressed them back, flexing those pectorals. Then he ambled toward her, his cock bobbing ahead of him like a dowsing rod.

A succession of erotic waves washed over Alice. With her back braced against the wall in case her knees buckled, she reached around the corner of the doorway. Keeping her eyes focused on his clavicle, she fumbled open the utility closet door with one hand and grabbed the nearest item. The old sponge mop wasn't much of a weapon but it had a long reach. Unlike the wimpy new plastic variety, the rectangular metal plate bolted to the business end gave it some heft. She brandished it like a major leaguer.

"Get the hell out of my house!" She was too focused to appreciate the relevance of the phrasing, and he kept coming anyway.

What would happen if she hit him? An explosion? Electrocution? Immolation on contact? A troop of hell's cavalry riding to his rescue?

None of that mattered. When he got within range she swung, then choked midway. The end of the mop missed his nose by inches, but she saw alarm flicker in his spaniel eyes. Had no one ever physically attacked him before? She struck again, this time at his midsection, and she put her back into it.

The mop's collision with Harry produced the Fourth of July. He cried "eek" like Mrs. Two Shoes in a Tom and Jerry cartoon. He disappeared in a flash of pure blue flame the size of a large garment bag. It gave off the suffocating odor of a few million kitchen matches igniting. As it burned down, a cascade of confetti-sized particles followed, glittering golden in a shaft of sunlight as they fell.

Who knew Harry was a drama queen.

Coughing and still brandishing the mop she leaned forward. Harry's clothes had disappeared, and a viscous puddle remained. It glistened blood-red.

She sidled around it to reach the phone. Faye was probably asleep, but today she didn't care. With a wary eye on the living room in case Harry pulled off a resurrection, she backed into the kitchen. Her hand shook as she measured out the coffee and dumped it into the filter. She didn't drink coffee herself, but even if this were the Apocalypse Faye would want some.

Faye blew on her coffee while she and Alice stared at what was left of Harry. As it dried, the puddle turned from crimson to dark orange, to amber to saffron yellow.

"Looks like sulfur," Faye said. "Used to be called brimstone."

"As in fire and brimstone?"

"As in Ezekiel throwing the devil into a lake of…. Along with the faithless, the polluted, murderers, fornicators, sorcerers, idolators, and the cowardly." Faye glanced at the metal head of the mop with its bright yellow sponge leaning against the wall like a gawker at a freeway pile-up. "Damn, Alice, whatever possessed you to attack a fucking demon?"

"I did it to keep from being damned, possessed, and fucked."

"Let's hope Harry doesn't like it rough."

"Is it safe to say his name?"

"Harry isn't his name. And who knows what's safe or not? We're off all known sea-lanes here."

Sea lanes sent Alice's mind meandering. She knew about those ancient sea-farers' flat-earth charts. At the horizon the cartographers had elegantly inked the warning, "Hic sunt dracones. Here be dragons." Maybe not such a divergence.

Faye crouched down for a closer look. "I've read lots of accounts of first-hand encounters with incubi, but I've never heard of anybody attacking one." She glanced up at Alice. "I'd say you scared the crap out of him."

"How do I get rid of this mess?"

Faye exhaled a coffee-scented gust. "Maybe it's just what it looks like. Sulfur slag. Lots of that around. It boils up from deep vents and collects in the calderas of volcanos. Molten, blood-red lakes of brimstone inspired the Hell that bible-thumpers love to hate." For someone who didn't read much, Faye had collected a lot of information on hell.

"So, you think it's harmless?"

"Probably. One theory holds that demons have to co-opt some physical substance in order to interact with humans. Although for incubi that can be a re-animated corpse."

"Don't even say that."

"It's just a theory, like everything else about the little freaks." Faye took the fireplace shovel and broom from the stand on the hearth. She shook them at Alice. "It's August, Al, and almost eighty-five degrees in here. Why do you still have your fireplace tools out?"

"Why not?" Alice fetched a heavy-duty freezer bag and held it open while Faye swept the crumbled sulfur crystals onto the hearth shovel.

"Now what?"

"It's garbage day." Faye headed for the door. "The truck hasn't come through yet and the gnome guy is at work."

The two of them walked up the street to the house of Logan's neighbor, Bernie. Faye cracked the lid on the large trash can by the curb and slid the bag of sulfur inside. They paused to look at the rotting array of herbicide-zapped dandelions, rag weed, loosestrife, and honey suckle. They were the latest casualties in Syl's assaults on the lawn. Alice almost felt sorry for the gnomes standing in the middle of it all, like loyal dogs stuck with an unworthy master.

As they walked home Faye said, "You're remarkably calm, Al."

"Does this look calm?" Alice held out her trembling hands. "Do you think we got rid of Harry?"

"Probably not. I can call Jake."

"Who's Jake?"

"He hangs out at the Red Eye sometimes. He mentioned once that his line of work is kind of like exorcism."

"What's his line of work?"

"He's an exterminator."

"You mean like termites?"

"Yeah. But he's read up on all kinds of pests, including the ones that aren't your garden variety. He says infestations by ghosts and poltergeists and such are one of the four types of demonic activity."

"Harry's a pest alright, but he isn't a ghost or a poltergeist. Anyway, as many wifty enthusiasms as you've explored, you must know people who perform exorcisms." She reconsidered. "No offense meant with the wifty thing."

"None taken. And yes, I know a few who say they can do exorcisms, but, honestly, I think Jake is more genuine."

"Has he ever gotten rid of a demonic infestation?"

"I don't think so."

"Let's keep his name on file, and I'll see what I can find out."

They parted company and Alice opened her front door cautiously. All seemed quiet, but now she had to face her computer again. She could work on her book without going on-line, but what if the whole machine had been corrupted? She put Waits on the stereo and sang along as she went back to her desk.

"You got to tell me brave captain, why are the wicked so strong? How do the angels get to sleep, when the devil leaves the porch light on?"

Chapter Twenty-Eight

"One Hundred Thousand Trillion Synapses – Give or Take a Few"

Only two things are infinite,
the universe and human stupidity,
and I'm not sure about the former.
Albert Einstein (1879-1955)

Felons and miscreants, the drunk, drugged-out, psychopathic, sociopathic, and mildly unhinged were not what Nick disliked most about his job. Not even garden variety street-stupidity topped the list. What challenged his patience was the paperwork required for every encounter with them.

He had never calculated the hours, but he would have bet that street time and station time ran neck-and-neck. Now and then, though, all the forms and reports proved worth the effort. Tonight would be one of those occasions.

The hoarder's demise was officially listed as "Unattended Death – Natural Causes." Nick was not the primary, but he still had to explain how he had earned his paycheck this evening. He went to the records room and retrieved the file with Len Smoot's report on the hoarder's grandson. With the manila folder tucked under his arm, he and his mug of coffee headed for the Bullpen.

Before he ventured inside he stood in the doorway and scanned it. The room was Stone-free, and he realized he hadn't seen the reporter lately. Maybe Joe had found a girlfriend, although more likely than that, ten-thirty was past his bedtime.

He opened the folder and skimmed the booker's fill-in-the-blanks information. Rip van Wrinkled's real name was Ezekiel Boyd and his grandmother's messy hacienda was listed as his home address. Len had added a note. The Sanitation Department had condemned the house a week before. The rest of the file consisted of write-ups for drunk-and-disorderly arrests going back fifteen years. A series of Public Defenders had represented him in court.

Nick closed the folder and stared at it while his brain's one hundred thousand trillion synapses sent electrical connections off to approximately eighty-six billion neurons. He opened the folder again and stared at the surname. Boyd. The same as Emanuel, aka Hot Dog.

Nick took van Wrinkled back to the records room. He pulled Emanuel Boyd's file and laid the opened folders next to each other. He leaned over, rested his knuckles on the table and studied them. Hot Dog's last known address was listed as "unknown," with "home-less" in parentheses. The investigative team had added nothing to his original report–no driver's license or learner's permit, no social security number. But one thing had been added after the interview.

He turned over the last page and discovered an envelope from East Creek Elementary School tucked in at the back. It contained three sheets of paper, folded in thirds– Emanuel's student record. Nathan Hale had signed off on it. It included Emanuel's address, the same one as Ezekiel Boyd. Nick made a mental note to buy Nat a drink at the Red Eye. He added a mental post script not to call him Nat.

He already had looked all over town for anyone with connections to Emanuel, but no one had admitted knowing him. Now he had found someone—a brother. And if that was so, the late hoarder must be Hot Dog's grandmother.

He would drive to the Juvenile Detention Center, and see if dropping Ezekiel's name prompted a response from Hot Dog. Plus he had the school file. He could talk to Hot Dog's teachers. Right now he would see if Ezekiel Boyd was still in custody and sober enough for a chat.

The clock registered midnight-thirty when Nick finished his report and the rest of the paperwork. As he headed for booking, his sergeant beckoned from the communication center that housed the dispatcher's desk and the monitors for the closed circuit cameras. Len Smoot sat in front of the console with several other late-shifters and a janitor clustered behind him. Kimberly, the dispatcher, was on the phone at her desk nearby.

They looked up when Nick walked in. The greeting came in a chorus. "Holy crap, what's that stench?"

They all moved away from him, except for Len who was engrossed in the bank of monitors. The first camera kept a glass eye on the parking lot, the second was trained on the lobby. The third panned down the length of the rear hallway and holding cells. The fourth gave a view of the semi-feral hens, silhouetted in moonlight as they slept on their roosts in the tree by the back door.

Real-time video from the second camera had everyone's attention. In it a man was making a call from the wall phone in the lobby. He obviously didn't know he was on a direct line to the dispatcher. Kimberly switched to speaker so everyone could hear the obscenity-laced invitation. When the first come-on didn't get a positive response he became more descriptive.

Nick leaned in for a closer look at the screen. "Is that Rip van Wrinkled?"

"It is."

"What the hell does he think he's doing?"

"He thinks he's going to get laid." Len glanced at Nick. To his credit he gave no indication of distaste at Nick's aroma. "A Mensa candidate he ain't."

Kimberly kept her admirer on the phone while Len and three other cops headed for the lobby. Nick watched on the monitor as they surrounded Ezekiel Boyd. They disappeared from the left frame of one screen then entered from the right frame of the next as they led him back to the recently-vacated holding cell.

Nick yawned and stretched. This was a stroke of luck for him. Ezekiel's latest idiocy would keep him behind bars for the night. He could go home and take a very long shower and a short nap. He'd return in three or four hours and wake Ezekiel up for a chat. Sleep-befuddled and maybe shaking with DT's, Van Wrinkled Boyd would be more likely to say something at four or five in the morning that he'd later wish he hadn't.

Nick walked out into a night warm as velvet, riffled by a light breeze, and sparkling with the light from a gibbous moon and stars. The river would be beautiful on a night like this. A quick dip at the Cliffs beach would be just the thing to clear his head, and get rid of the first layer of smell.

He would be going by way of the Cliffs anyhow. Dr. Logan Brant didn't know it, but after every shift he drove past her house in Cliffs of the Severn. He couldn't rest easy at home until he made sure all was quiet at her place.

CHAPTER TWENTY-NINE

"PEG O' MY HEART"

I can't take a well-tanned person seriously.
Cleveland Amory

Alice was not surprised to discover Harry's inept attempts at courtship appearing on her computer screen. She dealt with the erotic images the same way she did pop-up ads. She hit "delete" until they stopped appearing.

Try explaining this to my computer guy. She rocked back in her chair. *But I'm probably not the only one with this problem, so maybe he's had experience with it.*

She had seen her computer guy sitting on a high stool in his work shop like a cyber sorcerer's apprentice. Teetering towers of components, keyboards, tangled cords, and wires surrounded him. She was about to call him when the mantel clock struck nine and she realized she had not eaten.

Night had wrapped the house in darkness leaving only the bright corona of her desk lamp, plus the blue, red, orange, green, and white lights on the computer, monitor, printer, and phone. The path into the kitchen was lit by the glow of stereo, wireless router, DVD player, and strip plugs at every outlet.

Alice opened the refrigerator and stood in its arctic light. The contents were uninspiring. Time to forage for food at the Red Eye. She headed for the garage.

"Alice." The woman's voice came from the shadows at the foot of the stairs, and a neighbor stepped into a pale puddle of starlight.

"Denise, you scared the crap out of me."

"Sorry. But I have to talk to you."

Alice wanted to ask, *Do you see a neon "Open 24 Hours" sign on my roof?*

"I'm headed out."

"This is kind of an emergency."

"What kind of 'kind of' an emergency?" She felt a pang of dread.

"It's about Syl."

Alice wished that for once her stomach's early warning system would be wrong. As soon as she asked, "What has Syl done?" she wished she hadn't.

Faye saw Alice crossing the empty dance floor and put in an order for a veggie burger with sweet potato fries. She passed out refills of whatever the five men, two women, and one demon at the bar were drinking. She knew they were going to request them anyway, so they might as well buy her time to talk to her friend. Her friend, after all, had had a very stressful day.

Alice settled onto a stool and Faye set a margarita in front of her.

She held it up in a toast to her. "I don't know what I would've done if you hadn't helped me get rid of… you know who."

"You know what they say, 'Friends help you move. Real friends help you move demons.'" Faye propped her elbows on the bar and rested her chin in her palms. "How you holding up?"

"Okay. The good news is Harry hasn't reappeared. The bad news is my computer is possessed."

"Whose isn't?"

"Good point." Alice glanced at the elbow-bender on the far side of the bar. His preppy appearance shifted as she watched. She leaned forward and lowered her voice. "Faye, do you notice anything odd about the guy behind you?

"The one sucking down a fog cutter?"

"The one with red dreads, eagle's beak, and wings big as shower curtains."

Faye glanced over her shoulder. "Now that you mention it, he usually wears a Raven's gimme cap. He says his name's Merv Griffin. Cute, huh?"

Faye topped off Alice's margarita. "Esme was here for happy hour."

"Esme doesn't hang out in bars."

"She came in with Nathan."

"The detective we met at the beach last night?"

When Faye nodded, her Mohawk bobbed in agreement. "She looked happier than I've seen her in a long time, Al."

"That's terrific." Alice hated to follow good news with bad. "Denise came by as I was leaving tonight."

"Syl's neighbor Denise?"

"Yeah. Syl's gotten Denise and three friends involved with Harry. He's causing trouble and they want to know how to get rid of him. She says Syl told them to talk to me."

"Oh, crap." Faye ran her fingers through her spiked hair, a sure sign of distress. "Crap." She leaned so far across the bar her shirt sponged up a spill. "It means Syl's recruiting for him."

"For Harry?"

"For Harry's boss. Recruiting other souls is what you promise to do when you sign a pact with the Devil."

Faye's cell phone rang. She put her palm over the speaker and handed it to Alice. "Speak of the devil's disciple."

Syl didn't waste time with chit-chat. "Why don't you answer your cell phone, Alice?"

"I never turn it on."

"Why do you have a cell phone if you don't turn it on?"

"It's for emergencies."

"This is an emergency." And without a pause, "You knit, don't you?"

Alice held the phone so Faye could lean across the bar and listen in.

"I used to knit. Why do you ask?"

"You still have the needles, right?"

"Are you taking up knitting?"

"Very funny. Do you have big wooden knitting needles? And a hammer?"

The pit of Alice's stomach did not like where this was going. "Are you implying what I think you are?"

"I'm not im-fucking-plying anything, Alice. I went down to the basement to do a load of wash and found Bela Lugosi's cousin snoring in the tanning bed." Her voice teetered on the edge of panic. "What if he bites me while I'm asleep?"

Alice glanced at be-winged and dreadlocked Merv the Griffin sitting across the horseshoe-shaped bar. What would he think of a plot to kill one of his demonic colleagues? Enchanted by the mortal wonder of inebriation, however, Merv continued staring into his glass. Alice moved to the empty end of the bar anyway and Faye followed.

"Syl, I can't kill a cricket or a snake in my own basement. I'm not pounding a stake into anything's chest."

"Faye doesn't get off work until two. You have to help me, Al."

Faye took the phone. "He'll probably leave at midnight, Syl. If he's gone by then turn on the light in the tanning bed." She handed the phone back and went to collect Alice's veggie burger and fries.

"Would you do it for me?"

Alice sighed. At least she'd be dealing with demons in someone else's house. Her stomach's early warning system didn't consider that good news.

"It's ten o'clock. My dinner just arrived. I'll come when I finish it."

"How can you eat at a time like this?"

"It's easier than I would've thought a week ago."

She hit the "end call" button, and started making short work of the veggie burger and fries.

"Good of you not to tell her to go to hell," said Faye.

"She's already there. And we can't risk her becoming a blood sucker on top of everything else, can we." It wasn't a question.

"To protect your own house cut up a few pounds of garlic and onions. Spread them on a tray and turn on a fan to circulate the smell." Faye recognized the *That's not going to happen* on her friend's face. She shrugged and added, "Or not."

Alice washed down the last of the sweet potato fries with her margarita and stood up. "Our friend is such a pain in the ass."

"Hold that thought, Al." Faye collected the plate. "In a fuck-up like this, anger is your friend."

"Faye, no one else gets sucked into fuck-ups like this."

She took a deep breath. This would be another test of that resolution she had made. The one about maintaining calm, courage and common sense.

Syl hovered behind Alice at the top of the basement stairs.

Alice whispered, "Where's the 'On' switch for the tanning bed?"

"Above the electrical outlet next to the washer."

She clutched a rubber mallet in one set of white knuckles and a seventeen-gauge wooden knitting needle in the other. In the back pocket of her jeans was a print-out of the five methods for killing the undead. Sunlight and a wooden stake were the best means to a vampire's end. The other three options – silver, fire, and decapitation—ranked behind them.

Holding the knitting needle and mallet in one hand, Alice crouched and gripped the door frame with the other. She leaned forward so she could see the other side of the cellar. Light from the low wattage bulb over the washer reached there and outlined Syl's dusty exercise equipment.

The centerpiece of that gathering of fitness exiles was the aluminum tanning bed. Only now did Alice notice how much the sleek, elongated clamshell resembled a coffin. She had started down the stairs when Elvis crooned the phrases that marked each quarter hour on the clock in the living room.

Love me tender, love me true;
Take me to your heart.
For my darling I love you,
And we'll never part.

Then it started chiming the slow strokes of midnight. She reached the basement as the tanning bed's lid started to open. The hinges creaked loudly and she caught a glimpse of movement inside.

Syl heard the hinges too. "Oh shit!"

She executed a one-eighty, ricocheted off the kitchen wall, and headed for the front door. The rapid slap of her $800 Louboutin sandals hitting the floor boards above proved she could move fast when she wanted to.

The dark form in the tanning bed stirred. Folds of black silk fell out.

Good grief! They still wear capes?

Alice had the plug of the electrical cord in her hand when the lid creaked open enough to see the occupant lying on his back in formal attire. He turned his head, looked directly at her and smiled. His teeth radiated the quintessence of white in a sharp-chinned face the color and texture of old joint compound. His two canines overshot the corners of his slit of a mouth like exclamation marks not on speaking terms. She froze with the plug inches from the outlet.

His smile morphed into a leer. He pushed the lid all the way open and dangled an elegantly-trousered shin and polished shoe over the rim. He was starting to swing the other leg out to join it when she shoved the plug into the wall. Even as she did it she wondered who put the shine on those shoes and tailored his trousers. Did Hell have a haberdashery?

The tanning bed's upper and lower ranks of 100-watt fluorescent bronzing tubes lit up like Broadway. Alice put all her hope into ultra-violet light being close enough to the real thing to do the job. The guest who came to dine threw an arm across his eyes. Shrieking, he writhed and shriveled inside his cape.

158

She dropped the knitting needle and mallet. She sprinted to the tanning bed and slammed the top down. Light streamed out in expanding rays from the slots that provided oxygen for the UV bathers who required it.

She pulled the weight bench over, stepped up on it, then scrambled onto the rounded lid. She lay down and held on as though clinging to the hull over a capsized lifeboat. She could feel the warmth of the aluminum, but the inner acrylic shield kept it from overheating. The shrieks subsided.

When several very long minutes passed and all was quiet, she slid off. She shoved the bench up onto the lid and positioned it lengthwise so the iron legs straddled it. She tilted the treadmill up so it rested against the front of the bed's lid, making it difficult to open. The cross-trainer machine was too heavy, but she upended the stationary bike and rowing machine next to the treadmill.

She found duct tape on a utility shelf and covered the slots on the ends. With the glow from the ultraviolet nova cut off, the dim light in the basement was a comfort. Alice sat on the stair step, listened to the surf of aortal blood in her temples, and stared at the scrimmage of metal frames, pulleys, and cables.

She knew she should go find Syl, but for now she would rather sit here with the fried husk of a vampire.

CHAPTER THIRTY

"A SKINFUL OF SULLEN"

Women and young men are very apt
to tell what secrets they know,
from the vanity of having been trusted.
Philip Dormer Stanhope, Earl of Chesterfield (1694-1773)

As Nick revved the Indian onto a winding stretch of two-lane blacktop through forested hills, he understood why dogs stuck their heads out of car windows. The wind's pressure on his skin riffled the thin interface between himself and that mixture of life-sustaining gases called air. Maybe this was close to what eagles felt, soaring on thermals.

Eagles. Two dead eagles in a suburban septic tank pit. Finding a connection between Hot Dog Boyd's attack on Logan and those eagles was the reason for this trip to the juvenile detention center again.

Nick had questioned Hot Dog's brother, Ezekiel, in the station's interrogation room much earlier this morning. Even considering Boyd had had only two hours' sleep, Nick could see the lights had been extinguished in his eyes a long time ago. The words "burn-out" fit him.

At the academy, John Reid's interrogation techniques had been required reading. Nick had had experience with Reid's two types of liars, those who felt remorse and those who had switched off their moral nanny, the conscience. Ezekiel Boyd was the latter. He confirmed that Emanuel was his younger brother, but he swore he hadn't seen the kid in more than a year.

As for Hot Dog, he had been either too cagey to give up information or he had been stoned for too long to remember much. At the station he claimed he had gone to the bingo hall's parking lot to score crack. He said when his connection didn't show he keyed the Prius because he was pissed. Then he made a grab for the old lady's purse so the morning wouldn't be a total loss.

Nick passed through the metal detector and signed in at the reception desk. He wasn't happy to see Dr. Logan Brant in the waiting room. She already had sprung Hot Dog so he could advance from purse-snatching to armed robbery.

A woman sat next to her. If he were describing her in an official report he would have written "African American female, between fifty-five and sixty-five years old." For all purposes other than booking a felony, he never tried to guess a woman's weight. Now, if pressed, he would estimate one-eighty, with an athletic body-mass index of twenty-two. She also wore a silver crucifix around her neck and a pillbox hat so pink and perky it commanded the title, "chapeau."

Logan Brant beamed at him. "Detective Shea, what a pleasure to see you."

"Good afternoon, Dr. Brant." He gave a smile his best effort.

"This is my dear friend Mrs. Marjorie Mayhew."

He already had guessed Mrs. Mayhew was no ordinary matron in a bargain-rack dress, sensible shoes, and Sunday-go-to-meeting hat. When she stood up he didn't have to lower his line of sight more than a few degrees. Her eyes reminded him of tiger's eye quartz – iridescent shades of brown, with flecks of amber and gold. All the lights were on in the windows of this particular soul.

And where had he seen the name Mayhew? Nick's synapses scurried around with headsets, clipboards, and manila file folders. His synapses were old school, but effective. A Marjorie Mayhew had signed off on Emanuel Boyd's school records.

"Logan speaks highly of you, Detective Shea." Mrs. Mayhew had the lingering hint of a southern accent. Nick would have guessed Georgia. Atlanta, to be exact, by way of the Sea Isles. He couldn't specify which one.

"A pleasure, Mrs. Mayhew." When he shook her hand the strength of her grip didn't surprise him. "You were Emanuel's teacher, weren't you?"

Marjorie Mayhew would be an excellent poker opponent, but Nick detected a one-showing-only flick of her left eyebrow. Why did he care that he had impressed her with attention to that particular detail? Christ in pajamas, as his Irish grandmother used to say, had he regressed to junior high school?

"I taught Emanuel in fifth grade. He was in class again for ninth grade English." She paused, maybe reassembling that class in her mind's eye. "That child is a skinful of sullen, but if you saw his grandmother's house where he grew up…"

"Do you know that Emanuel's grandmother is deceased?"

"Oh, no." Mrs. Mayhew covered the crucifix with her hand and closed her eyes for no more than a few seconds. "I hope she finally has found peace."

Nick did not admit he had walked through the pesthole the Boyds had called home. He didn't want to revisit the place, even in conversation. He already had had a nightmare about it in his few hours of sleep today.

"I'm sad to say I lost track of him when he started living on the street." With a gesture, Mrs. Mayhew indicated the maze of hallways behind the big metal door painted royal blue. "Did you know he once sneaked back in here?"

"No, I didn't."

"A year ago. He hid in the laundry truck. They found him giving out cigarettes to his friends in the recreation room." She glanced toward the blue door. "A bed of his own, three meals a day, friends his own age. It's no wonder he broke the law again."

Nick would have argued that drugs and general ass-holery had caused his recidivism. But the topic of Hot Dog's downward careen could be left for another day. The door buzzed and the guard at desk waved her in.

"I'm sure you have priority, Nick…"

He assumed that Logan's use of his first name would be followed by a request for a favor. He was right.

"…but I suggest you let Marjorie go first. Maybe he'll open up to her."

"We can wait, Logan. Detective Shea is here in an official capacity."

"You go on ahead, Mrs. Mayhew." His smile was genuine.

He had reached the conclusion that her presence was another gift of coincidence. More than that, she had made him feel, for a few seconds, like a fifth grader. No one had done that since he occupied a pint-sized desk in Miss Lindsey's class. Marjorie Mayhew was a double threat to the dark side: good cop and bad cop combined.

With a sad cast to that tiger's-eye gaze she stood up. "Children like Emanuel learn early on that they get punished more for telling the truth than for lying."

Nick stood politely and nodded. *Amen to that.*

He intended to hold the door open for her, but she reached it first. She straight-armed the hinged slab of blue-painted steel like a quarterback scattering a so-so defensive line. As she strode through it the set of her shoulders signaled anger. One of her students had assaulted her friend.

He knew that ten minutes or so would pass before Hot Dog arrived from the rec room, gym, kitchen, garden, shower room, crapper, or his own bunk. He went back and sat next to Logan Brant.

"Aren't you going to eavesdrop, Detective Shea?"

"Is it live or is it Memorex?" He was sure she'd get the old reference.

"Of course. You can watch the video tape later. I loved those commercials."

"Has anything suspicious or threatening happened in your vicinity lately? Any more dead rats in your mailbox?"

"No. But if any appear you'll be the first person I'll call."

"Do you know anyone who's into voodoo? Obeah? Witchcraft?"

"No. But that's not the sort of thing people admit to in polite society. Why?"

"Exploring possibilities. Rats used to be called the Devil's lapdog."

"Not surprising. They wiped out a fourth of Europe's population with the Black Death."

"What about Sam Hare and Longview Development?"

"His lawyers still send our group cease-and-desist letters full of legal gibberish about restraining orders, lawsuits, accusations of assault. I'm president of the group so they address it all to me." Logan sighed. "And I'm sure you've spoken to my nephew, Freddy."

"Still a person of interest." But Freddy wasn't high on Nick's list of suspects.

Either his performance as an intellectual under-achiever deserved an Oscar, or he wouldn't have had the brains to earn the several million dollars and a lion's share of Longview's stocks if he hadn't inherited them. Nick would bet a week's pay on the latter.

"I've invited him to dinner at my house tonight to discuss a land swap. It's not waterfront, but maybe I can convince Freddy to intervene with Hare."

Nick knew that was futile. He assumed Dr. Brant did too.

His inner alarm clock went off. They'd probably fetched Hot Dog by now. He excused himself and went to find the monitors. Despite what he had said, Memorex wasn't good enough. He wanted to watch Mrs. Mayhew and Emanuel Boyd in real time. She had known him for almost half his life, two years of which were on a day-to-day basis. Besides that, males of all ages tended to underestimate women when it came to information-gathering.

The visitors' room on the other side of the one-way glass had twelve cubicles lined up like library carrels across the long hall. Each of them had a plexiglass window with two telephone receivers. Only a few people occupied the steel stools bolted to the floor. On a Friday afternoon in summer people would rather be sitting in beach-bound traffic.

Nick selected a chair with a view of the last cubicle through one-way glass. He put on the headphones and turned up the volume. He took his small notebook and pen from his shirt pocket and rested his elbows on the window's wide sill. He leaned forward to focus on the boy's micro-expressions– the tics and twitches of his facial muscles.

Mrs. Mayhew didn't waste time. "Emanuel Morrison Boyd, what possessed you to attack a seventy-eight-year-old woman?"

Nick was impressed. Step one in Reid's interrogation technique: direct confrontation.

"I didn't attack her, Miss Marjorie."

"A witness and a surveillance camera say you did."

"Wasn't gonna hurt her."

"Why were you in that parking lot?"

"I was hungry," he mumbled. "I needed bank."

Nick noted the variation in his story, from scoring crack to buying food.

"Bank?"

"Money."

"So you thought the old people at the bingo hall would be easy pickings."

"I didn't go there to rob nobody."

She looked at him as if a teacher's oak desk stood between them.

"I mean anybody. I didn't go there to rob anybody."

"You said you needed money for food. Now you say you didn't intend to rob anyone. Were they giving away money in that parking lot?"

Nick could almost hear the boy's mental gears grinding.

"No, ma'am. My uncle gave me a Jackson to key the red Prius."

"Why?"

"I don't know." Hot Dog shrugged. "Maybe he was mad at her about something."

Nick leaned farther forward. *Get the uncle's name.*

"When the old la…, I mean when the woman showed up I made a grab for her purse. I figured she could spare some change."

Marjorie Mayhew's voice turned sorrowful. "Child, how many times have I told you not to let bad people lead you astray?"

She's good, he thought. Step two: shift the blame away from the suspect.

"Sometimes the Devil gets in me."

"What's your uncle's name?"

"Uncle Roy."

"The woman whose car you vandalized and whose purse you tried to steal is my best friend, Emanuel." Marjorie spoke softly now, her voice laced with sorrow.

"I'm sorry, Miss Marjorie." He looked and sounded as though he meant it. "I didn't know."

"What's your uncle last name?"

"Rogers."

"Roy Rogers?"

"Yes, ma'am."

"The same as the cowboy?"

"What cowboy?"

"Never mind. Did your uncle pay you to put a dead rat in any-one's mailbox?"

"No, ma'am."

"Do you know where your uncle lives? Where he works?"

"He used to live in Glenbrook, but I ain't, I mean I hadn't seen him in a couple years. He musta found out I live under the overpass near the bingo hall. He came there and gave me the twenty. He said the red Prius was in the parking lot every Wednesday."

Marjorie put her palm against the window. On the other side Hot Dog, reacting with jail reflexes, matched his palm to hers.

"Emanuel, I'm sorry about your grandmother's death."

"She died?"

"You didn't know?"

"No, ma'am."

A bell sounded. Time was up. Emanuel stood abruptly and walked away. Marjorie Mayhew glanced over at the one-way window before she left through the blue steel door. She walked more slowly on the way out.

Chapter Thirty-One

"Leapin' Lizard"

I am escaped with the skin of my teeth.
Job 19:20

Alice had left a light on at home when she went to help Syl with her vampire problem. On her return she planted her foot against the front door and shoved it open. The living room seemed clear of evil beings, but a single chime from the mantel clock startled her. As she tiptoed inside her mental state swung between a detached state of unreality and barely contained panic.

She stood at the bottom of the stairs and looked up, appreciating the irony of the term "stairwell." This well was a vertical shaft leading to an overhead abyss. The bed there was too far from the front door for escape. Alice went to the couch.

Before she lay down she reached a hand up to the slowly circulating blades of the ceiling fan where the sylphs hovered in a blue haze. A warm tingle coursed from her fingertips down through her arm. It spread across her chest as she stretched out on the sofa. She put a hand on her heart in an attempt to calm its rapid thumping. She expected to lie awake and watchful the rest of the night, but the gnomes' almost subsonic hum, in harmony with the sylphs' fragile descant like a desert zephyr, eased her into a peaceful sleep.

When she surfaced seven hours later she saw the light flashing on the landline phone. She had been too preoccupied the night before to notice. She checked caller ID for the five messages and wasn't surprised to recognize the names of a few women who were neighbors. She didn't expect to see a man's name too, and certainly not Jerry, Syl's ex, but there it was. She assumed all the calls, including Jerry's, had to do with Syl. She was in no mood to bother with any of them.

While she ate breakfast she started, as usual, at the back of the newspaper with the advice column, comics, and letters to the editor. Then she folded it to the front page and set it aside. She was about to carry her plate to the kitchen when she saw Russell Wright's face staring at her from above the fold.

The banner headline was in sixty-point font. "KILLER CAUGHT." A more modest forty-point read: "DNA Ends Reign of Terror." The by-line was Joseph Stone's, but she hardly noticed he finally had made page one. When she turned to the rest of the article, the paper shook in her hands.

She knew Faye would still be asleep, so she called Esme. "Have you seen the morning paper?"

"Not yet. Kenya just left for school."

"I thought classes start on Monday."

"The band members are going in today to get fitted for uniforms. Kenya took her cello to try out for the orchestra." Newsprint rustled, then Alice heard alarm in Esme's voice.

"Russell is a murderer?"

"Apparently so."

"Are you alright, Al?"

"A little shaky. A lot shaky." *If you only knew how shaky.* Her heart was beating out a tattoo and she felt dizzy.

"I'll be right over."

"No need, Es. I want to bring a treat for 'Zilla. He saved my life."

"Dear God in Heaven. He did, didn't he."

"What's his favorite food?"

"Watermelon. Strawberries. Raspberries. He's bananas about bananas."

"Thanks. I'll hit the produce section and see you in half an hour."

Alice and Esme sat on the kitchen floor and watched Godzilla lay waste to the chunks of watermelon covering a cookie sheet. He gave the impression that the watermelon was the only object in his universe.

"Stay here with Kenya and me for a few days."

"I'll be okay. He's in jail and I still have that deadline to meet."

Godzilla started on the last piece of watermelon.

"You'll finish it, Al." Esme got up and retrieved the bag of fruit on the counter. "You always do. I'm going to ask Nathan to check on you every day though." Esme handed a banana to Alice. With one gulp 'Zilla downed the last chunk of watermelon, and transferred his gaze, like a laser pointer, to the banana. When Alice started peeling it he trundled into her lap.

While she fed him pieces of banana she asked, "So, how are you and Nathan getting along?"

A peach-colored glow appeared on Esme's cheeks. It was the same reaction her friend had had when Detective Hale showed up at the beach last Wednesday.

"I like him. I like him a lot." Esme paused. "We both have crazy work schedules, but we see each other when we can."

"Has he found out anything about who's harassing Logan?"

"He says he can't talk about an on-going investigation, but he and his partner are working on it."

Alice came, with a cart-load of misgivings, to the subject she had been putting off. "I need to tell you something, Es."

"I've been wondering when you would."

"Then you know about Syl? And Harry?"

"I know something's up. The usual assortment of cars haven't been parked in her driveway at night. Is Harry her latest?"

"If only."

Godzilla finished the banana. Alice picked him up and followed Esme into the living room. He curled the bulk of his twenty-five pounds in her lap for a snooze while she lay back against sofa pillows and closed her eyes. Suddenly she felt weary, overwhelmed, weepy, and terrified.

"Syl summoned an incubus," she said. "Faye dubbed him Harry."

"What's an incubus and why does Faye call him Harry?"

"An incubus is a male sexual demon, and Faye says she calls him that because the name just popped into her head."

"An alias." Esme laughed. "That's rich. Which of Syl's friends took home the title of male sexual demon?"

"It's not a joke. Faye and I walked in on her in the basement while she was putting in the call, as it were. Harry's appeared in my house too, and now other supernatural creatures are showing up."

"There has to be a rational explanation." Esme picked up 'Zilla's long tail and laid it across her own lap so she could move close enough to put an arm around her friend. "Maybe it's sleep paralysis. I've read that can cause hallucinations."

"You believe in God, Es." It wasn't a question.

"Yes, I do."

"Then you probably accept the existence of the Devil."

"Yes, but…" Esme stopped. She moved away so she could make eye contact. It was a gesture of at least tentative belief in Al's story, if only to comfort her. "Does Logan know about this?"

"She's too busy harassing Longview Development."

"True. She and my mother are organizing a protest for tomorrow."

Alice stood up. "I'd better get home. I'm trying to start a new chapter." As she headed for the door she muttered, "All these damned interruptions are playing hell with my work schedule."

"Only you would consider demonic infestation an annoying distraction."

"Most writers would feel the same way."

Esme held up a hand. "Wait a sec." She burrowed in her large purse and came up with a canister of pepper spray. "Maybe this will help."

"Don't you need it?"

"I have half a dozen of them. You never know when things will get dicey at an airport." She held it up in front of her. "Do this to make sure you get the eyes and nose." She made a plus in the air with it.

The gesture also resembled the sign of the cross.

Pausing in the doorway had become a habit with Alice. The television was off. No Harry monster in sight, no serial killers, no vampires. The house was quiet except for the convivial murmur of the gnomes in the sun porch shrubbery.

She inhaled a lungful of courage and went upstairs to change clothes. When she got there she noticed the door of the utility closet was open. She reached out to close it and a creature the size and color of a toddler's rusty red tricycle rushed her on three legs. It waved all of its six arms, each of which ended with several talons. For good measure it raised a flap of scaly skin on its back into a threatening ruff, then bared its fangs and made a high-pitched tea kettle sort of whistle.

Alice screamed and gave him a blast of pepper spray. The steam whistle shrank to a squeak. The critter whirled and scuttled behind the air handler. From there he disappeared into the space between the inner and outer walls. She could hear his sneezes progressing toward the back of the house. Maybe the terrified look in the little demon's eyes affected her. Without conscious thought she named him.

"You scared the crap out of me, Trike," she yelled after him.

If the spray worked on him, it might discourage Harry too. As she headed back downstairs she wondered if Trike had always resided between the walls. If so, did he get along with the occasional bat and squirrel squatters?

Before she sat down to work, she went upstairs to leave the crumbs from the last of the chocolate chip cookies next to the air handler as a peace offering.

CHAPTER THIRTY-TWO

"THE FREEZER GEEZER"

When Baby's cries grew hard to bear,
I popped him in the Frigidaire.
I never would have done so if
I'd known that he'd be frozen stiff.
Harry Graham (1911- 1998)
Ruthless Rhymes for Heartless Homes

Nick parked his Bronco at the crumbling curb and got out. He took the notebook from the back pocket of his jeans and checked the address again. 2157 Bella Vista Road, Glenbrook.

He leaned against the car and stared at the house. The rental property was Roy Rogers' last known address as of five years ago. It was also the only mention Nick could find of Rogers anywhere online for criminal activity, tax records, hospital and morgue files, the Department of Motor Vehicles, the Social Security Administration. Nor was a Roy Rogers listed in that outdated source, the phone book.

The owner of this property had died a month ago and left no heirs. That meant Hot Dog and his older brother were the only links to Rogers so far. He would talk to Hot Dog again, but his instincts told him the kid wasn't lying when he said he didn't know where his uncle was. Maybe Hot Dog's older brother, Ezekiel, would have more information. Or maybe one of them knew what make and color car he drove. That they would know a license tag number was too much to wish for.

After returning from the juvenile detention center yesterday he had persuaded a judge to sign a search warrant. With its boarded-up windows and the roof's sagging ridge-line it looked like a derelict ship about to founder in a sea of thigh-high weeds. Kudzu, poison ivy, and briars engulfed the trash-strewn vacant lots on either side of it and flowed to the raised railroad bed a hundred feet behind.

Nick pushed off from the car and took a crowbar and flashlight from the cargo area. The sun was shining brightly this Saturday morning, but with the electricity cut off and plywood across the windows, the light would be necessary. The crowbar would do double duty as a weapon if any living thing larger than a breadbox with attitude lurked inside.

The crowbar made short work of the two one-by-sixes nailed in an elongated X across the door. He shoved it open and walked into the effluvium of equal parts mildew, rodent feces, and decay. Under stacks of boxes and over-flowing plastic bags, the rug was stained. The curtains were torn, and the faded, rose-motif wall paper was peeling away from the wall.

Although the house was dusty and disheveled, it didn't appear to have been ransacked. That indigents, addicts, and delinquents didn't consider it worth robbing made it look even more doleful.

He searched through the heaps of clutter in the living room and two small bedrooms, but he found no documents, no letters. The only reading material of any sort was a yellowed copy of the *Chronicle* on the floor next to the toilet. It was dated six months earlier. Nick laid it by the front door to take away with him.

A door at the rear of the kitchen led to a storeroom crammed with more boxes and bags of clothes and a sad life's detritus. A huge chest freezer took up most of one wall. Nick held his handkerchief over his nose and mouth with one hand while he opened the lid.

The stench of rotting meat rose from the mold-blackened interior. He let the lid slam shut, but the smell had already penetrated as far as his sinuses. Despite the handkerchief he could taste it in his mouth and throat.

He stared at the freezer, then at his notebook with the address written in it. No wonder it had seemed familiar. This could be the house where the elderly woman was found in cold storage a month ago. He'd reopen her file to see if any information had been added about the corpse his friend Will affectionately referred to as the Freezer Geezer.

He used his handkerchief to pick up the newspaper on his way out. Taking the faint impressions of finger tips from newsprint wasn't easy, but with rubber-gelatin lifters, it could be done. He'd also request that forensics sweep the place.

Nick considered the increasingly difficult weekday *New York Times* crossword puzzles as warm-ups for the challenge of Saturday's. He planned to stop at the convenience store only long enough to pick up the Saturday *Times* and a refill for his coffee cup. As he drove into the parking lot, a dumpster-green 1986 Buick Skylark with a scabrous cloth roof pulled in behind him and parked. He wondered if it was one of the cars known as a B2 Buick Iran, produced there after the Ayatollahs released the fifty-three American hostages in 1981. Around the station they were referred to as Contra Cars.

He was about to go ask the driver about it when a stocky twenty-something guy in a tee-shirt four sizes too large got out. He pulled the collar of his tee up over the lower half of his face, and slid a Beretta 9-millimeter Nano under the bottom of it . Keeping his hand on the gun inside the shirt, he walked toward the store. Nick glowered at his back. So much for making this a quick stop.

From habit he put a hand to his side. He knew the Sig Saur was in its holster under his jacket so the gesture was as much for reassurance and luck as it was for safety.

He started to open the Bronco's door when a second man scuttled out of the store. He was in a much lower weight class than the Beretta owner, and a low-riding ball cap put his face in shadow. Under his arm he carried a bulging bank deposit bag held tightly against his grimy plaid shirt. He walked with a limp caused by a stiff left leg. Nick figured he had stuck a weapon, most likely a sawed-off shotgun, down his baggy camo pants.

The two thieves must be partners. Nick had no way of knowing how many customers were inside, but the good news was he could have the show-down here in the open. He slumped out of sight in his seat, speed-dialed the station, and made a call for back-up.

He was about to get the drop on them both, when t-shirt pulled out the Beretta. He pointed the business end between the other man's eyes and backed him into the store. The glass door swung closed behind them.

"Damn." Nick said it softly, but with conviction. They weren't partners.

Using cars and dumpsters for cover he circled the parking lot's perimeter to approach the front wall from the side. He crouched and looked in the big window below the posters advertising energy drinks. He couldn't get an unobstructed view, but there was no sign of movement. Maybe they'd gone out the back door.

Still crouching, he cracked open the front door and with the Sig in hand slid inside. Keeping his back to the outer wall of shelving, he moved toward the rear of the store, looking down each aisle as he went. T-shirt came striding out from the storage area with the Beretta stuck under his belt, a sawed-off shotgun in one hand and the bank deposit bag dangling from the other. He looked as nonchalant as if he were a customer leaving with his purchases.

"Stop." Nick paused to let the order sink in. To his relief t-shirt halted and looked at him.

"Toss the bag over against the freezer case. Lay the guns on the floor, slowly, and slide them toward me. Then put your hands on your head."

He did as he was told, making a quick assessment of Nick in the process. Jeans with a dry cleaner's knife-edge crease down the legs, denim shirt, light-weight jacket, generic sneakers, and a policeman's haircut. The Sig Sauer disqualified him as an average-joe customer, but he probably was not convenience store robber number three either.

"I'm cool, man."

"Where's your friend?"

He gave his head a small jerk in the direction the storage area. "In the cooler."

"Is the clerk in there too?"

"Yeah."

Nick had him on the floor and cuffed when three county units arrived. Two cops frog-marched him out to their cruiser. The other four gathered around while he opened the cooler door. Two of them helped the shivering clerk to her feet and took her outside to warm up. Nick got a good look at the runner-up thief.

"Hello, Ezekiel."

How convenient for the author, he thought. Now he wouldn't have to go looking for Hot Dog Boyd's older brother. He could ask him about his uncle Roy Rogers in the comfort of another holding cell. And he could grill him about his relationship to the people who had lived in the house on Bella Vista.

While Nick cuffed him, Ezekiel kept up a steady drum roll of complaints. He was cold. He was hungry. He needed a drink to warm up. He had the right to call his lawyer. And finally...

"I want to press charges."

"Against whom?"

"The bastard that stole my money."

What was it Albert Einstein said? *Only two things are infinite, the universe and human stupidity, and I'm not sure about the former.*

Nick left him in the care of his two colleagues. As he headed for his car, the radio came on and the dispatcher's voice cut through the high-priced static of the new communication system.

"Detective Shea?"

"Yes, Kimberly."

"You won't believe this."

Sure I will. "What is it?"

"Doctor Brant's nephew, Frederick Brant, has been admitted to Arundel General. He says Dr. Brant poisoned him."

Nick remembered Logan Brant mentioning at the detention center yesterday that Freddy was coming to her house for dinner that night.

"The tox report will take a few days, but they're pumping his stomach now."

"They haven't taken Dr. Brant into custody, have they?"

"No. It could be salmonella. And the charge nurse said he came in with a hard-on like a titanium flag pole. A very short flag pole."

"So he'd taken a sexual performance enhancing drug at some point in the evening."

"A good guess."

"I'll go see him later."

Right now he had to read the file on the Freezer Geezer and get a description of Uncle Roy from his nephew Ezekiel. On a long shot he'd look through the newspaper he found in the Glenbrook house. Maybe there was a reason Roy Rogers had taken it into the bathroom to pass the time while he enjoyed a leisurely dump.

Chapter Thirty-Three

"The Devil to Pay"

The Prince of Darkness is a gentleman
William Shakespeare
King Lear

The clock struck seven in the evening. Its mellow resonance reminded Alice she had time to catch the last rays of the sun. She grabbed a book and slid into her flip-flops. She picked up one of the folding chairs on the brick patio by the pond, then headed downhill toward the river.

She set the chair in the shade thrown halfway to the water's edge by a huge oak and opened *A Deadly Shade of Gold*. She had read all of John D. McDonald's books about the lanky detective Travis McGee years ago. She was starting again, in order of the publication dates.

She got as far as the first line, "A smear of fresh blood has a metallic smell," when two of Syl's neighbors arrived and set their own chairs facing her.

Irene spoke first. "Alice, you have to help us."

Alice took longer than necessary to close the book before she looked up. "What's the problem, Reenie?"

Irene glanced at her companion and back to Alice. "You know."

"No, I don't." Alice wasn't a card player, but she could fake a poker face.

"It's Harry," said Mattie. "Syl says he hangs out at your house."

"Not recently." That was almost true. Alice hadn't seen him since the set-to with the sponge mop a couple days ago. "And besides,

Syl says Harry's a dream lay. What possibly could go wrong with a dream lay?"

Irene and Mattie exchanged looks again. They each seemed to be waiting for the other to explain. Alice didn't want to make this easy for them.

"Men stink," said Irene.

"You mean sex with Harry is so good real guys can't compete?"

"No," said Mattie. "She means men smell bad. And the better looking and more charming they are the more intense the odor."

"They reek like a diaper full of diarrhea," said Irene. "All of them."

"To me they smell like a tub full of vomit." Mattie paused, then added, "With chunks of rotten fish floating in it."

Alice put a hand to her brow as though to shield her eyes from the setting sun. Her poker face only went so far and the hand kept Irene and Matilda from detecting her total lack of sympathy.

"So when you made your deal with the Devil you got more than you thought you were bargaining for."

"I've been faking a cold at work so I can wear one of those white mask thingies." Irene started to cry. "But it doesn't help. Every time I get near a man I have to hurl."

"Yesterday…" said Mattie, "…a cop stops me for doing a measly eight miles over the limit. I roll down my window. The cop is freaking gorgeous so of course he reeks like Saturday night closing time in the alley behind a saloon with an all-you-can-eat raw bar."

While Mattie stopped to take a breath, Alice fought back a smile. Who knew the woman was funny? But she wasn't through.

"Plus, I'm trying to be all serious and 'So sorry, Officer,' and Harry starts messing with me and I'm having the grandmother of all orgasms. The cop thinks I'm drunk and makes me get out of the car for a breathalyzer, but the comes keep coming. I can hardly stand up. I pass the test, but he thinks I'm having a seizure and wants to call an ambulance. This was at a downtown intersection, mind you. I've never been so humiliated in my life. And now, to keep my license, I have to produce a doctor's note saying I don't have seizures."

"So, get a priest on the case."

"I'm Catholic," said Irene. "No way are we talking to a priest about this."

"And if we did," added Mattie, "Harry will just have us climaxing in the confessional."

Alice didn't have to ask them why they got into this mess in the first place. She knew what they'd say. Something to the effect that when it came to dating it wasn't a jungle out there. It was a desert.

She also knew she'd regret it, but she had to ask. "Why are you talking to me about it? I don't even go to church."

"Everyone knows you know stuff. And what you don't know, you know how to find out. And you probably don't like Harry hanging out at your house either."

"I have checked into it." She knew they wouldn't like what she'd found out.

"And…?" Reenie and Mattie leaned forward in their chairs.

"Incubi and succubi are the lowest order of demons." Alice paused. "They're too stupid to be affected by exorcism."

"Then why aren't you having these problems?"

"Because I said 'No.' "

Irene started to cry again and Alice took pity. "You could try pepper spray."

"Does that work?"

"It might. Have you signed anything?"

Mattie hesitated. "No."

Alice wondered if she was lying. "If I find out anything I'll let you know."

"Thanks, Al."

The sun dropped below the tree line. Alice folded her chair and started for home. As she headed for the wooden stairs up to her porch, the voice seemed to come out of the darkening air.

"Good evening, Alice. Lovely night, isn't it?"

In a dance choreographed by fear, she dropped the chair, pulled the pepper spray from her pocket, whirled to face the voice, lost her balance, and wind-milled to keep from toppling backwards into a flower bed.

"I apologize for startling you."

Alice recovered her bearings and the tattered shreds of her dignity and stared at the speaker. In the deepening twilight, a youthful James Coburn, her favorite actor from thirty years ago, sat by the pond in the mate to the canvas sling chair she had just dropped. He wore crisp new acid-washed jeans. One of his long legs was cocked and resting at a right angle on the other knee. The blue silk shirt and tweed jacket fit his lanky frame with a casual elegance. She would have recognized Coburn's angular face, sensual mouth, and mischievous eyes anywhere. Anywhere but here that is. And there-in lay the rub.

"Are you who I think you are?"

"I am God."

"No, you're not."

"There is nothing that is not God. Ergo, I am God. You are too, of course, but I'm much smarter."

"Cut the crap. Why are you here?"

"I wanted to get to know you better."

That can't be good.

"Over seven billion people on the planet and you want to talk to me."

"You happen to know the approximate number of people on this rock. That's the second reason you intrigue me." He glanced at a wrist watch the size of a macaroon. "Although technically, the number is seven billion, six hundred million, three hundred and twenty-seven thousand, two hundred and eighty-one, with about twelve million, seventy-three thousand women in labor this minute."

Alice figured that besides trivia like population figures, he had all the important answers, if she only knew what questions to ask. She stared at him while she tried to decide what to do. The Devil gazed affably back.

"If I talk to you out here, will you promise not to come inside my house?"

"Yes. And in case you're wondering, I keep my promises and I don't lie."

"If a liar swears he doesn't lie, how reassuring is that?" But Alice unfolded her chair and set it at the far end of the patio. The sound of the little waterfall in the pond usually soothed her, but not tonight. She perched on the edge of the chair, ready for flight. She wasn't as surprised to see him as she thought she'd be though.

"Okay," she said. "What's the first?"

"The first reason I wanted to have a chat with you?" He flashed her that devilish Coburn grin. "In the history of humankind, you're the only person to go after one of my associates with a sponge mop."

"Sponge mops are a recent invention so that's not a remarkable achievement. And did you call Harry an associate?"

The Devil shrugged. "Harry's not the brightest clinker in the firebox, but he doesn't have to be. When it comes to sex, most mortals will settle for feeling good even if it doesn't feel right. You recognize the difference, but most people don't."

"So let me get this straight. You claim to be a god..."

"Not a god. God."

"... and yet you're reduced to recruiting lonely and maybe not-so-bright women by using sex. Sounds like a pimp to me."

"I have other gifts to offer." He laced his long, tapering fingers behind his head and leaned back into his palms. "How's the book coming along?"

She sent him an irritated glance for an answer.

"You're a good writer, Alice. You deserve to be on the best seller lists."

"Don't insult my intelligence."

"You'd be surprised how many writers take me up on the offer."

"No, I wouldn't."

He regarded her with something akin to fondness. "There's something else I can do for you."

Alice made the mistake of looking into his eyes, like free-falling into a black abyss with white-hot fires burning at the bottom. A sink-hole opened in her chest. It took her lungs with it and threatened to suck in the heart that was thumping like a badly-aligned tire on a rough road.

"No."

"I can do it."

"No. No. No. And hell no."

"Imagine making love to him one more time."

"You liar." Alice fought back tears. "You try to pass yourself off as a gentleman, but you're hypocritical shit."

"God is a lot of things, but hypocrite isn't one of them."

"I would dispute that. And I may be a mere mortal, but I recognize bullshit, even when it's wearing designer jeans and claims to be God." She stood up. "I'm going inside where you promised you would not follow. Put an egg in your shoe and beat it. And don't leave any brimstone littering the patio."

"As you wish."

Alice expected him to vanish in a smoke and sulfur stench, or perhaps do a Cheshire Cat routine, fading slowly until only James Coburn's sexy grin remained. Instead he stood and gave a courtly gesture between a nod and a bow. He walked down the cement steps to the street, turned left, and sauntered in the direction of the community beach.

Chapter Thirty-Four

"Dancing in the Dark"

Little Willie from his mirror licked the mercury right off,
thinking in his childish error it would cure the whooping cough.
At the funeral his mother smartly said to Mrs. Brown,
'Twas a chilly day for Willie when the mercury went down.'
Anonymous

Nick stood in the doorway of the Lord Baltimore Ballroom and blinked to dispel a Twilight Zone deja vu. The last time he had stood here it was the bingo hall in whose parking lot Hot Dog Boyd had tried to mug Dr. Logan Brant. He had returned that day to ask if anyone knew Boyd or had seen him before. If anyone had they didn't let him interrupt their concentration by admitting it.

Now, he half expected to see photographs, religious icons, good luck charms, and a haze of smoke from candles. The tables had been moved back against the wall and what adorned them were beer bottles and wine glasses. A fifteen-piece band was doing Duke Ellington fairly proud with "It Don't Mean a Thing If It Ain't Got That Swing." Vivid splatters of colored light from the revolving mirror ball overhead made the lindy-hoppers and the jitter-buggers look even more frenetic. The industrial strength air conditioners were working overtime to offset the BTU's of body heat generated by the dancers.

Nick recognized Will's grin, rimless spectacles, and pine-straw hairdo on the far side of the dance floor, but he didn't recognize the pumping knees and flapping arms. Apparently swing music had charms not only to soothe the savage beast, but also to bring out the beast in the most laid-back person Nick knew.

The dance floor was almost as big as a basketball court. Its polished oak planks gleamed. As for its shadowy perimeter, Nick didn't need a detective's eye to notice that men were in short supply there. Clusters of single women stared at him as though he were a six-point buck at the opening of hunting season.

Desperate criminals were one thing. Desperate women were another. Nick considered waiting until Monday to ask Will about the freezer geezer, but he was on the scent and scents went cold. As he circled the room he tried not to make eye contact. He shook his head and mumbled "Sorry, I'm not staying," to the half dozen hopefuls who asked him to dance.

The band finished with a top-of-the-register blast of brass. Most of the dancers rushed to the bar, the water fountain or the bathrooms. Will steered his partner to where Nick stood. She was a striking brunette, about Will's age.

"Vivian, this is Detective Shea, the ne'er-do-well I told you about."

So this was Will's emergency room nurse, and coincidentally, the one who had admitted Logan Brant's nephew last night. Her smile had good-humored mischief in it. He liked her before she spoke.

She held out her hand. "Pleased to meet you, Nick."

Her grip strong and confident. If he ever ended up in the ER he would want her or someone like her on duty.

"Likewise. I finally get to meet the Circe who made a dancer out of Will."

Vivian laughed. "I'm going to the bar. What'll you have, Nick?"

"Whatever Will is drinking this week."

He pulled a chair close to Will's at the four-top. There was less likelihood of being overheard in the general chatter around them than outside where voices carried. But he still kept an eye out for anyone who looked like an eavesdropper.

Will leaned closer. "Did you find the King of the Cowboys in Glenbrook?"

"No."

"I assume you've checked Longview Development's personnel records for the past several years."

"Yeah. No Roy Rogers. But get this, the house he rented six years ago shares an address with Mary Rogers, affectionately known to us as the freezer geezer."

Will took a few moments to remember whom that was. "Y o u mean the old lady they found on ice?"

Nick nodded. "A neighbor said the people living with her were hired care-givers. They cleared out after the story hit the local news outlets. They wanted to avoid charges and they sure weren't going to find any more work in this state. The neighbor only knew their first names but Nathan's looking for them. For that matter, the neighbor only knew Mrs. Rogers' first name."

"Which is why she came to us as a Jane Doe. Is that the same neighbor who found the body?"

"Yeah. She went into the garage to collect the hindquarter of a Bambi her son had shot. I don't suppose anyone at your shop got her DNA."

"She died of natural causes. The police made no request for special treatment of the body. We had no name for her or family connections and no one claimed the body. We might have farmed it out to a funeral home that had her buried at state expense."

" 'Might have' being the operative words. They also could have gone with the more lucrative method of John or Jane Doe disposal."

"If someone did, it wasn't on my watch." Will held up both hands, to show he was not involved in selling cadavers on the black market. "Or, she might be on a shelf somewhere. Even reputable funeral homes have rooms full of boxes of unclaimed cremains. They have to keep them because there's no statute that says they can discard them." Will saw Nick's eyes narrow. "I'll look into it."

Vivian arrived and set the beers on the table. "Show me your badge and ID, Detective Shea."

He opened his wallet. She nodded, and he put it back in his pocket.

"Even with the badge you know I can't talk to you outside of the hospital about an on-going case. Or a cold case, for that matter. Patient confidentiality."

"Right. You need to see my badge so you can tell me you can't talk to me." But he said it with a smile. He knew she was telling him, in her round-about way, that she had information.

"I'll be working the night shift which starts…" She consulted her watch. "… in about an hour and a quarter. Why don't you drop by."

Nathan went to the hospital with Nick. Nick had noticed he'd developed a personal interest in the goings-on in Cliffs of the Severn.

Logan Brant's nephew Freddy was still unconscious, but his circulatory system had plenty to say. Vivian translated what his blood revealed.

"They found trace amounts of tetramethrin and peremethrin. Those are active ingredients in wasp spray. They're nasty stuff, but only zero point-four percent of the unlisted nasty stuff in any can. Wasp spray has twelve or so other chemicals that can cause headaches, nausea, stomach cramps, skin and eye irritation, pancreatitis, respiratory paralysis, comas, and even death."

Nathan glanced at Nick. "Looks like Dr. Brant has a dark side."

"Not necessarily," said Vivian. "There wasn't enough of it to cause more than the headache and nausea on that list."

"It's often used instead of pepper spray," said Nathan. "What if she sprayed him with it and it got into his lungs?"

"Irritation of eyes and nose would indicate that. And it would still make its way into his blood." Vivian pointed to the next two items on the list. "There are far more than traces of fluoxetine and sildenafil citrate. Fluoxetine is the generic term for an antidepressant and sildenafil citrate is taken for erectile dysfunction. Since anti-depressants suppress the sex drive, men often arrive here with Viagra in their systems as well as, shall we say, mood enhancers." Vivian caught Nick's and Nathan's grins. "Yeah, yeah. All of us have heard the street name for Viagra." She gave a gracious wave to invite their response.

Nathan supplied it. "Mycoxafloppin."

Nick chuckled and it felt good. It was beginning to look like Freddy was the captain of his own sinking ship. "So what's the prognosis?"

" 'Wait!' Vivian held up a hand. "There's more. In fact the nephew is a hot topic in the emergency ward. They also found evidence of fentanyl."

"The gel in pain patches," said Nathan.

"You mean Tango and Cash," added Nick. "Dance Fever. Murder 8. Jack Pot. Goodfellas. Apache."

Nathan continued. "China Girl, Poison, King Ivory, He-Man, Friend, Great Bear."

"I'm not surprised you guys have heard of it. When ingested it gives a high like heroin."

"So nephew Freddy is an ambulatory pharmacoepia," said Nathan.

"Well, he isn't ambulatory now or even conscious, but in answer to your next question, Detective Hale, he'll pull through."

They were about to part ways in the parking lot when Nick said, "Aren't you seeing someone in Dr. Brant's neighborhood?"

"I am. Her name's Esme."

" 'For Esme…' "

Nathan finished Salinger's short story title. " '…With Love and Squalor.' " He fished his car keys from his pocket. "The Cliffs is an interesting neighborhood. Did Len Smoot tell you they got an anonymous complaint about an alligator attack."

"Len mentioned it. What happened with that?"

"The alleged alligator owner denied having one. She let them search the house and they found no trace."

The complaint was probably someone's idea of a prank, but Nick filed away the information.

CHAPTER THIRTY-FIVE

"HE'D HAVE TO KISS
A LOT OF FROGS"

We are born naked, wet, and hungry. Then things get worse.
Unknown

Alice sat back down after the Devil sauntered away. The air was cooler here than inside, but she had another reason for staying by the pond.

She glanced up at the first floor of her house. It was located among the treetops, where the second floor of any normal flatland dwelling would be. The living room window framed the flickering glow of pixels. Harry had returned and must be watching one of his favorite reality shows, the more tasteless the better. The sponge mop would chase him away temporarily, but Alice hadn't slept much for over a week. She was too weary for another confrontation.

Too stupid for exorcism or not, the time to get rid of Harry once and for all had long since passed; but not tonight.

Besides, the full moon would clear the trees soon and the white noise of the pond's small waterfall was soothing. On a rock at the edge of the pond, Alice's favorite frog serenaded the evening. His torch song sounded like a broken banjo string, but Alice hoped he'd get lucky tonight. She had named him Al, in honor of Al Green. Faye called him Al-Too to avoid confusion.

Al-Too was the color of a UPS truck, if a truck had a lime green racing stripe along each side. In fact, he seemed to have a thing for UPS trucks. He'd start croaking whenever he heard one approaching. Female frogs were larger than males, but Al Green's amorous aspirations far surpassed realistic.

Alice slid down in the chair, stretched out her legs, and crossed her ankles. She lay back, letting the slack canvas enfold her while an almost-cool breeze riffled her hair. She fell asleep smiling.

She woke up with the half-moon beaming at her and a rival frog croaking counterpoint with Al-Too. When she heard a frog's release call she knew one of the males had tried to climb on top of the other and spray him with sperm. Al Green was the biggest male in the pond, so Alice assumed he was the one being mounted.

She sighed. Even for amphibians the path to progeny was a bumpy one. She knew frogs didn't have penises, which got her to wondering if they could experience the joys of orgasm without them.

She was about to go inside and chase Harry away when she noticed someone passing under the golden aura of the street lamp below. No mistaking the silhouette of Syl's ex, Jerry Gant. Five-eleven with slightly bowed legs evident in a pair of baggy Bermuda shorts and a baseball cap to cover his poker-chip-sized bald spot. He also had a deep tan and a middling beer belly that had replaced his six-pack abs. Alice couldn't see his feet, but she assumed he was wearing the usual deck shoes with no socks. Faye saw a lot of those at the Red Eye. She called them Boat Loafers.

Alice hoped Jerry would pass by, but he started up the cement steps to her yard. She had erased his phone message and the others without listening to them.

Jerry never had recognized her existence before, so he must have problems now and she could guess who was at the root of them.

She drew her feet under the chair and slumped lower into it. Maybe he wouldn't notice her in the shadows under the plum tree. A knock on her door would get no response and he would go away.

Instead, he turned on a pen light to help him make his way through the shrubbery and vines surrounding the pond. In its faint glow Alice saw that he carried a pole with a net on the end. Alice remembered Syl's off-hand remark about the special request she had made of the Devil, so she could guess what he was after and why.

Northern Green frogs were more docile than other species. In the spring she had succeeded in coaxing Al Green to take earthworms from the tip of a bamboo stem. By July his tongue flicked them from her fingers. He would be a sitting duck for a jerk with a butterfly net. And where, Alice wondered, did a hot-shot lawyer get a butterfly net?

Jerry crouched at the edge of the pond and made a slow sweep with the light. When it illuminated Al Green he kept it there and slowly raised the net.

Alice shouted so loudly she startled herself. "What the hell do you think you're doing?"

Jerry yelped. He tried to stand up and whirl around at the same time. While executing the maneuver he flung the net up with such force it caught in a low-hanging branch of the plum tree. He lost his balance and pitched sideways, arms flailing. He and the two frogs hit the water at the same time. The frogs' plunges were more graceful.

Jerry's water landing sent spray as far as Alice's chair. His flashlight continued to radiate a beam from the pond's murky depths. He surfaced briefly, then his boat shoes slipped on the slimy liner and he fell backwards. He grabbed the large rocks around the rim and managed to climb out and stand dripping on the patio. He was missing one deck shoe and long, tangled runners of duckweed draped across his head and shoulders.

He pulled off the duckweed and threw it back in the water. "You scared the crap out of me, Alice."

"Well, the crap had better still be in your pants and not in the pond."

"You didn't return my call."

"Is that why you decided to kidnap my frog?"

She regretted the sarcasm as soon as she said it. It might encourage him to tell her the real reason and suck her into yet another set of problems. She assumed he would lie and try to bluff his way out, so she didn't expect what happened next.

Jerry dropped suddenly in a sodden heap. He rested his elbows on his knees, put his face in his hands, and sobbed. Alice hitched the canvas deck chair closer and leaned forward to try to make out what he was saying.

"I don't know how she did it, but I know she did."

"Who did what, Jerry?"

"Warts." Jerry wiped his nose on the soggy hem of his shirt. "The crotch kind." He started to unbutton his shorts.

"No, Jerry. For pete's sake. I don't want to see them."

"The doctor says it's the worst case he's ever seen. He freezes them and they come right back."

"You're an educated guy, Jerry. You know toads and frogs don't give you warts and they don't cure them either."

"I'm desperate."

"Let me guess. You found a phony hoo-doo hack who promises to cure you."

"She comes highly recommended."

"By whom? Morticia Addams?"

"I've heard rumors about Syl. That she's dabbling in the black arts."

If only she were merely dabbling.

"I'll make a deal with you," she said.

"What deal?"

"If your law firm stops trying to persuade county governments to challenge the Chesapeake Bay cleanup efforts I'll talk to Syl."

"Not my area. Someone else in the firm is working that angle."

"You're a partner. Make them quit. Also, get Hare to leave Logan alone."

"I'll see what I can do, but I can't make any promises. The firm's making a lot of money off those lawsuits." He got to his feet.

Alice pulled the butterfly net from the tree and tossed it at him. "Get your shoe and flashlight out of my pond."

After he fished them out she watched him limp away, the sound of water sloshing from his shoes with every step. She almost felt sorry for him.

When he disappeared from sight she glanced up at her house. The window was dark. Maybe Harry had gone off to work his wiles somewhere else.

Maybe tonight she'd finally get some sleep.

Chapter Thirty-Six

"Matchless"

"If it is your time, love will
track you down like a cruise missile."
Lynda Barry

Nick was perhaps the only non-musician on the force who knew why Nathan called his 1975 Buick Electra 225 "Lucille." The Electra was the longest four-door hardtop General Motors had produced. Its black lacquer finish gleamed like obsidian. With a 455 four-barrel V8 and 360 horses, the deuce-and-a-quarter was a twentieth-century chariot. Nick could see how somebody who drove one would be man enough to name it Lucille.

Most in law enforcement could only afford the sort of jalopies they called "beaters." Among those who didn't know Nathan well the Electra raised suspicions he was on the take. Nick knew the real story.

Nathan's father had bought the car in Atlanta the year it came out and had maintained it with meticulous care. When The Old Man, as Nathan referred to him, died of a heart attack, his only child inherited it. Nathan was the kind of guy who would have kept it pristine anyway, but Nick suspected he did it for The Old Man.

He leaned back into the tufted plush of the passenger seat and stifled a yawn. Saturday had been a very long day, and at one o'clock Sunday morning it wasn't over yet. He glanced at Nathan, left arm resting on the window sill, left hand draped over the top of the wheel. He had the look of a contented man, and not just because his shift had ended. It was a look Nick didn't often see in this line of work. He hated to interrupt bliss with business, but necessity obliged.

"I talked to Hot Dog Boyd's brother Ezekiel again. He's a dead end. And Hot Dog still claims he doesn't have any idea where his uncle Roy lives. He's sticking with his story that Rogers came to his camp under the bridge and gave him money to trash Dr. Brant's car. Says he hasn't seen or heard from him since."

"Any record on his phone of his uncle Roy?"

"He says it was stolen. He didn't have one on him when he tried to mug Dr. Brant, and who doesn't carry their phones even into the john these days? A search of his digs under the bridge didn't turn up one."

Nick had conducted that search. Hot Dog's sad assortment of ripped and filthy bedding and cast-off belongings had looked so forlorn he had felt a pang of sympathy for the kid.

As they waited on the red light at the turn into Cliffs of the Severn he said, "Thanks again for the ride. My car should be ready by noon tomorrow. I'll take the motor to work in the morning."

"I won't stay long at Esme's. I'm dropping off my forensics text for her daughter. Es says Kenya's thinking of majoring in it next year. I'll pick you up at Dr. Brant's." Nathan glanced at Nick and saw him grinning. "What?"

"So it's going well with Ms. Esme?"

"We're taking it slow on account of her daughter."

Nick figured there was more and he waited for it.

"I like Esme a lot and I think she likes me a little bit."

"You're a lucky guy."

"I know. Not only is she fine as frog's hair, but her work schedule is as crazy as mine. She had the four-to-midnight shift today."

"Fine as frog's hair?"

"Just an old southren country-boy saying." Nathan pulled in behind a crime lab van and two police cars. The lights were on in the van.

Nick opened the car door. "I won't stay long enough to get in the way."

"You just want to make sure Dr. Brant's okay."

"Yes, I do." He started to get out.

"One more thing, Nick. This neighborhood, at least down there by the water, has a weird vibe. I get the feeling Esme knows something she's not telling me."

"You think she's involved in wrong-doing?"

"No. I think she's protecting someone. A friend maybe."

"Have you asked her about it?"

"I'm working up to it. Did I mention I really like her?" Nathan fell silent and Nick waited again for him to finish. "I'm trying to get her used to being around a cop. I don't want her to think I'm suspicious of her and spook her, you know?"

"Yeah." Nick got out. "I know."

He closed the door gently. Owners of rides like this resented passengers who slammed the doors. He watched the big Buick glide downhill toward the river. The luminescence of the full moon made the midnight-black deuce-and-a-quarter look like the Millennium Falcon about to make the jump into hyperspace.

All the lights were on in Dr. Brant's house. The other houses were dark, but Nick knew their occupants were peering from behind closed curtains. The yard gnome neighbor, Bernie, however, stood at the edge of his lawn. Nick turned to face him. His stare communicated enough menace to send Bernie back inside. Dr. Brant believed he hadn't put the eagles and the human heart in her septic tank pit, but Nick still considered him a suspect.

Len Smoot had drawn door duty. "You just missed Mini-you, Shea. No one would give him the time of day or let him within sixty feet of the front door."

"Stone?"

"He was waiting for us. The guy must sleep with a scanner in his skivvies."

Inside, five members of the crime scene team were busy. Sergeant Wilson knew what answers he would want.

"Dr. Brant volunteered to have blood drawn to look for tetramethrin, peremethrin, and the other nasties. They're checking it now." He led Nick into the kitchen where a member of the team was taking photographs.

"Hi, Nick." She lowered the camera long enough to smile. "Did someone report a body here we don't know about?"

"Just a social call, Megan."

Wilson nodded to the red can of wasp spray on the counter next to the stove. "Fredrick Brant says his aunt cooked the fried rice in that wok. He said it tasted a little funny but he took extra helpings so he wouldn't hurt her feelings. When he started feeling nauseated he left. The wok's been washed, but we're testing it and the plates for traces of the toxin."

"Did Fred Brant leave right away?"

"He said he thought he might throw up so he went into the bathroom first. We found the packaging for a gel pain pack in the trash there. Looks like someone ingested the contents. They're checking for prints."

"Did Dr. Brant eat the fried rice?"

"She said she had some digestive distress earlier so she only ate a little. And a cold has knocked out her sense of smell and taste."

"Anything of interest in the cupboards?"

With a latex-gloved hand the sergeant opened the cupboard above the counter. He moved aside so Megan could photograph the contents.

"That can of cooking oil spray in there is red too." Nick knew he was pointing out the obvious.

"So you think she grabbed the wrong can by mistake?"

"She needs reading glasses. She might not have had them on." He phrased the next question carefully. "Has anyone been to the hospital?"

"Staub and Ebson are on their way there now."

Wilson gave him a sideways look and he figured it was time to get out of the way. He found Logan Brant leaning against the railing on the back deck.

"I'm so glad to see you, Detective Shea. All they'll tell me is that before Freddy passed out in the ambulance, he said I poisoned him. Poor Freddy. Will he be alright?"

"The charge nurse says he's pull through. Have they asked you to go to the station?"

"Nine o'clock tomorrow morning. I'd like to visit Freddy tomorrow too."

"Just tell them what happened. As for visiting your nephew, not a good idea."

"I suppose not. Will you let me know how he's doing?"

"Sure." He gave her what he hoped was a reassuring smile as he left. She caught up with him on the front porch and handed him a slip of paper.

"Nick, please talk to a friend of mine. She lives close by."

He glanced at the name and address on the paper. "My partner interviewed her at the beach a few days ago."

"You should talk to her too. She's a nexus. People connect through her. They tell her things. Besides that, she's a writer. She has a writer's eye."

"Does she go to church?"

"I'm pretty sure she doesn't."

"Then I'll stop by first thing in the morning."

"Good. And thank you for coming tonight, Detective."

Nick heard her mutter, "Poor, Freddy," as she went back inside.

"Alice Lewis!" Len Smoot peered at the paper. "Stan and I checked out a complaint about an alligator attack at that house five or six days ago."

"You mean the anonymous complaint?"

"Turned out to be bogus."

"Did you trace the call and ID the caller?"

Len looked sheepish. "It was probably just a prank."

"Do it anyway. It'll be good practice."

As Nick walked to the street to wait for Nathan, he put the scrap of paper in his pocket. So many people had tried to set him up with women he suspected Dr. Brant of doing the same. He'd read that about seventy percent of successfully married couples had been introduced by mutual friends. But then, forty-two percent of people believed the sun revolved around the earth, and more than that number also claimed the Devil really did make them do it.

Only his cynical friend Will knew he was a true romantic. Where love was concerned, Nick believed in fate. Or as he called it, kismet.

Chapter Thirty-Seven

"Incubus Addicts Anonymous"

I'm trying to arrange my life so that
I don't even have to be present.
Unknown

The ring of the bedside telephone woke Alice. It triggered the usual late-night, heart-flutter of a question. *Who died?*

She rubbed her eyes and looked at the clock. 1:45 Sunday morning. She picked up the receiver, saw Syl's number on caller ID, and fumbled it back onto its base. When it rang a second time she grabbed it and slammed it down. She rolled over and pretended to believe that was the last she'd hear from Syl tonight.

She had just drifted off when the ding-dong, ding-dong, ding-damned-dong of the doorbell jerked her awake. No one except delivery folk and solicitors used the doorbell, and they rarely rang it at 1:58 on a Sunday morning. Nor at any time of day did they continue to lean on it.

She almost fell down the stairs in her haste to make it stop. She switched on the porch light and flung open the door. Syl squinted in the glare. Her hair was uncombed, her clothes rumpled.

"Dammit, Syl. What have you done now?" Alice held up a hand, palm out, even though she knew it was like trying to stop a runaway train. "On second thought, I don't want to know." She was right about the runaway train. Syl started talking.

"Logan called. The cops are at her house. She says they're going to arrest her for attempted murder."

"I'll get some jeans on." She started back inside, then turned around. "Sylvana, you'd better not be responsible for this."

"I'm not, Alice. I swear."

As soon as Alice reappeared Syl ran down the steps and started up the street at a slow jog. Alice hustled to keep up with her.

"What happened?"

"That twerp, cousin Freddy, claims Logan poisoned him Friday night."

"Friday night? This is Sunday morning."

"Logan said he was in a coma for a while. When he came out of it he started throwing accusations around. He's still in the hospital and the cops are tearing her house apart." Syl was so irate the street's steep slope hardly slowed her down. "That rat bastard weasel. I'll bet Hare put him up to this. I'll kill them both."

The upward tilt of headlights behind them lit the dense tree canopy overhead. Alice pulled Syl out of the way to let the long, sleek black car glide past. As distracted as Syl was, she muttered, "Nice Buick. '75, I think."

When they reached the top of the hill they saw a white van and three patrol cars parked in front of Logan's house. The big Buick stopped under a street lamp and someone tall, slender, and male got in. While the car had Syl's was attention, Alice stepped in front of her.

"What?"

Alice caught a worrisome whiff of alcohol in the exhale. How much Syl had had to drink could make a difference in any encounter with the police. She assumed the neighbors were watching so she kept her voice low.

"We both know Logan didn't poison anyone. The cops will figure that out."

"I have to make sure she's okay."

"They won't to let you inside"

"The hell they won't. She's my mother."

"Creating a scene will only make matters worse."

"My mother's been accused of murder. How could matters be worse?"

If Alice hadn't been so exasperated she would have laughed.

"You're right. You invited Evil, with a capital 'E,' into the place where we all live. How *could* matters be worse?"

Syl stared at the strangers silhouetted on the other side of Logan's brightly lit windows. "Now's not the time to discuss this, Al." Syl started toward the house.

"Yes, it is." Alice caught her arm. "Listen, I don't have much sympathy for Irene and Mattie and Denise. Their own stupidity got them into this. But you have to call off the curse on Jerry."

"Why?"

"That was a vicious thing to do. You're impulsive and careless and spiteful, but not vicious."

"Don't sugar coat it."

"I like you in spite of it, Syl. You know that, don't you?"

"Yes, I do." Syl seemed surprised by her own answer. "But I'm in a delicate situation, bargaining-wise."

"Delicate, my ass. You've inflicted your ex with the worst possible case of genital warts, which, by the way, he offered to show me a few hours ago. And your boyfriend from hell has taken up residence in *my* house. We have to make Harry and his hooligans go away. Forever."

"I don't want to lose him."

"Who? Harry?"

"Elvis."

Oh shit. Alice had suspected that Syl was addicted. This would be as much intervention as exorcism, and she was pretty sure she wouldn't find any organization called Incubus Addicts Anonymous.

"You know how sick that is, don't you?"

"Don't get high-and-mighty with me, Al. The world is a lonely place and some of us… a lot of us… have never had what you did with Charlie."

"Harry has nothing to do with love. You know that."

"I don't care. I'm fucking Elvis Presley. The *young* one."

Before Alice could answer, Syl marched off across the sod covering Logan's new septic tank. The cop on the porch moved to the windward railing where the storm cloud in very expensive sandals was unsteadily approaching.

"Ladies, I have to ask you to stay off this property."

"Okay officer," said Syl.

Alice's relief lasted until Syl finished the sentence. "You had to ask and you did." Syl started up the wooden porch steps.

The cop moved to bar her way and Alice grabbed the waistband at the back of Syl's designer jeans. Better they both be arrested for brawling than Syl land in jail for assaulting a police officer. She planted one foot and braced the other against the bottom step. She heaved and swiveled with more strength than she knew she had.

The good news was, Syl had lost weight, probably thanks to the Devil's diet plan. Alice created enough centrifugal force to fling her in an arc. Syl flew a few feet and landed face-down in the dew-soaked grass.

Alice set her left knee in the small of her back and shifted her weight onto it. She bent Syl's arm into a vee and shoved the hand, fingers folded, into her armpit. She put just enough torque on the elbow to make resistance extremely painful. She was more astonished than Syl that those long-ago hapkido lessons had kicked in.

Syl managed to turn her head enough to glare at her. "Fuck you."

"You'll thank me in the morning, Sylvana, and so will your mother."

"I can take it from here, ma'am." The cop's voice sounded familiar.

Alice looked up. "Hello, Officer Smoot."

"Good evening, Miss Lewis." Len Smoot put two fingers to the brim of the hat he wasn't wearing. "You'll vouch for her?'

"Yes, sir. She's distraught. Her mother's elderly and she's been under a lot of stress lately."

"I understand." As he helped Alice haul Syl to her feet he asked, "No more alligator problems, Miss Lewis?"

"No." She gave a flicker of a grin. "Never had an alligator problem."

Alice entwined her arm with Syl's, as much to reassure as to restrain her, and felt the fight drain out of her. She hugged her and whispered, "I'll find out what's going on and let you know in the morning. Stand Elvis up for one night and get some sleep."

She rotated her in the direction of home and gave her a gentle push between the shoulder blades. Syl walked off as though half-asleep already. Alice turned back to Officer Smoot.

"Will they arrest Dr. Brant?"

"I don't know." He took a pen and notebook from his pocket, wrote a name and phone number, tore out the page, and handed it to her. "Call the Eastern Division station tomorrow. Ask for Detective Nicolas Shea. He's been handling Dr. Brant's other… uh… issues. Maybe he can help you."

"Thank you, Officer Smoot."

As Alice walked away her rubber thongs felt like lead. She didn't see the grin on Officer Smoot's face as he watched her go. He looked positively conspiratorial.

Sunday sun was streaming in the bedroom window when the sound of voices downstairs woke Alice. She pulled a pair of Charlie's fatigue pants and put the pepper spray in one of the many pockets. She put on his olive drab t-shirt and arranged the silver chain around her neck so his ring hung inside it.

Harry, wearing red silk boxer shorts, lounged on the couch with his bare feet resting on the coffee trunk. He was drinking beer from the bottle, eating nachos out of the bag, and watching the 7:30am rerun of "I Love Lucy." He winced at the sight of the sponge mop, but laid a muscular arm along the top of the sofa as if to invite her to snuggle up.

Several questions occurred to her. Was he in seduction mode all the time? And if not where did he go on his off-hours? Did he hang out in Hell's bars with other incubi and succubi? Where did he get his disguises? Did the Devil pick out his clothes, or did Hell have a wardrobe department? And did those boxer shorts just appear on him or did he have to climb into them?

She settled for asking, "Why 'I Love Lucy'?" And as usual she heard his reply inside her head.

Not many laughs where I'm from. He gave her a rueful smile.

His azure gaze had the usual affect of sending sexual tremors up from her core. Her inner wench desperately wanted to ride them, but she shook the sponge mop with one hand and aimed the pepper spray with the other. He blew her a kiss and vanished.

She spoke aloud to the empty room. "You could at least turn off the TV."

When Syl didn't answer her phone Alice hoped she was asleep and not raising hell at the police station or reaching a sexual apogee under the young Elvis. She left a message about Detective Shea. She put Bob Seger on the stereo and was in the kitchen when the toaster rang in concert with the doorbell. She opened the door, expecting to tell Syl to come back later. Instead, she faced the abbreviated version of Indiana Jones in the same safari jacket, slouch hat, and shoes manufactured to climb mountains, not stairs. He held up his press badge.

"Joe Stone from the *Chronicle,* Miss Lewis.

"I remember you."

"I want to ask a few questions about Dr. Logan Brant. Do you think the alleged poisoning of her nephew is related to the eagles found in her yard?"

Alice slammed the door and returned to the kitchen. He came around to the back screen door and she held up the pepper spray. He backed away so fast she figured he must have had experience with it. From the kitchen window she watched him cruise down the hill in a flashy vintage Mustang instead of his battered clunker. He was probably headed for Syl's house, but Syl hated him for the trash he'd been writing about her mother.

If Syl didn't deck him outright, Alice doubted he'd get anything from her except the evil eye, and maybe a case of head lice. Or worse.

Chapter Thirty-Eight

"First Love at Second Sight"

What is irritating about love is that it is
a crime that requires an accomplice.
Charles Baudelaire (1821-1867)

On Sunday morning Nick coasted the Indian down the hill and parked it next to Logan's friend's garage. He glanced up at the house perched among the tall trees on the ridge. It was the same one he had been called to a year before. Alice Lewis was probably the one he heard crying that night.

He climbed the stairs to the porch and knocked on the front door. He was about to assume Miss Lewis was asleep when she came to the door and looked warily up at him through the screen door. Bob Seger's "Old Time Rock and Roll" drifted out around her.

He held up his badge so she could see it. While he was at it, he looked over her shoulder. He didn't expect to see an alligator roaming free in the living room, but Smoot said that was what the anonymous caller claimed. He wondered why someone would pull a mean trick like that on a woman who'd been recently widowed.

She came outside and closed the front door behind her. Her brown hair was pulled back in a pony tail. In the morning sunshine he could see auburn highlights and threads of silver. She was barefoot and wearing an over-sized olive drab t-shirt. The army-issue fatigue pants were several sizes too big for her and he assumed they had belonged to her late husband. He noticed the silver chain around her neck, but the shirt hid whatever was hanging on it. He glanced down and noted an unusual silver ring on her right hand. He had a feeling the t-shirt hid a larger version of it.

Her eyes went from the badge to Nick's face. She recognized him the same instant he knew he had seen those blue eyes before.

"You're the Undercover Cop. You got rid of the drunk with the snake."

"At the DMV. Yes, ma'am."

Nick wanted to tell Alice Lewis he remembered the exact moment he saw her there for those few seconds. He wanted to tell her how beautiful she had looked. He wanted to tell her how much her composure had impressed him when those around her were in full panic.

He thought of what Victor Hugo had written in *Les Miserables* about the power of a glance. *It is in this way that love begins, and in this way only.*

He wanted to tell her what he only now realized. He had fallen in love with her at the DMV.

Once Nick reassured Alice Lewis that Logan Brant hadn't been arrested, she went inside with an "I'll be right back." While she was gone he whipped off his tie and put it in his trouser pocket. He rolled up the sleeves of his white broadcloth shirt, and opened the top two buttons.

He settled into the canvas sling chair with a contented sigh. He extended the thirty-six-inch inseams of his starched and mangle-pressed chinos and rested his feet on a lower board of the porch railing. It wasn't proper posture for an official interview, but he was pretty sure Dr. Brant hadn't had anything official in mind when she told him to come here. Besides, unless Fred Brant died, this wasn't officially his investigation.

The small, oak-shaded deck was more like a large balcony. A cool breeze blew from the river, visible in glints of silvery light through the leafy canopy on the slope below. At least five noisy blue jays perched at eye level in the nearby fruit tree. They gave him the feeling he was the object of their racket. A squirrel dropped onto the railing from the oak and scampered to within a foot of his shoes. He sat up and stared fixedly at Nick.

Alice reappeared with a pitcher and two tumblers. Ice cubes chimed when she set the pitcher on the small glass table.

"Lemon or sugar in your tea, Detective Shea?"

"Straight, thanks."

While he poured a glass for himself and one for her, she went back inside. She returned with a plate of cookies and a bag of peanuts in their shells. Seger's "Night Moves" filtered through the screen door.

Nick nodded at the squirrel. "Miss Lewis, does he think I owe him money?"

Her laugh made him happier than a laugh usually would. He wondered if she had laughed much in the past year.

"Please call me Alice, Detective Shea."

He wanted to ask her to call him Nick, but if this wasn't an official visit it wasn't a social call either. At least that's how he rationalized his diffidence.

She held out a peanut for the squirrel who took it politely. Then she walked to the far end of the deck and distributed the rest of them along the railing. In the seconds she took to return, two more squirrels and the birds swarmed around the breakfast buffet.

"Looks like feeding time at the Aquarium in Baltimore." Alice sat in the chair on the other side of the table and put her bare feet near Nick's on the rail. "I love to visit the Aquarium then. It's a rush to watch the divers and the fish fraternize."

He didn't mention that he was one of those volunteer divers, and that he and a clown fish had a little something going on at feeding time.

She raised her glass of tea. Nick tapped it with his.

"To our noble selves," she said. "Damned few of us left."

"I'll drink to that."

He noticed that Alice had exchanged the baggy fatigue pants and tee for a blue chambray shirt and jeans with just the right amount of spandex. Watching the motion in those jeans when she walked to the other end of the deck had brightened his morning considerably.

The cookies were chocolate chip. He and Alice each took a couple and sat for a while in that rare phenomenon, a comfortable silence.

"I was going to call you at the police station this morning, Detective Shea."

"Me? Why?"

"Officer Smoot gave me the number. He said you're the one to talk to about what's going to happen to Logan."

"I'm not in charge of this case." Nick didn't know whether to growl at Smoot the next time he saw him, or buy him a beer. "But if I were, I couldn't give you that information anyway."

"Then why would Officer Smoot tell me to ca…." She stopped in mid-word and glanced away.

So now they both knew they'd been set up. Nick interrupted the silence that was no longer comfortable.

"I'm working on a couple other cases that concern Dr. Brant. She thinks you might have a fresh perspective on this one."

"I can't imagine why. I do know Logan wouldn't poison anybody."

"Here's what bothers me. They found tetramethrin and a lot of other nasty bug spray ingredients in Fred Brant's system the night he had dinner at his aunt's house, but Dr. Brant doesn't seem the type to keep stuff like that around."

"She can't abide it. The neighbor across the street uses gallons of herbicides and pesticides on his lawn. It's a constant source of friction."

"And yet a can of wasp spray was sitting on the counter by the stove. Wasp spray has all those ingredients and more."

"That's strange."

He wanted to tell her the cookies were the best he'd ever tasted, but he could see she was thinking. He was glad he waited. She dropped her feet to the deck planks and sat up straight. Her expression was pure "Eureka!" So pure, he would have bet his motorcycle that what she was about to say would be the truth.

"A week ago this past Thursday, Logan invited several of us from the neighborhood for dinner. Just the day before, some hooligan tried to mug her at the bingo hall."

"I was there."

"At the bingo hall?"

"I happened to be nearby. That's how I met Dr. Brant."

"Well, we wanted to make sure she was okay, you know?" She glanced at him. "Where is the mugger, by the way?"

"Juvie."

"For some reason Logan believes she can turn that kid." Alice sighed. "But anyway, at Logan's house that night her daughter Syl showed up with a can of waspicide. She set it on the kitchen counter and said it was more effective than pepper spray for fending off attackers."

"Very bad idea."

"Syl was worried. Can't say as I blame her."

"So why do you think Dr. Brant didn't get rid of it?"

"Logan keeps a lot of things on her kitchen counters. Her sight is failing, and she complains about her memory. She might not have noticed it or she forgot what it was."

"Would you be willing to testify in court?"

"Of course."

"I've been investigating the two eagles found in Dr. Brant's yard."

"Any leads?" She caught his glance. "Of course. You can't discuss it."

"I can tell you that a neighbor also claims Logan's into witchcraft. He's reported that he often sees a... how did he put it... a 'gi-normous colored woman' at the house. He's convinced she's a 'hoodoo priestess.' He says she and Dr. Brant put the bondage gear on his yard statues as a hex."

"Bernie Robertson? The gnome guy? You've figured out he's nuts, right? He's talking about Logan's best friend, Marjorie

Mayhew. There isn't a better person than Miss Marjorie anywhere on the planet."

Nick had already connected the "gi-normous colored woman" with Dr. Brant's friend. He didn't mention he had met Mrs. Mayhew. He was here to get information, not give it out.

"So you don't know of anything like that going on around here?"

"You mean covens and warlocks and Devil worship? No. Nothing like that."

"People commit horrific crimes in the name of the Devil — animal mutilation, child abuse, human sacrifice, cannibalism."

"Tell me, Detective Shea..." She turned to look directly at him. The glint in her eyes reminded him of sunlight on tropical waters. "If devil worshippers set out Chinese food at their rituals, is that a Hunan sacrifice or Schezhuan of those things?"

Nick stared at her for about a second before he let loose. When he finally stopped laughing he saw her glance toward the front door.

Of course. She was a writer. She probably wanted to get back to whatever she was working on. He took his feet off the railing and stood up.

"Thank you for your time, Miss Lewis. If you think of anything else that might be relevant, please call me." He handed her his card. She put the rest of the cookies into the bag recently occupied by peanuts and gave it to him.

When she stood up he realized her eyes were closer to being level with his than he had expected. They were smiling. So were her lips and he imagined brushing them lightly with his. His libido's reaction wasn't anything he hadn't felt before, but something subtly stunning had been added.

Subtly stunning. It described her.

"Thank you for your time."

Alice Lewis waved from the porch as he revved up the Indian. He raised a hand in acknowledgement. He didn't look back when he drove away, but he felt her eyes watching him.

So this is what love is.

The thought should have been more comforting. What was it Baudelaire said about the crime of love? It requires an accomplice.

Did he want his life to become even more complicated? Did he want to see hurt in another woman's eyes, especially a woman he already cared about as much as this one?

CHAPTER THIRTY-NINE

"SECOND LOVE AT FIRST SIGHT"

*" 'Of all the gin joints in all the towns in all the world
she walks into mine.' "*
Rick Blaine in *Casablanca*

Bob Seger's "Roll Me Away" was playing as Alice stood at the porch railing and watched Detective Nick Shea's motorcycle cruise up the street at a sedate, Sunday morning pace.

"What do you think, Charlie?" She cocked her head, as though listening. "Yeah. I like him too. So, does that mean you won't be coming back to haunt me?"

She was continuing a conversation she and Charlie had had a few days after the oncologist told him, "If you don't get hit by a bus, the cancer will kill you in six months." The doc's bedside manner could have used improvement.

"If you take up with someone unworthy of you…" Charlie had kept his tone light. "…I'll come back to haunt you."

She had kissed him. "Then I'll date sleazebags. "

Alice turned and stared at the small table and canvas chairs, the two glasses and the pitcher. She tried to supplement the space with the image of Detective Nick Shea, long, lean, broad-shouldered, dark-haired, dark-eyed, and at ease in his starched and pressed casual slacks and shirt.

She tried to hear his voice, the timbre and tempo of it. She had read that sound waves never totally flat-line, but the atmospheric perturbations of her conversation with him were already off on their inter-galactic journey.

Just as well. Better he occupy her daydreams than her reality, and not because of Charlie. Charlie would want her to be happy, and she was pretty sure he would approve of Detective Shea. The hitch was, she had too much to hide to start a flirtation with a cop. Esme was dating a policeman, but she didn't know how much trouble Syl had set loose, and she was skeptical about what she did know.

Technically, Alice hadn't lied. She really didn't know of any covens or warlocks or devil-worshippers in the neighborhood. He hadn't asked her if an incubus in silk boxer shorts watched TV in her living room. Or if the Devil had chatted with her by the pond the day before. Her answers might have misled Shea this time, but eventually he would find out the truth and that would be the end of it.

As she carried the pitcher, glasses, and plate back inside she muttered, "Of all the gin joints in all the towns in all the world he walks into mine."

Staring into the rectangular eye of the cyber Cyclops was how Alice spent most of her time. The rumble of Detective Shea's motorcycle had barely faded to silence when she sat down at her desk. The screen-saver of seahorses performing their courtship ballet would have mesmerized her if Shea and Logan hadn't been competing for her attention.

She went into the kitchen, put a dozen cookies in a plastic container, and headed for Logan's house. She was relieved to see no police cars parked out front. Logan never locked her door, so when no one answered her knock she let herself in. She followed the sound of laughter to the back deck and found Logan and Faye drinking margarita mix on the rocks. A large bottle of the mixer and couple more glasses sat on the old wooden cable spool Logan used as a table. She always set out extra glasses in case someone dropped by.

Logan held up her glass in greeting. "Such a beautiful day, Alice. So glad you came up for air."

"What's the joke, you two?" Alice pulled out a chair and put the cookies on the table. She poured herself a virgin margarita.

"Logan put your admirer, Stone, on a few mailing lists," said Faye.

"You mean the one who's been canvassing the neighbors like a Jehovah's Witness on safari?"

"Right." Faye turned to Logan. "Tell her which lists."

"Re-Treads, for one. That's a foreskin restoration association. Mr. Stone doesn't know it, but he asked for a consultation and all their literature."

"Any others?" Alice now saw where Syl got the penchant for revenge.

"The Hung Jury. Mr. Stone will be receiving their newsletter, *Measuring Up.*" Then there's the Tantric Love Society and a few others."

"Logan didn't want to invade Stone's privacy by giving his home address," added Faye, "So she had them sent to him at the newspaper office."

Alice chuckled. "I'm relieved to find you here. I thought I might have to schlep to the county lock-up to visit you. Stone would've had a field day with that."

"The police took that awful can of spray when they left. I'd been meaning to get rid of it right after Syl brought it over, but I lost track of it, then forgot I had it."

"Logan has a back channel at the hospital," said Faye.

"Why am I not surprised?"

"She says Freddy had ingested such a cocktail of drugs that the wasp spray was just the olive." Faye paused. "Even less. It was the pimento inside the olive.

"They're considering the possibility that the insecticide in the meal was an accident, and circumstantial in any case." Logan looked over the rail of the deck and into the ravine. "They wanted to test the rice, but I fed the leftovers to the raccoons. "I hope it didn't make them sick."

"I doubt it," said Faye. "Raccoons eat my week-old garbage when I put it out for pick-up."

"I'm still accountable for the pain gel Freddy ate." Logan looked stricken. "I'm a doctor and I should have known young people consider it a way to get high."

"You retired a couple years ago," said Faye. "No one expects you to be hip to the latest youthful idiocy. And the gel was in your medicine cabinet. He stole it."

Alice changed the subject. "Logan, you shouldn't have sicced that policeman on me."

"Did Detective Shea come to see you this morning?"

"He did."

"You didn't like him?"

"I did. I do. But that's not the point."

"Yes it is," said Logan.

Alice and Faye exchanged glances. Esme's new beau was risky enough. A second detective hanging around in the Lower Cliffs would be a disaster.

"I don't need the distraction of a policeman in my life."

"Love, my dear Alice, is not a distraction."

"It is not a distraction, Logan. It is *the* distraction."

"Some dude named Baudelaire said 'Love is a crime that requires an accomplice.'"

Alice and Logan stared at Faye. She was not in the habit of quoting long-dead French poets.

"Where did you hear that?"

Faye shrugged. "If the Detective Shea you're referring to is tall, fit, and fine, I know him. He hangs out at the bar with his friend, the coroner. And he's all the time quoting somebody or other. That's his answer when his friend tries to get him to chat up one of the women."

Alice desperately wanted to ask if Detective Shea flirted with women at the Red Eye, so she changed the subject. "Logan, has Syl come by to see you?"

"No. I reckon she's sleeping it off. Officer Smoot said she came here last night, but he wouldn't let her in. He mentioned that she might have been drinking."

"Knowing Syl, there's no 'might' about it," said Faye. "Sorry, Logan."

"It's alright, Faye."

"Did he tell you I came along?" asked Alice. "Syl was genuinely upset and worried about you."

"He said she had a friend with her."

"That's all?"

"Yes. Is there more?"

"Nothing important." Alice was grateful Officer Smoot hadn't mentioned to Logan that her daughter had engaged in a tussle with Alice on the front lawn. The neighbors would probably fill her in on it soon anyway.

The phone rang inside.

"I'll let it go to message," said Logan. "It's probably that Stone fellow."

They listened through the open sliding glass doors. "Hello, Logan? This is Betty. I'm so sorry I caused you all this trouble. I happened to see your nephew in town a couple days ago and I must have hexed him. Please call me."

"Who's that and what's she talking about?"

"Betty's one of the bingo regulars. She must have heard about Freddy on her scanner."

"Why is she apologizing?"

"She thinks she has the evil eye. Every morning she stares at a tree in her yard before she leaves the house. She believes it absorbs the malevolence and keeps her power from hurting people."

"So how's the tree doing," asked Faye.

"Actually, not so well as the trees around it." Logan turned to Alice. "My dear, would you please visit Freddy at the hospital this afternoon? It wouldn't be a good idea for me to go, and I want to make sure he's okay. Find out if there's anything he needs?"

Alice sighed too softly for Logan to hear. Maybe she should write a book about why books don't get written. She left without telling either of them what she really thought about Detective Nicholas Shea, the Undercover Cop at the Department of Motor Vehicles. He just might be her second love at first sight.

Chapter Forty

"Sorry"

A bird in the hand is dead.
Boozer's Revision to Murphy's Law

A single cubic centimeter of Nick's brain tissue might have as many neuron connections as the number of stars in the Milky Way galaxy, but he needed all of them for the case he was working on. He didn't have a billion or two to spare for an infatuation.

On the forty-five-minute motorcycle ride to the Juvenile Detention Center he thought about what he would ask Emanuel Hot Dog Boyd:

What work does your uncle Roy do?

Is your grandmother named Mary Rogers?

What are the names of your other relatives?

Do you know about the house in Glen Brooke?

Do you know a man named Sam Hare?

Granted, he'd asked most of those questions before, but maybe the kid had had a change of heart. Or memory. Or both. Maybe.

As the rural scenery flashed by, Nick rode with his brain in split-screen mode. On one side the pieces of the investigation's puzzle arranged and re-arranged themselves. On the other side ran the loop of his conversation with Alice Lewis intercut with the script of what he wished he had said to her. He thought he had detected a signal from her, but it was probably just a momentary flicker. She had a self-contained, independent air about her. Why would she want to become involved in a cop's complicated life?

The ambulance parked outside the Detention Center gave him a bad feeling. He wasn't surprised to find Emanuel Boyd surrounded by paramedics in the infirmary. When he held up his badge one of the EMT's took a moment to toss him a glance and shake his head.

The warden stood to one side with his arms folded across his chest. A clear plastic bag dangled from the fingers of one hand. Without unfolding his arms, the warden raised the bag for Nick to see. It contained a shiv of the familiar sort.

Prisons, even this lockup-lite, were war zones. Inmates fabricated weapons out of everything from dining hall plates to bed sheets. This shank was made from a metal bed slat, the point shaped and sharpened by rubbing it on a concrete wall or floor. The handle was wrapped with electrical tape.

"A dispute over drugs," the warden said. "The assailant is on his way to the county jail."

So, someone already in custody would soon be in more custody. This was not Nick's jurisdiction and he didn't bother asking how drugs got into the detention center. That would be like asking how flies got in.

He walked over to see if there was any chance Hot Dog would be able to talk. The boy's shirt was soaked in blood, but his eyes were open. When he saw Nick he mustered a smile, as though an old friend had come to visit him. He managed a slight gesture and Nick leaned down to hear him.

"They didn't get my dope, man."

"Take it easy, Emanuel. They're doing what they can for you."

The boy's next words were barely a whisper. Nick heard only the last one.

"Sorry."

Mortality's switch flipped and the light went out in his eyes. The paramedics started the task of trying to revive him and Nick returned to where the warden stood. He kept his voice low.

"Where did he get money for dope?"

"Someone named Logan Brant sends a little every week for his account at the cantina. Do you know him?"

"I know her."

"Oh."

"Still no relatives other than the brother?"

"No. And we have no address of record for him."

"His address of record is a holding cell at headquarters right now. He claims total ignorance of everything." Nick thought about Logan and her concern for the welfare of her attacker. "Has anyone told Dr. Brant?"

The warden shook his head. "She's not a relative. Privacy issues."

Nick followed the paramedics as they picked up the stretcher with Hot Dog's blanket-shrouded body and headed outside. He watched them load it into the back of the ambulance, then he threw a leg over the Indian. He turned on the petcock, put the gear in neutral, retarded the spark, and stamped on the kick starter.

Tonight he was glad that he had to stop at the station to write a report. It delayed the visit with Dr. Brant he must make on his way home. She never seemed to mind him showing up late at her door, but he wished he didn't have to deliver bad news.

After he left the station he stopped at a drive-through for an unfashionable dinner at a fashionable hour. When he turned at the narrow street into the Cliffs he decided to locate Sylvana Gant's house before paying Logan a visit. Mrs. Gant had connections with both sides of the environmental conflict. Her ex-husband was one of the partners in the law firm Sam Hare had hired. Maybe she had learned some new information since Nathan talked to her.

He turned off the ignition and coasted down the hill toward the river. He gave the brake a slight squeeze and looked up as he approached Alice Lewis's house. It was dark except a single light in the window overlooking the pond. Maybe she was at the computer now.

He wanted to walk up the stairs and knock on the door. He wanted to see what photographs hung on the walls, what books kept her company. He imagined a well-worn easy chair in her office. He wanted to sit in it and confide that he was trying to write a novel. He wanted to ask how she got past writer's block. He wanted to know if her fictional characters sometimes hijacked her stories the way his did. Instead, he released the brake and let the Indian carry him on downhill.

A vintage Mustang convertible was parked across the street and two houses uphill from Sylvana's place. He recognized the flawless paint job as Caspian Blue Metallic, one of the colors used on the '65 models. A placard with "PRESS" printed in large letters was affixed to the inside of the front window. The vanity plate read, "ROVN STN." Joe Stone must be doing well to replace his old clunker with this. It seemed odd though, even for Stone, to be skulking around at this hour when no crime or accident had been reported.

Nick diverted his attention from the Mustang to its owner. Stone was taking photos of Sylvana's house by the glow of the street light. Bats chasing moths around the arc lamp sent eerie shadows skittering across Mrs. Gant's lawn. Without dismounting, he walked the motorcycle into the deep shade of an oak. He only intended to escape Stone's notice, so what followed was a bonus.

Sylvana Gant came boiling out of the house like all three Stooges plus one Cat-on-a-Hot-Front-Porch. She carried a large cardboard box with her. Nick assumed she had left it by the front door for just such an occasion.

"You sorry son of a goddam bitch." She started flinging crockery and hardware at him. "You will regret libeling my mother and me, you freakin' cheeser."

Stone made a zig-zag dash for his car. He dodged a hammer's head-over-handle trajectory, but a dinner plate hit him between the shoulder blades with the force of a porcelain frisbee. He reached the Mustang and gunned it up the hill. He had had the foresight to make a u-turn at the river and park it headed out. He must have had to evade his news flashes' wrath before.

Sylvana left the hammer and broken plates where they had landed. She stormed back into the house and slammed the door. Nick decided this would not be a good time to talk to her about her mother's situation.

No more stalling. He had to tell Logan Brant that Emanuel had been murdered. He had to tell her what she probably already knew, that he would be stuffed into a body bag and buried in a modern day version of a Potters' Field. His grave would have no tombstone, no marker. No one would mourn him, except perhaps his former teacher, Mrs. Marjorie Mayhew, and Dr. Brant. He tried to take consolation in the fact that at least he could tell Logan that Emanuel's last word was "Sorry."

He rode back to Dr. Brant's house, and stood outside listening to Bach and the mocking bird soloist for a while before he knocked on the door.

Chapter Forty-One

"In a Rut"

Borrow trouble for yourself
if that is your nature,
but don't lend it to your neighbors.
Rudyard Kipling
(*Hot and Bothered*: Rectorial Address, 1923)

A lice thought she'd witnessed all the supernatural weirdness possible. As a scribbler of fiction she should have known better. On the way to her garage Monday morning she encountered a new surprise.

The two deer stood at an angle that blocked most of the narrow, dead-end street in front of the garage. Lots of deer roamed the neighborhood. At first glance these two seemed innocuous enough until the buck did something Alice doubted many people had seen. The doe stood motionless while he slowly licked the inner surfaces of her hind legs, then a circle around the base of her tail, and finally, long strokes with his tongue along her sides.

Alice stood as motionless as the doe. She couldn't help wondering if the buck's tongue was rough or smooth. The thought had its affect on her.

She also wondered if it was true that male deer were endowed with exceptionally large penises. The doe raised her tail in invitation. The buck reared on his hind legs to cover her. Alice could see that particular fact was true.

Deer wouldn't go into rut for a couple more months, though. Alice was sure the location for this pair's tryst wasn't a coincidence and that Harry was responsible for it.

The buck mounted the doe as a street model Humvee arrived. Judging by how hard the driver leaned on his horn, he must have been late for work. Another car pulled up behind him and a third tailgated that one. Folks straggled out to watch the show. Alice's neighbor, her hair in curlers, banged on a metal saucepan with an iron ladle. The buck ignored her and the blaring horns too.

The humvee driver threw open his door and stormed out, flapping one arm over his head and brandishing an umbrella like a rapier. Then he got a closer look at the buck's size. He saw the fierce stare of those brown eyes with their glaze of pure sex. He assessed the antlers and the sharp edges on the hooves and retreated back to the haven of his Hummer. Alice could see him dialing his phone there. Since he probably didn't have Animal Control on speed-dial, she guessed he was calling 911.

Alice opened the garage door and backed the Corvette out slowly. In the rear view mirror she caught a glimpse of Harry among the on-lookers. He was dressed only in the red silk boxers he favored. He winked at her. She had no doubt he was behind this scene. She had no clue as to why, but she wasn't going to ask him.

As soon as the Vette's long, low left front fender cleared the door she hauled on the steering wheel and swore at 1974's definition of power steering. She had to ride up over the curb, but the left rear end missed the deer, if only by inches. That was lucky. The buck looked ready to take on whatever Chevrolet or General Motors or any other company produced, and repairing dents in shiny red fiberglass was expensive. Alice got some satisfaction from knowing that even rolling over the curb, the Hummer would be too wide to pass the deer.

Alice drove a block, then had to stop. Two dogs stood in the middle of the road. They had finished the main event, but Reggie's cock hadn't gotten the memo. He had managed to maneuver until he stood tail-to-tail with the poodle named Ginger, but he was still stuck. Reggie's owner stood on the sidelines, fists on hips like a coach watching a member of his team make a bad play.

Alice knew Reggie was a mutt adopted from the animal shelter. She also knew Ginger was supposedly a registered pure-bred. As Alice inched the Vette forward, Reggie stared up at her with an expression that achieved chagrin, exhaustion, and triumph all in one. Alice had a feeling this was his first experience with love and probably his last.

Ginger's owner appeared dragging a heavy-duty garden hose and yelling.

"If you kept your mutt tied up, Jackson, this wouldn't happen."

Jackson shouted back. "He wouldn't have jumped the fence if you didn't let your bitch roam the streets while she's in heat."

"She's not in heat, you moron."

Alice drove around them and in the rearview mirror saw Ginger's owner blast Reggie with a stream of water powerful enough to put out a barn fire.

Poor Reggie.

Alice hadn't had a chance to look at the morning paper. As she passed the dispensers just inside the hospital's entryway a headline over Joseph Stone's byline caught her eye. *Dispute over Development Heats up.* The Baltimore paper also had a teaser about it at the top of the front page, which meant he had a byline inside. Stone's journalistic star was rising. Maybe he too had made a pact with the Devil.

That wasn't a laughing matter, but she smiled anyway, speculating on what would happen if two people who hated each other made pacts with Evil. Which one would prevail?

She deposited three quarters and stood there reading about Freddy's accusation and an account of the police visit to Logan's house. The piece continued on page four with a photograph of Syl sprawled on the ground with Alice on top of her. The good news was that only Alice's back was visible and she was referred to as an "unidentified assailant."

Alice hadn't seen Stone anywhere in the vicinity of Logan's house that night. How had he gotten the photo? Her next thought was that Syl would be out for more than Stone's blood when she saw this. She'd go after his soul.

She folded the paper, stuck it under her arm, and walked slowly to the information desk in the admittance area. She hadn't wanted to come here, but she couldn't refuse Logan. She only knew Freddy by sight, but at Logan's dinner party ten days ago Syl had regaled her and the others with details of his risky proclivities. That was the same night she brought the wasp spray for her mother to use on intruders.

Ten days ago. It seemed like a another lifetime. Ten days ago incubus was just a word and the Devil was a myth. Ten days ago she didn't know the Undercover Cop's name and assumed the brief encounter at the DMV would be the last time she saw him.

She hoped only relatives would be allowed to see Mr. Brant, but the volunteer cheerily looked up Freddy's room number and told Alice how to get there.

There was no way this visit could be anything but awkward. She felt remiss in not bringing a get-well gift, but he didn't seem the type to appreciate flowers or books. Since he claimed someone had tried to poison him, a box of bon-bons almost certainly would not be allowed. And the hospital's gift shop didn't carry cards that said "Sorry you think your aunt poisoned you. Get over it."

Freddy was sitting in bed hooked up to an IV and vital signs monitor. The eggplant-colored pouches under his eyes contrasted with the rest of his sallow face.

"Good morning, Fred. I'm Alice, your aunt's neighbor."

"Did Aunt Lo send you to help her weasel out of the attempted murder rap?"

So much for the amenities.

"She's worried about you."

"She hates me. She tried to kill me."

Alice sat on the edge of the bed. "You know that isn't true."

He looked away, suddenly attentive to the rectangle of blue sky outside his window. "Just because she didn't succeed in killing me doesn't mean she didn't try."

"Her eyesight's bad. The bug spray was a mistake." Alice handed him the newspaper. "You need to call this reporter and tell him that. I can give you his number."

"I have his card."

"So, he's been in touch with you."

"He's been bugging me for weeks." Freddy opened the paper to page four and saw the photo. When he stopped laughing he said, "Is that you on top of cousin Sylvana?"

"Yeah. Stone wasn't there and I'm wondering how he got that picture."

"Probably from Bernie."

"Bernie who?"

"Aunt Lo's neighbor. Across the street."

"The gnome guy?"

"Yeah. He takes pictures of her and her house. He's positive she's up to no good and he wants proof. He even installed a wide angle night vision camera."

"Fred, please call Logan. She's worried sick about you. She thinks of you as a son."

"What makes you think so?"

"She told me." Alice smiled. "A wayward, wrong-headed son, but a son nonetheless."

Logan also had called him a semi-likeable bobble-head, but she dialed that one back. Freddy returned a flicker of a grin. He could take a joke at his own expense. That was a good sign.

"I'll think about it."

"Thank you." She paused. "I have to ask you a question that's been bothering me."

"I didn't put the damned dead eagles in Aunt Lo's damned septic tank hole."

Alice recognized the *I'm telling you the truth. Please believe me* subtext in his reply.

She nodded and stood up. When she shook his hand, she held it firmly a few extra seconds. It was body-speak, making the tenuous connection between them a little more solid and personal.

As she headed for the parking lot her plan was to make a quick stop at the hardware store. By the time she got home she figured Reggie and Ginger would have parted company and the deer would be browsing in the ravine as if sex had never been invented.

She would stop by Logan's house and tell her about this visit. With errands and obligations taken care of she could mute the ring on her phone and spend the rest of the day trying to shove her story's plot up that steep slope.

Chapter Forty-Two

Taking a Ribbing

The most romantic thing a woman ever said to me in bed
was "Are you sure you're not a cop?"
Larry Brown

Nick had the usual early September conversation about the Orioles' prospects with Jim, the lone mechanic who kept the department's fleet running. He signed for the Crown Vic and had just cleared the gate when his cell phone rang. Caller ID showed Department of Natural Resources. He pulled into a convenience store parking lot and answered it. Fortunately no one was trying to rob the place.

"Good morning, Cindy, what do you have for me?"

"A one-legged floater."

"Where?"

"It got tangled in a chicken-necker's lines near Howlet's Pier." She chuckled. "Not the crab feast he was anticipating. It's on the way to the morgue now."

"Male or female?"

" Woman's clothes, man's equipment, or what's left of it. And there's a full set of choppers."

"Thanks."

"You're welcome. Have a good one."

Nick's to-do list now included finding out if this body's DNA matched the leg found washed up over two weeks ago. Also, checking the missing persons file for leads to people who might be able to identify him. At least he could narrow it down to lost cross-dressers, unless the one making the report didn't know he was. If that didn't pan out he and Nathan would have to subpoena the patient records of every dentist in the county and beyond.

He took the next on-ramp to the highway and immediately regretted it. Traffic started to slow at the bottom of a steep hill ahead and red lights flashed. He bumped along the shoulder and stopped behind the last police car in line. He stepped out into a horrific stench and hiked up the slope toward the source of it. The driver of the convertible had somehow made it to the shoulder and a septic tank pumper truck had parked in front of it.

The convertible's top was down. The thick coating of raw sewage inside and out made it hard to identify, but from the lines of it Nick guessed a Mustang from the '60's. Both doors were open to let the remaining sludge drain into the coffee-colored pond that had accumulated around the car.

The driver, covered in the end products of a large number of gastro-intestinal systems, sat on the ground. He was vomiting between his knees. Nick could easily have located him with his eyes closed, but he was impossible to identify by sight. A Good Samaritan of a state trooper with a bucket was sliding down the nearby embankment to a creek. Everyone else was giving him plenty of personal space. An ambulance and fire trucks, sirens wailing, crested the hill in the on-coming lane.

Trying to take in as little air as possible, Nick walked along the shoulder toward the pumper truck. As he approached the Mustang he caught sight of a patch of Cadmium Blue metallic paint and the partial letters R and O on the vanity plate.

The huddle of sewage sitting in the grass must be Joe Stone. He wondered how this could have happened. And what a coincidence that it had happened to Stone. Nick was so used to seeing him at crime scenes he wondered if a crime had occurred here too. Had Stone been at the wrong place at the wrong time?

The pump-out company's driver waved his arms like a symphony conductor as he delivered his account of the accident. The gist of it was that 1) the truck's vacuum system was designed so that no way an accident like this could happen. 2) he had unhooked the hoses and locked everything down tight before he got on the road. 3) this wasn't his fault, and 4) THIS WAS NOT HIS FAULT.

Nick walked to the back of the truck and studied the valve where the hose connected when in use. The metal intake pipe pointed downward. He sighted down the asphalt slope to the car. He had almost flunked trigonometry in college, but even eyeballing the angles he agreed with the driver. There was no way the truck's contents could have arced high enough to spew into the Mustang.

Puzzling, certainly, but not a case for Homicide. Shaking his head, he returned to his Crown Vic whose interior, he was convinced, would harbor the lingering bouquet of excrement for a long time to come.

Half an hour later Nick wore latex gloves and a surgical mask Will had thoughtfully provided. Will unzipped the body bag of heavy plastic, releasing the djin of decay. The escaping stench reminded Nick that there were worse smells than an aged blend of urine and feces simmering in a vintage Mustang parked in the sun. The two of them stared at the gelatinous mass of decay that once had been… someone.

"We estimate he was in the water at least three weeks, maybe four. Here's what he was wearing." Will retrieved a couple hangers from a hook on the back of a door. A water-logged turquoise silk spaghetti-strap mini-dress hung on one. A black satin strapless padded bra and matching thong, also wet, were draped over the other. Nick recognized the thong as a gaff panty, designed to flatten and disguise male genitals.

He leaned down for a closer look at the stump of the left femur.

"Not chewed off and spit out by a shark," Will said. "Unless the shark also swallowed a chainsaw."

"No ID on the vic, of course."

"Of course." Will pushed the shelf and its body back into the refrigerated compartment. "The handle on my rib-splitter broke. Can't finish here without one. Give me a ride to the hardware store and I'll stand you a beer afterward."

"Too early for a beer, but I need some air freshener for the car. I have to take a shower first though."

"You'll have to take another one after we finish the autopsy. But if you insist on the cleanliness-godliness thing, there's a bottle of patchouli oil in my locker, number seventeen. It's been in there a few years, but it's still good."

"Patchouli? The stuff hippies used to wear?"

"It promotes serenity and health. And they say it's an aphrodisiac."

Nick gave an eye-roll and headed for the locker room.

Nick picked up a six-pack of the pine tree air fresheners then went to the gardening tools section to look for Will. He was surprised to see him chatting with Alice Lewis. Will was using the long-handled loppers he called rib-splitters to point out the bladed garden tools on the wall display.

Damn! He had showered and washed his hair, but not his shoes and clothes. Pretending to straighten his collar he pulled it up for a quick sniff to see if the aroma of sewage had seeped into the warp and weft of his shirt. All he could smell was patchouli. He had dabbed on a miniscule amount of the stuff to mask the latrine odor. He had forgotten how far the scent of a tiny amount of patchouli could go. He was about to duck out of sight when Miss Lewis spotted him.

"Detective Shea."

"You know this ne'er-do-well?" asked Will.

Nick stopped at what he reckoned was a safe distance, windage-wise. "I was going to ask you the same thing about that miscreant, Miss Lewis."

"First time I've laid eyes on him. But your friend was advising me on the subject of pruning shears. He seems to know a lot about them." Her smile was as warm and enigmatic as he remembered. "And the name's Alice."

"In case he hasn't mentioned it, Alice, this is Will Mabry. Will, Alice is a friend of Logan Brant."

Will shifted the loppers so he could shake hands.

"Are you a weekend gardener, Will?"

"No. I use these tools in my line of work."

Before Nick could think of something, anything, that would change the subject Alice asked, "And what is your line of work?"

"I'm the County Coroner." Will held up the loppers. "We use these beauties to cut open rib cages. The pruning shears you're holding are handy for snip-work, separating organs for removal, etcetera."

This was not the way to make a third impression on a woman Nick really wanted to impress. When she spoke he realized he had underestimated her.

"I was just reading about the Samburu people in Africa. They believe a person isn't dead until hyenas will eat the body."

"Good to know, Alice. We could use some hyenas around the shop. I'll check eBay to see if any are for sale."

Alice laughed and Nick felt a twinge of jealousy.

"Detective, could I speak with you for a minute?"

Will took the package of air fresheners from his hand. "I'll be at the cashier's."

When he was out of ear-shot Alice came closer. Still worried about the mélange of sewage and patchouli, Nick had to struggle against the urge to back away.

"I saw Freddy Brant this morning." She spoke in a low voice and much too close for his comfort. "Logan asked me to visit him, to make sure he was alright."

"I talked to him yesterday. Looks like he'll be okay."

"So then you know about the photos and videos Logan's neighbor's been taking of her house."

"Mr. Brant didn't mention it. And if you mean the neighbor with the lawn ornaments, neither did he."

Nick had thought the sewage stench and the patchouli would be the worst embarrassment of the day. The fact that she knew something he didn't about this case topped it.

"Freddy only told me about it because he thinks that's probably where the reporter got the photo of Logan's daughter they printed in the paper this morning. As for the gnome guy not divulging it, do you think he might worry about being sued for stalking?"

"Could be. Thanks. I'll talk to him again."

Alice reached out and touched his arm lightly. "I'm relieved you're in Logan's corner. Thank you."

Nick muttered something about it being his job, and she headed off toward the wild bird section. On his way to the check-out counter he paused for a few heartbeats to stare at her back as she perused the suet and sunflower seed.

At the cash register he took out his wallet to pay for the airfresheners, but Will waved it away.

"My treat, since you won't have a beer with me." As they left the store Will said, "You talk alike."

"Who?"

"You and Alice. I read somewhere that speaking alike is a good predictor of romantic compatibility."

"You read somewhere? Romantic compatibility?" Nick stared at him. "Who the hell are you and what have you done with my friend?"

"I'm just saying."

"Aren't you the guy who claims the most romantic thing a woman ever said to you in bed is 'Are you sure you're not a cop?' "

"Rub it in, Shea. Just because you happen to look like Cary Grant. If Cary Grant were a whole lot uglier."

Chapter Forty-Three

" 'Call Alice' "

'For they were learning to draw,' the Dormouse went on....
'And they drew all manner of things –
everything that begins with an M.'"
'Why with an M?' said Alice.
'Why not?' said the March Hare.
Lewis Carroll (Alice in Wonderland)

Still riding a scent-induced high, Alice muttered to herself as she drove home.

"Patchouli? Patchouli!"

Wasn't Detective Nicholas Shea sexy enough? Did he have to call in the cavalry? Did his choice of after-shaves have to evoke memories of dancing with eyes closed, barefoot in the grass, to Grace Slick and "White Rabbit?"

Alice had been thirteen when her Flower Child parents took her with them to love-ins. The aroma of patchouli, along with incense and marijuana smoke, would always remind her of that brief bubble in eternity. Universal peace and love had seemed possible then, even if people had to get stoned and toasted to believe it.

The phone's message light was blinking when she put her car keys on the table near the door. Still distracted by the encounter in the hardware store she hit the play button. She was hanging her purse in its usual place on the back of a dining room chair when she heard Joe Stone's voice behind her.

"Good morning, Alice. Still sleeping?"

Without hesitation, she ripped a table lamp's cord from the wall. Brandishing it, she whirled so fast the room wobbled for a couple thumping heartbeats. The message machine continued Stone's pitch.

Every sentence had "I" in it. Where had she read that the frequent use of "I" in conversation indicated insecurity? She wondered how large a monetary grant some genius had cadged to come to that conclusion.

"I know you like vintage cars," Stone said, "what with the Vette and all. How about I take you on a tour in the '65 Mustang I just bought. I'll show you the house where I grew up and my old elementary school. I'll tell you all about my idea for the next Great American Novel."

The message machine couldn't capitalize Great American Novel, but Alice pictured trumpets sounding a fanfaronade. In her experience, those three words were the number-one indication that the writer would be wasting his time and readers' money. She wasn't surprised when Stone added, "It's autobiographical." Autobiographical and Great American Novel equaled redundancy.

Stone had more information about himself to share with her. Thankfully the machine cut him off. She checked the time on the message. He'd left it a few hours ago, while she was at the hospital visiting Freddy.

She fixed herself a peanut butter and chipotle pepper jelly sandwich and went to her office. She approached her computer with caution. The pornographic images Hell sent were hackneyed, disgusting, and in a way, sad. The same old graphic scenes of balloon boobs and super-sized salamies, served up as bestiality, sodomy, and threesomes.

Hell must lack a Creative Director for its outreach efforts. She worried that Hell's IT department would figure out a way to wrest control from her finger on the delete button, but so far they had displayed the same level of ineptitude as any government bureaucracy.

She spent the next few hours fidgeting at her desk and pacing the room, trying to organize the clutter. She had just made a start on chapter three when the phone rang. She let it go to message. She didn't immediately recognize the voice because Faye sounded like she was being throttled.

Alice picked up the receiver. "Faye, what's the matter?"

"Kelly's dead, Al. The police called me because of the missing person report I filed. They want me to ID his clothes."

"His clothes?" Alice regretted the words as soon as they cleared her larynx.

Faye teetered on the rim of hysteria. "The detective tried to find a diplomatic way to tell me his face is unrecognizable, but the dress he described sounds like my turquoise silk." Several moments of silence followed. Then, "Please go with me."

Alice wanted to ask Faye if she remembered the detective's name, but this was not the time.

"I'll drive."

What was the old saw? "Friends help you move. Best friends help you move bodies."

Kelly's remains bore little resemblance to a body, and thank goodness, Alice wouldn't have to help Faye move it. Even with the heavy-duty plastic bag zipped, the smell of decaying flesh and chemicals was enough to exorcize the lingering memory of patchouli. When Will brought out the turquoise silk dress Alice put her arm around Faye's shoulders.

"That's mine." Faye maintained a remarkable calm. Shock had its helpful side. "We wore the same size."

For his part, Will was the consummate professional, considerate and dignified. He gave no indication that he had exchanged pleasantries with Alice about rib-splitters, sinew-snips, autopsies, and cadaver-munching hyenas in the hardware store that morning.

Faye signed papers taking financial responsibility for Kelly's burial, then excused herself and headed for the restroom. Alice assumed she went there to cry. When the restroom door closed she asked Will the Question. She understood why Faye hadn't asked it. She had loved her husband with all her heart when they married, and she still considered him her dearest friend. Grief plays havoc with the rational thought process.

"Do they know who killed him?"

"I couldn't discuss the case even if I knew anything, Alice, but Nick's working on it. They don't come better than him."

"He'll be getting in touch with Faye, right?"

"I'm sure he will."

When Faye returned, Alice put an arm around her and walked her to the car. While she took the back route to avoid commuter traffic, she made quiet small talk, more to soothe than console. She knew words were inadequate for consolation.

As they neared the Cliffs, she said "You're not working tonight, so help me finish off the macaroni and cheese. Plus, I bought sweet corn and string beans at the farmers' market. We can bake cookies and watch *Casablanca*."

Faye smiled. "Thanks, Al, but I'd rather go home. I need to write an obituary and think about a memorial service. I'll have to contact his relatives. They haven't spoken to him since he came out, but they should be told."

"I'll help you write the obituary, and I'm here for anything else you need." Alice remembered how very "here" Faye had been for her after Charlie's death.

"Thanks."

"How will you contact his friends for the service?"

"I have a key to his apartment and I know where he keeps his little black address book. He was old-fashioned that way. I'll go by there tomorrow morning."

"I expect his place'll be a crime scene now and the address book will be impounded as evidence. The coroner said someone from Homicide will want to talk to you. You can ask him about it when he calls." Alice glanced over at her. "I'll drive you to the police station or anywhere else you need to go."

"Thanks." Faye leaned forward to peer out the windshield. "What's happening at your house, Al? I don't see any smoke or fire trucks."

"Oh, shit." Alice saw a few dozen people milling around in front of her garage. "What has Harry done now?"

"Looks like another truck took a wrong turn and jack-knifed."

Alice pulled into Faye's driveway which was upstream from what appeared to be a block party in progress. Someone's deck stereo was blasting sixties R & B. The centerpiece of the celebration was a beer company's refrigerated tanker truck. Beer trucks were a common sight in waterfront communities where crab feasts were annual events, but no such event was planned here on a Monday evening.

She turned the engine off. "Okay if I leave the Vette in your driveway?"

"Sure. It'll class-up the place." Still dazed with the shock of what she had seen, Faye went inside.

Alice wandered through the happy crowd to the source of merriment. The truck had rammed rear-end-first into that Humvee when the driver had tried to back and turn. Sitting on a tilt, it looked like a beached and wounded whale.

Alice stooped over to study the gash in the downhill side of the tilted truck. She didn't see how the wall could have breached the metal hull so easily. Beer splattered her as it gushed out, but it wasn't hitting the ground. A fifty-gallon trash can lined with a heavy-duty black plastic bag was catching it. Another one, already filled, stood nearby. Partiers were diligently lowering the level.

One of them must have already been drinking when the truck arrived. Holding up two large plastic cups, and enrapt by the magical rhythm of Bob Marley, he undulated toward her.

"Hey, Alice, how about a dance?"

"You're doing fine by yourself, Lenny." She started up her steps.

She wasn't surprised to find the TV on, but she didn't expect Harry to leave it tuned to the local newscast. She stared in horror at the footage, obviously shot earlier. It showed a pump-out truck, a convertible covered in sewage, and Joe Stone surrounded by EMTs.

Over the voice of the anchor came the "whup, whup" of a helicopter circling.

This had to be Syl's vengeance on Stone. She turned off the television. In the silence that followed she heard Harry's voice. He was practicing John Wayne this time.

You're welcome, little lady.

She didn't know if the "You're welcome" was for the free beer or the get-back visited on Stone, but it didn't matter. She had to end this and she had to do it before something lethal happened. The question was, how?

For some reason she remembered a line from the last verse of White Rabbit. "Remember what the Dormouse said."

What had the Dormouse said?

Sitting on the floor in front of the low bookcase, she leafed through her copy of Alice in Wonderland with the Tenniel illustrations until she found the tea party.

"They were learning to draw,' " the Dormouse went on, yawning and rubbing its eyes, for it was getting very sleepy; 'and they drew all manner of things–everything that begins with an M.'

'Why with an M?' said Alice.

'Why not?' said the March Hare.

Everything that begins with an M. That might not be the answer, but it was a place to start.

Chapter Forty-Four

"Lawn of the Living Dead"

Singularity is almost invariably a clue.
The more featureless and commonplace a crime is,
the more difficult it is to bring home.
Sir Arthur Conan Doyle (1859-1930)

Nick knew his colleagues referred to him as Old Stone Face. They never called him that to his old stone face, but he didn't mind the moniker. The tableau in Logan's neighbor's yard, however, defeated his ability to maintain composure. He slid back inside his cruiser, rolled up the window, and had the longest, loudest laugh in years. He was getting out of the car when Bernard Robertson, the unhappy homeowner, came boiling out his front door.

"That was quick!" Bernie double-timed down the front steps. "I just phoned in the complaint ten minutes ago." With his morning mug of coffee, he made a sweeping gesture that encompassed the zombie jamboree.

An assortment of skeletal gnomes seemed to rise from the grass. Some had staggered all the way out of their graves. Others were visible from the shoulders or waist up. All of them had bloody mouths, putrid green sagging plaster flesh, and hollow-eyed stares.

"Officer, that Brant bitch is a thief and a vandal. Make her return the yard art she stole and clean up this mess."

Nick focused on keeping a straight face. "This is not my jurisdiction, Mr. Robertson. Someone from crime investigation will be in touch with you."

Everyone at headquarters knew about Bernie and his feud with Logan's daughter. Nick imagined the CID unit drawing strips of shredded documents to see who got the ones with "Gnome Nut" written on them.

Bernie finally noticed that Nick had arrived in an unmarked car, and he wasn't wearing a uniform.

"Then why are you here?"

"I'm from homicide. I have a court-ordered subpoena for the footage you've been recording of your neighbor, Dr. Logan Brant."

In a flicker, Bernie's expression went from hunter to hunted. Nick could almost hear the collision and subsequent pile-up of fears. Was he a murder suspect? Would he be charged with stalking? Harassment? Invasion of privacy? Would he be written up in the newspaper's Police Beat as a peeping tom?

That might worry him the most. Joe Stone was writing under his own by-line now, but back when he was anonymous he had plagiarized his way into quite a following for the Police Beat.

If Sylvana Brant Gant had turned Bernie's yard into the Lawn of the Living Dead, she must have landed a starring role in his surveillance video. However, all of the foregoing possible misdemeanors would explain why Bernie never offered the video as evidence against her. That also might be what prompted him to take down the twin cameras when the police showed up to investigate the discoveries in Dr. Brant's septic pit. Nick was sure he would have noticed it that morning when Bernie was yelling about the sorry state of his "yard art."

Then again, maybe what turned Bernard shifty-eyed was an unrelated question. What scenes of a personal nature had he filmed?

Nathan pushed off from his desk and used his feet to roll his chair over to Nick's as he slid Bernie Robertson's SD card into his computer. Word had gotten out about the Gnome Nut's home video, and people wandered by as though they happened to be in the vicinity. By the time Bernie himself opened the show that had been shot inside his house, everyone in the station had gathered for his debut.

Bernie's attempt to recreate the dance bit in *Risky Business* didn't disappoint. In a rumpled white shirt, dirty crew socks, and baggy cotton briefs, he strutted and lip-synched to "Old Time Rock and Roll." The rear view of his satchel ass trying to bump and grind in the saggy briefs had everyone laughing too loudly to hear the music. When he threw himself on his back and kicked his hairy legs, the crotch shot made it clear his underwear hadn't been washed lately, if ever.

As a finale he pulled down his skivvies. Lifting his front shirttail and swiveling his hips forward he grasped his inconsequential dick in one hand and waved it at the camera. As everyone went back to their desks the reviews were loud and colorful.

Nick and Nathan were left to screen the remaining hours of Bernie's lawn at night, as well as the street and Logan's front yard. Whenever the camera's motion detector turned it on, the time and date glowed in small red letters at the lower right side of the frame.

Nick fast-forwarded through footage triggered by passing cars and the meanderings of deer and raccoons, foxes and cats. He hit "play" when August twenty-third appeared.

At 1:13a.m. a figure in camo shirt and pants and a baseball cap pulled low appeared carrying a shopping bag. He or she looked straight at the camera and gave a little wave. Whoever it was wore gloves and an Elvis mask.

"Gotta be Sylvana Gant," muttered Nathan. "Her house is full of Elvis stuff."

Nick never ruled out coincidence, but he too assumed Sylvana was the culprit. They watched her dress the gnomes in miniature bondage gear — push-up bra, corset, strap-on dildo, whip, and the leather mask that he had seen the next morning.

"Must've gotten all that on-line," said Nathan.

"Yeah, I checked."

That Nick was surprised there was a market for S&M doll clothes was a good sign. If something could surprise him the job hadn't completely jaded him yet.

An hour after Mrs. Gant left, another figure approached Logan's yard. He too carried a bag, but he was farther away, and his face was shaded by a baseball cap. Nick froze the frame where he passed Logan's mailbox and printed it out. They could measure the height of the mailbox and estimate how tall the intruder was.

"He looks short," said Nathan.

"Emanuel said his uncle Roy was short."

"What else did Hot Dog say about his uncle, the King of the Cowboys?"

"Nothing useful."

When the figure passed out of range the screen went dark. They waited for him to trigger it again, but the camera didn't come on until hours later when it filmed a pair of raccoons tumbling around in play among the gnomes.

"He must've left through the ravine."

"Hard to track him there."

"That could mean he's familiar with the neighborhood."

Nick fast-forwarded through almost a week's worth of film before he hit "play" again.

Nathan leaned closer. "Is that Alice Lewis and her neighbor, Faye? What kind of coincidence is that? Faye's ex-husband was the floater they found yesterday."

"A lot of coincidences in this neighborhood." Nick leaned in until he was shoulder to shoulder with Nathan. "What's Alice carrying?"

"Looks like a large freezer bag. And whatever's in it has a glow on."

They watched the two women drop the bag into Robertson's trash can. The bag's faint green glow radiated out of the can until Faye replaced the lid.

Nathan glanced over at Nick. "I told you something strange was going on in that neighborhood. And what was it Arthur Conan Doyle said about singularity?"

"That it's usually a clue. Everyday crimes of opportunity are harder to solve."

"This is the most singular case I've ever worked. And I walked a beat in Miami."

Len Smoot arrived in such a rush he almost overshot the desk. "You're not going to believe this about the Spitter."

Nick and Nathan glanced at each other, then at Len, and answered in unison. "Sure we will."

"I traced that anonymous complaint against Ms. Lewis. The one about the alligator."

Nick had a sudden feeling he knew where this was going. The premonition was accompanied by a churning sensation in the pit of his stomach.

"It was made from the phone in the custodian's office in the laundry room of the apartment building where Russell Wright lived."

"Oh shit." Nick whispered it.

"She's safe, Nick." Nathan put a hand on his shoulder. "They're not going to let this one out of jail."

"Shit." He whispered it again. "No wonder she seemed nervous when she answered the door."

Chapter Forty-Five

"Dead Broke"

There are more dead people than living,
and their numbers are increasing.
Eugene Ionesco (1909-1994)

Alice didn't know she knew where the county Potter's Field was. Over the years she had driven past the vacant lot with its rusting iron fence hundreds of times, but no headstones gave a clue to its purpose. Littered with trash, and surrounded by office buildings, it lay like an open sore at a busy intersection. Knee-high weeds obscured the low mounds that were the only signs of burials.

Alice parked behind the hybrid as Logan and Marjorie Mayhew got out of it. She didn't expect to see a crowd at Emanuel Hot Dog Boyd's send-off, and the gathering lived down to her expectations. So far Logan, Miss Marjorie, and herself were the only ones to show up, except for the two men who had dug the grave with the assistance of a back hoe.

One of them lounged on the mower that had cleared a narrow perimeter around the rectangular hole in the hard-packed soil. The other, chewing a blade of grass, sat the back hoe like a rodeo roper waiting for the chute to open.

As Alice, Logan, and Marjorie slogged through the tall weeds toward the mowed oasis, they kept an eye out for poison ivy. Marjorie carried a milk jug filled with water. Logan held a bouquet of flowers in a plastic vase against her chest.

"The brass ones disappear." Logan must have felt the cheap vase needed an explanation.

When Logan went to speak with the two men, Alice mused out loud. "I wonder if Potter's Field was named after someone called Potter."

"It was originally a field where potters dug their clay." Marjorie spoke in a low voice. Trashed and abandoned or not, this was still hallowed ground. "So it wasn't any good for planting crops. The Jewish priests and elders bought it with the thirty pieces of silver Judas Iscariot returned before he hanged himself."

Thirty pieces of silver. The image of Judas handing them to the head priest set the hair at the nape of Alice's neck to stirring.

" 'And they took counsel," Marjorie recited, "… and bought with them the potter's field to bury strangers in. Wherefore that the field was called Haceldama, the field of blood, unto this day.' Matthew. Chapter Three, verse eight."

Logan beckoned. As they walked over to her Marjorie said, "Esme sends regrets. She's working and Kenya is in school."

"She called to tell me," said Alice. "Faye called too. She'll try to make it. She's making arrangements for Kelly's funeral."

"Logan told me about Faye's husband. Such a tragedy."

Alice stopped with her toes a few inches from the rim of the grave and stared into the shallow hole. A narrow concrete box filled the bottom of it.

"So much for six feet under."

"There's a wooden coffin inside," said Logan, "but with a concrete container, four feet is deep enough."

Logan set the vase at one end of the grave and put the flowers in it. Marjorie filled it with water from the milk jug. The tears in their eyes didn't surprise Alice. They were grieving for the person Emanuel Boyd might have become, had the circumstances of his life been different.

"I didn't know what else to do." With a sweep of her hand Logan encompassed the bleak surroundings. "It costs so much to buy a plot in a cemetery and he would be just as alone there."

"He wouldn't be there at all, darlin.' " Marjorie put an arm around her shoulders. "And he's not here either."

"But wherever he is," said Alice, "...he'll know we wish him well."

A month ago she would have considered that thought to be nonsense. But if the Devil and his errand boy, Harry, were real, then angels, spirits, and God must exist too.

She stared at the rough gray slab of the cement box. *So where are you, Charlie? You don't write? You don't call? You don't visit?*

Logan seemed at a loss for words and Marjorie spoke up.

" 'Blessed are the poor in spirit: for theirs is the kingdom of heaven. Blessed are they that mourn: for they shall be comforted. Blessed are the meek: for they shall inherit the earth.'"

When Marjorie finished reciting all of the Beatitudes from the Sermon on the Mount, Logan gave a signal. The backhoe operator revved up his steed. Alice half expected him to attempt a wheelie on it. As he started herding dirt into the hole she thought, I doubt this is the inheritance of earth Jesus had in mind.

The two county workers were smoothing the excess dirt into a mound when Faye arrived.

"I'm sorry I'm late."

"That's okay, sweetheart," said Logan. "You didn't miss much. Now let's get something to eat. Some place with a bar. We all could use cheering up."

Logan and Marjorie discussed lunch venues with liquor licenses as they walked to the car. Alice put a hand on Faye's arm to slow her down so they lagged behind. She spoke barely above a whisper.

"We have to get rid of Harry and his boss."

"I know."

"Did you see the what happened to our least favorite reporter who's been hounding Logan and Syl?"

"The sewage spill? Yes, I did. I figure Syl's deal with the Devil caused it."

"Then there're Irene and Mattie, and Denise and goodness knows who else Syl's lured into this."

"We can't shoo him away with chanting and a sponge mop. We have to ask a priest to do a full-on exorcism. Maybe that won't affect Harry, but we'll burn that bridge when we come to it."

A priest. Alice hadn't been in a church in years and neither had Faye.

"Faye, do you remember the last two lines in "White Rabbit?"

"You mean this song?" Faye sang softly. " 'Remember what the dormouse said, Feed your head, feed you head.' What about it?"

"I looked up the tea party scene in Alice in Wonderland. What the dormouse said was that they drew everything that begins with an M." She recited, " 'Why with an M?' asked Alice. 'Why not?' said the March Hare.' "

"You think it's a message from Charlie?"

"He admired both of Carroll's *Alice* books. Used to quote from them. He kidded me about being the inspiration for them in a former life."

Faye and Alice looked at each other, then turned to stare at Marjorie's formidable back. Marjorie occupied a pew every Sunday in the Episcopal church started as a mission for freedmen a few years after the Civil War. Episcopalians had priests.

They hurried to catch up.

"Logan," said Alice. "Have you noticed anything different about Syl?"

"Now that you mention it, I have. She seems calmer these days. She's not cruising the bars every night. Maybe she's finally maturing." The hope in Logan's voice was audible. "They must have noticed it at the firm because they gave her a raise and a corner office. But she probably told you that."

While Logan was talking, Marjorie looked from Faye's face to Alice's. In a few seconds she read them.

"Alice, Faye, what's wrong?"

Since Alice had read what the dormouse said, she had been rehearsing what she would say to Marjorie Howard when she asked for her help. She was sure Esme had kept her promise and had not told anyone about Harry and Syl, not even her mother.

The time had come. Alice took a deep breath.

"Miss Marjorie, you're not going to believe this."

Chapter Forty-Six

Come into My Parlour

Laws are like spiders' webs:
if some poor weak creature comes up against them,
it is caught;
but a bigger one can break through and get away.
Solon (circa 630-555 B.C.)

The third floor window in the office building's stairwell gave the best view of the county's solution to its broke dead disposal problem. With forearms and ankles crossed, Nick leaned against the sill. He was watching the three women watching the back hoe shove topsoil into Emanuel Boyd's grave.

He had little-to-no expectation that Hot Dog Boyd's mysterious uncle, Roy Rogers, would show up. He also suspected the tell-tale heart in the fast food container had belonged to the elderly Mrs. Mary Rogers who, his friend Will assured him, had died of natural causes. When the DNA confirmed no one was murdered to obtain the heart, this would no longer be a case for Homicide. But Nick didn't like to leave a case once he started it.

Besides, Joe Stone had identified the heart as human in his front page series of articles about the bad blood between developers and environmentalists. That's when it became a homicide in the court of public opinion. It was the macabre sort of detail the general public got off on. The newspaper had sold out of that edition, and the same general public assumed a murder had been committed, and worse.

People still called the station about it. Not one of them had any useful information to add. Most of them wanted to know how to protect themselves against the Satanist cult that was preying on Christians. Some of them wanted to report satanic activity in their neighborhoods. Nick and Nathan had to follow up on those, and all of them had proven to be simple hostility between neighbors.

A few wanted confirmation that the heart in a septic tank hole was left by Mid-East terrorists. Others shouted their views on the only Road to Salvation and the Threat of the Anti-Christ in America. Sheila said they were the worst.

Sheila imperiled her immortal soul by following the instructions to lie. It was only a pig's heart, she told them. An easy mistake to make, she added. And that part, at least, was true. A pig's ticker and a human one were similar in size, function, and anatomy.

"In fact," Sheila told the callers, "they're so similar that pigs' hearts are used in medical schools to teach anatomy students about our own hearts."

Sheila said she didn't mind lying for a good cause. What depressed her was how often she had to define "Anatomy."

As irritating as the phone inquiries were, Nick wished they'd received more of them. The callers made up a small percentage of the tens of thousands of people who'd read Stone's account or had heard about it. The story was picked up by the Baltimore and Washington newspapers and some in surrounding states. Stone circulated a rumor that producers of a national TV exposé show were interested.

Stone had always been a minor nuisance at precinct headquarters. After his exposé came out, warnings blew like a draft through the building when he entered the front door. As word of his presence spread, uniforms and civilian staff alike found places to hide.

No one wanted to listen to Stone brag, again, that he had been nominated for a Pulitzer Prize. He was oblivious of the fact that claiming to be a Pulitzer nominee lowered the general estimation of him even more. Most journalists, plus Nick and now everyone in the precinct, knew that all it took to be nominated for a Pulitzer was fifty dollars and an entry form.

The Chief had convinced the newspaper's editor to print a correction about the human heart. Stone, however, worded it to imply that the police were conspiring to silence investigative journalists. Not that it mattered. When the small-print "Oops" appeared few readers noticed.

The news that the sewage truck had dumped its load on Stone had the whole department laughing, but Nick had witnessed the horrific scene. He knew there was nothing funny about it and he wished he could feel sorrier for the guy.

Standing watch now at the stairwell window, Nick saw Faye Clark cross the weed-grown lot below. After a short conversation with the other three women, they all went back to their cars. As they drove away he started down the stairs with his brain in gear.

Faye, the Red Eye's bartender with the magenta Mohawk, was friends with Alice Lewis. Alice. Al. Because of the recent discovery of Faye's ex-husband's body, he now knew she and Alice were next door neighbors.

Alice must have been on the other end of that telephone conversation he had overheard at the bar a couple weeks ago. He replayed Faye's side of it and the questions remained. Who preferred enclosed spaces and why should Al take refuge from them? Did Faye's advice have something to do with Russell Wright?

Nathan was waiting for him in the building's lobby and walked with him to the Crown Vic. Nick put the key in the ignition but didn't turn it. This was a secure place to talk.

"Anyone suspicious show up for the send-off?" Nathan asked.

"Only the usual non-suspects."

"We got the dump from Russell Wright's phone. Lots of calls and texts to Kelly Harris shortly before he disappeared. Or should I say 'she'? I guess it doesn't matter now, but Wright sounded like he thought he was talking to a woman." Nathan paused. "Well, anyway, Wright's last message arranged to meet Harris on his boat."

LUCIA ST. CLAIR ROBSON

"His ex-wife will know where that's docked." Nick closed his eyes, as if to shut out this latest messenger-of-death assignment. "Faye Clark was here with Ms. Lewis, Dr. Brant, and your future mother-in-law."

"I figured you'd appreciate having someone else along when you give Ms. Clark the news about Wright being the murderer. That's why I asked Len to drop me off. Two more units would create a stir in that neighborhood anyway."

"Cliffs of the Severn has had its share of cop cars lately." Nick turned the key in the ignition and pulled into mid-week traffic.

"Remember I said a while ago that I thought Esme might be hiding something to protect someone?" said Nathan. "I have a hunch she's protecting Alice."

"Why?"

"Just a feeling. Alice Lewis is Esme's best friend."

"If anyone's done something wrong it's Sylvana Gant."

Nathan chuckled. "I heard about her latest escapade with Bernie's trolls."

"Gnomes."

"Gnomes, trolls, dwarfs, whatever."

"They're for sale in black, you know. Gnomies, the Homies." Nick pretended to focus on the traffic.

Nathan pretended he hadn't heard him. "Have you contacted Ms. Lewis about a security assessment of her house?"

"I'm going to suggest it to her today."

"So you still haven't been inside her house."

"Not yet."

"Maybe she does have an alligator in there."

Nick could imagine Alice Lewis having an alligator for a pet. "Len Smoot said they didn't find one, but something scared Wright away."

"Why don't you ask her?" Nathan glanced out the window then back at Nick. "Don't bother answering that."

He didn't have to elaborate. They both had talked about the problem of mixing police business with a love life. And it was quite clear to Nathan that his partner was in love.

He changed the subject. "Let's get something to eat. I'm in the mood for barbecue."

"I need to go by Hare's office first and ask some more questions. He has a quote from Faust on his wall, by the way. 'With the Prince of Darkness I have gambled at dice.' "

"I'll bet a week's pay he's behind all this."

"I still think he's being set up."

"By that Roy Rogers guy? What stake could he have in it?"

"I wish I knew. I'll ask Hare if he knows Rogers. The prints on that newspaper didn't match any in the data base."

"There are thousands of developers like Hare busily buying off politicians in south Florida."

"Maryland isn't south Florida."

Nathan's grunt registered as disagreement. "What is it you said about laws and spider webs?"

"Spider webs, like laws, catch the weak while the bigger ones get away."

"Yeah. Some things never change. Which reminds me, I'm still hungry."

"I bought some bananas. They're in the bag on the back seat."

"Bananas?"

"A good source of potassium."

Nathan grumbled about fruit being no substitute for real food unless the barbecue sauce included mango. He retrieved the paper bag and opened it.

"Oh man!" He rolled the top of the bag shut. "Pull over!"

"What?"

"Pull over. Now!"

Nick steered into a gas station. Nathan opened the door and set the bag on the asphalt.

"Pop the trunk."

Nick didn't ask why. Nathan hustled to the rear of the car and returned with a plastic zippered evidence bag from Nick's stash. He shoved the paper bag inside and sealed it shut. He returned it to the trunk and closed the lid.

He sat back down in the passenger seat and Nick waited for an explanation.

"Spiders."

"I hadn't figured you to be afraid of spiders."

"These are Brazilian wandering spiders."

Nick waited for the punch line.

"I saw photographs of them when I worked in Miami. A woman noticed a white blotch on one of the bananas she had just bought. Turned out to be an egg case. Dozens of spiders hatched and scattered all across the table, in the rug, on the chairs. The family had to abandon the house."

"Why didn't they call an exterminator?"

"These things need the Terminator. They're the most poisonous spiders on the planet. Where'd you buy them?"

"The supermarket at the turn into the Cliffs. I pass it on the way to the station every morning."

"We'd better stop at that store and tell the management about this."

"We should warn Faye Clark, Dr. Brant, Esme, and Alice."

Nathan wasn't fooled. The spiders provided a good excuse for Nick to see Ms. Lewis again. "Alice? On a first name basis are we?"

CHAPTER FORTY-SEVEN

"PEST CONTROL"

You got to be careful if you
don't know where you're going,
because you might not get there.
Lawrence Peter Berra, aka Yogi Berra

When Alice opened Faye's front door, a zephyr of Navajo flute music greeted her. So did a gust of cold air. The mercury marked eighty-five degrees this fourth afternoon of September, but Alice had brought a sweater. Faye claimed she had been a Malamute in a former life and kept the air-con set at sixty-five degrees.

For Alice, walking next door was like visiting a foreign country. Faye's décor was more sixteenth-century Turkish seraglio than mid-Atlantic suburb. Brocade curtains sagged under their own weight and candles lit the permanent twilight they produced. Tapestries covered the walls. Religious icons, primitive artifacts, and fetish figures hung from them. Travel and movie posters papered the ceiling. In an alcove a jungle of plants and vines glistened in the warm glow of fluorescent grow-lights and an occasional fine spray of water from a mister.

Alice liked to visit Faye's house precisely because it was so different from her own. She knew about the problems there, but as with travel to a foreign country, they weren't her problems. Yes, Faye's furniture glowed and Alice caught glimpses of salamander elementals hovering around the candles. Sylphs occupied the air conditioning vents and earth elementals kept up their low hum among the plants. Water sprites bobbed about in the small fountain in the foyer, but Alice didn't feel the same familiarity with any of them as she did with her own.

Alice already had had a run-in with the purple demon that lived behind the bin of sunflower seeds in Faye's pantry. Warty as a cobblestone road and big as a badger, it had stubby red horns and a bad attitude. Faye's pantry hobgoblin sported a perpetual scowl whereas Alice's furnace-closet demon always looked apprehensive and woebegone. And he liked her chocolate chip cookies.

Alice had to smile. Life had indeed taken the strangest of turns when she preferred her own demon to her neighbor's.

"It's five o'clock somewhere." Faye handed her a frozen margarita. She glanced at the bulging manila folder in Alice's hand. "Been printing out wild-eyed speculation from the internet again, Al?"

"There might be something useful in all this nonsense."

"I suppose. And we need all the help we can get." Faye sank back into the soft foothills of pillows on her over-sized couch. She propped her bare feet on a big wicker steamer trunk with a wayfaring past.

"I think Miss Marjorie is our best hope." Alice sat on the edge of the couch with the folder on her knees. "When I dropped her off I asked her if you and I could meet her somewhere away from home and give her the details of what's been going on."

"Good idea. We don't want to introduce Harry to her house."

Alice flipped absent-mindedly through the print-outs in the folder. "No surprise that Logan pooh-poohs the whole notion."

The phone rang and Faye let it go to message.

Alice didn't expect to hear Elvis crooning "Are you lonely tonight, do you miss me tonight? Are you sorry we drifted apart?"

"It was cute at first." Faye hit "Erase."

"I thought you'd broken up with him. It? Them?"

"Trying to. For me he looks like the blind angel in *Barbarella*. Sapphire-blue eyes, that long, wavy, white-blond hair, perfect body. It all seemed harmless when it started. That's why I mentioned it, as an amusing anecdote, you know, like my bar stories. Then Syl got involved and upped the ante."

"So how did you get rid of Harry?"

"Obviously I haven't." Faye nodded at the phone. "A lot of our neighbors are getting calls from him too. They think the telemarketers have gone porno."

"That's ridiculous."

"Is it? Telemarketers are a lot like incubi. Too stupid and persistent and duplicitous to go away."

"Why don't you have caller ID?"

Faye shrugged. "What would Hell's number be?"

"Harry's still hanging around my house, but I haven't gotten any phone calls from him."

"Maybe that's because Charlie's voice is still on your machine."

"Marjorie said to let her know where we want to meet. She says she'll talk to her priest after she's heard the whole story." She finished the margarita and stood up. "I've got to try to get some work done."

"You can't possibly make your deadline, Al. What're you going to tell your editor when you blow through it?"

"I'm considering the truth as an option. I'll bet this is one excuse he hasn't heard before." She paused. "Or maybe he has."

Faye walked with her to the scraggly hedge that didn't so much divide their yards as unite them. They stopped at the widest gap in it, as if reluctant to part with the comfort and reassurance they gave each other.

"You know we'll be opening an even bigger can of worms by taking on the Devil." Faye glanced at the folder containing print-outs of speculation, supposition, and popular delusion. "Plus, it's hard to know which route to take when all the roadmaps are imaginary and contradict each other."

"We can't go on like this. Irene and Mattie have been leaving phone messages begging me to do something about the fix they got themselves into. They say the stench from men is so bad now they can't leave home without masks on. People avoid them like they're plague carriers. Mattie's been fired from her job, which might mean she hasn't signed on. The only way to get the gold-plated, sweet-smelling deal Syl has is to put her autograph on the Devil's dotted line."

Faye sighed. "I hope Miss Marjorie can help us." As she walked back to her own house she sang a passable impersonation of Grace Slick.

One pill makes you larger,
And one pill makes you small.
And the ones that mother gives you
Don't do anything at all.
Go ask Alice when she's ten feet tall.

The warmth of Alice's own house was a relief after the meat locker temperature in Faye's. As usual the TV was on and broadcasting a channel she never watched. Today Harry had left a mega-church preacher in full cry. Reverend Leroy was promising God's bounty of prosperity on earth for each of the 10,000 faithful in the amphitheater. Now, however, she could see the real creature in the pulpit. The word mammon merely meant wealth in Hebrew, but its proselytizing mouthpiece was a horror.

Reverend Leroy's mane of white hair was elaborately coiffed, his designer suit deftly tailored. Instead of fingers, six aortal-red talons emerged from his crisp white cuffs. A basketball-sized head, the color and texture of an unpeeled beet, rose above the open collar of its starched white shirt. Six huge, curly black horns parted the cadaver-white bouffant. Fangs as big as beer openers adorned a mouth that stretched from ear to ear.

As she reached for the remote to change the channel and turn off the TV she heard Harry's laugh from the kitchen.

"Yeah, yeah," she muttered. "Very funny. As if I didn't already know that greedy hypocrite is evil."

She assumed if she had an air conditioner installed and lowered the thermostat enough to require a sweater, Harry might not find the place so appealing. Faye said she was being stubborn to hold out, but she wasn't going to surrender. Not to Harry or his boss.

She gathered her damp hair into a ponytail, sat down at her desk, and opened the file with the chapter-in-progress. She'd only added a couple sentences when she felt the familiar breath, with a hot whiff of sulfur, stir the short hairs on her nape. Still reading back over what she'd written she picked up the fly swatter lying next to her monitor and gave it a whip-flick of the wrist behind her head. She knew the swatter didn't hurt Harry, but at least it confused him enough to stop bothering her for awhile. Harry was easily confused.

Chapter Forty-Eight

"Tread Lightly"

*It takes more love to share the saddle
than it does to share the bed.*
(unknown)

Alice Lewis and Brazil's wandering spider were distracting Nick from the task at hand. He had had a talk with the supermarket's produce manager about the deadly bonus in the bag of bananas. He wanted to go straight from there to Alice's house in case she already had bought some, but the weather report predicted clouds and a possible rain storm this afternoon. That made this visit to Dr. Logan Brant's abyss of a backyard a priority. It was a wild goose chase he hadn't even mentioned to Nathan for fear his partner would say he was crazy.

On a sunny afternoon, the light was dim in the densely wooded ravine behind Logan's house. Nick hunkered on a soggy carpet of dead leaves below vine-covered logs, fallen limbs, and cushions of moss. With thumb and forefinger he lifted a trio of large tulip tree leaves and shined his flashlight on the rest of the partial three dimensional shoe impression that had caught his eye. Deadly spiders and even the fair Alice were put on hold.

Sometimes the most improbable of possibilities occur.

Any kind of track was improbable in this forest litter. Maybe a foraging opossum or raccoon had exposed this small area of loam that captured part of a shoe print. These three leaves had formed an umbrella before yesterday's drizzle filtered through the trees' canopy.

Nick had seen a lot of shoe prints in his career. On the rare occasions he strayed into a store with a footwear department he headed for the racks. Oblivious to stares from staff and customers, he turned over examples of every model and studied the treads and brand names. Now he shuffled through his mental inventory for this sole's make.

He remembered the high-end sporting goods store where he had seen it. At the time, he had wondered if a prospective buyer would want this absurdly high-tech hiking shoe for climbing mountains, or for duping people into thinking he did.

He mixed dental gypsum with water from the thermos he had brought.

Cock-eyed optimism, he thought, *is bringing a casting kit two weeks late to a crime scene that's already been thoroughly swept.* Or almost thoroughly.

It had been easy to assume this wasn't an inviting exit route. Rumor had it that a pack of coyotes and an errant mountain lion had been spotted down here. Everyone assumed the perpetrator had left by the street side. Not even a felon would want to slog through this vine-tangled badland in the middle of the night.

Then Bernie the Gnome Nut's footage surfaced. Nick had played it several times. It didn't show the suspect leaving the scene.

As a rule, he didn't play the "what if" game, but while he waited for the dental stone to dry, he indulged in it. What if a heavy rain had fallen instead of a mist? What if these leaves hadn't fluttered down from a hundred feet up and settled on this exact spot? What if Sylvana Gant hadn't messed with a neighbor's precious yard art? What if Bernie hadn't pointed a camera at Dr. Brant's property? What if Alice Lewis hadn't mentioned Bernie's voyeuristic proclivities?

Alice Lewis. Nick smiled. He would see her as soon as he finished here. He decided not to call her first. She didn't strike him as the call-ahead type, and this wasn't an official visit. Besides, taking a chance she would be home appealed to his flirtation with the notion of kismet.

❧ ❧ ❧

When Nick knocked, he noticed that the solid front door was open. Only the screen door separated the outside from the inside. When Alice opened it Nick saw it was unlocked too. A serial killer had almost made mincemeat of her and she still left her doors unlocked. This visit was more important than he had thought.

"Miss Lewis…"

"Alice."

"Alice, I want to warn you about a possibly dangerous situation at the Buy Fresh." He followed her inside.

"Have a seat, Detective… Nick. I'll get the ice tea."

From a rattan chair on the sun porch Nick surveyed the living room. It radiated a feeling of serenity and comfort and a lingering fragrance of freshly-baked cookies. The furniture was mismatched, scarred, and worn. Artwork hung on every wall.

He was aware of an almost undetectable shimmer from the furniture. He had, on rare occasions, seen auras around people before, but never from a sofa. The faint susurrus of crickets in the nearby house plants raised goose bumps on his arms. The ceiling fan shimmered with a faint blue haze as it circled lazily.

Alice handed him a tall glass of iced tea and set a plate of cookies on the end table. "What's the situation at the Buy Fresh?"

With her long legs stretched out, ankles crossed, she settled into a chair across from him. To a casual observer she would have looked at ease, but Nick detected tension in the muscles around her mouth and eyes.

"I bought a bunch of bananas there today, but I didn't notice the white spots on them. They turned out to be spider egg cases."

"I don't mind spiders, but I don't want them in my cereal. I'll check the produce carefully. Thanks for the warning."

"They're called Brazilian wandering spiders. Their bite can be lethal."

"Good grief, Nick. Did they get into your car?"

"No. My partner caught them in time."

"I'll be careful. Thank you for telling me."

"I spoke to the store's produce manager. He said he'd take care of it."

"Our neighborhood has an email message system. I'll let them know."

Nick was trying to come up with a diplomatic way to give her the news about Faye Clark's husband's murderer when she made it easy for him.

"My friend Faye told me you called her a little while ago. She said you told her Russell Wright is a suspect."

"We don't have hard evidence yet, but their phone records indicate that."

"I went to the morgue with Faye when she had to identify Kelly's clothes." Alice pulled her feet up under her and clenched her hands. "Well, Faye's clothes, really."

Nick had seen the remains at the morgue. They were enough to shake anyone. Alice must know she had come close to ending up on one of those slabs. He almost asked about Wright and the mysterious alligator, but her experience at the morgue obviously had upset her more than enough already. She looked so stricken he wanted to put an arm around her. Instead, he sat forward in his chair and rested his forearms on his thighs.

"Would you show me around your house? I'd like to do a security check. It won't take long, but if this isn't a good time, we could schedule it for another day."

"But Russell is in jail." Her stare was steady. "Isn't he?"

So, she had guessed the real reason for his visit. And she'd probably guessed it right away.

"He is. But home intrusions are always a threat."

She took a couple extra seconds before saying, "I'll show you around."

Nick noted the delay. *Don't be so suspicious, Shea. Maybe the bed isn't made.*

As he followed her he made notes of vulnerable windows and doors in the basement and on the first floor. The second floor was sunlit and neat. The queen-sized bed's navy-blue coverlet lacked that avalanche of frilly pillows deemed essential in decorating magazines. Two pairs of pillows in white cotton cases were propped up against the headboard. They suggested that reading in bed was a habit here. The image of reading next to Alice late at night had a stronger affect on him than the bed itself.

They returned to the first floor and Alice went back to the kitchen to refill the glasses with tea while Nick checked out her office.

So this is where she keeps the clutter.

Book cases filled two walls. File folders, newspaper clippings, and scraps of paper covered with scribbled notes covered every horizontal surface. He made a mental note of everything, but he stood for at least a minute, staring at the large framed photo of the man whose death had brought him here before. He could have searched the internet for details and images of the guy on the gurney that night, but it seemed a breach of privacy.

The world was full of big, handsome guys. He stared at this one, looking for clues as to why she had picked him. Even in a photo they weren't hard to find. Charisma can create a third dimension in a two-dimensional format.

Alice had given him permission to check her computer. He turned away from the photo and brought up the screensaver and stood entranced by the video of a seahorse courting his mate. No matter how often he witnessed this sensuous ballet at the Aquarium it always affected him. The two graceful, delicate creatures, their bodies entwined, were close to the finale when Alice arrived. She stood next to him, her elbow barely brushing his.

"I've seen them do this." She spoke softly, as if reluctant to disturb them. "At the Aquarium in Baltimore."

"Do you go there often?"

"I've been a couple times. You know how it is. Life gets in the way."

"Would you like to go with me some day? I'm a volunteer. I can show you the off-limits areas."

"You've one of the divers?"

"Yes. I'm not scheduled to feed the critters this Sunday, so I can show you around.

"I'd like that."

"I won't be interrupting your work?"

"It'll be a welcome interruption." She hesitated. "Could we go on your motorcycle?"

"Sure." He said it with no hesitation, even though he had never let anyone share the Indian's saddle. "I'll pick you up at eight o'clock Sunday morning."

On his way out Nick handed Alice a list of companies that sold alarm systems. "I can't recommend any particular one, but I can make suggestions."

"Thank you." Alice folded it and added it to the pile of mail on the narrow table by the door.

"You aren't going to install an alarm system, are you."

"I'll put it on the to-do list."

"And you'll lock the doors?"

"I'll try to remember."

Nick knew from now on he would drive past two houses on his way home.

Chapter Forty-Nine

"The Kiss of the Sun"

The Devil is an ass
Ben Jonson (1572-1637)

The early September breeze and dappled sunlight felt good on Alice's skin. Birds warbled over the crickets' incessant percussion. A few last-call hummingbirds sipped from the nearby cardinal flowers. A huge oak shaded the child-sized playhouse built with books as bricks.

This lovely garden behind Alice's favorite book store was the perfect place to gather. The whir of hummingbird wings, the crickets, bird chorus, and warm sun should have soothed the jangle in her nervous system. Instead, she had a gut-wrenching fear she had made a terrible mistake inviting her friends to meet her here. Patio tables graced the open area among the ancient trees and the colorful riot in the flower beds. Alice, Faye, Logan, Marjorie, and Esme sat around one of them.

While Faye told their friends what Syl had been up to, Alice tried not to fidget, but her hand trembled when she picked up her tea cup. What if diabolism were like a contagious virus? What if she and Faye were now carriers of it? What if their presence here exposed her friend Mary and her bookstore to hell, Harry, and the Devil?

She knew what Charlie would say. "Don't ask what if. Enjoy what is."

When Faye finished her account of Harry and the demons, Logan said, "I know you're not a liar or a prankster, Faye, but this is all very hard to believe."

Faye looked over at Alice. "Tell them, Al."

"He showed up in my yard while I was sitting by the pond. "

"Who?" asked Logan. "Harry?"

"No. Harry watches TV at my place, but the creature in the lawn chair was his boss."

"Alice Lewis, are you claiming the Devil visited you?"

"If you and Faye think this is funny, kiddo, you're wrong."

"I wish I were joking, Logan."

Marjorie's smile was reassuring. "What did he look like, Alice?

"James Coburn."

"Our Man Flint, Waterhole Three, or The Magnificent Seven?"

"Flint."

"What was his pitch?"

"He said there's nothing that is not God. Ergo he is God."

"Standard premise. What did he promise you in exchange for your soul?"

"Number one best seller, and…" Alice whispered the next word. "Charlie."

"Or an unreasonable facsimile."

"I didn't fall for it. I told him I might be a mere mortal, but I recognized bullshit even when it was wearing Ralph-Lauren-lite. I told him to put an egg in his shoe and beat it. And not to leave any brimstone littering the patio."

Marjorie laughed out loud, but Esme leaned forward. She spoke in a low voice, as though the Devil were eavesdropping.

"You told the Prince of Darkness to put an egg in his shoe and beat it?"

"It's what Charlie would've said, Es. And I wasn't going to cower or grovel." But Alice's tea cup rattled as she set it back on the saucer.

"Did he leave?" Esme asked.

"Yes."

"How? Did he disappear in a clap of thunder? A burst of flame?"

"He walked down the steps and strolled toward the beach. Look, I won't blame you if you think we're crazy. But we have to get Syl out of this contract."

Logan did something totally out of character. She started to cry, silently, tears running down her cheeks. Marjorie put an arm around her shoulder.

"Don't worry, Logan. We'll fix this." She grinned at Alice. "Did you hear the one about the dyslexic devil worshipper?" Her perfect comedic pause must have resulted from all that time in classrooms. "He sold his soul to Santa."

Alice laughed so hard she sprayed tea on the table. Esme was not amused.

"Mama, how can you joke about…you know… Evil Incarnate?"

"Alice has the right idea, child. If he's so intent on making a deal with her, that means he can't get her soul without her consent. Nowadays, the Devil isn't trending, as they say. Science has side-lined him. Hundreds of years ago he got credit for floods and plagues, storms, and indigestion, but we know what causes those now."

"Marjorie has a point," said Faye. "Other than preachers in some hard-core churches, who even mentions him these days?"

"Are you all kidding me?" All the harassment Logan had endured so far hadn't rattled her this much. "Twenty minutes ago I would have said hell and the Devil were nonsense. But Alice talked to him. And Faye says my daughter has signed away her soul."

"That's my point, Logan," said Marjorie. "Old Scratch is going door-to-door selling corner offices, executive parking spaces, and fantasy sex like magazine subscriptions. And he's doing it in the guise of an actor who hasn't starred in a first-run movie since the eighties. Instead of an Auroch's horns and wings as big as bed sheets, he picked the celebrity equivalent of MySpace. Or worse… a chat room."

Alice muttered, "But a damned sexy celebrity."

Esme got back to the main point. "Then maybe whatever Syl thinks she signed is bogus."

"Oh, Satan's real, alright, child," said Marjorie. "And that contract probably is too."

"What should we do?" asked Faye. "How do we get her out of it?"

"He has superhuman powers, but he's not omnipotent. I'll talk to my priest about it. I'm sure he'll want to see you and Faye too, Alice."

"But what about Harry? They say incubi are too stupid for exorcism and I want him out of my house."

"We'll deal with the faucet leak after we fix the water main."

"Syl will never agree." Worries still nagged Alice. "We'd have to stage an exorcism intervention. I'd rather deal with the Devil than Syl. No offense, Logan."

"None taken."

"Alice is right about Syl," said Faye. "Does your priest make house calls, or do we have to slip Syl a mickey, tie her up, and lug her into the church? Because that's the only way we'll get her there."

"We could invite her here." The graceful wave of Marjorie's arm encompassed the beauty around them.

"Do you think it's wise to put Mary and her garden in jeopardy?"

"I've known Mary a long time. She'll be okay with it. In fact, I suspect she'll be intrigued."

" 'The kiss of the sun for pardon…'" Esme recited. "… 'the song of the birds for mirth, one is nearer God's heart in a garden, than anywhere else on earth.'"

Alice didn't voice her doubts, but she was certain Syl would never go along with this plan.

Chapter Fifty

"Dead Letter Office"

The postman is the agent of impolite surprises.
Nietzsche (1844-1900)
Human, All-Too-Human: A Book for Free Spirits

Nick was already on his way to have another chat with Samuel Hare when the call came. He turned on the flashers and siren, but he still had to park a few blocks from Hare's development company offices. The area swarmed with police cars, fire trucks, ambulances, and haz-mat vans.

As Nick approached the yellow crime scene tape, Corporal Smoot held out a half-face respirator.

"If you're going in you'll need this, Detective Shea."

"Have they found any dead bodies inside?"

"No, sir."

"Then I'll let you know if I need it."

Nick had already spotted Sam Hare standing apart from the huddle of Longview Development employees. Hare held a half-empty bottle of very expensive scotch sandwiched between his arm and ribs while he hunched over his phone.

When the apocalypse comes, people will be texting each other and drinking.

"Mr. Hare."

Hare held a finger up as a signal to wait until he finished.

Nick said it twice more before Hare stopped poking at the keypad with his thumbs and looked up.

"Detective Shea. Thank goodness you're here." He flipped the phone closed with an authoritative snap, but held it in his hand.

276

"That Brant woman and her tree hugging thugs are trying to kill me."

"I hear you received a suspicious letter." The dispatcher had filled Nick in.

"Yes. It was addressed to me."

"No return address, I assume."

"Just 'Save the Elfin Skimmer,' whatever that means. Probably some code for Brant and her gang of vandals. The mailroom clerk felt something grainy inside and called 911. The envelope had Bacillus anthra-something written on the back."

"Bacillus anthracis. Anthrax."

"Right! You have to arrest them immediately."

No, I don't. Nick knew why he disliked Hare. He dealt with a lot of low-lifes, but few of them had a superiority complex this size.

"It's probably a hoax, Mr. Hare. The perpetrator will be arrested when we have proof of guilt."

Over the years Nick had responded to a lot of anthrax hoaxes. They were easy and cheap and caused the maximum cost, disruption, waste of first-responders' time, and emotional distress. A tablespoon of baking soda in an envelope was the perfect gotcha for people who derived a high from delusions of power.

Nick knew Hare had zero interest in knowing anything more about anthrax than that it could kill him, but he gave him a brief history anyway, just to annoy him. The zinger at the end of the lecture would be sweet payback.

"Anthrax is a disease of sheep, cattle, horses, and camels. That's why it's called the Woolsorters' or Ragpickers' disease. Inhalation anthrax is highly contagious and it can be contracted from imported wool or hair. You might want to dispose of the horse hair shaving brush in your office."

"I have a camel hair coat. What should I do about that?"

Nick shrugged. "Call precinct headquarters and ask to speak to someone from the bio-hazard squad. They can advise you."

"What's the number?" Hare flipped open his phone.

Nick pretended not to hear him and ducked under the crime tape. From the corner of his eye, he noticed Joe Stone. Since Stone had bought the vintage Mustang he had adopted the mid-'60's button-down look. He had replaced his high-end, ace-reporter sneakers with penny loafers, and the loafers' occupant was scuttling his way. The sight of him re-ran the image of the shit-filled Mustang and the pump-out truck. Stone probably had spent hours in the shower since then, but Nick could sense the stench hovering around him like a ghostly aura.

He gave Hare a nod-off from the other side of the tape and accepted the respirator from Len Smoot. As he walked into the building he pretended he didn't hear Stone call to him. He was busy anyway, looking up photos of the Elfin Skimmer on his own phone. It was a delicate creation, the smallest of the dragonfly species. Its wetland habitats were fast disappearing under concrete, asphalt, and landscaping.

Aliens in bright yellow coveralls, booties, and nitrile gloves swarmed in the mailroom. One of them noticed Nick in the doorway. In defiance of HAZWOPER, the Hazardous Waste Operations and Emergency Response standard, Mick took off the hood with the full-face. He held up the plastic bag.

"Damnedest thing, Shea." His face glistened with sweat.

Nick took a closer look. "Are those cremains?"

"Yeah. Could be a decoy, so we'll be doing a sweep for the next couple days."

"Did they lift prints off the envelope?"

"No."

"Thanks." He nodded and turned to go. Ashes were useless as DNA evidence.

"Shea." Mick called after him. "We just got another call."

Nick turned around. "Where?"

"Law offices."

Nick was pretty sure he knew the answer but he asked anyway. "Whose?"

"Powell, Huddle, and Gant, over on Skipjack Street. The letter was addressed to Jerome Gant."

"Thanks. I'll head over there."

Nick didn't think Dr. Brant would pull an anthrax hoax, although her followers might, so he wasn't discounting them. But given Sylvana Gant's penchant for vindictive pranks, she was on the list of suspects.

Thoreau was right about circumstantial evidence. If there's a trout in the milk, it's probably been watered.

Chapter Fifty-One

"Syl Glimpses the Abyss"

Curses are like young chickens,
they always come home to roost.
Robert Southey (1774-1843)

Sharing the details of Syl's folly with Logan, Esme, and her mother had taken the edge off Alice's anxiety. Plus, the inevitable intervention with Syl could be postponed until Marjorie Mayhew consulted with a priest. When the show-down did come, having Miss Marjorie in the posse would be a significant comfort.

Alice knew the feeling of relief had an expiration date, so she savored it before it went sour. While she waited for her old computer to boot up she intertwined her fingers behind her head and rocked back in her desk chair. She took a gut-sucking breath, closed her eyes, and exhaled a gust of tension-laced CO2.

She hadn't known Syl long but in spite of everything she liked her. She sensed a lonely desperation under her friend's bravado. And Syl was loyal in her own way. Before Harry and his Handler showed up she was the friend to have in a bar-brawl or a greased watermelon race.

Thwarting her, however, invited consequences. Dead opossums in the air-conditioning ducts and genital warts for her unfortunate ex-husband for example. And that raw sewage dumped in Joe Stone's Mustang convertible. As irritating as Stone was, Alice was sure the Devil wouldn't have done that without Syl holding him to his bargain. That started her wondering exactly what clauses a contract for the sale of a soul included. She typed "exorcism" in the search box.

She discovered that like everything else on the internet, exorcism had become a commodity. *God's Miracle* website was the most blatant example. It asked visitors if they were experiencing any of a long list of symptoms —unexplained events, obsessions, sinful behavior, alarming computer pop-ups, unusual illness, spells and curses, deviant sexual cravings, and/or chronic bad luck. The symptoms sounded like life as usual to Alice. But wait… *God's Miracle* workers had the cure for all of them.

For $9.99, plus the $7.00 shipping and handling, Alice could receive her very own miracle-maker, an anointed prayer cloth that would free her from powerful evil spirits. For a mere $14.99, she could have the entire Miracle Pack including the anointed cloth, protective "thermoplastic" wristband, and the Prayer of God's Everlasting Power. She resisted the temptation to add "You're a bunch of crooks" to the testimonials.

Information on other exorcism sites wasn't so upbeat. Success was a sometime thing and few priests would do them. Alice hoped Miss Marjorie's priest was the exception, but she couldn't blame him if he refused.

By the time the printer shuddered to a stop, the out-flow of paper had spilled onto the carpet. Alice pulled manila folders from her file cabinet and sat on the floor among them. She sorted the print-outs into categories – pacts with the Devil, demonic possession, incubi, exorcism. Organizing was a comfort for Alice. If she couldn't control her life, at least she could control some file folders.

She labeled the thickest folder "Computer Demons." It held complaints about hell-possessed computers and claims for solving the problem. Only one of those pages had a lone preacher's enlightened advice. He must have grown weary of parishioners convinced that the Devil had taken over their desktops, laptops, or too-smart-for-them phones.

"Have a technician replace the hard drive and reinstall the software," he wrote. "That will get rid of the evil spirits permanently."

If only deleting the Devil from our lives were that easy.

When the door to her office slammed open, Alice jumped as if a firecracker had gone off. Maybe she should follow Nick Shea's advice and lock her doors twenty-four hours a day, although that would have no effect on supernatural home invaders.

She wasn't much relieved to find Syl standing in the doorway. Maybe Syl's mother had told her about yesterday's chat in the bookstore's garden. The confrontation with her had arrived ahead of schedule, and caught Alice without backup. The fact that Syl had a wild look in her eyes didn't help the situation.

"I'm going to die, Al."

"Are you sick? Hurt? Do you need a ride to the ER?"

"No. No. And no." Syl dropped into the easy chair near the door. "There was a pile-up on Route 50 just ahead of me. I managed to swerve around it, but I almost got clipped by a semi."

Alice sat cross-legged on the floor in front of her. "Take deep breaths."

"I almost ran over a woman lying on the pavement, Al. I got out to see if she could be helped. Her head was smashed. She looked like road kill, Alice." Syl collapsed back against the cushions. "A minute earlier and I would've been that woman in the road. I would've been road kill, Alice."

Sitting on the floor, Alice noticed globs of gray on Syl's shoes. "What's that?"

"What's what?" Syl stuck out her Manolo Blahniks and turned paler. "Is that what it looks like?"

What it looked like was the brain tissue and cranial fluid Alice had seen at the morgue two days ago. She made the mistake of saying so.

Syl screamed and kicked off the shoes. Then she hitched back in the chair, trying to get away from her own feet.

"Keep calm." Alice took the shoes outside and tossed them over the porch rail. She handed Syl a pair of her bargain bin thongs.

"What should I do, Alice? Please help me."

Syl had seen one of her many possible futures. There was no point reminding her that, deal with the Devil or not, she was mortal, and would be until mortality caught up with her. No point scolding her or asking what she had expected when she signed that crazy contract.

Alice nodded at the file folders spread out in front of the file cabinet. "I'm working on it. Miss Marjorie has offered to help."

"You told Mrs. Mayhew?"

"And your mother too."

"Oh, shit."

"Marjorie's going to ask her priest about an exorcism, although you aren't possessed in the usual way. You don't spit fire or speak in tongues or rotate your head 360 degrees. Do you?"

"No, I don't. It's just that damned paper I signed."

"You signed the agreement on actual paper?"

"Yeah. That stiff parchment sort of stuff."

"If only we knew what was in it."

"I can show it to you."

"You have a copy?" Alice knew she had to see it, but she didn't want to be on the same planet with it, much less hold it in her hands.

"It's in my safe deposit box in the vault at the bank."

Alice had a flash-image of the staid bank's vault full of satanic pacts in safe deposit boxes.

"I'll ask Marjorie whether we should bring it to the exorcism ritual or leave it in the vault."

"One other thing, Al."

"What?"

"Jerry called last night, pissed as hell and madder than that. Someone sent anthrax to the firm and the envelope was addressed to him. He'd been at the police station all day."

"Anthrax?"

"No, as it turned out. Just ashes in an envelope."

"What kind of ashes?"

"He said human ashes. He told the police he's sure I sent them."

"Did you send them?"

"No! Where would I get human ashes?"

Alice's left eyebrow must have twitched of its own accord.

"I swear, Al. I promised you I wouldn't do anything else bad to the twerp." Will you talk to Jerry? Will you tell him that? He won't listen to me."

"Okay." Alice sighed. "But you have to agree to the exorcism."

"If I agree, what about Harry?" Even now Syl couldn't keep the wistful out of the question.

"Let's deal with his boss first."

"You mean the Devil's bag man."

"Bag man?"

"Yeah. Calls himself Ass-moebius. He's a max-ugly freak, but I was drunk, so he didn't look all that different from some I've seen in bars."

"You signed a pact with Asmodeus?"

"Yeah. That's him."

Alice sorted through her print-outs. "Says here he's one of the seven princes of hell. He's in charge of the third deadly sin. Lust. What a surprise." Alice closed that folder and opened another one. "There's something you can do in the meantime."

"What?"

"Take the genital warts curse off Jerry."

"That's impossible."

"No it's not."

Alice read one of the print-outs aloud. It might not have been the most effective method of dispelling a hex, but the easiest. She put her faith in the human mind's healing powers into it.

" 'To heal the pain one has inflicted one must burn white candles and sandalwood incense.' I happen to have both. What are the odds? But let's do it out on the porch."

Alice continued reading while Syl lit three white candles and a dozen sticks of sandalwood.

" 'He shall presently spit in the middle of his hand...' "

Syl complied.

"Now repeat this. 'I ask that the spell of genital warts be removed from Jerome Gant, also known as Jerry.'"

Syl held up her hand with the blob of mucus in the palm, and repeated the request. Alice found a clean tissue in her pocket and handed it to her.

"The instructions say you have to give something of yours in return."

"I didn't bring anything. Give me a pair of scissors."

Alice brought out her sewing shears and Syl pulled her hair back. Before Alice could stop her, she cut off several inches and handed it over. "Now what?"

"Say that to prove your intentions are true you're transferring the spell to this lock of hair from your own head, thereby rendering the curse powerless. Say that no harm will come to you for canceling it."

When Syl had repeated that they both waited for a flash of light, a rumble of thunder, a fiendish laugh, some response. All they heard were the birds. Syl exhaled a sigh of relief and smiled for the first time in a while.

"Do you feel better?" asked Alice.

"Yes."

Alice hoped it had worked, although she would have been astonished if it did. She was thinking of how to bring up the subject of genital warts the next time she ran into Jerry when Syl grinned at her. Marjorie Mayhew agreeing to find a solution to her dealings with hell had cheered her considerably.

"You know what happens when you don't pay the exorcist?"

"I've read that priests ask only for a voluntary donation to the church."

"Work with me here, Al. What happens when you don't pay the exorcist?"

"I don't know. What happens when you don't pay the exorcist?"

"You get repossessed."

Syl chortled all the way down the stairs. Alice wished she could feel as cheerful. But then, if Syl were one to worry about consequences she wouldn't be in this mess.

Chapter Fifty-Two

Playing Dead

To play billiards well was a sign of an ill-spent youth.
Herbert Spencer (1820-1903)

Nathan and Will leaned on their pool sticks and watched Nick line up a draw shot. He leaned forward, positioned his stick, and with a flick of the wrist, hit the cue ball near its bottom. The tap caused it to collide with his own ball, and created backspin that returned it to him for the next set-up. He had used it often, but this time his one remaining ball bumped against the side cushion half an inch from the pocket's opening.

"Gotcha, Shea, you luckless son." Will turned heads at the bar with a passable imitation of Screamin' Jay Hawkins while he sang the first verse of "I Put a Spell on You." He didn't notice the glance that passed between Nick and Nathan.

The two of them had discussed satanic activity in the Cliffs of the Severn community. Nathan was positive it was going on. Nick was skeptical, but kept an open mind.

Nathan knew Nick also was preoccupied with the threats against Dr. Brant, but he hadn't suspected it was bad enough to make him miss a pool shot.

"The eagle case has been parceled out to four divisions." Nathan knew better than to make excuses for his partner. He kept his comments conversational. "Homicide is off the board."

The off-hand tone didn't fool Will.

"Nick doesn't miss pool shots, no matter what's going on back at the ranch. Our boy puts the mental in compartmentalized."

"I can hear you." But Nick was glad his friends were breaking the unspoken rule against discussing business while shooting pool. It kept them from guessing that the real reason for the missed shot was Alice Lewis. Much to his chagrin, his love life or lack of it, was always fair game for discussion among his friends.

While Will sank his three remaining balls and the eight, Nick's eyes focused on the future for a few heartbeats while he thought of cruising on the Indian with Alice's arms around his waist. He also breathed a small prayer that the weather would be sunny and no Saturday night mayhem would interfere with those plans.

Then he did the math. The time now, ten-fifteen Friday night. Thirty-four and a quarter hours until eight a.m. Sunday when he would see Alice again. That was not counting the time needed to shower, shave, and stand in front of the closet and chest of drawers deciding what to wear. He made a mental note to do laundry.

When Will had cleared the table, he and Nick and Nathan hung their cue sticks on the rack and collected their beer bottles from the shelf above it. On the way to the table farthest from the juke box, they stopped at the bar to order refills.

As they sat down, Will reopened the conversation about what he called "the case of the tell-no-tales heart." A large percentage of the clientele at Pete's pool hall were off-duty police, but he kept his voice low anyway.

"So they've divvied up the investigation. No surprise there. Let's summarize." He counted off the elements of the case on his fingers. "A rat in a mail box. An attempted granny-mugging. A pair of dead eagles. A ticker in a take-out box. A geezer in a freezer. The mysterious Roy Rogers. A dead juvie inmate. Zombie yard gnomes. Poisoning by wasp spray. And double anthrax hoaxes. That's enough to keep every division busy except the meter maids."

"Parking Enforcement Officers are city, not county," said Nick.

He could have added a couple more strange events — Hot Dog Boyd's mother buried under a noisome avalanche of her own chattel. And most puzzling, the sewage spill in Joe Stone's convertible from a pumper truck designed to prevent that sort of thing. Also, on Sunday he planned to ask Alice about the phantom alligator that had scared away Russell Wright.

"None of those turned out to be a homicide, Will," said Nathan, "…except the Boyd kid, and we know who did that."

"So they took you two off the case." Will grinned. "So what? Nick'll pursue it on his own time, what little he has of that. And I reckon you will too, Nathan."

"There are hundreds of Roy Rogers on Facebook alone," said Nathan. "I went through all of them."

"But we lucked out," said Nick. "This afternoon we got a copy of the death certificate for the guy we think is our Cowboy."

"Death certificate?"

"Practically had to get a subpoena to look at it. I was ready to drive up there and wring it out of them. The personal data on it matches up."

"It's from Cranesboro in northwest P.A.," said Nathan. "Population six thousand, four hundred and seventy-seven. They've been changing to a new system so their computers were down. According to the certificate, Rogers died six years ago."

"That rules out the King of the Cowboys as a suspect then."

Nick shook his head. "The death certificate says Roy Hooker Rogers died of 'Denzor Hemorrhagic Fever' in Harare, Zimbabwe."

"So it's a fake."

"Good guess."

"Falsifying a death certificate is easy," said Nathan. "I heard of a guy who did it a couple times to get out of going to court for traffic tickets."

"How about a birth certificate?"

"A fire destroyed those records seven years ago."

"How convenient."

The convenience of it had occurred to Nick and Nathan also.

"We found an article about the Cranesboro fire in the *Chronicle's* morgue," said Nick.

"So you think this Roger's guy is that important?"

"Yeah."

Important was an understatement. Nick had a feeling Rogers was central to everything, and the clock was ticking. The more time passed in any investigation, the less chance he had of solving the case. He didn't have to do the math now because he did it every morning. Workers had found the heart in Dr. Brant's septic tank pit two weeks ago.

Will glanced at his watch. "Vivian's shift ends at midnight."

"So does Esme's," said Nathan, "…and Kenya is at her grandmother's."

Nick knew what that meant. He raised a hand to call for the check. He was figuring his amount of the tab plus Will's, the price of losing the game, when the front door swung open. A lot of shouting followed Pete's next bar tab inside, but that wasn't all.

A piglet a little bigger than a six-pack of tall-boys darted between the legs of the prospective bar tab. He went sprawling and three cops leaped over him. One of them brandished a crab net.

The pig raced around the room like a slot car with greased axles. People jumped out of his way as he dodged under tables and chairs. He fishtailed on sharp turns, his hooves clicking on the hardwood floor under the litter of peanut shells. He left chaos in his path as his pursuers collided with Pete's regulars.

At the far end of the bar he made a high-performance right and headed for the table farthest from the juke box. Without slowing down he gathered himself for a leap four times his height. He landed, quaking, in Nick's lap and tried to burrow under his shirt. He stopped shaking as soon as Nick started stroking him.

The dimly-lit room lit up with the flashes and the blue glow from phone cameras. He knew the photos and videos would go viral. He also knew he could do nothing about it except keep his head down. He didn't look up until six city policemen formed a semi-circular screen between him and Pete's clientele.

"Where'd he come from?" Nick asked.

"Damned if we know. The seafood restaurant complained he was rooting in the overturned garbage cans in the alley." The uniform held out his arms for the hand-over and the piglet started shaking again.

Will stood up. "Shea, you realize your name will be 'the pig whisperer' from now on."

Nick ignored him and laid his and Will's share of the tab on the table. He cradled the pig in his arms and walked outside, followed by the cops, Will, and Nathan. When he tried to hand over his new charge, the pig gave a piteous squeak and started shaking again.

You little faker. He held him up, noted he was a male, and stared into his squinty eyes. *So, you think you've found the biggest softie in the room.* The pig grunted and stretched his snout toward his new friend's face. His breath smelled like aged rockfish.

Nick glanced up at the cop with the net. "Where will you take him?"

"Animal Control is on the way. They'll keep him at the shelter for five days."

"What are the chances of him being adopted?"

"Slim to none. If no one claims him they'll give him to a farmer in south County."

"I don't suppose he'll live out a happy life there."

"Sure he will, until he's big enough to be turned into pork chops."

Will interrupted. "Nick, you can't adopt a pig."

"I know." With one hand Nick opened his wallet to where he kept his badge and held it up. He turned to the cop who wielded the crab net like a scepter. "If I can't find a home for him tonight I'll bring him to the shelter in the morning."

By the light of the street lamp the patrolman squinted at the badge, making note of the number.

"Okay." He and the others sauntered off along Main Street.

Will and Nathan headed for their cars. Halfway down the block Will turned around and called out, "Don't name him."

Holding the pig under his arm like a rolled up newspaper, Nick took out his phone and tapped Logan's number on his speed dial.

When she answered he said, "Logan, this is Nick. Will you put up a friend of mine for the night?"

Chapter Fifty-Three

"Now What?"

For every problem there is one solution
which is simple, neat, and wrong.
H.L. Mencken

Alice said goodbye to Marjorie, hung up the phone, leaned back in her desk chair, and closed her eyes in relief. The priest was willing to talk to Syl this afternoon instead of tomorrow. Alice wouldn't have to break her Sunday aquarium date with Nick Shea. Even better, she wouldn't have to invent a lie for canceling. "I have to attend an exorcism" wasn't the best way to start any relationship, much less one with a policeman.

Through the open door of her office she saw the television light up. Harry shimmered into view on the living room sofa. As usual he was ripped and stripped, except for the red silk boxer shorts. He held a bottle of Horny Devil pale ale in one hand. The bag of nachos on his lap leaned against his large and perpetual hard-on.

One thing about Harry, he didn't hold a grudge. He turned that classic profile to look at her. His high beam of a smile started her heart industriously pumping blood south. It flowed into the soft tissue down there with an erotic pulse that was almost irresistible.

By now Alice had experienced Harry's wiles often enough to come up with a defense that didn't include flight, a cold shower or an ugly throw-down with the sponge mop. She had discovered that singing "Don't Fence Me In," loudly, distracted her. It required her to remember the lyrics and focus on staying somewhere in range of the correct key.

Today, however, she had a premonition that Harry would be a bad memory before long. She didn't know how that would happen, since exorcism didn't appear to be the answer. Marjorie had warned her not to get her hopes up about the priest even being able to help Syl, but she felt optimistic anyway. She leaned against the door frame of her office.

"Why my house, Harry?"

He ratcheted the smile up to dazzle.

I like you, Alice.

"Cut the crap." Alice said it out loud.

You don't have air-conditioning. He looked puppy dog hopeful, as if her willingness to talk meant he might be able to seduce her after all. *Turn on the heat and your house will be perfect.*

"Go bother some other poor sucker."

When she went to the kitchen he snapped to attention, as though he expected her to reappear with chocolate chip cookies. She returned with the sponge mop instead. He vanished, taking the beer and nachos with him. Alice knew he would be back.

Alice, Faye, and Marjorie stood with Syl in the church's parking lot. They could feel the afternoon heat of the asphalt through the soles of their shoes. Syl stalked toward her car and the other three followed.

"I'm sorry, Sylvana," said Marjorie. "Father Phelps did warn us not to get our hopes up."

Alice muttered, "What hopes?" too low for anyone to hear.

"I have to qualify for an exorcism?" Syl was furious. "I have to get my head candled by a shrink and a… who else did he say?"

"A neurologist," said Alice.

"Does he think I'm making this up?"

"Nine-hundred and ninety-nine out of a thousand do, Syl," said Faye.

On her fingers Syl ticked off the reasons why Fr. Phelps said he couldn't perform the exorcism.

"He has to get permission from some bishop who's off on a junket. They've mislaid the only copy of the book with the exorcism mumbo-jumbo in it. They require at least three witnesses who'll swear they've seen me do a Linda Blair. They expect me to pinwheel my eyes, spin my head, and babble like a demonic Cookie Monster."

Syl reached her Mercedes and stared at the trunk. The parchment with the pact was locked in a metal file box inside. Faye and Alice kept their distance from it. Marjorie, however, put a hand on Syl's shoulder.

"That part about head-spinning is the problem, Sylvana. You aren't possessed in the usual sense of the word."

"No offense, Miss Marjorie, but those prayers he mumbled over me as a consolation prize aren't going to help."

"You don't know that, child."

Alice understood her friend's skepticism about the power of prayer. She was pretty sure Syl had signed the Devil's contract assuming she could get out of it. Finding loopholes to wriggle her clients from under the control of the Internal Revenue Service was her job, and she was good at it. When it came to legalese, the IRS could go up against the Devil anytime.

"Where's Doc, Marjorie?" Syl asked. "Why didn't she come?"

Marjorie put an arm around her shoulders.

"This is not another one of those drunk and disorderly fixes you've gotten yourself into, Sylvana. Your mother coming down to the jail and writing a check for bail won't get you out of it. I can't speak for Logan, but if you were my child I'd think coming here with you today would imply I condoned what you did."

From the look in Syl's eyes, Alice could see the exact moment fear took control of her.

"I came with Faye," Alice said. "I can drive you home. I'll stay with you tonight if you want, but I have to leave early tomorrow morning."

Syl gave her a hug that lasted a few beats longer that the usual.

"Thank you, Al. I can drive myself. And I'll stay with Doc." Syl saw Marjorie raise an eyebrow. "She'll let me stay with her. I know she will."

"I hope you're okay with sleeping next to a pig," said Faye.

"What?"

"Detective Shea left an orphaned piglet with her last night."

Syl smiled. "If Doc'll give shelter to a pig, she'll let her daughter sleep on the sofa bed."

Chapter Fifty-Four

"Coming Almost Clean in the Rain Forest"

You may charge me with murder –
or want of sense-
(we are all of us weak at times);
but the slightest approach to a false pretense
was never one of my crimes.
Lewis Carroll (*Through the Looking Glass*
and What Alice Found There)

Without any need to confer, Nick and Alice walked straight to the Syngnathidae exhibit. The seahorses' ocean was a five-hundred-gallon tank with a curved window that took up most of the wall. Nick knew the Syngnathids had finished their daily courtship dances. Soon after the lights came on every morning the staff would find them paired off and in a tangle with tails entwined. By this hour, except for the occasional amorous maverick, the members of the dozen or so seahorse species were no longer in a wooing mood.

Nick figured that was just as well for two diffident humans on a first date. Seahorse courtships were sensual as well as graceful and he didn't want Alice to think he had brought her here with ulterior motives. But then, neither did he want her to think he had no ulterior motives.

He sensed Alice had something worrisome on her mind, but the anxiety in her eyes was understandable. Her friend, Logan Brant, had been attacked and harassed and she herself had had a close call with a serial killer.

She had perked up at the sight of the Indian though. She had buckled on the helmet while Nick got the engine started. She had put her hands on his shoulders, swung one long leg across the bike, and settled behind. Luckily she couldn't see his face. The grin would have given her the impression he had ulterior motives.

The only disappointment so far was that the ride to Baltimore was too short, but the day was about to get better.

"See that one?" Nick pointed to a very pregnant seahorse in the eel grass near the window.

"He's male, right? They carry the eggs in a pouch."

"Right."

"He's turning pale and panting. Is he sick?"

"He's fine."

The seahorse wrapped his tail around a narrow pipe and used it to anchor himself while a succession of contractions shook him. Alice watched, transfixed. All traces of whatever had been bothering her disappeared. Nick felt more relaxed than he had been since he had put on his wetsuit, goggles, and fins here a week ago.

Alice knelt on the floor to get as close to the seahorse's level as possible. She sat back on her heels and leaned forward until her face almost touched the window. She took shallow breaths so as not to fog the glass.

Nick hunkered next to her as the vertical slit opened in the middle of the seahorse's belly and a tiny head appeared. Alice gasped when a perfect miniature of the father popped out and swam away.

Nick turned his head slightly to watch her reaction to what was about to happen. With the next contraction dozens of tiny seahorses exploded outward as though blasted from a canon. Alice barely had time to shift to a cross-legged sitting position before the next spasm. The ones after that ejected scores more. When Dad finally sent the last few stragglers out into the watery world, the sum total of his brood clouded a cubic meter of water.

Alice couldn't take her eyes off them. "How many eggs does the female lay?"

"For this species, between eighteen hundred and two thousand. She deposits them directly into his pouch and he fertilizes them there."

"And yet…"

"Yes. They're disappearing in the wild."

The male unwound his tail from the chain and sank to lie inert in the fine gravel covering the bottom of the tank. His mate hovered around him.

"Looks like she's worried about him."

Nick suppressed a chuckle. "She wants to make him pregnant again."

"So soon?"

"He'll be up for it before long. That's why Chinese men grind seahorses up as a cure for impotence. More than a hundred and fifty million are caught and killed every year because of that delusion."

From there they walked up the spiral ramp through the middle of the five-story coral reef exhibit. Nick showed Alice where his favorite clown fish hung out, and introduced her to Ray, the manta. Neither of them recognized him without his wet suit, goggles and fins of course. He always felt like an alien when he was on this side of the glass.

The rain forest was their last destination. No glass separated them from the birds, mammals, reptiles, insects, and spiders living in the dense overhang of foliage there. While they watched the young sloth named Scout do absolutely nothing, Nick asked one of the questions that had been on his mind.

"A couple of our guys said Russell Wright called in a complaint about being attacked by an alligator at your house. It was an anonymous call, but they tracked the source."

"That was no alligator, Nick, that was Godzilla. I owe him my life."

"Godzilla?"

"Esme Mayhew's daughter's pet iguana. I was taking care of him for a few days."

"A lizard scared away a murderer?"

"You haven't met 'Zilla. I'll introduce you to him when we get home."

When we get home. Nick liked the sound of that.

"Nick, you offered to do that security check for my house because of Russell, didn't you."

"Yes. But it was also a good excuse to get to know you better."

Before asking the second question, Nick looked around. No one was in the vicinity. Scout was not the most vivacious attraction in the rain forest.

"Do your friends call you 'Al'?"

"Sure. Why?"

"I don't want you to think I'm prying into your personal life."

"I expect that's the major part of your job, Nick, and we're all safer for it."

"The evening of the day 'Zilla chased Wright out of your house, Will and Nathan and I were at the Red Eye. I happened to hear Faye talking on her phone to someone named Al." Nick noticed the tension return to Alice's jaw line. "I swear I wasn't listening in, but I caught a little of her end of the conversation."

Alice must have remembered the conversation too. "And you're wondering what Faye was afraid would happen, who 'they' were, and why I should leave the house?"

"Was Russell threatening to come back and bring an accomplice?"

Alice waited for a set of parents and three small children to pass by. When she spoke Nick had to lean close to hear her.

"If I tell you, you won't believe me."

"Tell me anyway."

"After 'Zilla chomped down on Russell's crotch I figured I'd better take him back to Esme's. I had dinner there and came home around ten. I hadn't planned to stay that late and didn't leave any lights on."

Nick didn't ask if she'd left her house unlocked. No sense beating that dead horse.

"When I opened the door, the living room was lit up. Auras like neon tubes rimmed the furniture. Sylph elementals were hovering around the ceiling fan."

"By elementals do you mean the mythical earth, wind, fire, and water creatures?"

"Yes, but they aren't mythical, and Faye says they've been there all along. I just hadn't been able to see them."

"Why do you think you could see them that night?"

"At midnight the night before, Syl chalked a pentagon in her basement and called up a demon. Faye and I happened in while she was in the middle of it. Apparently we were affected. I see supernatural creatures all the time now. A three-legged demon lives in my utility closet, for pete's sake." Alice sighed. " "I don't expect you to believe me."

"I know you don't lie, Alice, but you have to admit this is a lot to swallow."

"There's more." She took a deep breath. "Syl signed a pact with the Devil."

Nick might have laughed except he had a mental image of Joe Stone's Mustang overflowing with sewage. As crazy as it seemed, the Devil doing it was the only rational explanation. Nathan was right about the Cliffs after all.

"I'm serious, Nick."

He looked into her eyes. "I believe you."

"Thank God." She put her arms around him and held on as though he were a tree in a hurricane.

With one arm around her shoulders, he stroked her hair with his other hand. When she stood back a few paces he saw tears in her eyes.

"We tried to have an exorcism yesterday, but the priest said he couldn't do it. Syl isn't possessed in the traditional sense."

"Sounds like Mrs. Gant needs a Philadelphia lawyer."

Alice's eyes opened wide. "She has one, although he's angry with her."

Nick thought of the Gnome Nut, Joe Stone, and some of the Cliffs' dwellers he'd talked to and stifled his first response. *Who isn't?*

"Thank you." Alice kissed him on the cheek. "Why didn't I think of that? I just have to persuade him to help her."

"Glad to be of service, ma'am."

"How can you possibly believe all this? About the Devil and the elementals."

Nick cupped his hands around her face and kissed her lightly on the lips. "I do believe you."

He held her hand on the walk back through the humid concrete halls of the Aquarium and out into the bright sunshine.

As he steered the Indian through downtown Baltimore traffic with Alice's arms around his waist, he couldn't get one of Woody Guthrie's songs out of his head, and when he stopped at a traffic light he wasn't surprised to hear Alice singing it softly.

> Way out in Reno, Nevada,
> Where romance blooms and fades,
> A great Philadelphia lawyer
> Was in love with a Hollywood maid.

CHAPTER FIFTY-FIVE

"WHEN PIGS FLY"

The Eskimo had his own explanation.
Said he, "The devil is asleep or having trouble
with his wife, or we should never have
come back so easily."
Commander Robert Peary 1856-1920
(*The North Pole*)

"We've named him Piglet, from the Pooh books," said Kenya. "Dr. Brant brought him over. He and Zilla are best friends now."

In a sunny corner of Esme's enclosed porch, Godzilla and the pig from Pete's pool hall shared a cushion that would have accommodated a Great Dane. The tall window behind them provided a view of the creek. Piglet lay on his side with Zilla resting his chin on his plump mid-section. The rest of Zilla curled around his new friend. He measured four times the pig's length so the tip of his tail ended back where it started. Both of them were napping in the afternoon sunlight.

"This is what they mean by hog heaven," said Nick.

Piglet must have heard Nick's voice. He opened his eyes and struggled to get out from under the weight of Zilla's head and shoulders. Zilla woke up too. The ruff on his head and neck flared. He managed to stare fixedly at Nick while bobbing his head at the same time. He opened his mouth, exposing a multitude of teeth. And not just any teeth. These were tetrahedrons with razor-sharp serrations on all edges. He flicked his long, pointy tongue and hissed, in case Nick had missed the message.

"Don't look directly at him, Detective Shea," said Kenya. "He'll take that as a challenge. He's just protecting his friend."

"Now I see why Russell Wright ran."

"Not to worry." Alice handed him the plastic container of fruit chunks they'd bought on their way home. "His affections can be bought."

As soon as Zilla lumbered across the room to use those teeth on the pineapple and melon, Piglet scrambled to his feet. He trotted to Nick who picked him up, scratched behind his ears, and had a catch-up chat. He promised he'd come back to visit, and handed him to Kenya. Then he and Alice walked up the hill to where the Indian was parked in front of her house.

"I'd ask you to come in, but in an hour I have an appointment with that four-hundred-dollar-an-hour lawyer."

"Feel free to tell me to mind my own business, but why doesn't Mrs. Gant meet with him?"

"They aren't on speaking terms."

"You're not talking about her ex-husband, Jerry Gant, are you? The one whose firm represents Longview?"

"Yes."

"I checked out Sylvana Brant Gant. Even discounting Bernie Robertson's nuisance calls and her threats of murder and mayhem to that reporter, she's been busy. The neighbors called 911 to report the ruckus when she threw Mr. Gant's belongings out a third story window."

"That happened before I met her, but I heard about it."

"The cop on the scene moonlights in a band. He had tears in his eyes when he told me he got there just in time to see a three thousand dollar DW drum kit go airborne."

"Faye said the drums were the worst loss. She also said Jerry just kept them around as décor."

"And didn't Gant file a complaint accusing his ex-wife of putting dead possums in the air ducts of his house?"

"That's him."

You don't know the worst of it. Alice remembered Jerry knee-deep in her pond with duck weed in his hair, warts on his crotch, and no frogs in his hands.

"Promise you'll call me tonight and tell me what happens with Gant."

"Okay."

He laced his fingers at the nape of her neck with his thumbs lightly pressing the two accupressure spots at the base of her skull. He kissed her, twice.

"Not to make light of what you've told me, but I'm more worried about who's behind the harassment of Logan than her daughter's dealings with Old Scratch." He put on the helmet. "Be careful, Alice. Hare probably has flunkies far more nefarious than Jerry Gant."

"I'll keep my eyes open."

As Nick started the Indian, Alice considered telling him about Harry. She decided against it for the second time that day. She was honest, but she wasn't stupid. What could extinguish a spark of romance more effectively than mentioning to the guy that a male sexual demon was a frequent, if uninvited, houseguest?

Alice watched the Indian's tail lights disappear over the crest of the hill. She wished she could ride away with him instead of keeping her appointment with Jerry tonight. She glanced at the garage door. A copy of the Devil's pact lay in a plain brown envelope on the carpenter's bench inside.

After the non-exorcism the day before, she and Syl had gone to the copy center. They'd both been surprised that they'd been able to make a duplicate of the contract. Alice hoped the machine hadn't become possessed as a result. But she had made note of which one it was so she wouldn't use it in the future.

She pressed her fingers to the front of her shirt and felt the hard rim of Charlie's silver ring hanging on its chain underneath.

A dead guy, a vibrator, an imaginary dragon, and a sponge mop had protected her so far. Today a county police detective joined the team.

Jerry slammed his fist on the desk so hard the copy of Syl's contract jumped a millimeter off the surface.

"When pigs fly."

"I don't blame you."

"This is preposterous anyway. The Devil doesn't exist."

Alice waited several beats for him to get his dander down. "Have the warts gone away?"

"The warts? Oh, yeah." His cheeks turned pink. "I found a doctor who could cure them."

"No, you didn't. Syl called off the curse."

"There was no curse."

"That's not what you said when you tried to catch a frog in my pond. You said, and I quote, 'I don't know how she did it, but I know she did.'"

"If, for argument's sake, she could lay a curse on someone, she's not the type to call it off."

"But she did."

"She must have decided that scaring me to death with fake anthrax was a better idea."

"Syl didn't send the envelope with the cremains in it."

"How do you know?"

"She told me so, and she has never lied to me."

He stared at Alice without seeing her. She could tell he was going through the memory files marked "Syl."

"She's pulled a lot of mean, spiteful stunts, but I don't remember her ever lying to me either."

"So would you please look over that document?"

"I repeat. When pigs fly. Since the Devil doesn't exist, this paper is bogus. Must be another of her tricks."

"Those warts were real, Jerry." Alice pulled the ace out of her sleeve. "If you can get Syl out of this deal, you'll render her powerless to pull something like that again."

He picked up the document and scowled as he read it. "Very interesting. May I keep this to show some colleagues?"

"No."

He read it a second time. The third time through he said "Aha."

Alice sat forward on the chair. "Aha what?"

"She signed it Sylvana Gant."

"That was her name when she made the deal."

"No it wasn't. Someone else in the firm took care of the name change a couple months ago. I told him I'd let Syl know, but I was so pissed I didn't tell her. My assistant happened to run into her at the liquor store recently and congratulated her on getting her maiden name back."

"So Sylvana signed this with the wrong name."

"Exactly. You'd think the Devil would have known that."

"Here's what I've learned about the Devil. He's smarter than we are, but he's not omniscient. So what does Syl do now?"

Jerry turned in his chair and took a volume from the mahogany bookcase behind him. He held it up so she could read the title.

She put on her glasses. "Stephen Vincent Benet's *The Devil and Daniel Webster*?"

"It was required reading in one of my law classes."

"I forget how the story ends."

"Webster's oratory convinced a jury of the worst scoundrels in history to exonerate his client and release him from his contract with the Devil. The judge told Webster to tear up the document."

"Then we can tear up Syl's original and the copy?"

Jerry nodded and handed the copy back to her. "Let me know if the Devil gives Syl any trouble about it." He grinned. "I'll get to play Daniel Webster."

"Thank you for doing this, Jerry. We all appreciate it more than you'll ever know."

Alice wanted to feel relieved when she left his office, but she couldn't shake the dread. Getting rid of the Devil couldn't be this easy.

Chapter Fifty-Six

"Write On"

Every journalist has a novel in him,
which is an excellent place for it.
Russell Lynes (1910-1991)

Alice's number came up on Nick's caller ID. He answered it on the first ring. Alice sounded excited.

"Jerry found a loophole. We'll burn the contract tomorrow."

"You convinced Gant to help his ex? The State Department should send you as an envoy to the Middle East."

"May I ask your advice on a different matter?"

"Sure."

"When I came home I saw shoeprints in the dirt next to the stairs. The basement is above ground under the porch and there's a window."

"You think a peeping Tom left the tracks?"

"Not unless he's obsessed with watching women do laundry. But it is a means of entry."

"Have you noticed anyone suspicious in the area?" Given all the strange happenings in Cliffs of the Severn he hoped the question didn't sound as foolish to her as it did to him.

"That reporter Joe Stone has been here several times on the pretext of interviewing me."

"I know him."

"He calls a lot. When I don't pick up he leaves long messages."

"Why do you think Stone was the one who left the prints?"

"The treads look like they'd belong to those ridiculous high-tech shoes he wears."

"You mean the sneakers with airbags and turn signals?"

"No. The ones he wears when he comes here are I-want-you-to-think-I've-climbed-Mt.-Everest boots."

Nick looked at his watch and calculated. Seven-fifteen p.m. Drive time was almost over. "I'll be there in twelve minutes."

He parked parallel to the garage doors. He didn't care what the neighbors thought. If word got out there was a police presence at Ms. Lewis's house, so much the better.

He took the metal case with his casting equipment from the trunk and double-timed up the concrete steps. Alice sat at the bottom of the wooden stairs leading to her porch. A hundred-and-fifty watt trouble light was draped over her knees.

It was almost night under the porch and she held up the light so he could see. These were not prints but three-dimensional impressions. He could compare the wear patterns on the left one with the cast he'd taken in the ravine.

Alice held the light to one side and at a slant so it wouldn't wash out the details while Nick took a photograph of each impression. He took more photos with a ruler laid alongside the soles. He was almost certain this was the same brand of shoe as the one that had left the print in the ravine.

With water from the outside tap Nick mixed the Dental Stone in a large plastic bag. When it was the consistency of pancake batter he poured it onto a spatula to deflect and lighten the stream. He and Alice went inside while it dried. As the sepia twilight faded to black, Alice lit candles on the mantle.

Before he had a chance to sit down she asked, "Do you notice anything odd about this room? I mean except for the sponge mop."

He had noticed the mop leaning against the wall next to the sofa. It seemed out of character even with Alice's devil-may-care approach to décor, but he figured she must have used it recently. He saw the same faint radiance he had detected before.

"There's a translucent blue light around the ceiling fan, but it disappears when I look directly at it."

"Those are the sylphs I told you about. The air elementals." She took his wrist and raised his hand to just under the blades. "Do you feel anything?"

The hair on his arms stirred with the ancient response to a threat that his friend Will liked to call by its scientific name, *piloerection*. In polite society they were merely goose bumps.

"A slight tingling sensation."

"They have that effect on me too."

Nick sat on the couch and set his feet on the old trunk in front of it. Alice leaned against the armrest and laid her legs across his lap. He rested a hand on them. They sat for a minute or two in silence before Alice spoke.

"I can introduce you to the earth guys in the plants over there." She nodded toward the sun porch. "The fire salamanders live in the oven's pilot light. The water nymphs are called undines. They prefer the toilet in the basement, maybe because it doesn't get used much." She paused, as if deciding whether to tell him this. "Sometimes I put a rubber band on the spray nozzle in the kitchen sink to keep it going for a minute or two. The undines like to play in the rain."

Nick put an arm along the top of the sofa cushions, and drew her closer. "You're a strange one, Alice Lewis."

"You'd be surprised how quickly strangeness becomes normal." She rested her head in the lee angle of his elbow. "Although in your line of work you must run into a lot of strangeness."

"Yes, I do." Nick leaned against the cushion and closed his eyes while he made out his Monday morning to-do list. Thanks to Alice, Joe Stone had become a person of interest. That put him at the top of the to-do list.

He had never felt this comfortable not talking to a woman, especially one who was sitting less than a foot away. When he glanced at her she seemed to be deep in her own thoughts.

"What was your husband's name?"

"Charles O'Brien. Charlie."

"I was here the night he passed away."

"You were?"

"Kimberly, our dispatcher, told me someone called 911 about a death. My job is to check out those calls. Since he died from natural causes I wasn't needed."

"How do you do it?"

"Do what?"

"Live every day with 'the evil that men do?'"

"*Julius Caesar.*"

"Right."

Nick could have talked for the rest of the night about the evil men and women do and how it affected him. He edited it down. "At least I know when a case is closed I can see the bad guys get their come-uppance. Most of the time."

" 'Most of the time?' "

"If I tell you what I think of criminals and the justice system will I be reading my rant in one of your books some day?"

"Almost certainly."

He hesitated. "I write whenever I get a little free time. It relieves some of the tension."

"Fiction or non-fiction?"

"A crime novel. I'm about seventy-five pages in." He asked the question that bothered him most. "How do I know if the writing's passable or drek?"

"You won't know unless your ego is so performance-enhanced you believe, as they say in the army, that your shit don't stink."

Nick could see this was a sore subject with Alice, and she wasn't done with it.

"Like the phone messages Joe Stone's been leaving. He keeps offering me the privilege of first look at his unfinished autobiographical blockbuster. It's a crime novel, by the way. Going to be a world-wide best-seller, he says. His name will be a household word, he says. I predict it's drek."

Nick wanted to see the manuscript, but asking Stone for it might tip him off that he was on Homicide's radar. He couldn't tell Alice details of the investigation. She inadvertently had given him some good leads, but he couldn't officially enlist her help. He could ask her to agree to read the novel and report back to him, but that would give Stone the idea she was interested in him. Not good for her peace of mind, nor Nick's.

He also wanted to ask her what she and Faye had dumped into Bernie Robertson's trash can ten days ago and why it had been glowing. He was pretty sure their late-night visit was not merely another neighborhood prank on the Gnome Nut. Bringing it up now would divulge that he had watched Bernie's surveillance video. So much for his claim he wasn't checking up on her.

He always had known getting involved with someone connected to a case was not a good idea. Now he understood on a visceral level why it was true.

With his right hand around her shoulder, Nick drew her a few inches closer. They sat in relaxed silence for a while, but he remembered what he had said about the night he came to her house a year ago. *My job is to check out those calls.*

That line of thought led him back to the ubiquitous Joe Stone. Nick wasn't surprised that Stone had an unfinished manuscript in his drawers. What reporter didn't? He also must have a scanner in his car. He was always first at the scene of a murder or anything resembling one. Sometimes he was waiting when the police arrived. And the mountain boots. Why didn't he wear them when he came to the police station every week to copy Nick's police reports?

"I have to go, Alice. I'll call you tomorrow."

"I understand." She gave him a kiss on the cheek. "Deadline isn't a metaphor in your line of work."

After Nick retrieved the dried plaster cast of the shoe print, he didn't waste time getting started on his to-do list. As soon as he reached the highway he called Nathan to tell him about Stone's boot prints.

"I'll go by the newspaper's personnel office first thing in the morning," Nathan said. "I'll get his social and whatever other information they have."

Nick's next call was to Will's home number.

"Any luck finding where Mary Rogers' body might have been sent?"

"I've been going through all the files for unclaimed bodies and making a list of which funeral homes they went to and when. It's time-consuming."

"While you're at it, ask if Joseph Stone contacted any of them."

"The reporter? Why?"

"A hunch."

"I'll get back to you tomorrow."

"Thanks."

The Longview Development building was closed on a Sunday night. Nick's own workplace, however, was open twenty-four hours a day. Before he headed for home he left the boot casts at the forensic lab office for an expert cleaning. He put the casts and a note of explanation in the middle of the big green blotter on the examiner's desk to find first thing in the morning.

CHAPTER FIFTY-SEVEN

"MUCH TO DO"

And this is the way
We start the day,
In a corner of hell called home.
Louise Cass (1878-1917)

The mantel clock had only chimed eight o'clock in the morning, but Alice called Faye anyway. She heard the phone ring faintly next door. And ring. And ring.

It finally stopped and Faye mumbled, "This had better be life or death, Al."

"We have to get rid of Harry."

"What's he done to get your skivvies in a twist at…" Faye paused and Alice imagined her squinting at the big and little hands on the clock. "…O-dark-thirty?"

"It's after eight o'clock."

"Easy for you to say."

"Nick Shea came by for a visit last night."

"Oh, lord, did Harry screw that up?"

"He tried. He was vogueing in those red boxers in the doorway behind Nick. He was more ridiculous than usual and he had a boner you could do chin-ups on."

"Could Nick see him?"

"I don't think so. I pretended to stretch so I could put a hand on the sponge mop. Harry skedaddled to the back rooms, but the doors were open and I could see him prancing around there. He mooned me once with those buns you could bounce a quarter off of. I have to make him leave my house. Permanently."

"I need to get rid of him too. I've started spending time with Jake."

Alice heard something new in Faye's voice, a cautious optimism about a man.

"The pest control guy you met at the bar?"

"Yes. I told him about Harry and he's working on the problem. He said he can come by at two this afternoon. Tomorrow he'll have time to do a clearance. He likes to do it in daylight when they're most vulnerable. It'll only take an hour."

"What's a clearance?" Alice wasn't in the mood for any more surprises.

"He calls it an exorcism-lite to get rid of evil spirits. He says you have to dismiss them carefully so you don't piss them off."

"What about destroying Syl's contract?"

"She's agreed to meet us at the beach at six for a very Happy Hour. We'll burn it in one of the grills." Faye yawned loudly. "This is my day off. I'm going back to bed. I'll see you at two o'clock."

Alice's old roam-phone sat on a low cabinet next to the stairs. As she returned it to its cradle she heard the scratch and skitter of three-inch-long toenails on the second floor. The nightmare face and basset hound eyes of the three-legged closet demon, Trike, peered around the half-wall at the top of the stairwell.

Alice retrieved the last two stale chocolate chip cookies and shied them like frisbees to the top of the stairs. Trike wrapped its spidery fingers around them and backed out of sight.

She headed for her office, but screamed when a knobbly purple head with glowing red eyes popped up from the floor in front of her. A bristly crest of green hair sprouted just above the outcrop of its brow and continued over the top of its skull. Its bat-wing ears flared, folded flat, then flared again.

The whole preposterous enterprise was supported by bony shoulders the texture of 60-grade sandpaper and the color of an eggplant. It was staring at the kitchen door as fixedly as a cat an hour before feeding time.

This was a new apparition. How many more of them lurked in the crannies and crawlspaces of her old house?

Alice stamped her foot and shouted, "Scat!" The creature's glowing eyes dilated to tea-cup size. With a noise like a cat coughing up a hairball, it melted back down through the two-by-three-inch hole in the floor where an old electrical outlet had been. Alice covered the opening with "A through O" of her weighty two-volume set of the Oxford English Dictionary. She added "P through Z" on top of it. She knew the gesture was futile, but she had to do something.

"ELIMINATOR" was painted in eighteen-inch black letters on the sides of the white panel van. Alice and Faye helped Jake unload the cardboard boxes from the back of it. With Caribbean-blue eyes and streaked blond hair tied in a pony tail that reached below his deltoids, Jake himself looked angelic, if angels surfed. He explained the plan while they carried everything up the stairs.

"The minor rite consists of prayers for those afflicted by evil spirits, but not truly possessed. The *Malleus Maleficarum* claims it's one way to stop attacks by an incubus."

"It also says women are victims of incubi more often because they don't have the intellectual capacity of men," said Faye.

"It was written over five hundred years ago."

"The more things change...," Faye muttered.

"Other methods are the 'Sacramental Confession' and reciting the 'Angelic Salutation.' " Jake set the largest box inside the front door and sniffed. "Something smells good."

"I just took a batch of cookies out of the oven."

"Where do you usually see it?" He glanced up the stairs. "In the bedroom?"

"No. It prefers to sit on the sofa in front of the TV." Alice noticed Jake didn't refer to Harry by name or gender. She assumed he had his reasons.

"Good. That means it's easily distracted."

They cleared a space in the middle of the living room and Jake took his solution to the Harry problem out of the biggest box. The aluminum wire frame trap had glass sides. It looked big enough to catch large raccoons disgruntled at being interrupted while ransacking a pantry.

"I thought it would be better to get rid of the incubus before putting it on alert with an over-all cleansing of your house."

"Can't it hear us?"

"It can always hear us. Secrecy is not an option." He put the trap down in front of the TV with the opening facing the sofa. "We're counting on its stupidity and complacence."

"Amen to that," Alice muttered.

"The Franciscan friar Ludovico Maria Sinistrari wrote that incubi ignore exorcists. He said they're contemptuous of anything sacred. So I'm going to try trapping it."

"Why the glass sides on the trap?"

"Look inside."

Alice got down on hands and knees and peered in. The sides were one-way glass which meant the interior was surrounded by mirrors.

"Sexual demons feed off human energy. If all they can see is themselves they lose focus. They get confused and can't find the exit. That's the theory anyway."

"Have you ever caught one?"

"I just finished designing this. It's a trial run."

"How do we lure it in there?" Alice actually felt odd referring to Harry as "it." That she found using the impersonal pronoun odd was unsettling.

"Bait. I brought some pornography."

"Alice has something better," said Faye. "She bakes chocolate chip cookies with her grandmother's secret ingredient."

The three cookies were still warm when Jake put them on the metal platform on the floor of the trap. He distributed their weight so the rocker apparatus underneath was neutral and the platform level.

When he finished he looked up at Alice. "What's the secret ingredient in the cookies."

"Corn flakes."

"Really?"

"Really."

Jake set the trigger that would release the door and lock it down when the metal platform's delicate balance was disturbed. He made the sign of the cross over it and muttered something. Then he smiled at Alice and Faye.

"What was that?" asked Alice.

"An obeah incantation. It comes highly recommended by the folks at my favorite shop in Baltimore. Don't worry. It's a positive spell."

Alice brushed the crumbs off her hands. "Now what?"

"Turn on the TV to whatever channel it likes to watch." Jake picked up the big cardboard box, empty now. He left the smaller ones stacked against the wall. Alice assumed they contained the items he'd need for the Clearance.

"Let's go to Faye's house for beer while we wait."

"I'll stay here," said Alice.

Jake paused at the door. "If this trap works things could get ugly."

"I'll leave if there's any danger."

"Do you have your scapular medal?"

"Scapular medal?"

"Faye says you have an amulet that protects you."

"Charlie's ring," said Faye.

Alice pulled the dragon ring on its silver chain from inside the collar of her shirt. "I'll be okay."

The fact was, she refused to go next door because the house belonged to her and she would defend it. Besides, she wanted to see if Harry was stupid enough to crawl into a trap. And what would he look like when he did?

She crumbled several of the freshly-baked cookies and delivered them to the gnomes in the planters. She stood on tip-toe and sprayed organic lavender scent in among the fan blades. The tingling in her fingers and arm tickled more than usual whenever she did that. She was pretty sure the nymphs got a buzz from the spray.

She picked up the sponge mop on her way back to the kitchen and leaned it against the door frame. Out of habit, she ran a low stream of water down the sink drain and turned on one of the gas burners so the water and fire elementals could play for a few minutes. She put the rest of the cookies in a freezer container. She figured the freezer would be the last place a creature from hell would look, and she wanted the trap to be the only source of them for Harry.

Alice was not good at being on-hold even in everyday situations, and this situation was not everyday. While she waited for Harry she ran hot water into a plastic basin and added dish soap. As she washed the lunch dishes and baking utensils she sang Charlie's favorite Shel Silverstein song. Silverstein probably would have appreciated today's context.

> Well, a man came to our house, our house, our house.
> A man came to our house to sell some brooms.
> So we asked him to come in, and we
>   hit him with a hammer,
> And we hid him in the closet in my father's room.
>
> But you're always welcome at our house
>   Any time of day.
> Yes, you're always welcome at our house,
>   And we hope you will stay.

Chapter Fifty-Eight

"The Purloined Heart"

We make up most of our history around here, codger.
We'd put some zip into it.
add some character, some identity.
Leonard Franklin Slye
Aka Roy Rogers (1911-1998)

Nick had just set his coffee mug on the desk when Will's call came. Will got right to the point.

"Two and a half weeks ago the meat wagon brought the Freezer Geezer's body to the morgue. We were backed up so we kept her in cold storage a couple more days until Serenity Funeral Home offered to take her. The director told me Joseph Stone came in to order their cheapest cremation package for Mary Rogers."

Nick thought about the timing. "A couple days would be enough for the newspaper to print something about her. Even without a name, Stone would pick up on the address."

"Especially since he works for the paper. Should I call him Stone or Rogers, by the way?"

"We'll be arresting Stone, so let's stick with that."

"Listen, I'm sorry I didn't get you info about the funeral home back when they found the heart in the hole. By then the Freezer Geezer had gone from Jane Doe to Mary Rogers, then out the back door and onto the funeral home's loading dock. Our records didn't catch the connection. And then a second deceased with the same name arrived."

"That's the one Nathan just found. So, we've been working on the paper work to exhume the wrong Mary Rogers?"

"Looks like it, but we didn't have the Joe Stone connection back then."

"What was her relationship to Stone?"

"According to the funeral home's records he listed her as his mother."

"Hence Hot Dog Boyd's mention of his uncle Roy Rogers."

"Hence? Haven't had your coffee yet, Shea? You still think you're Shakespeare's stenographer? Okay, yes, hence... if Mary Rogers was Roy Rogers' mother and your hoarder's sister. And the hoarder was Hot Dog Boyd's grandmother then..." Will's voice trailed off.

"Hot Dog's great uncle, but 'Uncle' will do." Nick understood Will's confusion. Other people's family relationships had the same effect on him.

Still, he had to give Stone a little credit for doing what was right. He could've kept quiet while his mother was cremated at the county's expense. But then Will continued his report.

"The Serenity Funeral Home director's name is Dennis Ewell. He remembers Stone. He said Stone decided on cremation, but she had a pacemaker that had to be removed. He asked to see the preparation of the body. He flashed *Washington Post* press credentials. Claimed to be a *Post* reporter doing a thoughtful, in-depth article on 'death with dignity' for the Sunday supplement."

"The *Post*?"

"Go big or go home. Looks like he was planning to steal that heart from the git-go, Nick. He must've slipped someone a bribe to get it, or once in the back rooms he could've sneaked it from the waste before it was disposed of."

For Nick, the important question was, as always, why. Even random, casual violence, the sort the media liked to call "senseless," had some motivating force behind it.

"But here's the best part. Stone apparently didn't notice on the form he filled out that he was giving Serenity permission to take a

DNA sample. Ewell says they do that with everyone who's passed and passes through. They have some cockamamie idea that one day clients will want to clone Grannie."

"Thanks, Will. Nathan or I will talk to Ewell and whomever prepared the body."

"I thought they took you two off the case."

"Staub had a heart attack. I hear he's been putting the moves on every nurse in the cardiac ward. Ebson is on vacation. Everyone else is slammed with work, so the chief put us back on it."

"A wise decision."

Nick nodded silent agreement.

The case involved a threatening note on an elderly woman's windshield, a dead rat in her mailbox, a mugging and vandalism to her car, plus two dead eagles and a human heart in her yard. All of it added up to an attempt to scare her to death. That the perpetrator badly underestimated his victim didn't diminish his intent.

Nick stared at his coffee mug and thought of the faint, but visible finger prints lifted off the newspaper from Mary Rogers' house in Glenbrook. How many times had Joe Stone helped himself to an unclaimed mug in the station house kitchen and sipped coffee as he perused Nick's reports? Unfortunately, Sheila washed all stray cups at the end of each day.

Nathan had left an email with Stone's social security number he'd found on file at the newspaper office. Nick spent the next hour searching the department's data base for information on him. He discovered that Roy Rogers had created another identity, alright, but it belonged to a corpse.

Nathan arrived with search and arrest warrants in hand.

"Our boy's a ghoster," said Nick.

Ghosting put a ghoulish spin on identity theft. It meant stealing the name and life history of a dead person, preferably one who had lived in relative obscurity. The ghoster picked an individual who would have been about the same age. Any documents showing a birth date wouldn't run up a red flag.

"That's a relief," said Nathan. "I checked out the name Joseph Stone on facebook last night. I stopped counting at a hundred and fifty. What lucky stiff is our perp impersonating?"

"Someone out in Wyoming."

"That explains 'Wyoming' as Stone's previous address in the *Chronicle's* personnel files."

"Not so easy to pull that off nowadays, what with global data-sharing. Looks like he managed it though. Roger's dead alter-ego led a remarkably unremarkable life."

The two of them were looking at Nick's photos of the shoe soles when Sheila brought the cleaned-up dental stone casts from the lab. Nick set the partial left foot impression from the ravine next to the one he took under Alice's porch. Nathan hitched up a chair and he and Nick almost bumped heads studying them. The wear pattern was identical.

" 'Mountain Warrior,'" said Nick. "Ripple pattern. Gore-Tex. Sold in three local sporting goods outlets."

"You are the Sole Man, Shea."

They looked at each other.

"Bernie's video." They said it in unison.

The computer's software enabled them to focus in, enlarge, and advance the film frame by frame. The image was slightly blurry, but recognizable.

"That's the boot," said Nick. "It has the mountain logo on the side."

"We can check his closet for the clothes he was wearing in this clip. There'll be beaucoup fingerprints to compare with the ones from Mrs. Rogers' house."

"Let's go get him."

Chapter Fifty-Nine

"Come and Get It"

In baiting a mousetrap with cheese,
always leave room for the mouse.
H. H. Munro/Saki (1870-1916)

A lice sang to herself while she dried the dishes.

> When you come to our house we'll have some fun.
> We'll ask you to come in and we'll take you
>   to the kitchen
> And we'll put you in the oven until you're done.

She had almost finished putting the dishes away when Harry signaled his presence as usual. Alice sang the chorus louder in an effort to keep her head above the sensual surf washing over her. She was only partially successful. The exhilaration of sex was evolution's crowning achievement, and she wasn't immune.

> But you're always welcome at our house
>   any time of the day.
> Yes, you're always welcome at our house,
> And we hope you will stay.
> And we *know* you will stay.

She turned to face the doorway. In the living room, Harry stood with his knuckles on his hips. Alice noticed he left more than critical distance between himself and the sponge mop. She gripped the spatula she'd just dried. It would be useful for smacking him if he rushed her.

He wore a pair of tabi, gray with road dust, a shabby black hakima whose hems had frayed to fringes, and a haori coat with the sash riding low on his hips. He sported a steel-brush stubble on his jaw. His black hair was tied into a short ponytail with a strand of straw raffia.

Where did he get all his costumes?

"You think you can get to me with Toshiro Mifuni?"

Alice had to admit the resemblance to her favorite actor was uncanny, and the coating of road dust was a good touch.

Harry tried to growl like Mifuni-san, even though what sounded inside her skull was, *Do I smell cookies?*

"I fed most of them to the gnomes." Alice pointed the spatula at the trap. "I left a few in there though."

Will you get them for me? He stepped back to clear a path for her.

"Get them yourself. I put extra chocolate chips in this batch."

With the spatula in one hand and the other gripping the mop handle she watched him circle the trap twice. On the third lap he began to shrink inside his clothes. As each item of samurai attire fell off him it dissolved and vanished.

Naked and covered with warts, he shriveled to the size of a large badger. His chest bulged and sprouted a shag carpet of black hair. His legs shortened and bowed backwards. His elbows looked like the galls insects made on oak leaves. His arms shortened too, making his hands seem enormous. The nails grew until they curled around underneath the knobby fingers.

The homunculus Faye had named Harry had pointy, translucent ears. When he got on his hands and knees and crawled into the trap his cock dragged on the floor between his legs. He filled the cage, which left little maneuvering room. He made a grab for the cookies and disturbed the delicate balance of the shelf on which they sat. The door clanged shut and locked behind him.

He howled. He kicked the door. He flung himself from side to side.

Harry's caterwauling attracted assorted house imps Alice hadn't met yet. They popped up from the furnace vents, and the nickel-sized hole in the floor for the TV cable. They oozed from the electrical outlets, and one appeared hanging upside down in the fireplace. The eggplant-colored demon that recently had made her acquaintance slithered out from under the A to O volume of the Oxford English Dictionary.

The supernatural vermin situation was clearly out of control. Alice wondered if she was in violation of the health code. Local news shows often aired footage of homes overrun with cats. She'd seen the clips of the owners, usually clutching one scrawny, restive stray, while dozens of others milled in the background. What would a TV field reporter make of this?

Added to that problem, Harry was contained for the time being, but now arose the problem of disposal. Alice threw an afghan over the trap and called Faye.

"Harry fell for it. What should we do with him? And how soon can you and Jake do the clearance? I have an infestation situation here."

Faye held three large hula hoops in her left hand and a carton of sea salt under her arm. Alice had a can of paint stripper in her right. Between them they carried the heavy trap, still wrapped in the afghan. Harry called to Alice on the way down the two flights of stairs to the garage. Fortunately, she and Faye were the only ones who could hear him.

Ally. Ally. Please let me out, Ally. The nickname was the one Charlie used.

Tears stung her eyes. "Shut up, Harry."

He didn't of course.

They put the trap on the cement floor of the garage. Faye pulled a tarp over it. She stood back and gave it one more zap with a psalm. Alice was surprised she also remembered it and recited along with Faye.

"The Lord is my shepherd; I shall not want." The words meant more than they had before, particularly the line, "Yea, though I walk through the valley of the shadow of death, I will fear no evil."

They shoved the trap as far as it would go under the hulking wooden work table at the back corner of the garage. They both made the sign of the cross, picked up the envelope with the copy of Syl's pact with the Devil, and hurried out. Alice hit the button and the garage door rolled down behind them.

"Do you have Charlie's ring, Al?"

"I always do."

Faye nodded and they headed for the river.

They found Syl and her metal courier case sitting on a picnic bench set in the grass at the edge of the beach. Slate gray clouds huddled at the horizon and thunder grumbled.

"Let's do it," said Faye.

Syl laid the case on the picnic table. "Maybe we don't have to."

"Don't have to what?" asked Alice. "Destroy the contract?"

"I did a little research on this."

"Where?"

"Someone at the office mentioned she was a witch. She says the Devil's bound by certain laws, and it's possible to get his help without losing one's soul."

"Let me get this straight." Faye didn't try to hide her exasperation. "You want to renegotiate the deal?"

"No. I'm just saying…" Syl glanced at the hula hoops. "Are we going to have an exercise class afterwards?"

"Circles can provide some protection, at least from lesser demons, and maybe even from Scratch himself."

Faye carried the hula hoops and box of sea salt to the barbecue grill perched atop its post on a grassy point of land near the water. Alice followed with the metal case. Syl trailed behind, shaking each foot like a wet dog as she tried to keep the sand out of her high-end footwear.

"That damned reporter's career took off," she grumbled. "Do you suppose he made a deal too?"

"If he did, it proves the Devil can provide wealth and success," said Faye, "but he can't make people more talented than they already are."

"That explains a lot of best-sellers," muttered Alice.

Faye brought up the question both she and Alice had wondered about. "If he made a deal, Syl, it didn't protect him from the high-test shit fill-up you arranged for his Mustang, now did it."

"What makes you think I was responsible?" Syl's grin dispelled any doubt.

Alice wondered which hellish perks and curses trumped whose when two enemies signed agreements with the Devil. With any luck, the question would soon be irrelevant.

Faye laid the three hoops out on the ground. She sprinkled salt around the inside perimeters of each.

"Circles can ward off evil and the salt is extra protection." Holding the two copies of the contract, she stood inside the middle ring directly in front of the metal fire box.

"Can I share your hoop, Al?"

"Sure."

Syl linked arms with Alice in the center of the second hoop. Faye held the papers over the grill, struck a match, and lit them. She gripped a corner as long as she could, then dropped the flaming sheets onto the weathered charcoal ash and congealed grease of cook-outs past.

Alice poured the paint stripper over all of it, fusing it into a redolent mass. She intended to clean out the fire-box later, assuming she and Faye and Syl escaped with their souls today. They took shallow breaths while they waited for a response. They didn't have to wait long.

The low roar sounded like a chimney fire in a smelter. About fifty feet away a funnel of flame descended until it hovered a few inches over the beach. It looked like a dust-devil set ablaze and whipped hotter by the wind it created as it spun. Faye hurried to join Alice and Syl inside their hoop. The three of them put their arms around each other.

As if on cue, a neighbor strolled across the beach and stooped to let his golden retriever off the leash. He seemed oblivious to the whirling inferno raging twenty feet away.

"Damn," murmured Syl.

"It's okay," said Faye. "He can't see the fire."

"You girls having an exercise class?" he called out.

"You bet," said Faye.

The retriever, however, saw everything, or at least sensed it. When the Devil appeared the dog tucked tail and howled up the stairs to the road. His owner chased after him.

Scratch stepped from the swirl of flames as though he were leaving an elevator. He still looked like Our Man Flint. He shot the cuffs of a crisp white shirt tucked into jeans that fit like a second skin. When he took off his reflector sunglasses his eyes gleamed yellow as a cat's. He did not look pleased.

Alice felt Charlie's ring stir and expand and she pulled it up by the silver chain. The dragon called the Worm Ouroboros unfolded its wings and spit out its tail, leaving it free of the chain.

It grew to the size of a seagull and scrambled up to perch on her shoulder. Its scaly tail draped around her neck. The tip of it snaked under her shirt's lapel and tickled her collarbone. The vibrations of its joy at being released caused goose bumps on Alice's arms.

Its left wing collided with her head when it stretched, probably to make itself look larger. It hissed menace at the Devil. The wary glance Scratch gave it encouraged Alice. Encouragement was a good thing, because Faye and Syl had lost the ability to speak, much less make small talk with Ultimate Evil.

Alice pulled a sheet of paper from her back pocket, unfolded it, and held it up. It was the dated, notarized document notifying Sylvana that her name had been legally changed from Gant to Brant.

"The contract with Sylvana Brant is null and void, *ab initio*. And everyone involved with her is *indemnis*, without hurt, harm or damage."

The Devil chuckled. "Well played, Ms. Lewis."

"I can't take credit."

"Wisdom is knowing whom to ask for help. And I trust his warts are cured."

"They are. Thanks for asking." Alice glanced at her wrist where a watch would be if she wore one. "I imagine you have a lot more business to transact today. Don't let us keep you."

He bowed in the old manner, with a sweep of his hand as though taking his nonexistent hat off to her. "Have a nice day."

He turned and walked back into the fire. The whirling inferno spun into itself, dwindled, and vanished. The dragon shrank, took its tail back in its mouth, and rolled down into Alice's left shirt pocket.

She put her right hand over it and felt it rise and fall with the pounding of her heart.

CHAPTER SIXTY

"IF THE SHOE FITS..."

*The difference between literature
and journalism is that journalism
is unreadable,
and literature is not read.*
Oscar Wilde
(*The Critic as Artist*)

They all decided Nick should not be the first one through the door. Everyone assumed Joe Stone fantasized some sort of professional and maybe even personal relationship with him. No sense adding awkward to an already tense situation.

Joe Stone's shabby bungalow was half hidden under a shroud of Virginia creeper and poison ivy. Nick waited with Stan and Len behind a wisteria trellis in the side yard of the house down the street from it. Nathan and the two surveillance detectives had taken up positions behind the high fence at the back of Stone's house. Other members of the force were scattered throughout the neighborhood.

Someone had tipped off Detective Staub about the pending take-down and had smuggled street clothes into his room in the cardiac ward. He had discharged himself, sneaking out in time for this. Standing five-foot-six and weighing one-forty, Staub wore granny glasses and a wispy comb-over. He looked like the grown-up version of the kid that bullies gave wedgies and stuffed into lockers. But everyone in the department knew woe betided anyone who messed with him.

Two other officers waited at the bottom of the two steps. Nick and the rest listened on their radios as Staub rapped on the front door. Stone must have replied from inside.

"I'm a police officer, Mr. Stone," said Staub. "I need to talk to you."

No matter how often Nick stood in Staub's place or watched a fellow policeman wait at a felon's door, time always slowed between the knock and the response. Would this particular response be a barrage of bullets? Nick didn't think so, but the possibility was always present.

Stone opened the door and Staub and the other two went in. As Nick and the rest of the team converged on the house he could hear Staub reading Stone his Miranda rights. Nick stood at the back of the eight or so men outside the door, but Stone glared at him as he was led down the steps in handcuffs. Nick expected humiliation, defiance maybe, or anger at his part in the arrest. What he saw was hatred. He had a feeling it had little to do with the arrest and everything to do with the fact that he had been keeping company with Alice Lewis.

Once the squad car pulled away, he and Nathan went in first. At the far end a half-wall separated the narrow living room from a kitchen and dining area that stretched across the back of the house. Paralleling the left side was an entry to a hallway with three closed doors. A fireplace occupied the right side of the room. A 250-channel scanner with Trunk Tracker III technology sat on the mantle.

A maroon leather couch and over-stuffed easy chair faced a high-def flat screen that took up most of the wall next to the fireplace. Rock concert posters and knock-off art covered the others. Wireless surround-sound speakers seemed to float in the corners near the ceiling. A pair of bass woofers sat on either end of a tall bookcase containing a matched set of literary classics. Against the half-wall separating the living room from the kitchen stood a metal wine rack and wet-bar.

Nathan asked the question that had been on Nick's mind too.

"Stone claimed he got a six-figure book contract and a movie deal for his novel, so why didn't he buy a bigger house?"

"He'd have to hire movers. No way he could carry that couch out by himself."

"And he has something to hide."

"Right." Nick opened one of the doors in the hallway while the rest of the team fanned out on the hunt for evidence.

A plaster bust of Ernest Hemingway and an older model police scanner sat on a cluttered desk along with a 1950's-vintage Royal typewriter. Next to it was a three-inch-tall stack of paper, the unfinished novel Stone referred to as his killer thriller. Nick glanced at the title, *A Revolting Development.* He knew from his own attempt at fiction it would contain autobiographical references that could answer questions about this case

On a wall shelf sat a gaudy urn of the sort to hold human ashes. Next to them were a half-dozen eight-by-ten photos pinned to a bulletin board. Alice was the subject of all of them, and obviously photographed without her knowledge. Nick felt a churning in his stomach at the sight of them.

He shook it off as he and Nathan made a preliminary search of the desk drawers. They were heading for the bedroom to see what their colleagues had found in Stone's bureau and closet, when they heard Len's voice from the kitchen.

"Holy moley!"

Nick's smile was grim. "I predict we're about to learn why Stone hasn't moved on up."

They joined the members of the team watching Len empty the refrigerator's tightly packed freezer compartment. He handed the plastic bags to Stan who laid them next to another scanner on the kitchen table. The bags' contents were wrapped in butcher paper and neatly labeled in capital letters.

"Rats." Nathan held up the first one. He read the other labels aloud. "'Liver.' 'Kidney.' 'Lungs.' 'Small Intestines.' 'Eyeballs.' 'Tongue,' 'Foot.' 'Femur.' " He paused. "This one is labeled 'Penis.' "

"He didn't get that from his mother," muttered Nick.

Staub appeared in the doorway leading from the kitchen to the garage. "Cricket fixings out here."

Stored on a shelf in the cluttered garage were motor oil, turtle wax, battery charger, window cleaner, and a squeegee, and of course a scanner. Next to them sat CO_2 cartridges, a canister of smokeless rifle powder, a roll of timer fuse, and a box of ball bearings to act as shrapnel. They were the ingredients for the do-it-yourself explosives called crickets.

When Megan had finished photographing everything, the investigators put the carefully-wrapped body parts on ice in a cooler. They hauled it away along with boxes of evidence including the contents of Stone's closet. Before they packed the shoes, Nick checked the sole on the left Mountain Warrior boot. It had the same wear pattern as the print in the ravine and the one under Alice's porch.

Nick and Nathan rode in silence for most of the way back to the station. What the team had found in Joe Stone's freezer and garage gave them plenty to think about, but Nick focused on the photos of Alice on the wall in the office. Stone and his zoom lens had taken them at the grocery store, the river beach, in her yard, and most disturbing of all, doing laundry in her own basement. He had a strong urge to detour past her house to make sure she was all right.

When Nathan spoke it was obvious his mind had been elsewhere too.

"I asked Esme to marry me. A couple weeks ago her daughter Kenya told me to go for it. That cleared away the only uncertainty."

"And...?"

"Esme said 'yes.' "

"Congratulations." Nick positively beamed at him, something he hadn't done in years. "You two are perfect for each other."

"We're thinking about October. Would you be my best man?"

"I'd be honored."

"How are things going with the fair Alice?"

"By all accounts her late husband was a one-off. Best to take it slow. I don't want to be the fall-back."

"A very wise woman once said, 'He who hesitates is a damned fool.'"

"Who said that?"

"Mae West."

Nick was reading Joe Stone's manuscript when Sheila stopped by his desk.

"Stone says he'll only talk to you, Shea."

Nick had hoped to avoid a face-to-face with Stone. Best to ask Nathan to come with him and conduct the interview. When the occasion called for it, good-humored, easy-going Nathan could emanate more menace than anyone on the force. Plus, he'd make sure Nick didn't lose control and attack the suspect.

Nathan didn't have to go bad-cop. Stone seemed eager to tell his story. In short order he and Nathan learned that Stone had escalated the feud between Longview Development and the Defenders of the Chesapeake to provide more sensational copy for the *Chronicle*, under his byline, of course.

Yes, he had left the note on Dr. Brant's windshield. Yes, he had put the dead rat in her mailbox, but he swore he had paid his nephew merely to vandalize her car, not mug her. The anthrax scare was also his doing. He said it had been an afterthought, but he seemed particularly proud of the idea.

He said he hadn't stored his sister in the freezer. The first he heard of it was when the report came in to the newspaper office. He had filched her heart, though, and put it and the eagles in Logan's septic pit. He figured the heart would indicate a possible homicide and likely involve Nick.

"Why Nick?"

"He writes the best reports."

"And the other human organs and parts?"

"Mary's heart gave me the idea. I got the rest of the things from a guy who knows a guy at the crematorium. I don't know their names.

It was all anonymous through the internet. Maybe the funeral director can tell you who they are. Hell, a lot of people are selling body parts, some legit, some not. It's a billion dollar business."

Nathan nodded. In his search for the owner of the heart in the take-out box, he had learned that shady funeral home directors and crematorium operators were selling corpses for a thousand dollars each and passing off the ashes of farm animals as Aunt Sadie and Uncle Herman.

Nick had one more question. "Did the Devil make you do it, Stone?"

Nathan flashed him a what the hell are you talking about look. Stone had been calm, as if expecting them to be impressed by his cleverness. Now he went pale.

"Why would you ask a crazy question like that?" A muscle in his jaw twitched and his left eye started blinking uncontrollably.

Nathan caught the cues. He had been attentive throughout the interrogation, but now he sat up straighter.

"I've read enough of your manuscript to know it didn't deserve a six-figure advance," said Nick. "Not even compared to the other drivel being published."

Stone went belligerent. Apparently being accused of body-parts theft, harassment of a senior citizen, and anthrax hoaxes was okay, but to have his work rated below "drivel" was cause for *code duello*. Nick expected him to stand up and issue a challenge.

Stone tried to gather his scattered aplomb. "The publisher thinks it's worth that."

Nick realized that even if Stone hadn't made a deal with the Devil, his "killer thriller" probably would hit the best-seller list when the details came out about the author's shenanigans, arrest, and trial. A brilliant marketing plan, really, even if it wasn't the one Stone had in mind.

As Sheila led Stone out Nathan turned to Nick.

"What was all that about the Devil?"

"I'll tell you later."

CHAPTER SIXTY-ONE

"RETURN OF THE ELIMINATOR"

In case of Emergency:
1) Grab your coat
2) Get your hat
3) Leave your worries on the doorstep
4) Direct your feet to the sunny side of the street
Unknown

Alice could sense Esme's wariness as soon as she walked through the door. Esme opened with an apology.

"I'm sorry I didn't come to the beach last night for the burning of Syl's contract. I had to work, but I wouldn't have come anyway. I have a child. I can't risk… you know."

"We all understand." Alice hugged her. "Faye and her friend Jake are on their way now. They're going to clear my house of…" Alice did a quick search for a neutral term. "…negative influences."

"Faye mentioned she'd taken on a second career."

"Her official title is 'Entity Release Therapist,' but she calls herself 'Boo-a-Bug.' "

"Cute. I guess 'Spook' wouldn't do as a nickname in her new line of work." Esme looked around the living room, as if expecting to see negative influences lounging on the sofa and chairs. "I've always felt an odd vibe from your house, but in a good way. I figured it was the residual history of all that hand-me-down furniture you've scrounged over the years. I get the feeling they're as grateful to be pulled from dumpsters as dogs and cats are to be rescued from the pound.

Faye arrived and kissed Esme on the cheek. "Jake is on his way, Al."

"I have to run," said Esme. "Lots of errands."

"You're welcome to stay, Es."

"We have a saying at the airport, Faye. 'Never fly in the same cockpit with someone braver than you.' "

Esme almost collided with Jake in the doorway. After introductions she continued out, but she turned, and behind his back, gave Faye the thumbs-up sign of approval.

"We have lupine and lousewort, sage, rosemary, and garlic." Faye held up a bouquet of plants. "Logan didn't know her yard was a cornucopia of the plants we need. I told her Syl's temporary insanity had been cured, by the way."

"I notice she's been keeping her distance."

"Can you blame her?"

Jake was ready to get the party started. "What are you seeing here, Alice?"

"Each one's different, but they're all small and ugly, except Trike. He's about knee high."

"Trike?"

"He's a three-legged creature that lives in the upstairs utility closet. From there he has access to the space between the exterior and interior walls."

"The good news is you have imps, not demons. Imps are more mischievous than harmful. It's the difference between cockroaches and rats with rabies."

"If the good news is an infestation of cockroaches from hell, what's the bad news?"

"There is no bad news. We can take care of them."

"They're lonely really," said Faye. "But they do pull pranks. Jake says they're trying to be friends with humans, but they're not very good at it."

"That explains Trike's woebegone look."

"We use deliverance prayers that don't require a priest or bishop's permission."

"I'm not much on religion."

"So you say." Jake smiled. "What matters is your good intent and conviction. Since you had a conversation with the Devil, and you weren't on an acid trip, I'd say you were convinced."

"You could say that."

"Cleansing can be done in a variety of ways," said Faye. "Opening windows, ringing bells, smudging, putting bowls of salt in the corners. But we keep it as simple as possible. We dismiss them politely. We don't want to make them cranky."

Faye opened a package of stick incense and stuck its contents into a bowl filled with sand. Jake unplugged Alice's old land line and made sure all cell phones were off.

"Phones ringing disrupts the focus. Cell phones are free-roving and radiate a particularly pernicious influence."

Alice followed Jake and Faye and their cloud of incense smoke through the house. Jake recited the Sarum Missal as they entered each room.

> God be in my head,
> and in my understanding.
> God be in my eyes,
> and in my looking;
> God be in my mouth
> and in my speaking;
> God be in my heart
> and in my thinking;
> God be at my end
> and at my departing.

Alice pretended to have something in her eyes so she could wipe them. She was still uncertain about a Supreme Being, but she now knew for a fact that death was a departing, not an ending.

When they finished in the basement Faye extinguished the incense.

"What about the elementals?" Alice had grown fond of them, even the rowdy gnomes.

"The prayer might drive them away," said Jake, "But a cleansing is a blessing, not an exorcism. If you want them back, we can invoke them again."

"How much do I owe you?"

"Nothing. You're Faye's friend, so we'll consider it an introductory offer."

"How's the eliminator business going, if you don't mind my asking?"

"It's booming," said Faye. "I've turned in my notice at the Red Eye."

Alice still had one important question. "What about Harry?"

"We can take it for a drive in the country and dump it." Jake handed her a sheet of follow-up instructions. "It's unlikely it'll return to your house again if you do this simple weekly cleansing maintenance. But it'll always be looking for an opening."

"We need to give Harry a better alternative than a pasture in the boonies," said Faye. "Someplace with plenty of horny numbskulls to keep him busy."

Alice knew what she was thinking. "I'll take you to work tonight, Faye."

The Vette wasn't big enough for Alice, Faye and the large live trap still covered with an afghan. She took her CRV instead and Charlie's song filled it. She tried to focus on the road, but it was difficult.

Harry was singing "The Little Beggar Man," One of Charlie's favorite ditties. He even tried, without much success, to accompany his mimicry with the virtuoso rhythms Charlie could create with a pair of metal spoons. Like any Irish tune worth its salt, "The Little Beggar Man" had numerous verses. Every now and then Harry would stop in the middle of the chorus and plead to be set free.

A thought occurred to Alice, and not for the first time. Satan and his henchmen bungled many of the details, and yet they managed to know exactly what would affect her the most.

Alice had considered strapping the trap onto the rack on the roof, but she didn't want to chance it falling off into traffic. Some truck might roll over it, break the mirrors, and release Harry before they reached their destination.

As she pulled into the employees' area of the Red Eye Dock Bar's parking lot, Faye muttered, "This is the longest damn ride to work I've ever taken."

The Red Eye's kitchen was on dry land. They carried the trap behind the building to where a dozen large trash bins were lined up by the back door. This was Tuesday evening, and the weekend's abundance of empty bottles had topped off the nearby dumpster.

"We could stuff him into one of the garbage cans," said Faye.

"Let's set him loose in that stand of sea oats by the water."

They were watching him scamper on all four of his distorted limbs into the acre of tall grass when a voice boomed behind them.

"What are you doing back here, Faye?"

They both gave a start, but Faye recovered first.

"Hi, D.W. We're relocating a squirrel that got into Alice's ceiling."

She lifted one of his arms, and a heavy lift it was. She slipped under it with headroom to spare. With his arm around her shoulder the three of them headed for D.W.'s post at the large gateway separating the parking lot from the sprawling, open-air bar.

D.W. was Faye's favorite bouncer and the affection was mutual. His name was Ralph, but Faye called him D.W. for the Drunk Whisperer. All the Red Eye's bouncers were professionals, but Ralph was large and in charge.

A man staggered past Alice and Faye as they walked through the gateway. Alice heard him mumble something and then D.W.'s booming reply.

"Yes, I do have handcuffs. And no, you may not borrow them."

Alice sat at the bar and was still giggling when Faye set a margarita in front of her.

"It's light on tequila since you have to drive home tonight. Jake'll give me a ride at closing time."

Alice nodded toward Merv Griffin who was staring into his fogcutter as usual. "Do you suppose Hell considers him AWOL? I mean, isn't he supposed to report in now and then, and do something to earn his keep, whatever that may be?"

"Darned if I know. But he always has money to pay for his drinks and he's a good tipper." Faye leaned forward. "Want to bet how long it takes Harry to show up?"

"No point. I think he just walked in."

Tonight Harry was the nacho-eating, beer-drinking, America's Stupidest Reality Show-watching, hound-dog-eyed hunk who had camped on Alice's couch for the past two weeks. Except now he was a ringer for James Dean and instead of the red silk boxers, he wore tight black jeans, motorcycle boots, black leather jacket, and no shirt. As he came through the gate he unzipped the jacket so it framed his rippling abs.

D.W. saw him do it. He caught up with Harry, tapped him on the shoulder, and pantomimed zipping up a jacket. Harry complied, but not before a lot of Dock-siders had noticed him.

A few moments passed before Alice realized that the usual rush of sensuality wasn't happening. The cleansing must have gotten him out of her system as well as her house. The other women weren't immune though. As he swaggered across the dance floor they turned to watch him pass. He reached the other side, crossed his boots at the ankles, leaned a slender hip against one of the posts supporting a thatched tiki hut, and struck a Rebel Without a Cause pose.

Sexual tension always hung in the air at the Red Eye, but now the wattage had amped up. Several women drifted in Harry's direction and joined those who were already making his acquaintance.

"How the hell did he come up with that outfit so fast?" asked Faye.

"Beats me. And why can everyone here see him? For that matter, why can they see Merv over there, but don't notice he has wings and a hawk's face?"

Faye shrugged. "I've given up trying to understand the rules of other planes of existence, if there are any rules."

"Ditto." Alice held up her margarita glass. "Would you put this in a doggie jar? I can't hang around and watch."

CHAPTER SIXTY-TWO

"THE NERVE"

Is that a gun in your pocket,
or are you just glad to see me?
Mae West (1893-1980)

No one in the department had seen Nick rattled before. Those who weren't worried about him were amused.

He fidgeted. He paced. He tapped his pen on the desk. He either made a call or checked his cell phone messages every five minutes.

When Nathan reported in, Sheila grabbed his arm, stood on tiptoe, and whispered in his ear. Nathan nodded and ambled over to Nick's desk. He perched on a corner of it with his leg dangling. He leaned close and kept his voice low.

"On behalf of the entire personnel roster, Sheila wants me to find out what's eating you."

"It's private."

"Alice is okay, Nick. You caught the bad guy."

"Guys. We caught the bad guys. Remember Russell Wright?"

"Yes, I do. He's locked up too."

"Her phone has been off the hook all afternoon."

"Esme told me you called to ask if she knew where Alice was."

"She said she saw Alice at home around noon, and has no idea why her phone's not working. She knows *something* though. They should recruit your fiancee for the C.I.A. She can keep secrets."

"But she doesn't lie. If she said she doesn't know where Alice is, then she doesn't."

Nick spoke so low Nathan had to lean closer to hear him.

"The thing is, Nathan, one maniac planned to kill Alice and carve her up, and another has been stalking her. How would you feel if that were happening to Esme?"

"I get it." Nathan reached over and closed the file folders scattered in rare disarray on Nick's desk. "You were here until daybreak working on that report, and then back before lunch. Sheila says you've been at this all afternoon."

"It's a complicated case. I'm double-dogging details, in case I missed something."

"I'll finish the paperwork. Go check on Alice."

"I just called her and Faye again. Alice's phone is connected now, but both hers and Faye's are going to message. I haven't had a chance to tell her Stone's behind bars."

Nathan gathered up the folders. Nick knew if it came to arm-wrestling for them he would lose. He took his shoulder holster from the back of the chair, but continued staring at his phone.

"What else is bothering you, Sole Man?"

"I'm an idiot."

"In which respect?"

"I sent Alice an email with a link to the novel I've been working on."

"The novel you haven't told anyone about, much less let any of us read?"

"Yeah." Nick pulled his jacket on over the holster.

"You're right. You are an idiot."

As Alice drove home in the darkening twilight, one name headed the list of living individuals she most wanted to be with. To tell the truth, the list only had one name on it. As she came in sight of her garage she saw the big cream and white motorcycle parked next to it. She parked inside, combed her hair and turned on the four-by-four's interior light. While she checked herself in the rear view mirror, she took deep breaths to calm the jitters.

Nick was sitting in a porch chair in the deepening dusk. He stood up, put his arms around her, and held her close. For the first time in more than a year she felt what it was like to be inside a force field of love and protection. This protection was armed, however.

She laid her palm against the right side of his jacket. "Is that a gun in your pocket or are you just glad to see me?"

He laughed. He couldn't remember being this happy on dry land before.

"It is a gun and I am happy to see you." His kiss was brief but long on promise. "We arrested Joe Stone."

"Why?"

"He's the one who's been harassing Logan and bothering you. The boot prints under your porch were the final clue. I tried to call you all afternoon."

"Faye and Jake unplugged the phone while they were clearing my house of negative energy. Then I took Faye to the Red Eye."

"Speaking of negative energy, I don't need a detailed report now about Sylvana Gant's deal with the devil..." He kissed her again to emphasize his disinterest in a detailed report. "...but did the Philadelphia lawyer get her out of it?"

"He did." *Some day,* she thought, *I'll tell you about Harry. Some day we'll both laugh about it.*

"Did Faye and Jake banish your elementals too?"

"Yes, but they said they can bring them back if I want them."

"Good. I want to meet them. Maybe Faye can show me how to do that."

Alice opened the front door, chagrinned that she had forgotten to lock it. Had the Eliminators' de-bug-a-booing worked? She made a quick scan before she beckoned him to follow her in.

The living room was dark and quiet. The furniture didn't glow. No toenails scrabbled across the pine floor. No orange eyes glowed from the corners. No sylphs twinkled around the ceiling fan. No muttering came from the planters. She stepped out of her sandals and lit the three candles on the mantle. She stared at them for a few seconds, but the flames attracted no fire elementals.

Nick set his shoes neatly next to hers and locked the door. He hung his jacket, tie, and shoulder holster on the coat hooks above the shoes. He loosened his collar and pulled out his shirt tails. Without saying anything, Alice took his hand and led him upstairs.

The almost full moon sent light through the wall of windows by the bed. Alice unclasped the chain and the dragon ring and hung it on the peg with her few other necklaces.

Nick rested his hands at the base of her neck. "Are you sure?"

"Yes. Are you?"

He answered by lifting her hair with his thumb and the palm of his hand. He kissed her behind the ear where the vagus nerve's bundle of sensory and motor filaments started their journey from the brain to her pharynx, esophagus, heart, and diaphragm. The nervous system was wired for sex and the residual sensuality radiated to her viscera and points south.

They undressed slowly, taking time to run their hands lightly over each part of the other's body as it was exposed. Every millimeter of skin had become a conductor of peace, joy, and total trust.

Nick murmured, "So this is what it's like."

He always had been cynical about humanity's preoccupation with love. Now he understood it. Words were inadequate to describe something so transcendent in its purest form but, still and all, people wanted to try.

Nick picked Alice up, laid her on the bed, and stretched out on his side next to her. Neither of them was in a hurry. Without conferring on the matter they both knew they would make love again and again in the years to come. They wanted to take their time now. They wanted to make this night one they would remember for all of those years.

❧ ❧ ❧

When Nick's phone rang they were lying side by side on their backs. His arm was around Alice. Her head rested in the hollow below his shoulder. Her arm and hand extended along his leg. The phone rang again.

"That's Kimberly."

"The dispatcher?"

"Yes. I have to answer it."

"It's okay."

When he hung up he kissed her and started gathering his clothes.

"What's happened?"

"Highway patrol found a guy in a 55-gallon drum. Must've been there a long time. They said his body poured out."

This was not the sort of pillow talk that should follow the experience they had shared, but there was nothing he could do about it. And he needed to know how she would react.

"Janitor in a Drum." She did a pretty good imitation of the voice in the old TV commercial. "'Specially formulated to suspend grease from floors.'"

She said it without cracking a smile, but Nick laughed so hard he had to sit on the side of the bed.

She got dressed and went downstairs with him. While he was putting on his tie, holster, jacket, and shoes he remembered what he had meant to tell her earlier.

"I sent you a very nervy email. Delete it without opening the attachment." He didn't have to explain. He could see from her expression she had guessed what it was about.

"Did you attach all of your novel or a few sample chapters?"

"It doesn't matter. Really. Delete it."

"People talk about writer's block." Alice kissed him. "Welcome to the world of writer's doubt."

The night sky was getting dawn's glow on when they kissed on the porch. Alice watched from there as he rode away. She was smiling when she turned on her desk lamp and fired up her computer. She said good morning to the seahorses on the screen and opened Nick's email attachment.

Nick's book's title was *Done to Death*. The first line read, "Performing a swan dive down the concrete mixer truck's chute and into the rotating drum was Louie's second mistake of the day." She chuckled and finished reading the chapter. He could write.

Alice was creating a new folder for her own work when she felt in her bones the ambient syncopation of metal spoons. She looked up, hoping to see Charlie. The doorway was empty and the room became quiet, but she could feel his presence and that overwhelming sense of love.

"I take it that means you like him, Charlie."

The spoons began again, tapping out a fast and complicated percussion line to "The Little Beggar Man." Gradually the lilting rhythm grew fainter as if whoever was playing them had someplace to go and was on his way.

Alice typed "Chapter One" on the blank screen and added the first line.

"Do seahorses sing when they make love?"

ABOUT THE AUTHOR

Lucia St. Clair Robson was born in Baltimore, Maryland, and raised in West Palm Beach, Florida. She has lived in Japan, New York City, and Arizona and served in the Peace Corps in Venezuela. She has written nine other novels — *Ride the Wind, Walk in My Soul, Light a Distant Fire, Tokaido Road, Mary's Land, Fearless: A Novel of Sarah Bowman, Ghost Warrior, Shadow Patriots,* and *Last Train from Cuernavaca.*

"Love all, trust a few,
do wrong to none."

William Shakespeare
All's Well that Ends Well

www.ingramcontent.com/pod-product-compliance
Lightning Source LLC
Chambersburg PA
CBHW071211250626
47159CB00001B/285